Watch Me

A Jefferson Winter Thriller

James Carol

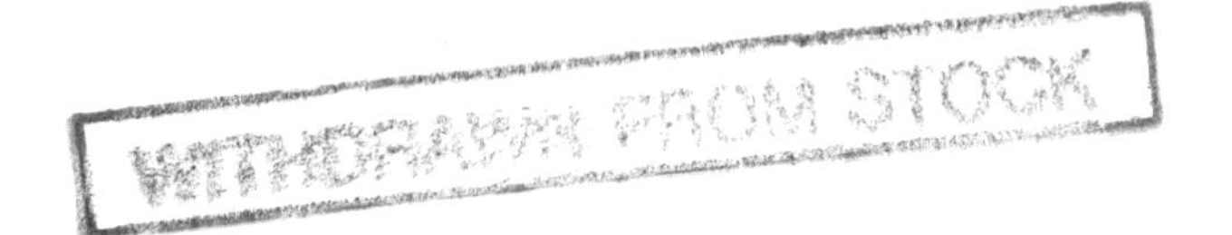

First published in Great Britain 2014
by
Faber & Faber Ltd.

First Isis Edition
published 2015
by arrangement with
Faber & Faber Ltd.

A catalogue record for this book is available from the British Library.

ISBN 978–1–78541–084–0 (hb)
ISBN 978–1–78541–090–1 (pb)

Published by
F. A. Thorpe (Publishing)
Anstey, Leicestershire

Set by Words & Graphics Ltd.
Anstey, Leicestershire
Printed and bound in Great Britain by
T. J. International Ltd., Padstow, Cornwall

This book is printed on acid-free paper

For Cam, co-conspirator and partner in crime.

CHAPTER ONE

Sam Galloway died slow, and he died hard. His death was completely at odds with the way he'd lived his life, and completely at odds with the sort of death he should have had. Men like Sam slipped away peacefully in their sleep, or they were felled by a heart attack on the back nine of the golf course, they did not die because they'd been doused in gasoline and set alight. And they sure as hell didn't die screaming their final breaths into a filthy rag while the flesh melted from their bones.

It would be easy to categorise Sam as a victim of circumstance, to file him away under "wrong place, wrong time". This was a common mistake in these situations, one that was rooted in fear. Saying that Sam had been in the wrong place at the wrong time meant his murder could be blamed on fate, or chance, or the whims of the gods.

Alternatively if this murder wasn't random, then it became much easier to believe that what had happened to Sam could happen to anyone. Follow the logic, and it wasn't that huge a leap to believe that you might be next.

But Sam hadn't been in the wrong place at the wrong time. There was nothing random about his murder. Whoever had done this had targeted him. They'd fantasised about what they wanted to do, then they'd worked out a way to turn fantasy into reality. Most importantly, they'd looked long and hard at how they could burn Sam up and get away with it.

That last detail was crucial. *Getting away with it*. That's what separates the amateurs from the pros. Committing a crime is relatively easy. Any fool can do that. Committing a crime and getting away with it, now that's tough.

So far the plan was working just fine. Sam was dead and the guy responsible was out there somewhere, free to go on living his life as though nothing had ever happened. Right now, he was probably enjoying a celebratory breakfast in a diner somewhere. Eggs sunny side up, a tower of pancakes drenched in maple syrup, bacon crisped to perfection, and a gallon of coffee to wash it all down.

Or maybe he was at work, doing the nine-to-five thing. Handshakes and backslaps and a post-mortem of last night's ball game around the water cooler, a game he hadn't seen because he'd been busy elsewhere. A game whose details he'd picked up from the sports pages.

Until the email dropped into my inbox ten minutes ago, I'd never heard of Sam Galloway. Now all I could think about was Sam, and what had happened to him, and who might be responsible. Particularly that last one.

I glanced at the laptop screen, glanced at the suitcase on the bed. I'd been in South Carolina for the past two weeks hunting down a killer called Carl Tindle, and now Carl was in custody it was time to move on to the next case.

Up until five minutes ago that had been a serial rapist who was targeting prostitutes in Honolulu. These weren't your high-end girls, these were your nickel-and-dime whores, the lowest of the low, girls that the world had all but given up on. That didn't mean they shouldn't have justice. As far as I'm concerned every victim matters. You could be royalty or a junkie whore, it makes no difference to me.

The flights and hotel were booked, my suitcase packed, and I was more than ready to get out of Charleston. Not because there was anything wrong with Charleston. There wasn't. It's just that I'd been here for two weeks, and two weeks is pretty much my limit for staying anywhere these days.

I glanced at the laptop again. One thing I'd had to learn fast during my FBI days was how to prioritise. Resources were always stretched to breaking point because there were too many bad guys out there. The latest victim had just been found in Hawaii so time was on our side there. It would be a while before that guy struck again. But with this Sam Galloway thing, the clock was ticking loud and fast. The way I figured it, I could postpone going to Hawaii for a few days and it wouldn't make that much of a difference to what was happening over there.

The email had come from Sheriff Peter Fortier of the Dayton Parish Sheriff's Department, down in Eagle Creek, Louisiana. I'd never heard of Dayton or

Eagle Creek or Sheriff Fortier, which wasn't surprising considering the US has a land mass of 3.8 million square miles and a population in the region of a third of a billion.

The video clip attached to the email was interesting because I rarely got to see killers at work. Usually all I saw was the end result. Sometimes there was a corpse, sometimes not. Sometimes there wasn't even a crime scene. During my time with the FBI I'd interviewed dozens of serial criminals, so I had plenty of first-hand accounts stored away, albeit biased ones. But it didn't matter how fresh the body was, or how detailed the account, there was no substitute for witnessing something with your own two eyes, even if you were only witnessing it through the lens of someone else's camera.

This guy wasn't the first killer to film his work, and he wouldn't be the last. However, this was the exception rather than the rule. It's common knowledge that serial killers often keep trophies to fuel their fantasies, but these tended to be obscure, innocent-looking mementos that hold significance only for the killer: an article of clothing, a lock of hair, maybe an earring. Filming was rare because it was risky. If the wrong person saw it, how the hell did you explain that one away?

I played the film clip a second time. The picture quality was good, sharp and defined. No shake, which meant the camera had been mounted on a tripod. It also meant that Sheriff Fortier was dealing with a single unsub here. If there had been two unknown subjects, one of them would have wanted to play with the camera and I'd now be watching something that resembled a badly shot home movie. There was no sound. In some ways it would have been less unsettling if there had been. My imagination had gone into overdrive, filling the silence, and what it was coming up with was probably way worse than the reality.

Most of the screen was taken up with Sam Galloway. He was lying on the floor, hog-tied and gagged and scared out of his mind. His face had turned bright red from the exertion, eyes popping. His suit was crumpled and dirty, the collar of his white shirt smeared with grime.

It was difficult to tell exactly where he was being held. The floor was dirt-streaked concrete, and the one wall I could see was constructed from cinderblock. I had a sense of an industrial, utilitarian space, and I also had a sense of confinement, which made me think this was some sort of garage or bunker rather than a warehouse. According to the numbers in the bottom right-hand corner of the screen, the video had been filmed at a little after eleven o'clock yesterday evening.

The clock on the screen jumped forward a minute to 23:04, and a short while later a second man appeared on the screen. The new guy was thin, slightly built, somewhere around five-nine.

And he was carrying a jerry can.

The thin guy walked up to Sam, careful to keep his back to the camera. Sam saw him and froze. He stared at the guy, stared at the can, then he started thrashing around again, more desperate than ever to get free.

The guy unscrewed the jerry can's lid and tipped the contents over Sam. Gasoline sloshed everywhere. It got into Sam's eyes, his nose. He was drowning in the stuff. His clothes were drenched. His hair was dripping. The thin guy shook the last drops from the can and placed it on the concrete floor. Then he took out a matchbook. The cover was white and blank. No restaurant logos, no bar names. He lit a match, tossed it casually onto Sam, then disappeared from the screen.

It took Sam more than two minutes to die, which was two minutes longer than anyone should have to suffer. The pain would have been excruciating. Nobody should have to die like that.

The hyperlink in Sheriff Fortier's email took me to a crude webpage. Large white numbers on a black background. 13:29:23. To the right of the numbers was a stick-figure diagram straight from a game of hangman. This particular game was almost at an end. All that was missing were the limbs.

The three became a two, then a one. Arms and legs appeared. *Blip, blip*. Two limbs for each second. The last digit turned to a zero, the diagram turned red, then it disappeared.

Twenty became nineteen, and the base of the gallows flashed up onto the screen. With each passing second more parts were added. The tall back post, the top beam, the diagonal brace, the rope. Head, body, arms, legs. The last digit changed from a one to a zero, the diagram turned red then disappeared, and the whole ten-second process started over again.

I ran the mouse across the screen, looking for hidden links. There hadn't been any the first time I'd done this, and there weren't any now. The web address didn't tell me much, either: www.violescent.com. A Google search revealed violescent to be an obscure word that meant "tending to a violet colour".

My guess was that the unsub had used a random word generator. That's what I would have done. If you try to think up a random word, it's never going to be truly random because your subconscious gets in the way. The domain name would need checking out, but my money was on it being another dead end. Registering a domain name under a fake identity was a fairly straightforward process.

It had crossed my mind that this could be an elaborate hoax. There was no body, no crime scene, no physical evidence whatsoever. All the cops had was the video clip and the website. It wasn't much to go on, but I was convinced this was the real deal.

First off, Sam Galloway was missing.

Secondly, the person on the film had been positively identified as Sam.

Thirdly, and this was the big one, what did they have to gain? You don't do anything without a reason. It was the effort/outcome principle at play. The benefit gained from an activity had to outweigh the amount of energy expended. If Sam wanted to fake his death, there were a lot of easier ways to do it.

Fourthly, and this was the clincher for me, there was no way that film had been faked. If it had been then you were looking at an acting performance worthy of an Oscar.

For a long couple of minutes I sat there considering my options, a steady stream of numbers and hangman figures filing across the screen.

It was eleven-thirty in the morning here in Charleston. Dayton was an hour behind, so it was only ten-thirty there. The countdown was due to run out at the stroke of midnight Louisiana time. During that time another 4,860 stick figures would die.

Louisiana or Honolulu?

Swamps or bikinis?

It was a no-brainer. I've always been a sucker for the dramatic gesture, and there was no doubt that this unsub had a flair for the dramatic. The truth was that this guy had got me at hello.

CHAPTER TWO

"Jefferson Winter?"

The question echoed around the vast hangar. I traced the sound to its origin and saw a giant bald black guy standing by the steps of a Gulfstream G550. The size of the hangar made the private jet look like a toy, yet this guy still looked huge in comparison to the plane. All the perspectives were wrong.

I walked over to the jet, my footsteps disappearing into the girders. Up close, the black guy really was a giant. Six-six and at least two-eighty pounds of solid muscle. I'm only five-nine, so he towered above me by almost a whole foot. The conflicting shadows cast by the overhead lights spread from his feet in all directions, creating a lake of grey with him standing slap bang in the middle. His black uniform had a shiny gold star on the chest, and Dayton Sheriff's Department patches on both arms. It looked brand new.

He was younger than I'd first thought. Early twenties, maybe even late teens. He had one of those baby faces, a trust-me face. It was open and honest, and I wondered how long that would last. This job wore everyone down, some faster than others. Given enough time, the darkness always found a way in.

I was also wondering about that private jet. The FBI could afford a Gulfstream, it could actually afford two, but the FBI had an annual budget in excess of eight billion dollars. From what little I'd gleaned off the internet, it was a safe bet that the Dayton Sheriff's Department was not operating on a ten-figure budget. Six figures was probably closer to the mark, and once the day-to-day expenses were taken care of there wouldn't be much left for those little luxuries.

Like a Gulfstream.

There were no clues on the plane itself. Gleaming white paintwork, a number on the tail, and that was it. No logos, which was unusual. People who owned private jets wanted you to know who they were. They wanted to advertise their wealth and status. They wanted to fly that flag from the highest mast, and that mast went all the way up to 51,000 feet. Owning a private jet had nothing to do with getting from A to B, and everything to do with showing the world how important you were. There was a reason the president had his own 747 rather than flying coach, and, as much as the White House PR department would like you to believe otherwise, that reason had little to do with pragmatism.

The big guy was hiding his nerves well. There was an electrical buzz in his movements, and he kept checking the far shadows for snipers. He didn't know what to do with his hands. Should he offer one so we could shake? Should he offer to take my suitcase? In the end, I made the decision for him. I put my case down and held out my hand. He hesitated, then shook it. His hand swallowed mine, completely engulfed it. At the same time, there was a gentleness that surprised me.

"Nice ride you've got there," I said, nodding to the plane.

"I wish."

That deep resonant bear growl again, a low rumble that started way down in his diaphragm. The voice was still young enough to lack authority, but something about this guy hinted that this would come in time. There were no rank markings on his uniform, which meant he was right down at the bottom of the pecking order. The spark of intelligence in his eyes indicated this was a temporary state of affairs.

Big, yes. Stupid, not a chance.

"What's your name?" I asked.

"Taylor."

"That's it? Just Taylor?"

A nod. "Just Taylor."

"Which means your first name must be something really embarrassing." I grinned. "You might as well tell me now. I will find out."

"No you won't," he said, mirroring my grin.

An airport worker appeared from nowhere and magicked my suitcase off into the hold. Everything I needed to get through the day was in it. Since my father's execution I had spent my life travelling the world hunting serial criminals, and I'd travelled light. I'd chased monsters in Paris and Sydney, LA and

London, Johannesburg and Buenos Aires. Evil had no respect for borders.

These days home was whatever hotel suite I found myself booked into, which suited me fine. Some were more comfortable than others, but that didn't worry me. Even the most basic suite was going to be better than a crappy motel room, and believe me I'd seen more than my share of those.

I did own a house. It was up in Virginia, within easy commuting distance of Quantico. I hadn't been back there in years, and had no intention of doing so any time soon, but I couldn't quite bring myself to sell it. I'm sure a psychiatrist could give a dozen good reasons why I hadn't, and I'm sure some of those might even have been valid. I guess that everyone needs somewhere they can call home, even if it's an empty gesture.

Before I quit the FBI I was their lead profiler, the youngest in the history of the Behavioral Analysis Unit. I had the G-man suit, the shiny shoes and worked from dawn until dusk for a faceless master I respected less and less with each and every passing day. The execution was my personal Road to Damascus. A couple of days after the state of California pumped a lethal chemical cocktail into my father, I quit.

Whenever I picture my father, it's in that execution chamber. It took six minutes and twenty-three seconds for him to die and for most of that time he was unconscious. Unlike Sam Galloway, he got off far too easy.

Way too easy.

I've seen the case files. Seen the photographs. My father murdered fifteen women before he was caught. He abducted them and took them to the wide rolling forests of Oregon, then hunted them down with a high-powered rifle and a night scope.

My father had left those girls where they died. He hadn't even bothered to dig them a shallow grave. Exposure to the elements had sped up the decomposition process. The insects and animals had feasted on their flesh. It's amazing how quickly Mother Nature can strip away beauty, how merciless she can be.

In my opinion, they should have skipped the pentobarbital. My father should have left this world struggling for his last breath, fully awake and fully aware. That still wouldn't have come close to making amends, but it would have been a start.

"Marion," I said. "Your parents were big John Wayne fans."

"Not even close."

"Chuck?"

Taylor laughed and made an "after-you" gesture and we climbed the stairs. The flight attendant who greeted us when we ducked into the cabin was in her early fifties. Hair dyed black to disguise the grey, sensible flat shoes. She'd been hired for her ability to do the job, not her looks, which said a lot about the person who owned the plane. There was a time for looks and a time for efficiency. When it came to flight attendants, I'd take efficiency over looks any day. Flying was tedious enough without adding incompetence into the mix.

The interior of the Gulfstream was understated and subdued and reminded me of the FBI's jets. There were none of the ostentatious touches you associated with rock stars or the Hollywood glitterati. None of the bling.

Toward the back there was a table with four black leather chairs surrounding a walnut-topped table. I got comfy in the forward-facing window seat and put my laptop case on the table. Taylor folded himself into the aisle seat opposite and stretched his legs out as far as he could. The jet started rolling and he reached for his seatbelt.

"I wouldn't bother," I told him. "One perk of flying in a private jet is that you don't have to wear a seatbelt."

"What if we crash?"

"If we crash, we die. That seatbelt won't save you. Twenty-five tons of metal smashing into the ground at five hundred miles an hour, you really think that tiny strap is going to save your life?"

Taylor gave me the look. His eyes were narrowed, his brow furrowed, and he was staring at me like I'd grown an extra head. It was a look I was used to.

"The reason the FAA insist you wear a seatbelt on take-off and landing comes down to crowd control," I continued. "If there's an emergency the last thing you want are three hundred hysterical people running up and down the aisles. The same thing goes for the oxygen masks. That's all about crowd control, too. Those things pump out pure oxygen. Breathe that stuff in and it leaves you feeling euphoric. Would you rather your last moments were filled with terror, or would you rather believe that you were about to reach out and touch the hand of God?"

Taylor looked at me again.

A minute later we turned onto the runway and stopped. The engines whined, and then we were propelled forward like a pebble from a slingshot. The Gulfstream lifted off in a fraction of the distance a passenger jet needed. A grind and a whine as the undercarriage retracted, then we carried on climbing at a comfortable twenty degrees. Whoever was at the stick knew his stuff. The take-off was a textbook civilian effort. No drama, no fuss, and boring as hell.

Outside the tiny porthole window, Charleston shrunk to toy-town size and Carl Tindle became nothing more than a memory. Carl wasn't the worst I'd come across, but that didn't make him a saint. Far from it. Carl had a thing for coeds, and once he'd done his thing he suffocated them with a plastic bag and a leather belt. By the time I came on board his body count was up to eight.

Identifying Carl was straightforward enough and I'd managed that by the end of day one. The challenge was catching him. There was plenty of empty space in South Carolina, lots of places to hide. We eventually tracked Carl down to a remote cabin near the coast, and when he realised he was surrounded he came in quietly enough.

Unlike my father, Carl would not live long enough for the death sentence appeals to play out. Carl Tindle was a small man, a weak man, a dead man walking. He wouldn't see the end of the year. There was every chance he'd be dead before the week was out, suicide or shanked. Prison justice was harsh and brutal, and so much more effective than the courtroom variety.

When it came to getting the job done, I knew which one I put my faith in.

CHAPTER THREE

The flight attendant appeared shortly after we'd passed through the clouds. She handed us a couple of menus, asked what we wanted to eat and drink, then disappeared to the galley at the rear. When she returned with our drinks we were still climbing. I was thinking about who owned the Gulfstream again. If I owned a private jet I'd be fussy about who borrowed it. The local sheriff's department would be way down the list. The easiest thing would be to ask Taylor, but I wasn't ready to go there yet.

I booted up my laptop, clicked open the film clip of Sam Galloway's last moments, hit play and turned the computer around so Taylor could see the screen. The smell of beef bourguignon drifted from the back. If the smell was anything to go by, I'd made a good choice.

"Watch carefully, then tell me what you see."

I reached for my coffee and took a sip. It had come from the Blue Mountains of Jamaica and was spectacularly smooth. The conditions in the Blue Mountains are perfect for growing coffee. Rich soil, good drainage, and a climate that's cool, misty and wet. Put that all together and you end up with some of the finest coffee known to man.

Taylor was drinking a Pepsi. He didn't know what he was missing.

I looked over at him. Light from the screen flickered and reflected in his eyes, a series of warped, indistinct images. His discomfort was obvious in his facial expressions, and a couple of times he winced as though what he was seeing on the screen was happening to him. Taylor would also be overcompensating for the lack of sound. He wouldn't be able to help himself. His imagination would be providing a soundtrack that owed more to every horror movie he'd ever seen than to what he was actually watching.

The grey and white in his eyes turned to orange and yellow and he winced again. He rubbed his hands together like there were flames on his fingertips and he was trying to extinguish them. Orange became black and he turned the laptop back around so it was facing me.

"So?" I asked.

Taylor shook his head. "I don't get paid enough to have opinions on something like this, Mr Winter. This goes way above my pay grade."

I let loose with a mock yawn, really milked it.

"Look, I've been a cop for six months. I know how to write tickets. I'm so integral to the running of the department that they can afford to send me all the way up to Charleston to meet you. I don't know if you've noticed, but this isn't a sheriff's uniform I'm wearing."

"First off, call me Winter. Secondly, interesting choice of words. You could have chosen any rank, but you chose sheriff. The man at the top. That means at some point in time, probably more than once, you've stood in front of a mirror and imagined yourself in a brand new sheriff's uniform."

Taylor's cheeks darkened with a blush. The contrast was nowhere near as pronounced as red on white skin, but it was definitely there. For a moment it wasn't a two-hundred-and-eighty-pound giant sitting opposite me, it was a school kid who stood out because he'd always been a foot taller and a hundred pounds heavier than his classmates.

"Also," I added, "you're smart enough to realise the chances of that happening in northern Louisiana are zilch. So your game plan is to keep your head down, work hard, and progress through the ranks as far as you can until you've racked up enough experience to move to a more racially enlightened part of the country."

Taylor reached for his Pepsi and took a drink.

"I'm not hearing any rebuttals," I said.

"There's nothing wrong with being ambitious."

"Nothing at all. What's more, I promise that if you answer my question I won't let on to your colleagues how smart you really are."

Another long look, but, again, no denials.

"You dumbed down on the entrance exam, didn't you? Played it so you passed comfortably? You could have excelled, you probably could have got the highest score in the whole history of the Dayton Sheriff's Department, but you didn't because the last thing you need is for your colleagues to feel uncomfortable when they're around you. My guess is that you've got that whole dumb, gentle giant act down to a fine art. You've had plenty of practice, right?"

Taylor didn't deny this, either, but he didn't have to because the guilt was written all over his face.

"George," I said.

"Like Steinbeck's George?" Taylor shook his head. "I credited you with more imagination."

I nodded to the laptop. "Okay, back to business. What do you think?"

Taylor sighed and chewed at his lip, then he shook his head and said, "Nobody should have to die like that."

Which echoed my first impressions. Unfortunately that was an emotional response and no use to us whatsoever. "Try again, but this time put your emotions aside."

Taylor went to say something. He hesitated, smiled. "Emotion."

"Go on."

"The killer could be a robot for all the emotion he's showing. He comes onto the screen, tips gasoline all over Sam Galloway, tosses a match on him, then walks off. He could have been lighting a barbecue. This guy's a psychopath. It's textbook."

I shook my head. "You're right about one thing. The lack of emotion is key here. Where you went wrong was your assumption that our firestarter is a psychopath. He isn't."

"Of course he is. He didn't just murder Galloway, he *torched* him. He could have killed him a dozen ways that were quicker, a bullet to the head, for example, but he didn't. He set him on fire, and the only reason you'd do something like that is because you want your victim to suffer."

"And you've just put two and two together and got five. Sometimes that's a good thing, but not this time."

"So what does four look like?"

"Good question."

"You're not going to answer, are you?"

"Not yet."

A couple of clicks was all it took to navigate to the webpage.

10:42:08.

This game of hangman had just started. At the moment there was only the base of the gallows and a tall back post. Another second passed and the top beam appeared. It was currently eighteen minutes after one in Dayton. Time was marching on, getting ever closer to midnight. The fact that this unsub had chosen midnight as his zero hour was another example of his flair for the dramatic. I turned the computer around so Taylor could see the screen.

"And what do you think of this?"

White light flickered in Taylor's eyes. One flash for every second, like a slow, steady, relaxed heartbeat. Ten seconds passed, twenty. Two more stick figures bit the dust. Taylor stared at the screen, entranced.

Thinking.

He looked over at me, grim-faced. "It's a promise. He's telling us that Sam Galloway was just the start. He's going to kill again."

CHAPTER FOUR

"I've got a question," said Taylor.

I pulled out my earbuds and opened my eyes. The second movement of Mozart's Jupiter Symphony turned to tin and lost its richness. I reached for my laptop and killed the sound. We were an hour into the flight, halfway to Louisiana, and 51,000 feet below us the wide empty spaces of Alabama would soon give way to Mississippi. The beef bourguignon had been every bit as good as I'd anticipated. Almost as good as the coffee.

Taylor had an earnest expression on his face and I knew what was coming next. I'd heard this particular question a thousand times. What my father had done was no secret, and people were naturally curious.

There were two main variations of the question. The first was to ask how I couldn't have known. How was it possible to live under the same roof as a serial killer and not know what he really was?

The answer to that one was simple. My father was intelligent, manipulative and completely plausible. Unlike our firestarter, my father *was* a textbook psychopath. He taught math at college and was well liked by both his students and his colleagues. He created the illusion of a real life that was so believable nobody suspected a thing.

Variation number two of the question: what was it like to have a serial killer for a father? Usually I'd answer this with another question. What's it like to have a father who's a doctor, or an accountant, or a garbage man? More often than not, this answer was taken for rudeness and tended to stop the conversation dead. Ironically, if the person doing the asking actually stopped to think about what I'd said they would have realised they'd got their answer.

Put aside the fact that my father was a serial killer, he was just some guy who taught math and had a wife and kid at home. He worked hard to be normal. He blended in. He never beat or abused me or my mother. His worst crime was that he could occasionally be distant and controlling, but there were millions of fathers who fell into those two categories.

Until the FBI came crashing into our lives we were your average family. A little more dysfunctional than some, a little less dysfunctional than others. There were arguments and reconciliations, holidays and good times. Plenty of bad times, too. We had our share of Norman Rockwell moments, and we had our Hieronymus Bosch moments, too. Sometimes we hated each other, sometimes we tolerated each other, and occasionally we loved one another. Just a normal family, in other words.

"Go on. Ask away," I said.

Taylor hesitated, which again was pretty much par for the course. He gazed out the small porthole window, stared deep into the blue and white haze. When he turned back, the earnest expression had gone.

"What's with the white hair?"

I laughed and shook my head, and Taylor said "What?" He was back to looking like a kid trapped in a giant's body again.

Lost and uncertain, and overly defensive.

"It's nothing. That wasn't the question I was expecting, that's all."

"If you don't want to answer, I understand."

I waved his comment away. "The white hair's a genetic thing. My father went white in his twenties. My grandfather, too. I was only twenty-one."

"That wasn't what I was getting at. Why don't you dye it? I mean, you're what, early thirties? You could pull it off. It's not like you're some loser who's pretending he's still young."

There were a dozen ways to answer that, some more truthful than others. The real truth went back to that execution chamber in San Quentin. My father's last words were aimed directly at me. He'd stared through the Plexiglas, stared straight at me, and mouthed three words: *We're the same*. I knew he was just messing with my head, but I'd be lying to myself if I didn't acknowledge that there was some truth in those three words.

There's a reason I'm good at what I do. My training at Quantico is part of it, but only a small part. I know how serial criminals think. Except that doesn't quite cut it. What I do goes deeper than just knowing. I understand them. I've been inside their heads, walked in their shoes. There's something embedded in my DNA that enables me to get up close and personal with these monsters, and that DNA had to come from somewhere.

I wasn't about to get into all that with Taylor though. A lesser truth would be to tell him that I didn't dye my hair because my father had dyed his, but I wasn't about to go there, either.

"Why do you hunch your shoulders when you walk? Why do you keep your fingers curled into your palms?"

"I don't know what you're talking about."

"Most people travel the middle road, but occasionally you get people who exist at the edge of that road. The outsiders. You and me, we're more alike than you realise."

Taylor snorted a laugh. "Yeah, right. You're the genius profiler, and I'm the rookie cop. I could see how people might confuse us. And that's before you get into the whole size and race thing."

"I said alike, not the same. Big difference. You stand out because you're built like a mountain. I stand out because I'm good at what I do and my father murdered fifteen women. Your way of dealing with that is to try and make yourself appear smaller. That's why you walk with a stoop and hide your hands."

"And your way of dealing with it is to stand out. That's why you don't dye your hair. And that's why you dress like you're in a grunge band."

I raised an eyebrow. "Grunge?"

"You know what I'm talking about. The designer jeans, the scuffed boots, the T-shirt, the leather jacket, that hair." Taylor laughed. "You might look like you've just stepped out of a dumpster, but it takes time to cultivate a look like that."

That was worth a laugh.

"Okay," Taylor continued. "Here's another question. Do you have any idea who the bad guy is?"

"I've got a few ideas, but nothing I'm willing to share. And before you ask, it's because a bad profile is one of the best ways to screw up a case. We need to see that crime scene before I say anything."

"He's got to be smart, though. Programming that webpage couldn't have been easy."

"Stop fishing."

Taylor ignored me and said, "So we're looking for someone whose computer skills are above average. I mean, I couldn't knock up a website with a countdown on it, never mind that whole hangman thing."

"You really want to go there?"

Taylor answered with a nod.

"Outsourcing," I said, and he gave me a puzzled look.

"You were right about one thing: this guy is smart. How many people in Eagle Creek have those sorts of computer skills? The answer is probably none. However, for the purpose of this exercise, let's say you have two or three. So you round them up, interview them until one of them cracks and confesses, case closed. No, if this guy had those sort of computer skills there's no way he'd advertise the fact. He's too smart for that."

"So he does what everybody else does," said Taylor, the words rolling out on a sigh. "He outsources. He gets some programmer in Mumbai or the Philippines or Thailand to write the code. They'll do it for peanuts, and we could spend a year chasing down that lead and still be no further forward. Okay, say it: it was a dumb idea."

Taylor's expression reminded me of a puppy dog who'd been scolded for chewing up the sofa.

"Don't be so hard on yourself. It would make life so much easier if this guy was some sort of megalomaniacal computer genius straight from the pages of a Marvel comic, but he's not. Unfortunately, it's never that easy."

Tell me about it, Taylor said with a roll of the eyes, and for a second he looked a whole lot older than he was. "And what if we don't find the crime scene, Winter? What then?"

"You'll find it. This unsub's a performer. He's a show-off. He thinks he's smarter than we are, and he wants to rub our faces in it."

"So we'll find the scene because he wants us to find it."

"Got it in one. So what can you tell me about Sam Galloway?"

"Nothing you haven't seen in the files Sheriff Fortier sent you."

I gave a derisory snort and shook my head. "The problem with files is that people are inherently lazy. When you write out a report, you cut corners. Everyone does. It takes time to write something down and there just aren't enough hours in the day. Never trust reports, okay?"

"Okay."

"Sam Galloway," I prompted.

"Galloway was five-ten, forty-two years old, black hair turned mostly to grey."

I let loose with another fake yawn. "Boring. I don't need his shirt size, I need to know who he was. What made him tick. What made him get out of bed in the morning."

"He was a lawyer. Married for twenty years. He had three kids. A son and two daughters."

"Now you're getting warmer. Did he have enemies? Affairs? The kids, are they on drugs?"

"How the hell should I know?"

"You know because Eagle Creek has a population of less than ten thousand people and Sam has just been murdered. That means there will be all sorts of rumours flying around right now."

"Cops are supposed to deal with facts, not rumours."

"And that sounds like a line that's been fed to you. Fortier, perhaps?"

Taylor nodded.

"Okay, forget what Fortier's told you. Cops don't deal with facts, they deal with information. Facts are great, but rumours can be just as useful."

Taylor thought for a second, then shook his head. "No affairs that I've heard about. The marriage was solid. As for the kids, they're a dead end too. They're aged ten to fifteen and, by all accounts, they're good kids. No drugs, no arrests, and no pregnancies. And, as for work, Galloway dealt with the dull end of the law. Divorces, wills, property, that sort of thing. It's not like he was a criminal lawyer who'd made a load of enemies."

"Except he did make one enemy."

"And what if his murder was random?"

"It wasn't. The person responsible for this is a highly organised serial killer. Nothing he does is random."

"Don't you have to kill a minimum of three people to get serial-killer status?"

"That's just a detail. Trust me, this guy's a serial killer. The film clip and the countdown prove that. No one except a serial killer would go to those sort of lengths. By the way, the film was attached to an email, right? I take it you've tried to trace it?"

"Not me personally, but yeah it's been looked into."

"And nothing?"

Taylor shook his head slowly. "Nothing."

I clapped my hands and rubbed them together. "Okay, are you ready for some fun? You might want to fasten your safety belt for this."

Taylor's eyes narrowed. "What are you up to?"

"Get the flight attendant to buckle herself in, too."

"But you said safety belts were a waste of time."

"No, what I said was that they would be useless if we crashed. I can assure you that we're not about to crash any time soon."

I jumped from my seat and headed to the front of the plane. Since 9/11 the pilots on passenger jets have been locked away on the flight deck. But this wasn't a passenger plane. The rules were different here. One law for the rich, one for the poor. I did a sharp *rat-a-tat* knock on the flight deck door then pushed it open.

The pilot was in his late fifties, and had ex-military written all over him. He was sizing me up over his shoulder, trying to decide if I was a friend or foe. Trying to decide if I was crazy.

"Can I help you, sir?"

"I really do hope so. You have the ultimate boy's toy here, right? We're talking at least fifty million dollars' worth of fun, yet you're flying it like you're taking a load of old folks out to Florida. That must kill you."

The pilot's face relaxed. His whole body relaxed. He gave a knowing smile. "Yes, sir, there are times when it can get a little frustrating."

"Okay, so how about for the rest of the flight you fly this plane like it belongs to you?"

"I can't do that."

"Of course you can. What's more, I'm betting that every time you take the controls you dream of doing just that. Compared to flying fighter jets this has got to be so boring."

"How did you know I flew fighter jets?"

"Call it a gift."

I smiled conspiratorially. The pilot stared at me for a moment, then a slow smile spread over his face.

"Get back to your seat and get buckled in. Give me a holler when you're ready."

I jogged back to my seat, strapped myself in, grinned at Taylor.

"You've no idea how many times I wanted to do this when I was with the FBI."

"What the hell are you up to, Winter?" Taylor was tugging at his safety belt, pulling it as tight as it would go.

"You'll see. Okay," I shouted up to the pilot. "We're good to go back here."

The first barrel roll took my breath away.

CHAPTER FIVE

The pilot did a low pass from the north so I could see Dayton Parish in all its glory. We came in over the Arkansas–Louisiana border at three thousand feet. Low enough to get an impression of what lay below us, but without the fine detail you get at a thousand feet. There were forests and lakes and farms, hills that would never be mistaken for mountains, and a scattering of small towns connected by winding two-lane roads. Lots of space, not very many people.

Every state claims to be unique, but some are more unique than others, and Louisiana was right up there in the top three. The state wears its differences like a badge of honour. For a start, it's the only state divided into parishes rather than counties. Louisiana was formed from a mix of Spanish and French colonies, and the carve-up into parishes reflects those Roman Catholic roots.

The French and Spanish influence stretches way beyond the geographical borders, though. It can be seen in the architecture and the food, and in a hundred other ways both big and small that make Louisiana stand out from the other forty-nine states.

The first thing that struck me about Dayton was the lack of swampland. Think of Louisiana and you think of swamps and alligators and Cajun food and Mardi Gras. You don't think of farms, yet that's what was below us, a patchwork of fields in various shades of green and brown.

Dayton was two hundred feet above sea level, whereas parts of New Orleans were six feet below, and that simple fact separated north from south. To all intents and purposes we could have been in a completely different state from the Louisiana that everyone thought they knew.

Eagle Creek was at the bottom end of Dayton, sitting ten miles to the north of I-20, a six-lane interstate that cuts across the top end of the state from east to west. The town was laid out like thousands of other small towns. Offices and factories and a shopping mall on the outer ring where land was cheap. Move to the middle ring and that's where you found the people. Apartments and houses, school buildings and community centres, parks and a Little League field. Move on to the centre and there were the municipal buildings.

On the south side of the interstate was the sprawling expanse of an abandoned oil refinery. Grey concrete and scorched earth and tons of steel. The refinery shimmered in the summer sun, a confusion of pipework and tanks and tall metal. A railroad ran parallel to I-20 and split the town neatly in two, and a disused branch line led out to the refinery.

The big fancy houses were clustered in their own perfect sea of green to the north-west. Well out of earshot of the interstate, and well out of eyesight of the old refinery, and just a short drive from the golf course.

We banked sharply to the right and made our final approach into Eagle Creek's tiny airfield. For a few seconds we were flying so low over the fields that you could have reached out and touched them. There was that moment where you hoped the pilot knew what he was doing, then the runway appeared from nowhere and we touched down, the reverse thrusters bringing us to a virtual standstill.

We taxied past a line of small private propeller planes and pulled into a hangar that had been built away from the other buildings. Like the Gulfstream, the hangar was painted white and had no markings to indicate who owned it. The only other vehicles inside the hangar were a helicopter and a black police cruiser covered in Dayton Sheriff's Department markings. The Gulfstream rolled to a halt beside the car, and the jets idled then died.

It was almost three in the afternoon. The journey from Charleston to Eagle Creek had taken exactly two hours. I could picture those white numbers counting down to zero against that pitch-black background: 09:06:34.

At the door we said thanks and bye to the pilot and flight attendant, then climbed down the steps. The heat hit me straight away. It was like getting off a plane in the tropics. It smelled the same, too. Kerosene and sun-baked vegetation.

I got into the passenger seat of the police cruiser. Taylor squashed himself behind the wheel. The partition had been removed and his seat was racked back as far as it would go, but he still looked like he was squeezing himself into a toy car. My suitcase and laptop bag went onto the back seat and Taylor started the engine.

"Sue," I said. "You're the boy called Sue."

"What the hell are you talking about?"

"It's a Johnny Cash song."

"My parents are more into Motown."

"How about Marvin, then? Like Marvin Gaye. Marvin Taylor? Yeah I can see that. It's got a nice ring to it."

Taylor laughed. We pulled out of the hangar and the sound of the engine changed from a muted throb to a distant growl. Bright sunshine flooded the car and I put on my sunglasses.

"You might as well quit now, Winter. You're not going to get it."

"And that sounds like a challenge."

"Not a challenge, a fact."

"And you're prepared to put your money where your mouth is? How about fifty bucks?"

"Fifty? Let's make it really interesting. How about two hundred?"

"You sure you can afford to lose that on a rookie's salary?"

Taylor let loose with a deep belly laugh. "No way am I going to lose this one."

"Okay, here's the deal. If I don't find out what your first name is by the time I leave, then I'll happily pay you two hundred bucks."

I reached across and we shook, Taylor's gentle hand swallowing mine.

"You might as well pay up now, Winter. Save yourself the trouble."

I smiled and settled back in my seat, the sun blazing through the windshield warming my skin. "Funnily enough, I was just about to say the exact same thing to you."

CHAPTER SIX

Five minutes after leaving the airfield we hit Main Street. We came in from the south and kept to the speed limit all the way. The first structure I saw was a church, and the first billboard had a large poster proclaiming that JESUS DIED FOR YOU! WOULD YOU DIE FOR HIM? in four-foot-high blood-red letters.

Get this far into the Southern badlands and poverty was rife. Small towns were dying. That's a fact. It's like a plague had hit. Abandoned, ruined buildings littered the landscape, and boarded-up shops were the rule rather than the exception. Most of the houses were rundown with dirt yards and rusty chicken-wire fencing.

That wasn't the case in Eagle Creek. There was bright, shiny paintwork wherever you looked, and every single window sparkled. The road was so smooth it could have been resurfaced a week ago.

The park in the town centre was surrounded by buildings that shimmered in the afternoon heat. Large, important-looking grey and white monuments as opposed to the squat two-storey structures on the rest of Main Street. The courthouse, the mayor's office, the library.

The Eagle Creek Police Department's HQ was next to the courthouse, a couple of cruisers and a 4×4 parked out front. The sheriff's department had got in there first and claimed black for its cars and uniforms, which meant the police department had to settle for tan. Black on a cop car was always going to look way cooler than tan. The police department vehicles looked as bright and shiny as everything else on Main Street, like they'd just rolled off the factory floor.

In the middle of the park was a tall white statue of a stern-looking man. The Stars and Stripes hung from a flagpole beside the statue. There was no breeze to stir the flag and it clung limply to the pole. The red, white and blue was so bright it hurt your eyes. The manicured grass could have been a golf green.

We carried on north and the buildings dropped down in size to two storeys again. Shops on the first floor, apartments on the second. The sheriff department's station house was based in a large building right up at the north end of Main Street.

Taylor pulled into the lot at the back and reversed into a slot beside all the other police vehicles. There were four vehicles on our left, five on the right, a mix of sedans and 4×4s, the oldest only a couple of years old. A ten-car fleet like this indicated a recent investment in the hundreds of thousands.

On the other side of the lot were two rows of vehicles that weren't cop cars. These cars didn't look brand new. Most were at least five years old, and almost all of them were American. There was a mix of makes and models, a mix of conditions. Some were well loved while others were suffering from a serious case of neglect.

Stepping outside again was like stepping into a blast furnace. Mid-afternoon and the mercury had to be pushing past the hundred mark. The heat was a solid thing that slammed into you and stole your breath away. By the time we'd crossed the parking lot, I'd already worked up a sweat. I wiped the drops from my forehead as we walked into the air-conditioned cool of the station house. The heat was bad, but the humidity was the real killer.

The dispatcher at the front desk told us that Sheriff Fortier was expecting us, and Taylor led the way through a maze of corridors to a door with a smoked-glass window and SHERIFF PETER FORTIER stencilled in gold. Taylor knocked once and a voice on the other side told us to enter.

Like the rest of the station house, Fortier's office was immaculate. A tidy oak desk with a large leather chair dominated the space, and the in- and out-trays looked well under control. The whitewashed walls were actually white, and the striplight had been cleaned this side of Christmas.

One wall was taken up with pictures of boats and fish. Fortier was in all of them, either standing at the wheel wearing a battered blue cap with a red anchor stitched on the front, or standing in that same cap holding up the catch of the day. There was a marked difference between the grim-faced man behind the oak desk and the smiling, tanned fisherman in the photographs.

Fortier came around to the front of the desk, arm outstretched, and we shook. He had a grip like a bear and I could feel my bones grinding together. He gave me the once-over, trying not to make it too obvious. I was used to being stared at so it didn't bother me.

While Fortier looked me over, I checked him out. The sheriff was in his mid-fifties and stood at five-five, four inches shorter than me, and a whole foot and an inch shorter than Taylor. Put us in a line and we could have been the three bears. He had grey hair and a ruddy outdoors complexion from all that time spent fishing. There were red blooms on his cheek, and the skin was tight and shiny. His uniform was as immaculate as his office. Creases in all the right places and shoes spit-shined.

He looked tired, though, bone-weary, like all the fight had been knocked out of him. My guess was that he wouldn't be running for sheriff in the next election. If that decision hadn't already been made, then what happened to Sam Galloway had tipped the scales. Here was someone desperate to leave the troubles of the real world behind, someone who spent his days staring at the pictures on his office wall and dreaming of a time when he could while away his remaining years fishing for marlin and drinking bourbon.

"Thanks for coming at such short notice," said Fortier.

"No problem."

"I've got to admit, though, I'm surprised you came at all. When I contacted you, it was a real long shot. I know you usually only deal with serial killers and this guy isn't a serial killer, but I'd been following what you'd been up to in South Carolina, and since Charleston is only a short plane hop away, I thought what the hell. Nothing ventured. Anyway, anything you can do to help, we're all ears. Anything you need, just ask."

The speech sounded rehearsed, like he'd spent all morning in here practising. "Serial criminals," I told him.

"Excuse me?"

"Serial criminals. I deal with them all. Kidnappers, rapists, arsonists, extortionists, murderers. And I hate to be the bearer of bad news, but this guy *is* a serial killer."

"How do you figure that one?"

"Because Sam Galloway's murder was pure theatre. Here's a question for you: what do you think's going to happen when the countdown hits zero?" I could tell by the look on his face that he'd already considered this, and that we'd come to the same conclusion. "Unless you catch this guy, and catch him quickly, he will kill again, and again. He's going to keep going until someone stops him. Believe me, he's just got started."

"So you don't think this is a one-off?"

"Not a chance."

Fortier seemed to shrink in front of me. He'd clearly wanted a different answer. All the same, nothing I'd said had come as a great surprise. If this murder had been a one-off it would have made his life easier. One murder was a headache, but a series of them was a nightmare.

"What's the situation with the press?" I asked.

"All quiet on that front. The town has a weekly newspaper, the *Eagle Creek Courier*. It's pretty much a one-man show. Harry Spindler, the fellow who runs it, prefers drinking to writing. The next edition doesn't come out until next week. So long as he's got something to put on his front page by then he won't give us any trouble."

"What about outside town?"

"Shreveport and Monroe are the closest big cities. Nothing much happens in Eagle Creek, so I doubt the media folks there could even find us on a map."

"Nothing much happened until now."

"I'm confident that when they come knocking, I can handle them."

I didn't doubt that. In my experience a typical sheriff was five per cent cop and ninety-five per cent politician. Fortier might look like he was on the ropes, but he also looked as though he'd been doing the job long enough that he could successfully run interference with the press without breaking much of a sweat.

"It would be good if we could keep this as quiet as possible for as long as possible," I said. "This guy's looking for an audience and if we can deny him that then it might push him into doing something dumb in order to get attention. The dumber they act the easier they are to catch."

Fortier smiled and for a brief moment I caught a glimpse of the man he'd been three decades ago, someone with ambitions, and dreams that didn't end at the rippling line where water met land.

"I'll do what I can."

"Same goes for the website. We need to keep that one quiet too. That's another cry for attention. Who knows about it?"

The smile slipped, and the old guy who dreamt of marlin and bourbon was back. "Too many people. It's common knowledge within the department, and I obviously told the police chief. And the mayor, of course, he needed to know."

"Damage limitation's the name of the game there. Put the word out to keep this as quiet as possible. I doubt it'll do much good, but you never know."

"Horses and unbolted stable doors." Fortier shook his head. "I should have thought that one through."

"The fact the media aren't camped out in your parking lot is a good indicator that they haven't picked up on the website yet. That's going to get them more excited than a dead lawyer, you can bet on that. Who knows, maybe you can keep a lid on this." I thought for a second then added, "Silly question, but I'm guessing that everyone in town has heard about Sam Galloway by now?"

Fortier snorted a laugh. "What do you think?"

"A town this small, I think it would be a miracle if they hadn't, and I'm not a great believer in miracles."

"We haven't discussed your fee yet."

"Don't worry about that. I charge what I think people can afford. For me the case is more important than the money. I promise I won't bankrupt you."

Fortier chuckled at that. "I'd like to see you try."

"What's that supposed to mean?"

The sheriff waved the question away. "Send your bill through when you're done. And make sure you include all your expenses. I'm taking it you'll need a little time to get up to speed before you give us a profile."

I glanced over at Taylor, waited until he met my eye, then said, "Officer Taylor brought me up to speed on the plane. I'm ready to give the profile whenever you are."

CHAPTER SEVEN

Sheriff Fortier led us along a corridor and stopped at a door that had CAPTAIN ANTHONY SHEPHERD, CRIMINAL INVESTIGATION DIVISION stencilled in gold on the smoked glass. He knocked once and pushed the door open. Shepherd was on the phone. He looked over at us, indicated that he'd just be a second, then wound up the call.

We went through the introductions and the handshakes. Shepherd did the staring thing. He was in his mid-forties, fit and lean, with salt-and-pepper hair. His moustache was neatly trimmed and his glasses had thick black frames. He was wearing a plain brown seersucker suit, a white shirt and a red tie.

Unlike Fortier, Shepherd still had plenty of fight left in him. I wouldn't be surprised if he'd snuck into Fortier's office and tried that big leather chair on for size.

Shepherd did look stressed, but the reason was obvious. It had been ten years since the last murder happened in Dayton. In the last century there had only been twenty murders, an average of one every five years. The one thing those murders had in common was that the victims were killed by someone they knew.

A husband, a brother, a friend. In a couple of instances the murderer had been a wife and the victim was her spouse. Nothing unusual there. Most murderers are known to their victims.

Sam Galloway's murder was a whole new ball game. Shepherd might have had his name stencilled in fancy gold letters on the door, but the reality of the situation was that Dayton's Criminal Investigation Division was made up of Shepherd and two investigators, and things didn't tend to get much more exciting than the occasional housebreak, and high-school kids selling dope.

"Mr Winter is ready to give his profile," Fortier told him.

"Already."

"I'm a fast worker," I said, and I could feel Taylor's eyes burning into the back of my head. "And, please, just Winter is fine. 'Mister' makes me feel old."

"Winter it is, then. It's probably best if we do this next door. There's more space."

Fortier glanced at his watch. "Unfortunately, I've got to go to a meeting. Tony, you can fill me in later?"

"Yes, sir."

Fortier used both hands to shake mine this time, his left grasping my arm. It was a politician's handshake, one that said *I'm here for you*.

"Winter, it's been a pleasure meeting you. And remember what I said. Anything you need, just holler."

"I'll do that."

We filed out of the office, and Fortier peeled off to the right and headed quickly down the corridor.

Whoever he was meeting with was important enough for him to want to be on time. He was one of the big bosses around here. The only people who ranked above him were his wife and the mayor. My money was on his meeting being with the mayor, probably to bring him up to speed on the investigation. Not that there was much to tell.

Shepherd led the way to the next office and entered without knocking. There were two plain-clothed cops in the room. Both male, both in their thirties. Both of them had black hair and blue eyes. They could have been twins except for the fact that one of them had a thirty-inch waist and the other's was forty inches.

There were sweat stains under their armpits, so they'd probably spent the morning out in the heat playing detective and been called back here to meet me. A murder happens in a place like this, the last thing you're going to do is have your entire squad of investigators sat around the office twiddling their thumbs.

The desks were pushed flat against the walls, which was a mistake since it meant the two men spent most of their working days with their backs to one another. The desks should have been pushed together in the middle of the room so they were eye to eye. Brainstorming was much more efficient when you could see the person you were brainstorming with.

They turned from their desks when we entered the room and gave me the new-kid stare. It was a look that combined suspicion and curiosity, a look that said *Who the hell do you think you are?* It was another look I was used to.

After my father's arrest, my mother went into flight mode. She started running the day they came for him, and kept running until she'd drunk herself into an early grave. Between the ages of eleven and seventeen I lived in fifteen different cities in ten different states, so I was used to being the new kid. Even now, whenever I step into a situation like this, it's as though the clock has been wound back. I reckon I'll always be the new kid, no matter how old I get.

Shepherd turned to Taylor and dismissed him with a curt "You can go now."

"Actually," I said, "if it's okay with you, I'd like him to stay. I'm working on the assumption that this unsub's a serial killer. If that's the case then we're going to need all the help we can get."

It sounded like a request, but wasn't, and we both knew it. Everyone in the room knew it. Taylor was frozen to the spot, halfway to the door, unsure what to do. All eyes had turned towards him.

"Okay, you can stay," said Shepherd.

"A serial killer?" This came from the skinny guy.

Shepherd nodded towards the skinny guy. "This is Barker." A nod in the direction of the fat guy. "And this is Romero."

The way he introduced them told me everything I needed to know about the pecking order. Shepherd at the top, then Barker, then Romero. Taylor didn't even figure on the radar, which was crazy, but understandable. Understandable because of his gentle giant act.

Crazy because he was probably smarter than Barker and Romero combined.

Handshakes all around, then I perched on the windowsill. There weren't any spare seats. Barker and Romero didn't look as if they were about to give theirs up any time soon, and Shepherd didn't look like he was about to make them. Even with the blinds down I could feel the burn of the sun. It was twenty-two minutes after three. I pictured the website page, pictured those white numbers glowing on a pitch-black background, pictured another stick figure about to hang.

08:37:23.

"So far you've got one victim, but there are going to be more. By my reckoning the next one is going to turn up in a little over eight and a half hours' time."

"The countdown on that website," Shepherd said. "You think this guy's telling us when he's going to kill again?"

"What else could it be for?"

"But that's crazy. Why the hell do something like that?"

"Okay, the first thing you need to understand here is that serial criminals don't think like normal people. Everything they do is informed by their fantasies. The logic that governs their lives is driven by that. What seems crazy to us seems completely rational to them because the fantasy is everything. Have any of you heard of Richard Trenton Chase?"

Three heads went from side to side. Taylor's stayed very still for a fraction of a second, then followed the rest. You don't need to open your mouth to tell a lie.

"Richard Chase was a serial killer who was active during the seventies. After he was sentenced he was interviewed by the FBI. Chase believed that his blood was turning to powder and he needed the blood of his victims to replenish his. During the interview he talked about 'soap dish poisoning'. When asked what he meant, he said that you could tell who's been poisoned by checking beneath the soap. If the underneath of the soap is gooey, you're okay, but if it's dry then you've been poisoned and your blood is turning to powder."

"Now *that* is crazy," Barker said.

"By normal standards, yes, but the point is that this fantasy made perfect sense to Chase. Our unsub has already done a number of things that seem crazy when taken at face value. The countdown, the fact he filmed the murder and sent it to the police, the fact he chose fire as his murder weapon. To catch this guy we need to forget about what's crazy and concentrate on what his actions tell us."

"And what do his actions tell us?" Romero asked.

"That he's anything but crazy. Serial killers fall into two broad categories. Organised and disorganised. Chase was a classic example of a disorganised killer. He was a paranoid schizophrenic. There was no real planning behind his murders. His first murder was a drive-by shooting. The victim just happened to be in the wrong place at the wrong time. The same could be said for his other five victims. Wrong time, wrong place."

"Surely you could say the same thing about Sam Galloway," said Barker.

"And you'd be wrong. The unsub who killed Sam is highly organised. Everything he does is done for a reason."

"What can you tell us about the unsub?" asked Shepherd.

"You're looking for a white male, five foot nine, who's in his thirties. He's slim-built and he's college-educated."

"Hey, Barker, he could be talking about you," Romero called across the room.

"My alibi's solid," Barker shot back. "I was with your wife last night."

"You two knock it off." Shepherd turned to me. "Okay, what else have you got?"

"That's it for just now. I need to see the crime scene, or a body. Preferably both. You need to get every spare man you've got out there looking."

"Maybe we'll get lucky. Maybe we'll find this guy before he strikes again."

"And maybe the Tooth Fairy and Father Christmas do exist."

Shepherd gave me a sharp look.

"I don't believe in luck. Never have, never will. Luck is the last resort of people who lack imagination. What I believe in is hard work. That's how we're going to catch this guy. Honest, hard work."

Shepherd opened his mouth to say something, and I had a pretty good idea what was coming next. Over the years I've pissed off more than my share of authority figures, sometimes by design and sometimes by accident. This time it had been an accident. On the plus side, I'd just managed to find the limit of how far Shepherd could be pushed. Whenever I walked into a new situation I always liked to know where the lines were drawn.

"Captain Shepherd," I said, respectful and compliant, like a good Boy Scout. "Can I have a quick word in your office?"

CHAPTER EIGHT

We headed next door in silence. Shepherd's shoulders were tense, his movements stiff. He was pretty pissed, and understandably so. On the way out, Taylor caught my eye. His expression was neutral, but the cogs inside his head were spinning and his eyes were burning with questions. He must have been wondering what the hell I was up to.

Shepherd pulled the door closed behind us. He sat down at his desk and motioned for me to take the chair on the other side. A stroke of his neat moustache, then he locked eyes with mine.

"The last resort of people who lack imagination?"

I met his gaze without flinching and said nothing.

"I do not appreciate being made to look a fool in front of my men."

"I can assure you that was not my intention."

"Whether you intended it or not, that's how it came across."

"I know. It's just that sometimes I get so wrapped up in the case, I end up saying things without thinking. I didn't mean any disrespect."

Shepherd considered this for a moment, a heavy silence filling the space between us. He was still staring, and I was still meeting his eye.

"You look at me and see a small-town cop who's way out of his depth. And you know something, you're right. I have no experience with something of this magnitude. No reference point. You, on the other hand, do. If the only way to catch this bastard is to cut you some slack, I'm prepared to cut as much as you need." A pause, another stroke of that neat moustache. His gaze drilled deep into me. "However, please do not disrespect me in front of my men again."

"Understood."

Shepherd settled back in his chair and shook his head. "I just don't get it. How can someone do something like this? Pour gasoline on a fellow human being then stand back and watch them burn? It's sick." He shook his head again, looked at me. "How do you deal with this sort of stuff day in and day out and stay sane? How do you sleep at night?"

"Whisky and sleeping tablets, and who says I've managed to stay sane?"

Shepherd almost laughed. "Does that work, the sleeping pills?"

"Most of the time."

"All I want is for this nightmare to be over, and for things to get back to some semblance of normality."

"You and me both. You're planning on buddying me up with Barker, aren't you?"

"He's a good man. The best I've got."

"No, he's not."

"He can run circles around Romero."

"I don't doubt that for a second."

"So why would you want to work with Romero rather than Barker?"

It took a second for the penny to drop.

"Because you don't want to work with either of them. You want Taylor."

I nodded.

"Why? He's just a rookie. Barker has seventeen years' experience on him."

"I have my reasons."

"And I'd like to hear those reasons."

"You spoke earlier about cutting me some slack." I smiled. "It's time to start cutting."

"Okay, you can have Taylor. But if you change your mind, I can get Barker assigned to you."

"I'm not going to change my mind. Taylor's my wingman on this one." I got up to leave, stopped at the door. "One more thing. I don't suppose you know his first name?"

CHAPTER NINE

Taylor didn't say a word all the way to the car. He didn't say a word when he started up the engine and pulled out of the parking lot. We cruised in silence along Main Street, past the municipal buildings and that tall white statue of the stern-looking man, the engine rumbling, smooth pavement sliding away beneath our tyres. Traffic was light and it only took a couple of minutes to reach the Imperial Hotel at the south end of the street. Taylor killed the engine.

"At some point you're going to have to tell me what you're up to," he said.

"You're right. But now isn't the time."

I opened the passenger door, stepped out into the heat, then leant back into the open doorway, careful to avoid the hot metal.

"I need you to sit tight while I go and check in."

Taylor nodded to my suitcase on the back seat. "Aren't you forgetting something?"

"No." I banged the door shut.

Because of the geography, the Imperial Hotel was one of the newer buildings on Main Street, dating back to sometime around the mid-twentieth century. The really old buildings were the ones surrounding the town square. As you moved outwards the buildings got progressively newer, as dictated by the rules that governed the slow crawl of urban sprawl. Even though the Imperial had first opened its doors just after the Second World War, those windows still gleamed and the facade was shining like it was new.

A blast of cool air hit me as I stepped from the outside brightness into the tomblike gloom created by the hotel's heavy stonework. I pushed my sunglasses up onto the top of my head and made my way to the reception desk. There was worn dark wood everywhere and the lights were shielded by green shades. The carpet was red and gold, but repeated cleaning had dulled the colours. The outside of the building might have suggested the 1950s, but inside it was 1850.

It took a couple of minutes to go through the check-in procedure. When we were done the concierge handed me a key with a wooden fob that had *The Senator's Suite* carved into it.

I have two conditions when I take a case. The first condition is that I get a suite rather than a room. This went back to my FBI days. Despite that multibillion-dollar annual budget, federal agents still had to watch the nickels and dimes. I'd seen the inside of more cheap motel rooms than I care to remember, and that was enough of a reason to insist on a suite. Being a nomad doesn't mean you have to live in a tent.

The second condition was a bottle of single malt. Anything over twelve years was acceptable, but eighteen years plus was preferable.

I told the guy at the desk that my luggage would be along later, then headed back outside and climbed into the passenger seat. Taylor had kept the engine running, and the air-conditioning was turned to full. He was watching stick figures being massacred on his cellphone.

"Tommy Taylor. Someone your size, that would be suitably embarrassing. Little Tommy Taylor. Kind of rolls off the tongue, don't you think?"

He closed his phone and put it away. "So Shepherd wasn't able to help you out?"

"Who said I asked Shepherd?"

Taylor raised an eyebrow.

"I'm going to need a different hotel."

"Why? This one's the best in town."

"I know, and as far as your work buddies are concerned this is where I'm staying."

"You want me to lie."

"Only if they ask."

"And I'm guessing you're still not ready to talk."

"Soon. So, do you know another place or not? I'm looking for quiet and anonymous. Somewhere they don't ask too many questions."

"Yeah, I know a place."

Taylor put the car into gear and pulled away from the side-walk. Fifty yards on he hung a right, and five minutes later we reached the railroad line. The car bumped gently over the tracks, the heavy chassis rising up before settling back on its shocks.

The roads in this part of town were still in good condition, but they weren't as pristine as Main Street.

There was the occasional pothole, and the occasional stray piece of litter blew through like a tumbleweed. The state of the houses was consistent with what you'd expect to find in a relatively prosperous white-collar neighbourhood. Some were cared for like palaces. Paintwork in good order, grass neatly mowed and a flag drooping from a pole in the airless afternoon. Others were crumbling wrecks with overgrown lawns, missing roof tiles, and paintwork that was worn back to the wood. Most fell somewhere between those two extremes.

Morrow Street was lined with bars on both sides, grey two-storey buildings with dark windows. Interspersed amongst these were a couple of guesthouses and diners. Mostly it was just bars, though. This was the dark heart of Eagle Creek. Every town had one, because every town needed one. This was a place where a college kid could get served with ID that was obviously faked, a place where a horny guy with a pocketful of cash could find some relief. If you wanted to score some weed, this was the place to come.

We pulled up outside a guesthouse two-thirds of the way along the street. The door and window frames were bright red, a splash of colour in amongst all the grey. *Hannah's Place* was painted in red on the sign above the door, the letters swirly and flamboyant. I got out of the car, retrieved my suitcase and laptop bag from the back. Taylor took the case from me and I followed him across the sidewalk.

It had just gone four and Morrow Street was deserted. The place had a desolate, lonely feel, like a film set that was about to be dismantled. A couple of bars were advertising Happy Hour from 5.30 'til 7.30. Bad math aside, that was when the area would start to come alive. By nine o'clock enough alcohol would have been consumed to get the place really rocking. I wasn't expecting things to get busy this evening. A Wednesday night the day after a brutal murder, everyone would be staying away in droves.

The inside of the guesthouse was cool, clean and spacious. The scuffed red and white floor tiles were laid out like a chessboard, and there was a faint smell of lemons in the air. A red leather sofa had been pushed into the nook below the staircase. The Fifties Americana feel was enhanced by the black and white stills from old Hollywood that hung on the walls. Marilyn Monroe and Tony Curtis. Rock Hudson and Doris Day. Paul Newman. Marlon Brando. We walked over to reception and Taylor dinged the old-fashioned brass bell.

"One second," a voice called from the back room.

The girl who followed the voice into the room was in her early to mid-twenties but looked at least thirty. Her hands had seen their share of hard work, and she was lean from being busy rather than hours spent in a gym.

She had big brown fawn eyes, and her blonde hair was short and spiky. Piercings in her ears and nose, and a baggy Gutterpigs T-shirt. It looked like she'd cut her hair herself. It was a practical style for someone who didn't have any spare hours in the day. No time wasted in beauty parlours. No time wasted brushing it through. No time wasted, period, because time was precious.

I subscribed to a similar school of thought. My hair was a scruffy white mess that hung to my shoulders. Getting ready meant scrubbing a hand across my head a couple of times after I'd gotten out the shower.

The girl saw Taylor and her smile made the years melt away. For a brief moment she looked her real age. There was an understated beauty there that a tough life had tried hard to steal away.

"Hey, Hannah."

"Hey, Taylor."

Taylor turned to me. "Jefferson Winter meet Hannah Hayden." He turned to the girl. "Hannah meet Jefferson Winter."

"Cool name," I said. "You're a palindrome."

She smiled. "I can honestly say that's the first time anyone's called me that."

"Winter needs a room."

"Well he's in luck, since that's what we do here."

"I don't suppose you've got any suites?" I asked.

"Yeah, they're all up on the third floor. They've got great views."

"Since there are only two floors, I'll take that as a 'no' ".

"I could give you our best room. It's no suite, but it does have its own bathroom."

"Chocolates on the pillows?"

Hannah raised an eyebrow.

"How about a candy bar, then? It's been a while since lunch and my blood sugar level is starting to dip."

She gave me the look, then shrugged. "I don't have any chocolates, but I'm sure I can find you a candy bar."

"In that case you've got a deal."

Hannah looked me up and down and reeled off a price that was probably twenty per cent higher than the going rate. I paid for two nights in advance, then put down an extra hundred and turned it so Benjamin Franklin was staring straight at her.

"I'd appreciate it if you didn't mention to anyone that I'm staying here."

"Sure." The money disappeared.

She handed me the key and Taylor grabbed my suitcase before I could get to it. He led the way up to the second floor and we walked along a narrow corridor to the door at the far end. Hannah was right. The room was no suite. But it was clean and tidy, and the mattress was firm, and there were no alien life forms growing in the bathroom. It would never feature in my top ten, it probably wouldn't even figure in my top fifty, but I'd stayed in a hell of a lot worse.

The drapes were pulled to keep the heat out and the way the material glowed reminded me of a Chinese lantern. Taylor had dumped my case on the bed and was standing there staring at me.

"I want answers, Winter."

"I'm betting you do. If you didn't, it would mean I've completely misjudged you."

"Seriously, I want some answers."

"And you'll get them. First, though, there are a couple of things you need to get for me."

I reeled off my list then handed him the key for the Senator's Suite at the Imperial. Taylor narrowed his eyes at me as if he was trying to peer inside my head.

"If you want, I can write that all down," I offered.

Taylor just stared.

"And change your clothes. That uniform's got to go."

Taylor's stare turned into a glare, then he walked over to the door. He stopped with his hand on the handle and glanced over his shoulder.

"When I get back I want those answers."

CHAPTER TEN

The door clicked shut and Taylor's footsteps faded away. I spent the next five minutes rearranging the room, fussing and moving stuff around and getting comfortable. Then I plugged in my laptop speakers and set the computer to play some tracks at random.

The first act of *The Marriage of Figaro* filled the room. The act opens with Figaro measuring the space where his bridal bed is going to go. This was Mozart at his most playful and it never failed to make me smile. Even when things got really dark this had the power to bring light back into the world.

I phoned down to Hannah and asked for the Wi-Fi password and some coffee. In addition to the usual junk, my inbox contained an email from Chief Olina Kalani of the Honolulu Police Department, and a new request from the New York Police Department.

Requests like the one from the NYPD came in on a daily basis. Two or three requests wasn't unusual. The problem was that there were too many for me to deal with, so inevitably I ended up letting down more people than I helped. This was something I'd had to learn to live with, but it wasn't easy. Some days I feel like that Dutch kid who tried to stop the leaks in the dyke with his fingers, but instead of water it's blood leaking through my dam.

The tone of the email from Chief Kalani was polite but pissed. The media had jumped on the story of his rapist, and the news was filled with scare headlines. An investigation like this was bad enough without fear being added into the mix. I typed out a quick reply asking him to send everything he had on the case, and signed off by saying that if anything jumped out at me I'd let him know. Once that was done, I logged onto the webpage the unsub had set up.

07:22:20.

For a whole minute I just watched the screen, the seconds ticking away, those numbers marching ever closer to zero. During that time another six pixelated stick figures went off to meet their maker. It was one of the longest minutes I'd ever known.

I put the laptop to one side then lay down on the bed and closed my eyes and thought about what I'd learned so far. While *The Marriage of Figaro* played in the background, I thought about Gulfstreams and brand-new cop cars, and a small-town sheriff's department that could afford to issue me with a blank cheque. I thought about paintwork that gleamed and windows that shone. Mostly I thought about Sam Galloway's final moments, about flames licking at his skin, and that infinitely slow slide into agonised madness. I thought about the minutes leading up to his death and wondered about what he might have seen. In particular, I wondered about *who* he might have seen.

So far there were three things I knew for sure.

Firstly, wherever Sam's killer was, whatever he was doing, he would be blending in like a chameleon right now, because that's what killers like this one were exceptional at. They blended in. This guy was the quiet neighbour who always gave you a cheery wave and a polite hello. He was that work colleague who helped you out last fall when your car broke down. Who knows, he might even be the buddy whose barbecue you attended at the weekend.

That's the thing with this type of killer. Bump into them on the street and you'd never know what they really were. They had wives and kids and jobs. They had lives. But those lives were an illusion, smoke and mirrors to hide their true selves.

I knew all about the smoke, and the mirrors. My father was a master illusionist. Fifteen murders over a twelve-year period and nobody suspected a thing.

The second thing I knew for sure was that Sam's killer would be obsessing over what he'd done. Even if he'd wanted to, he wouldn't be able to stop himself. He would be doing his best to treat today like it was just any other day. He'd be saying all the right things and making all the appropriate responses. If anything, he'd be even more careful than usual to make sure he blended in.

And all the time last night's events would be playing on a loop inside his head, an endless procession of sounds and images intruding into his every waking thought. In quieter moments, when he was sure he was alone, he might steal a few seconds to fully immerse himself in the memories, but the rest of the time he'd be making sure it was business as usual.

The third thing I was absolutely certain of was that unless somebody stopped this guy he would strike again.

There was one other thing that I was ninety-nine per cent certain of. That bombshell was going to be dropped on Taylor when he returned. I wasn't sure how he'd react. Hopefully he'd be able to put his personal feelings aside and view things objectively. If he didn't then I was on my own. That said, unless I'd read Taylor all wrong, I was confident it wouldn't come to that.

A soft knock on the door brought me back into the here and now. I closed the laptop lid, got up off the bed and let Hannah in. She carried her tray to the bedside table and put it down, the smell of fresh coffee following her across the room. There was a banana on the tray. I looked at the banana, looked at Hannah.

"That's not a candy bar."

Hannah smiled. "Ten out of ten for observation. Taylor said you were good. If you've got a problem with your blood sugar level, fruit is better. It's a proven fact."

"It doesn't taste as good, though."

"You'll thank me later."

I reached for the banana, looked at it like it was some sort of torture device, then peeled it and started eating.

Hannah's smile turned into a grin. "You're looking healthier already."

"I'm expecting a discount on the room."

The grin turned into a laugh. "Yeah, right."

I tipped two sugars into my mug and took a sip. It wasn't in the same league as the Blue Mountain coffee served on the Gulfstream, but it was strong and packed with caffeine and it would get the job done.

"Unless you've found the secret to eternal youth, I'm guessing you're not the original Hannah."

Hannah laughed. It was a great laugh, melodic and inviting. I wanted to hear more of that laughter. A lot more. Occasionally you meet people in life who you're immediately drawn to. Something just clicks into place, and you instinctively want to know everything about them.

"That was my grandmother," she was saying. "She bought this place back in the sixties. It's been in the family for more than fifty years."

"You've known Taylor for a while, haven't you?"

Hannah nodded. "We went to high school together. I was a couple of grades above him."

"The older girls don't tend to give the younger guys the time of day. At any rate, that's how it was when I was at high school."

"It sounds like you're talking from experience."

"Hard, bitter experience."

"What was her name?"

"Alison Blane. She was two grades above me."

"And she broke your heart."

"Shattered it into a thousand pieces. So how come you were even aware of Taylor's existence?"

"Because he was the best defensive tackle Eagle Creek High has ever seen, or is ever likely to see. He was a legend."

"That figures."

Her eyes narrowed and she smiled a smile that made her look much older. "You're circling around something, and I've a pretty good idea what that something is, so I'd appreciate it if you'd get to the point. As much as I'm enjoying this little trip down memory lane, I've got work to do."

"What's Taylor's first name?"

"And why would I tell you a thing like that? Especially since Taylor's just given me fifty bucks not to tell you."

I pulled a hundred-dollar bill from my wallet and waved it in front of her. "Because Ben Franklin trumps Ulysses S. Grant any day."

Hannah plucked it from my fingers. "I reckon that might just about do it."

CHAPTER ELEVEN

Taylor arrived back twenty minutes later, lugging a whiteboard that was as big as he was, a plastic shopping bag hooked around one meaty finger. He shook the bag onto the bed beside me. Inside was a collection of different coloured marker pens and the bottle of single malt that had been left in my suite at the Imperial. The whisky was a thirty-year-old Glenmorangie. Very classy indeed. It was rarer than diamonds. Whoever bought it knew their stuff.

I cracked the seal, opened the bottle, put my nose to the mouth and inhaled deeply. For a moment I was transported to a cold, wild place that was light years away from Louisiana in August. I could smell the peat and the heather. A cold, hard rain pricked at my face, while dark storm clouds roiled above my head. I put the cork back in and placed the bottle on the dresser.

Taylor was dressed in black jeans and a plain black shirt. Black sneakers and black socks. There was a Glock in the holster around his waist. It wasn't much of an improvement, but it was a step in the right direction, albeit a small one.

"What?" he asked.

"You look like a cop who's had all his badges stolen."

"Better than looking like a fading rock star who's desperate to relive his glory days." He nodded to the whiteboard. "Where do you want this?"

"Over there by the wardrobe, please."

Taylor propped the whiteboard up against the wall. It needed to go end-on because of the lack of space.

"Answers, Winter."

"You'll get them once you've passed the third test."

"Test? What are you talking about?"

"It's just a couple of questions. Nothing to worry about." I made a sour face. "At least I hope there's nothing to worry about. Okay, question one: have you ever murdered anyone?"

"What! Of course I've never murdered anyone."

"Question two: is lying ever acceptable?"

Taylor just glared.

"Answer the question."

"No."

"So little Jimmy's puppy has just died and his mom tells him that Scraps has gone over Rainbow Bridge to live at Sunshine Farm where he's going to spend all his days chasing rabbits and eating prime rib-eye steak."

"Okay, I guess there are times when white lies are acceptable."

"And that's what you truly believe. You wouldn't be lying about that now, would you?"

"Enough already. I have no idea what you're up to, but if you don't start making sense in the next two seconds, then I'm walking and you can find yourself another sucker to play your mind games with."

I cracked a smile. "Congratulations. You've passed with flying colours."

Taylor shook his head and made for the door.

"A bad profile is the best way to screw up a case."

He froze with his hand on the handle.

"You've got a whole load of questions running around your head, but that one's up there at the top of the list." Taylor stared at me, and I stared right back. A nod towards the bed. "Have a seat. Let's talk."

Taylor walked over to the bed and sat down.

"I needed to know if I could trust you," I said.

"Why?"

"We'll get on to that. The other thing I needed to know was whether I could work with you. On the plane when I asked your opinion on the film clip, I wanted to find out if you'd tell me what you thought rather than what I wanted to hear. I hate 'yes' people. Then back at the station house, I needed to know if you could think on your feet. You knew the profile I gave was bullshit, but you kept your mouth shut. Good call, by the way."

"But why? I don't get it. *Really* don't get it. Why go to all the trouble?"

"Because there's one massive assumption that's been made with this case, an assumption that's based on a piece of misdirection that even I'll admit is pretty impressive." I paused for a second to catch my thoughts. "Okay, when I gave the profile I said we were looking for a white male who's five foot nine and in his thirties, slim-built and college-educated. Five pieces of information. Two of those pieces of information are correct, and three might be correct." A shrug. "Then again they might not be. So, which two are correct?"

"It's a trick question," said Taylor. "All five are correct. You got the information from the film clip. The guy who tossed the match was definitely white and slim-built, and five-nine is in the right ballpark. The nature of the crime, chances are he was college-educated and in his thirties. It's not exactly rocket science, Winter."

I kept my mouth shut, gave Taylor a couple of seconds to think through what he'd just said.

"Shit. The guy who tossed the match isn't the unsub. That's the assumption, right?"

"You almost had it earlier back on the plane when you said the firestarter could have been a robot." I held up my hand, thumb and forefinger an inch apart. "You were that close. The lack of emotion was the key. You were right about that. And there are easier ways to kill people, more efficient ways. You were right about that, too."

Taylor's eyes were wide open and he was giving me his complete and undivided attention. Any thoughts of leaving had dissipated.

"Fire is a nasty way to kill someone. The only person who would choose fire as a murder weapon is a sadist, and a sadist would react very differently from the guy in the film. A sadist would draw things out as long as possible. He'd take his time. He'd play around with his props. He'd shake the jerry can so his victim would hear the gasoline sloshing around inside. He'd light a couple of matches and let them burn down to his fingertips before blowing them out. He'd taunt his victim until he broke. Then he'd torch him."

"Jesus," Taylor whispered. The faraway look on his face was made up of a mix of horror and revulsion.

"The one thing a sadist would never do, not in a million years, is march straight up to his victim, douse him in gasoline then toss a lit match on him. Where's the fun in that? Our firestarter was coerced into doing this."

"How?"

I shrugged. "He was threatened somehow. Maybe a family member. Have you had any missing person reports come in over the last forty-eight hours?"

Taylor shook his head. "Not that I'm aware of."

"So probably not a family member, then. Not unless there's a house full of bodies that hasn't been discovered yet. Anyway that's not the important question here. The important question is why? Why didn't our unsub do his own dirty work?"

"No idea, but I'm guessing he had a really good reason."

"What makes you say that?"

"The fact he chose fire as a murder weapon means he's got sadistic tendencies. However, the fact he got someone else to light the fire means he's suppressing those tendencies. He wouldn't do that without a good reason."

"And he's got a very good reason. Gasoline is horrible stuff to work with. The smell sticks to your clothing, your hair, your skin, and once that smell is on you, it's difficult to get rid of it. Then there's the smell of burning to take into account. That sticks to you, too. Have you ever sat around a camp fire? You're still smelling the wood smoke days later. Fire is a stupid way to kill someone. You might as well stick a neon sign above your head advertising the fact that you're the killer."

"But our unsub isn't stupid. That's why he gets someone else to torch the victims. He's aware of the sort of evidence that forensics look for when dealing with arsonists."

"Go on," I encouraged. "You're almost there. Take that final step. If it helps, the answer is in your earlier question. Why do I need to know if I can trust you?"

Taylor opened his mouth to tell me he didn't have a clue what I was talking about. Nothing came out. His eyes widened with realisation.

"Jesus. You think the unsub's a cop."

CHAPTER TWELVE

"There's no way this guy's a cop, Winter. Absolutely no way. I work with these people day in, day out. If one of them was a murderer, I'd know."

I walked over to the window and parted the drapes with one finger. There were a couple of early birds walking along Morrow Street, just in time for Happy Hour. These were your hardened drinkers, lonely lost souls who wouldn't let something like a murder get between them and a bottle. The sun was a ferocious ball of yellow that was closing in on the horizon but it still had a way to go. I let the drape flutter down.

"No, you wouldn't know. For eleven years I lived with one of this country's most notorious serial killers and I didn't suspect a thing. My mother was with him for seventeen years. We're talking almost two decades. For thirteen of those years they were married. They shared a bed, shared a life together, and she didn't suspect anything. My father lived in the same small town all his life, one not much different from Eagle Creek, except it was on the other side of the country in California. Some of his friends went way back to his school days, and they didn't suspect anything, either."

"You were just a kid. It's no wonder you didn't suspect anything. Nobody would have expected you to."

"And you're missing the point. We all have multiple personalities. The average is three, but some people have more. There's the face you wear for your friends and family, the one you let the outside world see. Then there's the face you see every time you look in the mirror. Everyone has a dark side. We all have thoughts and feelings we'd rather not share. We've all lain wide awake in the dead of night and wished someone dead."

"You're wrong."

"Am I? So you've never wished anyone dead." I shook my head. "You can try telling me that, but you'd be lying. Did you know that studies have shown there are an alarming number of similarities between psychopaths and teenagers? Psychologically speaking they're almost identical."

"So what?"

"So you were a football star in college. Back then you would have been pumped so full of testosterone your brain would have temporarily shut down for a few years. You wouldn't have been able to help it. Now add in the fact that you were a teenage psychopath, and it would be nothing short of a miracle if you hadn't wished someone dead. Probably more than one someone."

A faint blush rose up in Taylor's cheeks, a hint of red against a dark background.

"I don't want details. I just want you to admit I'm right."

"You're wrong. What about Gandhi, or Mother Teresa? Are you telling me that they had a dark side, too? That they went around wishing people dead?"

"Interesting you should choose two people who aren't alive to defend themselves, but, yeah, I'm sure they had their demons."

"And what about you?"

An image of my father strapped to a padded prison gurney in the execution chamber reared up in my mind. It was followed by an image of a young girl with a plastic bag over her head, a leather belt cinched tight around her neck, eyes wide and skin blue from cyanosis. I wondered how Carl Tindle was getting on in prison. Hopefully his new friends would be making him feel right at home.

"We've all got a dark side. Face it, Taylor, you cannot ever fully know another human being. How many times have you heard that cliché?"

"I'm telling you, Winter, he's not a cop."

"And you can vouch for every one of your colleagues, from the sheriff himself all the way down to the dispatchers?"

Taylor nodded.

"Even though you've only been there six months?"

Another nod, but this one wasn't quite so vehement.

"And what about the police department? Can you vouch for every single person that works there, too?"

There was no nod, not this time. I'd been aiming for reasonable doubt, and that's what I'd got.

"Be careful with assumptions, Taylor. They have their uses, but if you abuse them they're going to turn around and bite you on the ass. I said the unsub was a cop, I didn't say he was from the sheriff's department."

"Are you a hundred per cent positive this guy's a cop?"

I shook my head. "No, but I am up to ninety-nine per cent, and believe me, until this guy's in custody that's as good as it gets."

Taylor fell silent, the gears in his head turning. He was looking for a counter-argument, something to prove me wrong, anything. He was grabbing for straws in a pitch-black room.

"Okay," he said at last. "Let's assume for a second you're wrong. You just said yourself that there's a one in a hundred chance that this guy isn't a cop. If it turns out that you are wrong, then we're going to waste a load of time chasing a ghost, time that could have been spent doing something useful, like chasing down someone who isn't a cop. In the meantime, the countdown hits zero and someone else ends up being burnt alive."

"We're not wasting our time. First off, this guy is a cop. Secondly, you have the whole of the sheriff's department *and* the police department out there looking for a killer who isn't a cop. That's a lot of manpower. If by some miracle I am wrong, then we need to have faith that they're going to do their jobs and catch this guy. Thirdly, if it does turn out I'm wrong, I'll be the first to put my hands up and admit it. If the cops haven't caught him by then, we change tack and try a different approach."

"And in the meantime, someone else dies."

"And that's the reality of this business. You make a plan based on the information you have to hand, then hope and pray you've got it right. Sometimes you win, sometimes you lose."

Taylor said nothing.

"Worst-case scenario, I'm wrong and someone else ends up getting torched. Best-case scenario, I'm right and we catch this guy before he kills again."

Still nothing.

"You're smart and you can think on your feet, and that's what we need right now. I can do this on my own, but I'd appreciate your help. It's your call, though. If you decide that you can't help me, then I'll go it alone. However, I'd appreciate it if you kept your mouth shut about my theory that this unsub is a cop." I smiled. "But that's all academic since you're going to help me."

Taylor let out a long sigh. His broad shoulders slumped as a heavy weight settled on them.

"It gets worse," I added. "You realise that until this is over we're effectively the Dayton Sheriff's Department? It's just you and me, my friend."

"You're full of good news, aren't you?"

"Hey, it's not all bad. You're now the new head of the Dayton Sheriff's Department Criminal Investigation Division. You're sprinting up that career ladder. Keep on at this rate and they'll be fitting you for that brand-new sheriff's uniform in no time."

"So what happens now?"

"Now we work the case. We start by having a good look at Sam Galloway. If in doubt, always go back to the victim. It's amazing what the dead can tell you if you take the time to listen."

I took out a quarter and flipped it. Dull metal spun through the air, throwing off sparks of muted light. I slapped the coin down onto the back of my hand.

"Heads we go talk to the widow. Tails we check out Sam's office."

CHAPTER THIRTEEN

McArthur Heights was to the north-west of Eagle Creek, out where the houses were cathedrals and the golf club was just a short drive away. Taylor stuck to the speed limit, eyes glued to the road even though traffic was light, signalling even when it wasn't necessary.

"My turn for some questions," I told Taylor. "I've dealt with a lot of sheriff's departments, and do you know how many own a Gulfstream 550? Zero, zilch, nada. Go out and buy one tomorrow and you're not going to have much change out of fifty million bucks. And we're talking second hand. Budgets are being cut all the time. There's barely enough money for paperclips, never mind a personal jet."

"We don't own our own Gulfstream."

I laughed. "Yeah, I'd already worked that one out. What I want to know is who you borrowed it from, and, more importantly, why they let you borrow it. If I owned a Gulfstream, I wouldn't let you borrow it, and I like you."

"The plane is owned by Morgan Holdings. The Morgan family have been in Eagle Creek since forever. They own a large chunk of Dayton. Did you see the statue in the town square?"

I nodded. "It's hard to miss."

"That was Randall Morgan. He discovered oil on his farm back in the early 1900s, the first oil strike in Dayton. Local history has him painted as some sort of saint. It's like he was one of the Founding Fathers. Let me tell you, he was no saint. As soon as the money started rolling in, he started buying up land, anywhere he thought might have oil. When it came to getting people to sell up, he could be very persuasive, if you know what I mean."

"Broken limb persuasive."

Taylor was nodding and staring straight ahead at the road. There was tension in his shoulders that hadn't been there a minute ago, tension in his face. Tension all over. His fingers tightened and relaxed on the wheel, knuckles turning brown to white then back again.

"Grandfather or great-grandfather?" I asked softly.

"My great-grandfather. He had a smallholding twenty miles north of Eagle Creek. He grew some corn, raised some livestock, scratched out something that might have been called a living. Which was really no life at all. Go back to the start of the last century and there weren't many black men who owned land in the South, and any that did, you can guarantee that the land wasn't up to much."

"So Randall offers to buy the land for a pittance. Your great-grandfather tells him to shove it, and Randall sends in the heavies to make him an offer he couldn't refuse."

"Not quite."

Taylor's fingers were still kneading the steering wheel. Over a century had passed yet the anger was still there. Memories run particularly long in this part of the world, and I was getting first-hand experience of just how deep those ancient resentments went.

"What happened?"

"Randall sent in a lynch mob. Half a dozen men on horses dressed in white sheets and wearing white hoods. They dragged my great-grandfather from his house in the middle of the night, strung him up from the first tree they found and erected a burning cross in the yard. Next day Randall turns up with a lawyer and a contract and gets my great-grandmother to put her mark on it." Taylor shook his head. "Do you want to know the real tragedy, Winter? There was no oil on that land. It was just a worthless couple of acres. My great-grandfather was murdered for nothing."

We'd left Eagle Creek behind, houses and concrete replaced with fields and trees. There wasn't a soul in sight. It was easy to imagine it was a century earlier, easy to imagine we were back in a time when a rich white man could arrange to murder a poor black man without fear of repercussions.

"When Randall died, his son Randall Morgan Junior took over," Taylor continued. "Junior was ambitious, but he wasn't ruthless like his father. And he was clever, too. He'd worked out early on that the oil was a temporary thing, so he spread his investments. You name it, he invested in it, anything and everything. The one thing that most of his investments had in common was that they turned a profit. Newspapers, radio, banks, construction."

"When did the oil run out?"

"A couple of decades ago."

"Morgan Holdings, is it still owned by the Morgans?"

Taylor nodded. "Lock, stock and barrel. This is one family business that's staying in the family."

"And judging by the Gulfstream, the company's doing all right for itself."

"Yeah, you could say that. Its net worth is easily into ten figures. And it's just had a bumper payday. Dayton sits on top of the Haynesville Shale, so the Morgans got in on the recent gas boom. It's been known for a while that the gas was there, but it was too expensive to get to. Improvements in technology and drilling techniques have changed all that."

"So who's in charge of the company these days?"

Taylor smiled. The tension was gone and he'd stopped doing that thing with his fingers on the steering wheel. We were back on safer ground again. Whatever the set-up was now, the present didn't bother Taylor anywhere near as much as the past. I could relate.

"Technically it's Clayton Morgan. He's been the CEO since his father, Jasper, stepped down a few years back. Jasper is still the president. It's supposed to be an honorary position, but the general consensus is that he still calls the shots."

"Okay, that answers the who. What about the why? Why did Morgan Holdings lend their Gulfstream to you guys?"

"Because Jasper Morgan stepped down to become Eagle Creek's mayor. Anything that happens to the town, he takes personally. Very personally indeed. He loves this place like it's his own flesh and blood. When he saw the film he told us to do whatever we needed to do to catch this guy. Money was no object. He gave us a complete free rein. He wants this guy brought down hard and fast. Dead or alive, he doesn't care. He just wants him put out of business."

That explained Sheriff Fortier's reaction when we were discussing my fee. At least I now knew whose signature was at the bottom of my blank cheque.

CHAPTER FOURTEEN

Sam Galloway's McMansion sat on its own five-acre plot amongst all the other big houses in McArthur Heights. A black wrought-iron fence set on a four-foot brick wall marked the boundary. The top of the fence curved gently. Smooth, long curves that reminded me of the way a kid would draw a bird.

A row of trees had been planted to shield the house from the street, but they still had some growing to do. They weren't quite tall enough, the foliage wasn't quite thick enough, and we kept getting flickering glimpses of the house as we cruised along the boundary.

Taylor pulled up at a big set of double gates. Like the boundary fence, they were also made from black wrought iron. Unlike the fence, they made me think of a prison rather than a kid's drawing. They were ten feet tall with rose patterns wound into the metalwork. Our police cruiser was a solid enough piece of American engineering, but if we tried to ram those gates we'd definitely come off worse.

The driver's window went down and a wave of superheated air came crashing in. There was a microphone on a column like you'd see at a drive-through restaurant. No keypad. The only way you were getting in was if someone up at the house let you in, or you had a remote-controlled gate key. Taylor reached through the window and hit the buzzer. One beat, two beats, then a click and static.

"Can I help you?"

A female voice. Maybe Sam's wife, or maybe the maid. The sound was scratchy and lacked any sort of bass definition, making it difficult to tell.

"Sheriff's department. We need to talk with Mrs Galloway."

Another click, then the static died and the gates slowly parted. The silence coming in through the window was eerie. There was no sound whatsoever. It was too hot for the insects and the birds, and there was no wind to stir the leaves and the branches. Taylor shut the window as the gates finished opening and we headed up the long winding driveway.

A large antebellum plantation house came into view by degrees. By the time the air-conditioning had dispersed the heat, we could see the whole building in its full glory. Sam might have worked at the dull end of the law, but it had certainly paid well. The house was impressive. It had the columns and the symmetry. There were an equal number of windows on both sides of the wide entrance porch and all those windows were exactly the same size. The white brick-work glowed bright and celestial in the harsh sunlight.

But the white was too white, and everything about the house was just that little bit too perfect for this to be the real deal. There was no way this house dated back to before the Civil War. Even a building that had been loved and cherished was going to show some signs of wear and tear after two centuries.

Taylor drove slowly. A thin ribbon of blacktop stretched out in front of us, and the pristine green grass flowing gently away on either side reminded me of a cemetery. All that was missing were the headstones.

We followed the road around to the side of the house where a three-car garage was hidden away behind a tall hedge. Taylor pulled up next to a brand-new top-of-the-range Mercedes and killed the engine.

We got out of the car and the heat was enough to take my breath away. Although it was nearing 6p.m. the temperature was still in the high eighties, maybe even pushing ninety. Taylor took out his cellphone and checked the website. 06:19:23. White numbers on a black background and another stick figure dangling from a noose.

Unless there was a major break in the case, this guy was going to be adding a second corpse to his body count very soon. That was the problem when you were dealing with an unsub who was a cop. They were perfectly placed to mislead the investigation, to push resources in a direction they wanted rather than a direction that would yield results. It was like going into a boxing ring wearing handcuffs. What we needed was a miracle. The problem was that I believed in miracles as much as I believed in luck.

The front door was already open when we reached it, a maid waiting to show us in. The interior of the house was cool and cavernous, big and open like a church.

Every light was burning, but they seemed dull after the supernova brightness outside.

We followed the maid through the entrance hall, past a wide stairway that was made from dark wood and had a bright crimson carpet. The deeper into the house we went, the cooler it got, like we were burrowing underground. The maid stopped at a door, knocked once, then pushed it open and stepped aside to let us past.

The room was large with expensive-looking furniture and no personality. All the drapes were drawn to keep out the worst of the heat, and the elaborate crystal chandelier above our heads scattered jewels of light across the wooden floor. That chandelier was impressive, but it had more serious competition from the ornate fireplace and the Steinway to be the room's focal point. For me, the piano won hands down. Steinway make beautiful pianos. I had a strong urge to go and play it, but this was neither the time nor the place.

Barbara Galloway was standing beside the fireplace. She was exquisitely beautiful, like a china doll but without the fragility. Early forties, brunette, hazel eyes. She was dressed casually in jeans and a plain black blouse. The details of her grief were evident in a dozen different ways, some subtle, some not so subtle. She wasn't wearing make-up, and the only jewellery she had on was her engagement ring and a wedding band. She kept twisting the wedding ring around and around, but I doubted she was aware of this.

There was a space on her wrist where her watch should have been. When your world comes crashing to an abrupt halt, time ceases to have any real meaning. Every second is filled with thoughts and memories of the dead. Hours become your own personal hell. There was a small forgotten coffee stain on the front of her jeans that would not have been there under normal circumstances. Her eyes were bloodshot and heavy.

The painting hanging above her showed the whole family. Sam, Barbara and the three kids. No smiles and serious faces, because this was a portrait rather than a photograph. Taylor had said the kids were aged ten to fifteen, but those in the portrait were younger than that by two or three years. Barbara's eyes followed mine to the painting.

"The children are staying with my parents."

The statement was ambiguous and irrelevant, a way to fill the silence. Right now her parents could be in Miami or New York or Chicago. They might not even be in the country. Not that it mattered where they were. We weren't here to see them or the kids.

"We need to ask some questions, if that's okay."

"Of course. Please sit down."

She waved us towards a sofa that wouldn't have looked out of place in the Palace of Versailles. Taylor took one end and I took the other. Barbara Galloway was in a matching chair that had been positioned at ninety degrees to the sofa. She'd angled herself so she could face us, legs crossed, hands placed primly on her lap.

"I have spoken to the police already."

"I'm aware of that, Mrs Galloway. I just have a few additional questions."

"You're not from around here, are you?"

"No, ma'am. My name's Jefferson Winter. The sheriff's department has called me in to consult on this case."

She stared for a moment at my Hendrix T-shirt and my hair, then her gaze found my eyes.

"My husband called me at around five o'clock yesterday evening to tell me he was working late and wouldn't be home for dinner. This wasn't unusual. My husband often works late. Usually he's back by nine, though, so when he hadn't got home by ten I started to worry. I tried his cellphone but it went straight through to his voicemail."

The information was unsolicited, and felt rehearsed. A statement rather than any sort of actual answer. I wondered how often Sam had worked late, and how often he'd "worked late". A rich guy like him, living the Southern plantation owner cliché, I would be surprised if he didn't have a mistress.

Barbara Galloway struck me as a strong woman, a proud woman, but she was teetering on the brink. Right now she needed the denial, she needed to keep that mask in place. I could break her down easily enough, but that would have been unnecessarily cruel. There were truths here that we could find elsewhere. Barbara had arrived in hell, and assuming she was going to survive this, it would take a long time to get back. It wasn't my job to add to her agony.

CHAPTER FIFTEEN

"Mrs Galloway," I began. "What I'm trying to do here is build up a picture of what your husband was like."

"Was," she whispered. She was gazing down at her hands, the wedding band turning around and around. She looked up, searching for my eyes, stared deep into them. This level of scrutiny would have been uncomfortable if I hadn't been used to it. "How long does it take for the present tense to become the past tense?"

"That depends on how much you loved the person. If you hated them the crossover can be instantaneous. If you loved them, that's another matter altogether. For some people it takes months, for others, years. And then there are a few people who never make that transition."

I hesitated, wondering how far I should go with this. Wondering how much Barbara needed to hear, and how much she could take.

"Please," she said. "Just say what's on your mind."

I hesitated a moment longer then said, "Some people get stuck in time. For them the world stops turning when they get that phone call or that midnight knock on the door. It doesn't matter what they do, they can't move on. Then again, they don't try too hard. Survivor guilt keeps them locked in the past. Ten years after the event, fifteen years, and they still lay an extra place at the table."

I was thinking of my mother. She was the wife of a killer rather than the wife of a victim, but, in every way that mattered, her situation had been identical to Barbara Galloway's. My mother had never come to terms with what my father was, or what he had done. On numerous occasions, usually when she was drunk, she had laid an extra place at the dinner table. Whenever that happened, I'd just sit down at the table and eat whatever she'd served up and do my best to ignore the elephant sharing the room with us.

There was one other group that I hadn't mentioned to Barbara, the ones where the pain of living got so bad they couldn't go on. My mother had belonged to that group, too. She'd been labelled an alcoholic, but suicide can take many different forms.

"Thank you for your honesty, Mr Winter. I appreciate it. You said you had some questions?"

Her smile was strained. Good manners had been instilled into her since the cradle. Even now, she couldn't help herself. No matter how hard you try, how hard you run, you can't escape who you are.

"Run me through a typical day for your husband."

The flash of surprise that flickered across Barbara's face was there and gone in the blink of an eye. The mask of grief slid back into place. She would have endured plenty of questions since the sheriff's department got hold of that film clip, and I had a pretty good idea of the direction those questions had taken.

Shepherd and his men would have hit things head-on. They would have focussed on Sam Galloway's last day on the planet, and the reason they would have started there was because they were desperate to make sense of a situation that went way outside their usual frame of reference. They were trying to bring some equilibrium back into that tiny little space that Eagle Creek occupied in the universe. By piecing together Sam Galloway's final hours they would have been hoping to find a way to turn back time. They wanted things back to how they'd been before Sam went up in flames.

But time can't be reversed. It doesn't matter what the theoretical physicists would have you believe, that's not how things work in the real world. In the real world, time marches resolutely forward. There is nothing anyone can do to change that fact. The tides come in and soak the feet of kings, and the hours, minutes and seconds move inexorably into the future, and that's just the way it is.

"A typical working day starts at around seven." Barbara realised what she'd said and corrected herself. "*Started* at around seven. While Sam showered and got dressed, I'd wake the children and start getting them ready for school. Then we'd all sit down for breakfast. Sam always had cereal."

For a second I thought she might lose it. She took a deep breath, shook off her grief, and pulled herself back together. The transformation was impressive, a display of sheer will trumping emotion.

"If he was in court he'd leave the house around eight. Otherwise he tended to leave around quarter after eight. He always tried to get home for six whenever possible so we could eat dinner together as a family." Barbara met my eye. "Family meant everything to him."

"But, like you said earlier, he often worked late."

Barbara nodded. "He dealt with everything except criminal law, which, believe me, even in a small place like Eagle Creek, meant he kept busy. The law firm was founded by Sam's grandfather. After he died, Sam's father took it over, and then Sam. Three generations of continuous ownership by one family. We'd always thought that our son would take over when my husband retired. Maybe we'll be able to find a way to ensure that still happens."

Her voice trailed off and whatever she was about to say next was lost in the silence.

"What about weekends?"

"Saturday mornings Sam played golf. Sundays were for family. We would usually visit my parents, or Sam's mother."

"Did he ever work weekends?"

"Hardly ever. He did his best to keep weekends free so we could spend some quality time together as a family. I'm sorry, Mr Winter. Do you have many more questions? I'm finding this rather difficult."

"Just one. If you only had one word to describe your husband, what word would you choose?"

Barbara thought about this for a moment. "Honest. He was the most honest man I'd ever met."

CHAPTER SIXTEEN

Taylor found first gear and we pulled away from that brand-new top-of-the-range Mercedes. The air-conditioning was running full blast, but the car still felt like an oven. We passed the front of the house and turned onto the driveway and drove back towards the main gates. Heat shimmered up from the road in front of us and a rolling sea of perfect green stretched out on either side. That big white pretend plantation mansion slowly shrank in the car's side mirror.

The gates were already wide open when we got there. The maid had probably hit the button when she heard us coming around to the front of the house, timing it just right. She'd probably done the same for Sam Galloway. Sam had been a busy man, a man who often worked late, a man who didn't have time to waste hanging around waiting for the gates to open.

Taylor hung a right and we retraced our way back to Eagle Creek, steady and slow and sticking to the speed limit. I didn't get it. Taylor was driving like he had Miss Daisy in the back. One of the few perks of being a cop was that you didn't have to worry about tickets.

"What did you make of Barbara Galloway?" asked Taylor.

"She's a gold digger."

He glanced over, an incredulous expression on his face. "And how do you figure that?"

"You've seen the photographs. Sam wasn't exactly an oil painting. Barbara, on the other hand, is. She looks good now, she would have been stunning when they first met. She could have had her pick of men, and she chose Sam. Why? Because he was loaded."

"Maybe they married for love. It does happen, you know."

"Not in this case. The love came later. I don't doubt that for a second. In her own way, Barbara loved Sam. I've seen plenty of grieving widows, and her grief was real. But she married Sam for money and status, not for love."

Taylor was looking at me like he was about to slap down a winning hand. "You're wrong. Barbara Galloway is not a gold digger."

"Why? Because she comes from a good family? Because she didn't follow that worn old route from trailer park to strip club to meal ticket? Barbara Galloway is a gold digger, albeit a very classy one. Just one look and you know she was born into money. This is not someone who fought their way up from the gutter. There's a hardness missing that you usually find in gold diggers, but she's tough in her own way. Her toughness is born from generations of privileged breeding. It's a specific sort of toughness that comes from having everything, and wanting to make damn sure that you keep hold of it."

Taylor was still smiling that full-house smile. "You're right, she was born into a good family. A family with plenty of money. And that's where your argument falls down. Barbara Galloway didn't need Sam's money."

"There's an old saying: it takes one generation to make a fortune, the second generation to build it up, and the third generation to lose it. Plenty of fortunes have been squandered. My guess is that's what happened here. Barbara saw the writing on the wall and married Sam to maintain a standard of living that she'd got far too used to."

The smile disappeared from Taylor's face. "You can't know that for sure."

"You're right, I can't." It was my turn to flash a winning smile. "You're the new head of the investigation division. Go do some investigating and prove me wrong."

We drove on in silence for another mile or so, the road rumbling beneath the tyres.

"I've heard lawyers called a lot of things, but I've never heard one described as honest."

"You think she's lying?"

I shook my head. "That's the thing, I don't. She really believed what she was saying. What makes her statement ambiguous is the fact that Sam was having an affair." Taylor gave me a questioning look from the driver's seat, and I added, "If you're so busy that you're regularly working into the evenings, then you're going to be working weekends, too."

"Barbara Galloway isn't stupid. If her husband was having an affair then she would have known, and she wouldn't be describing him as the most honest man she'd ever met."

"Honesty is a continuum, not an absolute. She could have found out about the affair, but chose to keep quiet because the status and money were more important to her than fidelity. It happens. Or maybe this was a regular thing and they'd come to some sort of arrangement. She'd turn a blind eye so long as he didn't embarrass her."

I glanced out the window at the still trees and thought this over.

"Door number two fits better. They'd talked this over, put all their cards on the table, and come to an arrangement that worked for them both."

"What if she was just trying to save face?"

I shook my head. "The way she's perceived is obviously important to her, but it's not everything. When she said he was honest, I'm pretty sure she was talking about the pragmatic honesty between them."

I thought about this a while longer, then nodded and smiled to myself. "You're right, though: Barbara Galloway isn't stupid. She's smart enough to know that we're going to find out about the affair. That's the second reason she made that comment. She was telling us that she was okay about the affair."

"Why would she do that?"

"Because she doesn't want us to go digging too deep into Sam's past. She wants us to leave well alone."

"Same question as before, Winter: why would she do that?"

"To make sure Sam's reputation doesn't get tarnished. With Barbara Galloway it's always going to come back to status and money."

"Her husband's just died. Do you really think she's going to be worried about something like that? You said yourself her grief was real. That she loved him."

I looked over at Taylor. "You can grieve and still be pragmatic. Right now the thing that worries Barbara Galloway most is making sure that her son takes over the family firm one day. Sam is her past. Her son is the future. She wants to maintain her current lifestyle indefinitely, and it's her son who's going to help her do that."

"You don't have a very high opinion of her. First she's a gold digger. Now she's some sort of ice maiden."

"On the contrary, I've got nothing but respect for her. I've seen far too many people in her situation who've gone completely to pieces. People who went down so deep they couldn't find their way out again. Barbara Galloway's going to get through this, and that's a good thing because it means one less victim for our unsub."

We drove on in silence for a while, rolling on through the heat, slow and steady, heading for Main Street. The greens and browns of nature gave way to the dull muted monochrome of urban development when we hit the town limits.

"Okay, so what now?" asked Taylor. "Do we stop digging?"

I looked over at him again. "Of course not, you never stop digging."

CHAPTER SEVENTEEN

Taylor parked in an empty slot outside the police department's big white building and we stepped into the sun. Early evening and it was still hot. I lit a cigarette with my battered old Zippo and pushed my sunglasses as far back as they would go to block out as much of that white-hot glare as possible.

Our car was one of two sedans parked in front of the station house. Both were as new as you were going to get. The only real difference between our car and the police department's car were the markings and the colour.

When we'd passed by earlier there had been three police cruisers parked here, all in a neat row. Those other cars would no doubt be taking part in the hunt for Sam Galloway's killer. From a police perspective, it was the only story in town right now.

There were spaces for five cars, and, from what I'd seen of Eagle Creek, the police department would have enough vehicles to fill all five slots, and probably some spares. Ten cars in the sheriff department's lot and at least another five here meant an investment of around 400,000 dollars. In light of what I'd learned about Jasper Morgan this made a lot more sense than when I first drove up Main Street. When you had a billion in the bank, four hundred grand was pocket change.

It also went a long way to explaining why Main Street, Eagle Creek, reminded me of Main Street, Disneyland. Jasper Morgan loved his town. Taylor had told me that much. Jasper would want Eagle Creek to look its best. He'd want to win awards for having the finest Main Street in the whole of Louisiana, probably the whole of the South. But that beauty only went skin deep. Strip away the facade and things weren't quite so pristine. Look at the Imperial Hotel. Perfect on the outside, faded carpets and worn woodwork inside.

Sam's office was in a prime location overlooking the town square. It was a good spot for a criminal lawyer, since the courthouse and jail were only a stone's throw away. It wasn't so good for a lawyer who worked at the other end of the law and spent most of his billable hours shuffling paper. An office further up Main Street made more sense. Property was cheaper, but it would still be close enough for those rare courthouse appearances.

Now we were out of the car a new sense of urgency had infected Taylor. He was already up on the sidewalk, moving fast to escape the heat.

"Hold on," I called out. "There's something I want to check out."

I drew on my cigarette and walked over to the town square. The place was deserted, all the benches empty. The shade from the trees was non-existent and it was much too hot to be sitting outside.

Randall Morgan Senior stood larger than life on a six-foot plinth. It was at least fifteen feet from the ground to the top of his head. No matter where you stood in the west half of the park he would be staring down at you, disapproval carved into his stone features. It was almost as if he was casting his disapproval across the whole of Eagle Creek, the whole parish, the whole state. RANDALL JEBEDIAH MORGAN 1863–1934 was written on the plaque. And underneath: A GIANT AMONGST MEN.

Randall's expression was hard and unforgiving. It was easy to imagine him getting furious that a black man would have the audacity to defy him, easy to imagine him outlining exactly what needed to be done to right that wrong.

It was also easy to imagine him sitting on a horse dressed in a white sheet and a white hood. The first man in and the last man out. Last because he would have wanted to watch the flames lick and spit from the burning cross for as long as possible. To watch the fire shadows of a hanged man swinging in the night.

Taylor was standing beside me, arms folded, face grim. He shook his head and muttered, "Two lousy acres of nothing." Then he turned on his heel and headed back the way we'd come, out of the park and across the street towards Sam Galloway's office. His stride was much longer than mine and he pulled further away with every step.

I caught up with him in the shade of the entrance porch. *Galloway & Galloway Attorneys-At-Law* was engraved on a bronze plaque that had been screwed into the wall. The plaque was decades old. Despite regular cleaning the letters had a shadow of dirt ground into them, and there were faint streaks of green on the bronze caused by oxidisation.

Who had put the plaque up? My money was on Sam's grandfather. It looked old enough. When Barbara Galloway had talked about her eldest son taking over the family business, for a beat her grief had been replaced with the sort of pride that had its roots buried deep into history.

We'd been outside for five minutes, long enough to smoke the whole cigarette down to the butt. The humidity was more brutal than ever and my Hendrix T-shirt was sticking to me. Taylor's shirt was sticking to him too. I wondered if he owned any white T-shirts, and if he did, why the hell wasn't he wearing one?

Taylor pushed the heavy wooden door open and we went inside. I removed my sunglasses and hooked them onto the neck of my T-shirt. It took a few moments for my eyes to adjust to the change in light. The interior of the building was at least thirty degrees cooler, but it still felt warm. The heat didn't bother me. Give me sunshine over Siberia any day. I'd spent my first eleven years in northern California and the summers there could get pretty vicious. I'd also spent a summer in Arizona, where it got even hotter. In some ways that had been easier to handle since it was a dry heat.

A wide stairway led to the reception area on the second floor. The receptionist who greeted us had a sad smile that struggled to get past her lips. It was a gesture born out of conditioned politeness rather than one that carried any sort of honest emotion. In that respect she reminded me a lot of Barbara Galloway. In every other way, though, they were polar opposites. Looks, status, the fact that she had worked a day in her life.

The receptionist was well into her fifties. Grey hair, and an appropriate amount of make-up given her age and position. She was dressed conservatively in a plain white blouse and a navy skirt. She had an efficient desk. A computer keyboard and screen directly in front of her, the phone positioned off to her right within easy reach.

Taylor held up his badge. "I'm Officer Taylor and this is Jefferson Winter. He's helping us out with the investigation into Sam Galloway's murder. Thank you for waiting. We appreciate it."

The receptionist's face seemed to collapse in on itself. She looked on the verge of tears. "I can't believe Mr Galloway's gone."

"What's your name?" I asked her.

"Mary. Mary Sanders."

"Have you worked here long, Mary?"

"Since I left high school. Mr Galloway's father hired me." She shook her head. "It doesn't seem real. Every time I hear someone come in, I keep expecting to see Mr Galloway."

I nodded that I understood, but I was thinking about how we could get information from her. If anybody knew the details of Sam's extra-curricular activities, Mary would. The problem was that she would be fiercely loyal to her former employer. Particularly right now when the wounds were so raw.

"Who else is here?"

"Josh Landry. He deals mainly with property issues. Judy Dufrene is here as well. She's our legal secretary."

"I take it you have a conference room?"

Mary nodded.

"We'd like to talk to Judy and Josh, please."

"Certainly."

Mary got up and led the way through to a large wood-panelled room with a high ceiling and a twenty-seat oak conference table. I tried to think of a single situation that would merit a table this big in a place as small as Eagle Creek. All that sprung to mind was a will reading.

"Can I get you anything to drink?" More of that conditioned politeness, and another fake plastic smile.

"I'll have a coffee, please. Black, two sugars."

"An iced water would be good, thanks ma'am," said Taylor.

Mary gave a slight nod and slipped out the door. The conference room was on the opposite side of the building from the park, which figured. Sam's office would have been on the park side of the building. That was the prime position, and status had meant everything to him too.

That's why he hadn't downsized to cheaper premises further along the street, and that's why he had the big house out on McArthur Heights with a three-car garage and too many cars to fill it. A place like Dayton, in this heat, you didn't leave your car out in the sun unless you had to. The car that had been left out was a top-of-the-range Merc. Chances were that was just the runaround, which meant the cars in the garage were the really expensive ones.

There'd be a sports car, for sure. Possibly a Porsche, although I was veering towards a Ferrari, something red and flashy with a roaring engine that would turn heads when he drove up to the golf club. There'd be a luxurious sporty number for Barbara, too, possibly a soft-top Jaguar.

Then there'd be a big gas-guzzling SUV to ferry the three children around in, something more expensive than a top-of-the-range Merc, something like a Range Rover, one with tinted windows and heated seats and screens in the backs of the headrests for the kids, added extras whose main purpose was to underline just how rich he was.

Barbara had said that family was everything to Sam. She was wrong. From what I'd seen status trumped that one by a mile. In that respect the two of them had been more similar than either had probably realised. This table, this room, this whole building, it was just another way for Sam to display his wealth. Like the house up in McArthur Heights, and the Ferrari I was sure he had parked in his garage.

"Does anybody around here drive a Ferrari?"

Taylor narrowed his eyes. "Why do you ask?"

"No reason."

Taylor gave a deep belly laugh that rumbled through the room like an earthquake. "Yeah, right. You expect me to believe that. Why don't you ask me the question you really want to ask?"

"Did Sam Galloway drive a Ferrari?"

A nod. "I guess this is the point where you tell me which model."

"A Testarossa."

Taylor just stared. "How the hell did you know that?"

CHAPTER EIGHTEEN

Mary returned with our drinks on a tray, Josh Landry and Judy Dufrene tagging behind like a couple of reluctant kids. She handed me a coffee, then passed a tall glass streaked with condensation to Taylor.

Judy was in her mid-twenties, plain-looking and demure, and dressed conservatively in a navy skirt and white blouse. The skirt was similar to Mary's, but shorter and a little tighter. Judy had the sort of porcelain complexion that burnt at the first glimpse of the sun, a light sprinkling of freckles across her nose. I couldn't see any signs of sunburn, so she'd been careful, plenty of sunscreen. Her long red hair was wound up into a tight bun and her eyes were as green as mine.

Josh was a middle-aged heart attack just waiting to happen. Short and wide, and florid-faced. A drinker's face. He wore red suspenders over a white shirt. No tie and the top button undone. The bright red neck indicated unhealthily high blood pressure. His weight indicated high cholesterol, and a future filled with insulin shots to fight off the effects of type-two diabetes. He didn't look happy. Then again, he gave the impression that he never looked happy. Josh was one of those people who trailed their own personal thundercloud behind them wherever they went.

Judy and Josh sat down on the opposite side of the conference table and got themselves comfortable. Mary made to leave and I asked her to stay. She stared at me for a moment to make sure I was serious, then placed the empty tray on the table, shuffled a chair out from under it and sat down next to Josh.

"What can we do for you, Mr Winter?"

The question came from Josh. Sharp, direct, to the point. Sam Galloway's passing had created a power vacuum and Josh obviously had ambitions to fill it.

"What was Sam Galloway like to work for?"

Josh shrugged. "Most of the time he was okay."

"And at other times he could be a pain in the ass," I finished for him.

Another shrug. "What do you want me to say?"

"I don't want you to say anything."

Josh gave me a tight look, then sighed and scratched his nose. He glanced down at the table, stared at his reflection in the polished oak, looked back at me.

"Sam's gone, and I'm going to miss the guy. I worked with him for almost a decade. This sort of thing happens, and it's easy to turn a person into a saint." Josh sighed. "I spend my days helping people out when they want to buy or sell a house. This goes way outside my frame of reference." He paused, took a deep breath. "I guess what I'm trying to say is that Sam was a pretty decent guy. Some days he was happy, some days he wasn't. I'm sure he had his problems. Everyone does."

"You know that for a fact, or are you just speculating?"

"Pure speculation. At the end of the day he was my boss. We didn't socialise, didn't move in the same circles, didn't go out for drinks. That said, he was a good boss. One of the best I've worked for."

I glanced at Mary's left hand, saw a wedding ring and an engagement ring with a tiny diamond set in it. "And what about you Mrs Sanders? Would you agree with that?"

Mary nodded. "Mr Galloway was a complete gentleman, just like his father. I couldn't have asked for a better employer."

"What about you?" I turned to Judy.

"I've only been here seven months, so I didn't know Sam that well."

"Still, seven months is enough time to form an opinion."

"I'd have to agree with Mrs Sanders and Mr Landry. Mr Galloway was a good boss. He always treated me well."

I smiled at Josh, then Mary. "Thanks for your time."

They looked at each other uncertainly then got to their feet. Judy made to follow and I waved her back down.

"I've just got a couple more questions. It won't take long."

Judy watched Josh and Mary make their way around the large conference table and head for the door. She watched the door swing slowly shut, then looked back across the table at me. Her worried eyes met mine. She was holding her breath, waiting for that axe to fall.

"You're a liar. You might have only been here for seven months, but you knew Sam pretty well, didn't you? Better than well."

"I don't know what you're talking about."

"And that's another lie."

Judy stood up. "I think I'm going to leave now."

"No you're not. You're going to sit down and tell me how long you'd been sleeping with Sam."

Judy slumped back into her chair. "I wasn't sleeping with Mr Galloway."

"And that's another lie."

"Why would he be sleeping with me? He was married."

"And married men never have affairs."

"I was not sleeping with him."

"The first time you referred to him as Sam, but every other time you've called him Mr Galloway. Now, you could argue that the first time was a slip of the tongue, you'd meant to call him Mr Galloway, and I could believe that, but not in the way you want me to believe it."

"I don't understand."

"Okay, try this. You're right down at the bottom of the food chain here at Galloway and Galloway. Josh has way more experience, and, even though Mary's only educated to high-school level, she outranks you because she's been here since the start of time. Now, I can see Josh using Sam's first name because he knew him for a decade and would want to believe they were equals, even if they weren't. For Mary, Sam is Mr Galloway, always and for ever. She'd never slip up and call him Sam because that's not who he was to her. You, on the other hand, you're the new girl, so when you were in the office you would have been very careful to call him Mr Galloway. However, when the two of you were alone he would have insisted you call him Sam."

"You're wrong," she maintained, but there was no conviction in her voice.

I shook my head. "No, Judy, I'm not. The fact that you would accidentally call him Sam, even just once, implies familiarity and a degree of intimacy that goes outside the boundaries of the type of worker/boss relationship you should have had. So, I'll ask again: how well did you know Sam?"

Silence fell between us, a long silence that filled the large high-ceilinged room. I was prepared to wait this out as long as it took because the outcome was a foregone conclusion. Judy was staring at her reflection in the table. Taylor was sitting quietly beside me, looking across the table at Judy. He was completely still, barely breathing. For such a large person, there were times when he left a very small dent on the world. He reached for his water glass and the rattle of the ice cubes made more noise than he did.

"I didn't want anything to happen," Judy whispered. She was still staring at her reflection.

"And that's another lie."

CHAPTER NINETEEN

"I'm not a marriage wrecker."

"No you're not. You weren't Sam's first. And, if things had turned out differently, you wouldn't have been the last."

"It's not what you think."

I shook my head. "It's exactly what I think."

"We were in love."

"That's what he told you?"

Judy nodded. She looked up and stared defiantly across the table. I studied her for a moment, then shook my head and sighed.

"And you believed him?"

Judy nodded again. A single tear slid down her right cheek, closely followed by a second one down the left, shiny wet tracks on her porcelain skin. Her bright green eyes were full of tears.

"He told you he was going to leave his wife and family, didn't he?"

Another nod. "He said they didn't love each other any more. That they'd fallen out of love years ago. They slept in separate beds."

"And when exactly was he planning to leave her? Next week? Next month? Next year?"

"He *was* going to leave her."

"No he wasn't." I said softly.

"How can you say that? You didn't know him."

"Sam was never going to leave his wife, Judy. Do you really think that he was going to give up that big house over in McArthur Heights for you? No way. It was never going to happen. You deal with divorces here so you know how messy they can get."

Judy was staring at her reflection in the table top again. "He said he was going to leave her," she whispered, but all the fight had gone.

I leant forward and placed my hands on the table. "Why don't you tell me what happened?"

She spent the next ten minutes talking, detailing her affair with Sam in halting, tearful sentences. Her story was almost as old as time itself. A young girl gets her head turned by an older rich guy. He promises the moon and she believes him because she was brought up to believe that fairy tales can come true. In her world, Cinderella marries Prince Charming, and they live happily ever after.

Sam had told his wife he was working late the night he died because he was meeting Judy. Their liaisons followed a tried and tested routine. Judy would leave work somewhere between five-thirty and quarter to six and head home so she could shower and slip into her best underwear. Red was Sam's favourite colour. Victoria's Secret was his preferred brand. Sam would wait until the office was empty before locking up and heading out. Usually he'd leave by six-thirty, but that depended on how late Josh was working.

Judy's apartment was a five-minute walk from the office, a couple of streets back from Main Street. Sam always walked there because Judy lived in the sort of neighbourhood where a Ferrari or a top-of-the-range Mercedes would stand out. His wife had told him to be discreet. That was the deal, and Sam would have complied. The last thing he wanted was to embarrass her. He had a good thing going, and there was no way he was going to screw it up.

So he'd sneak around to Judy's place, being careful to make sure he wasn't seen. They'd do whatever it was they did, then Sam would sneak back to the office, pick up his car and head home to McArthur Heights. Back into the warm embrace of his loving family.

Except last night Sam never made it to Judy's apartment.

I sent Judy out and asked her to send Mary back in. The door swung shut and I stood up and stretched. "So where was Sam abducted?"

"It's got to have been here at the office," Taylor replied. "Snatching someone off the sidewalk is too risky. This isn't New York, or one of those other big cities where, even when people do see something, they don't see it. If Sam had been bundled into the back of a panel van, someone would have seen, and within five minutes everyone would have known about it."

"Yeah, that's what I figure."

"How did you know Sam drove a Testarossa?"

Before I could answer there was a gentle knock on the door. Mary came back in and took the same seat as earlier, but only after she'd tidied the other two back into their rightful places under the large oak conference table. It was a habitual response, one born from years of conditioning. Mary had spent a large part of her life tidying up after people. Her husband, her kids. Her employer.

She looked me straight in the eye, defiant and challenging. "Mr Galloway wasn't a bad person."

"But he was an adulterer. That's one of the big ten. It's right there at number eight, one place after don't kill and one place before don't steal."

"He was a happily married man."

"A happily married man who had affairs."

"Just the one affair."

I shook my head and Mary sighed.

"I never understood it. He had a beautiful wife. Beautiful children. A beautiful home."

"His wife knew about the affairs."

"And I don't understand that either. I've been married for thirty-three years. For better or for worse, and forsaking all others. Those were the vows we made, and we've stuck to them all these years."

"Those vows don't work for everyone."

"Evidently." Another sigh. "His father was the same. He was married to a beautiful woman who turned a blind eye. Rich folk just live by different rules, I guess."

"Was it always with the staff?"

"No, not always."

"But there was always someone, wasn't there?"

A nod. "Most of the time. He was always discreet, though."

"That would have been part of the arrangement he had with his wife."

Mary sighed again and shook her head. "How can you live like that? Sharing your bed with a man after you knew that he'd been with another woman?"

"Judy said they slept in separate rooms."

Mary raised an eyebrow.

"I didn't buy that one either. Anyway, back to your earlier question. Barbara Galloway accepted the situation because of the money. Like you said: rich folks live by different rules."

"She could have divorced him. Mr Galloway would have made sure that she and the children never wanted for anything."

"But then she'd have lost the status that comes from being married to one of Eagle Creek's most important men."

"Is status really that important?"

"For some people, yes. Okay, according to your interview with the sheriff's department you left after Josh last night."

"That's right. I left at around twenty to six."

"So, aside from the killer, you were the last person to see Sam alive."

Mary's eyes widened and she put a hand across her mouth. She looked shocked, like this had only just occurred to her.

"Was there anything about Sam's behaviour that struck you as out of the ordinary?"

Mary shook her head. "No."

"So he didn't seem stressed or worried? Frightened?"

Another shake of the head, and another "No".

"Where was he when you last saw him?"

"In his office. If he was still here when I was leaving, I'd always go and say goodnight."

"Can you show me his office, please?"

CHAPTER TWENTY

Like I thought, Sam's office overlooked the park. It would have belonged to his father, and, before that, his grandfather. If Barbara Galloway had her way, one day it would belong to her son. I parted the blinds with my hands and peered through the crack. From this angle all I could see was the back of Randall Morgan's head, but it was easy to imagine him staring back at me, as disapproving now as he had been when he was alive and breathing nearly a century ago.

Mary was hovering in the doorway. She looked worried, like she was witnessing a grave robbing. I sat down in Sam's big leather chair, rocked back and put my feet up on the big old mahogany desk. Mary just stared at me like I was the one wielding the shovel.

"Please sit down."

I waved her into the seat opposite me. She hesitated then sat down.

"Most interviews follow a tried and tested course. The interviewer asks questions and the interviewee answers them. The theory is fine, but the reality is that a lot of details are missed or skipped over. Worse still, answers are occasionally censored, with the interviewee saying what they think the interviewer wants to hear.

Sometimes they do this because they're trying to be helpful. Other times they're being disingenuous."

Mary nodded like this all made perfect sense. Keen to please. Keen to give me the answers I was looking for.

"I want to try a cognitive interview. The difference with this sort of interview is that you revisit the incident through sense memory. Sight, sound and smells are explored to build up a more accurate picture of the event. Because of the way we access memories, a secondary benefit is that it's much easier to spot a lie."

"I don't lie."

"I'm glad to hear it," I said, even though this was a lie. We all lie. Politicians, priests, everyone. From our first words to our last we'll tell a million lies. And the person we lie to most is ourselves. "I'd like you to close your eyes, please."

Mary gave me a concerned look. Modern society has conditioned us to trust our sight above the other four senses, so when a stranger asks you to make yourself temporarily blind, you're going to be suspicious. She looked at me for a few seconds more then shut her eyes.

"Talk me through what you do when you're getting ready to go home."

"I always check my emails one last time before I shut my computer down. Then I tidy my desk and switch on the answering machine. Like I said earlier, if Mr Galloway was still here, I'd go and say goodbye."

"Okay, let's go back to last night. You've shut down your computer and put the answer machine on. Mr

Galloway is still working, so you head along to his office. How fast are you walking?"

"Quickly. I need to get home to cook dinner. We're having lasagne and that always takes a while to prepare."

"What can you hear?"

"My footsteps echoing on the wooden floor."

"What can you smell?"

"Museums." A faint smile. "It's a dusty, old smell. I think it's from the wood. This place has always reminded me of a museum."

"Okay, you've reached Mr Galloway's office. Do you walk straight in?"

A shake of the head. "No, never. I straighten my skirt, make sure I'm presentable, then knock on the door and wait."

"Is that what happened last night?"

Mary's head dipped three times. Three barely perceptible nods as she checked each action off against her memory. This was where I wanted her, living and breathing the past.

"Yes."

"Then what?"

"Mr Galloway calls out for me to come in and I open the door. He's busy with some paperwork so I say a quick goodbye and leave."

"Does he say anything?"

A shake of the head. "No."

"Does he seem stressed or worried?"

"No, he's just his normal self."

Mary smiled.

"What?" I prompted.

She opened her eyes. "When I closed the door he started humming to himself. It was something he did when he was concentrating. It was one of those unconscious habits, like a child biting their tongue when they're trying to solve a math problem."

"Thanks. You've been really helpful."

CHAPTER TWENTY-ONE

The first thing I did when we got outside was light a cigarette. The second thing I did was put my sunglasses back on. Even though my eyeballs were melting under the relentless onslaught of the sun, that's the order it happened. Cigarette then shades. It was the prioritisation of an addict.

"The interview with Mary Sanders was interesting."

Taylor came to an abrupt halt and stared at me, eyes narrowed, brow furrowing. "You're not joking, are you? Okay, this I've got to hear."

"Well, for a start, we know that the spirit of Martha Stewart is alive and well in Eagle Creek, Louisiana. I mean, how many people do you know would go home and bake a lasagne after a hard day at work? You just wouldn't. You'd open the freezer, take out that plastic container, pierce that film lid and a few minutes later you'd be sitting down to eat."

"Seriously, Winter, how does any of what Mary Sanders said help us?"

"Well, we now know with absolute certainty that Sam Galloway did not see this coming. What happened to him came as a complete bolt out of the blue. You don't make a date with your lover if you think there's even an outside possibility that someone's going to abduct you, douse you in gasoline and set you alight."

"Great. But you got that from Judy Dufrene, not Mary Sanders."

"You're the lead investigator here, you figure it out."

I took a long drag on my cigarette. It was nine minutes to seven. I pictured the countdown in my head. White numbers on black. 05:08:32. In my mind's eye, I saw a snaking line of 1,851 stick figures queuing up to climb the gallows. The line disappeared into the distance, stick figures getting smaller and smaller until they were just a pixelated blur.

Unless we found this unsub soon someone else was going to die. There was still time, but that time was running shorter and faster with every passing minute. I would chase this one down to the very last second, but I was enough of a pragmatist to acknowledge that things were not looking good.

I called Shepherd. It took ten rings before he picked up, which didn't surprise me. Shepherd was old school. He didn't strike me as someone who would walk around with a cell-phone surgically grafted to the palm of his hand. I could see him in my mind's eye, harassed and harried and stroking that neat moustache, while he tried to be in a dozen places simultaneously.

"Have you found the crime scene yet?"

"We're working on it, Winter. I've got everyone out looking. The police department is out searching, too. We're checking factories, storage units, the old refinery plant. We're even looking at residential garages. But these things take time, you know how it is."

I did. My perfect universe was a place where I had unlimited resources at my disposal twenty-four/seven. It was a complete fantasy. There was no way that was ever going to happen, but that didn't stop me dreaming.

"Have any missing person reports been filed recently?"

"No, why?"

"I'm wondering about possible victims. It's a long shot, though. He didn't keep Sam Galloway for long, and chances are he's going to stick to this MO."

"Even still, it's a good thought. I'll make sure that I'm alerted immediately if anyone does get reported missing. How are you getting on?"

"Sam Galloway was having an affair with one of his work colleagues."

Taylor was watching me closely, ears tuned into the conversation.

"How serious?"

"Serious enough."

The implications hung between us in hundreds of miles of empty air. Geographically speaking, there was maybe a half mile between us, but our conversation was taking the long way around.

"I'll get someone to look into it," said Shepherd finally.

"As soon as you find that crime scene, I want to be the first to know."

"You can be sure of that."

I killed the call, took a final drag on my cigarette and crushed it out in a nearby trash can. We got into the car and Taylor got the motor running and turned the air-conditioning to full. I could feel him staring from the driver's seat.

"What was that all about?" he asked.

"I was just giving Shepherd an update."

"No you weren't. You were giving Shepherd a motive."

"And why would I do that?"

"Oh, I don't know. To muddy the waters, perhaps."

I smiled. "By his own admission, Shepherd is a small-town cop, which means he thinks like a small-town cop. A good old-fashioned motive like a spurned wife hiring someone to murder her cheating husband is going to make more sense to him than some sicko who gets off on setting people alight for the sheer pleasure of watching them burn."

"This theory about the unsub being a cop, you realise you're gambling everything on it."

"It's only a gamble when the outcome is uncertain."

"Ninety-nine per cent, remember?"

"This guy's a cop."

"Sam was humming to himself," Taylor went on. "If he'd been worried he would have been pacing his office or chewing his fingernails, or whatever he did when he got stressed. He wouldn't be absorbed by his work. He'd be looking over his shoulder, waiting for that other shoe to drop."

I nodded. "That's how I see it."

"So what now?"

"Now we eat. It's going to be a long night."

CHAPTER TWENTY-TWO

Taylor drove slow and steady, heading back to Morrow Street. We bumped gently across to the other side of the rail tracks, and I made an executive decision to do the driving in future. When you hit rail tracks you wanted to have a bit of speed up. You wanted to feel the car lift off. You wanted to hear the shock absorbers complain. Being a cop gave you driving privileges that your average Joe could only dream of, and ignoring those privileges was both pointless and crazy.

We parked outside Apollo's, a squat one-storey diner with big windows and a flickering blue and red neon rocket blasting off from the sign that hung the length of the frontage. The diner was right across the street from Hannah's Place. I could see my room from the doorway. Second floor, second window to the right.

There were rows of empty tables inside the diner and not a single customer. Not good. Empty seats usually equated to lousy food. I glanced up and down Morrow Street. It was like a ghost town. I looked back at the empty tables.

Taylor saw me staring. "It's usually busier at this time of the evening. Sam's murder has got everyone scared."

"Is the food here any good?"

"Better than good. Would I be eating here if it wasn't?"

That was good enough for me. One thing cops know are their diners. Which to use, which to avoid. When it comes to greasy, unhealthy food, they're walking Michelin Guides. Even a rookie would be a connoisseur after six months on the force.

We went inside and a bell jangled above our heads. The smell of fried food hit us the second we stepped through the door. It was grafted into the worn black vinyl seats, the yellowing Formica tables, the once-white walls and the scuffed white floor tiles. It was embedded into the very fabric of the place. Black and white framed photographs from the Apollo space missions hung on the wall. In pride of place behind the counter was a shot of Neil Armstrong taking that one giant leap for mankind.

Because the place was empty we had our pick of the seats. I opted for a window table. Always my first choice since I like to people watch, although on this occasion the pickings were going to be slim. I didn't bother checking the menu. A place like this, it was pretty much a done deal.

A waitress hustled over from behind the counter. Her hair was piled up into a beehive and her clothes were retro, like she'd been beamed in from the sixties. She looked familiar, but it took a second to work out why since I'd never seen her before. Her big brown fawn eyes gave it away in the end.

"How's it going, Taylor?" she asked.

"Great, Lori." Taylor nodded in my direction. "This is Jefferson Winter."

"Glad to meet you."

"Are you related to Hannah, by any chance?" I asked.

"I'm her aunt."

"Did your mother own this place, too?"

"Kind of. My parents owned this place and the guesthouse. This was my father's domain and the guesthouse was my mother's. My mother said she liked to be somewhere she could keep an eye on him. After they died I got this place and Cissy got the guesthouse." She pulled a pad and pen out of the pocket of her apron. "So, what can I get for you gentlemen?"

"I'll have a burger and fries and a large chocolate shake. Coffee as well, please. Lots of coffee."

She scribbled this down onto her pad and turned to Taylor.

"Same to eat, thanks, but double of everything. And I'll have a Pepsi. No coffee, no shake."

"Coming right up."

Lori flashed a cheery smile then hustled back behind the counter. She shouted our order through the hatch and a world-weary voice replied that it would be a pleasure. Thirty seconds later she was back with our drinks. I tipped two sugars into my coffee and took a sip. Any other day it would have ranked right up there with the best, but the Blue Mountain coffee on the Morgan's Gulfstream had raised the bar pretty high.

Taylor had his cellphone out and was checking the website again. 04:52:19. The phone was flat on the table so I could see, too. We watched a couple more stick men go to their deaths, then Taylor slid the cell off the table top and put it back in his pocket.

"You owe me two hundred bucks."

"And how do you figure that?"

I answered with a smile and a name. "Alvin."

Taylor responded with a deep belly laugh that I didn't like one bit. "How much did she take you for?"

"Your name's not Alvin?"

A shake of the head. "So answer my question, Winter. How much?"

"A hundred. But you're down by fifty."

Taylor said nothing.

"You didn't pay her fifty bucks, did you?"

"No way."

"She lied to me."

"It happens, Winter. Sometimes people lie."

"You're enjoying this, aren't you?"

Taylor let loose with another one of those deep, rumbling belly laughs. "Loving every second."

"I will find out what your name is, you know that, don't you? From here on in I will make this my life's mission. My sole reason for being."

Taylor just smiled.

"Back to business," I went on. "So everyone has gone home, leaving Sam all alone, hard at work in his office. The unsub turns up and somehow manages to kidnap him. Now I need you to think back to when you were in Sam's office. What was missing?"

Taylor thought for a moment. "There were no signs of a struggle. If there had been then his office would have been a crime scene."

"What does this tell you?"

"That the unsub was armed."

"He probably was, but I don't think he went in there waving a gun around and shouting for Sam to get down. I think he was more subtle than that. Okay, what else have you got?"

"I guess it's possible Sam knew the unsub."

"More than possible. He knew him. And the third thing this tells us is that the unsub was a person in authority. A cop, for example."

Taylor shook his head and made a face. "That's a pretty big leap, Winter."

"Not that big. Put it all together and it makes for a compelling picture. A cop walks into his office, the first thing Sam's going to do is wonder what he's done wrong. In a situation like that, even a saint would be trawling his memory for misdemeanours, because that's how we're wired. A cop comes up to you and you're going to feel guilty, even if you're as innocent as a newborn. Question: what's the best thing about being a cop?"

"You mean aside from the uniform and the groupies, and that overwhelming sense of power you get from being out on the streets with the whole weight of the law behind you."

I laughed. "Maybe that does it for you. However, what does it for our unsub is the fact that he gets to carry a gun. It's right there in his holster for the whole world to see. He won't want to use it, because that could lead to things spiralling out of control, but he's got it there if he needs it."

I took a sip of coffee. Taylor said nothing, just reached for his Pepsi.

"Okay, now that the unsub has got Sam's attention, he feeds him a story. Maybe he tells him that his wife has been in a car crash. Maybe he tells him the kids are involved as well, that they're all badly injured and the paramedics have rushed them over to the hospital in Shreveport. It's touch and go. Sam hears all this without really hearing. He's in a state of shock. He's just realised how fragile his world actually is."

I paused and waited for my imagination to catch up with itself before continuing.

"The cop then turns all Good Samaritan. He offers to drive Sam to the hospital, tells him they'll take the interstate at a hundred miles an hour, the blues and reds flashing. Sam doesn't walk downstairs, he sprints. He gets in the car, straps himself in, and the unsub hits him with a tranquilliser."

"Why bother tranquillising him? He's already in the car."

"Because the unsub won't be driving like a lunatic, and he won't have the lights and sirens going. He'll be sticking to the speed limit and trying to remain as inconspicuous as possible. Dazed and confused as he is, at some point Sam would have realised something was up. The last thing the unsub needed was for that epiphany to hit while he was busy driving. That would get messy. It makes more sense for the unsub to neutralise Sam before they hit the road."

"Sounds great. Except for one tiny little detail. This is all just speculation."

I shook my head. "No it's not. That's exactly how it went down."

"And how can you be so sure of that?"

"Because that's how I would have done it."

CHAPTER TWENTY-THREE

Lori returned with our food, topped up my coffee, told us to enjoy, then went back behind the counter and picked up a glossy magazine that had a rich, perfectly Photoshopped couple on the cover. We were still the only customers. The way things were going, we'd probably be the only customers for the rest of the night.

Since we'd got here I'd seen two high-school kids disappear into one of the bars, and that was it. I doubted the kids would need their fake IDs tonight. The bar owner would be glad of any customers he could get. This highlighted a major difference between big cities and small towns. Something like this happens in LA and nobody cares, they just get on with their lives like it's no big deal. Here, everybody had headed for the hills and battened down the hatches.

The amount of food on Taylor's plate was obscene. Two massive half-pound burgers and enough fries to feed four. He picked up a burger, took a large bite, then another, stuffed a couple of fries in his mouth. He was eating like a man who'd just invented food.

I looked at my meal. The burger and fries, the coffee and the shake. All the major food groups were represented. Carbs, protein, sugar and caffeine. I picked up my burger and took a bite. Taylor was right. The food was good.

"Assuming for a second that this guy is a cop, how do you know I'm not the killer?" Taylor shrugged. "After all, I'm a cop."

"Because back in my room you told me you'd never killed anyone."

Taylor snorted. "We've got penitentiaries that are fit to bursting with people who'll tell you they've never killed anyone. Maybe we should take them all at their word and set them free. How does that sound?"

"You didn't do it, Taylor. No way. And the real reason is because you don't fit the profile."

Another snort, this one followed by a shake of the head. "You mean that piece of fiction you told Shepherd back at the station house."

I tapped my temple. "No, I mean the profile that's up here. Anyway, it wasn't a complete work of fiction. Two of the details are correct, remember."

"But which two?"

I stuffed a handful of fries into my mouth. "You're the head of the Criminal Investigation Division, you tell me."

Taylor looked around, a puzzled expression on his face.

"What?" I said.

"I'm just wondering where my investigators are. If I'm the head of the Criminal Investigation Division then I'm going to need investigators, right?"

"Just answer the question. Our unsub is a white male, five foot nine, in his thirties, slim-built, college-educated, which two of those details are correct?"

Taylor ate in silence for a while, thinking hard. His face kept scrunching up into different expressions then relaxing again.

"He's a white male and he's college-educated," he said at last.

"Take a gold star and go to the top of the class. But why are you right? For all I know you just picked those two at random. You've got a one in ten chance of doing that and getting it right, which isn't too far out there. I've played longer odds and won."

"Sam was a white male, and serial killers tend to stick with their own racial group."

"Not always."

Taylor finished his first burger, licked his fingers and picked up the second. "No, not always, but it happens often enough for us to be able to make that generalisation with a fair degree of accuracy. He's got to be college-educated because of how elaborate and well-executed the murder was. This is not someone who failed their General Educational Development tests. He managed to get through high school, and make it all the way through college. No, this guy is way smarter than your average bear."

"I can buy that. Okay, what about the other three things?"

"He's probably in his thirties."

"Not younger?"

"Unlikely. This crime shows a high degree of self-control. A younger person would struggle with that. They wouldn't have the patience."

"I can buy that, too. And it's unlikely he's older. Suppressing his fantasies up until his thirties is one thing, keeping them in check for another decade is another matter altogether. And before you say anything, Sam was this guy's first. This unsub is a performer. If he'd killed before, you'd know about it. So what about his height and build? Five-nine and slim? What do you say?"

"It's possible."

I made the noise of a buzzer. "Wrong answer. Controlling one person is tough, but controlling two takes it up to a whole new level. Physically he's going to be big enough to be taken seriously, but not so big that he stands out." I glanced over at Taylor when I said this last bit. "You're looking for someone in good physical shape who measures in at somewhere around the six-foot mark. Someone who inspires trust and confidence rather than some black bald giant who'd scare the bejesus out of you just by saying hello."

"You saying I'm some sort of boogeyman, Winter?"

"No, what I'm saying is that there are some people out there who would find someone of your size intimidating. Little old ladies, Girl Scouts, babies in strollers."

"And this unsub isn't intimidating?"

"Oh, he's intimidating all right, but the sort of intimidation he employs will be more subtle than using his size to scare some soft lawyer into submission. Size isn't everything, you know. Okay, any more questions?"

Taylor shook his head. "Not just now."

We finished our meal in silence. Taylor cleared his plate first and nodded to the leftovers on mine.

"You going to finish those fries?"

"Be my guest."

He reached over for my plate and swapped it with his empty one. The fries disappeared in three mouthfuls. Taylor settled back on his seat, wiped his mouth with a napkin, then belched. It was barely audible, an old lady belch. It wasn't the belch of someone who'd just eaten enough to feed a family of four.

"I've got a job for you," I told him. "You'll need to be discreet, though. I want the names of everyone who works for the sheriff's department. Everyone. I'm talking the sheriff all the way down to the janitor. Same for the police department. Also, while you're back at the station house, keep your eyes open for anyone acting odd. Even a little bit odd. You can go in there and be invisible. I can't. I'm the new kid at school. As soon as I step through the door everyone's going to be looking at me."

"If you're so sure this guy's a cop, why do you need to know who the janitor is?"

"To cover all the bases. I'm ninety-nine per cent sure, which is different from being a hundred per cent certain. That unaccounted one per cent drives me nuts. You've no idea."

Taylor was staring across the table at me, a playful grin pulling at the corners of his mouth. "What are you actually saying here, Winter? That you might be wrong?"

"I'm not wrong. This guy's a cop. I just want to expand the parameters a little. That's all."

"But the janitor, Winter? That's really stretching things."

"A janitor would have easy access to a police uniform."

"And a cop car?" Taylor shook his head. "I don't think so."

"You took an exam and did an interview before they let you in. The reason they do that is because there are some people who shouldn't be cops. Psychos and people with anger management issues, for example. A lot of people who fail the entrance exams want to be cops so badly they end up taking jobs as security guards or private investigators, anything where they get to play cop. Some even take on menial roles in police departments. Like janitorial positions."

"And what about the cop car?"

"You can get hold of one of those second hand, no problems whatsoever. That's what the internet's for."

CHAPTER TWENTY-FOUR

The first name that went up on the whiteboard was Taylor's. Second on the list was Sheriff Peter Fortier, then Captain Tony Shepherd, then Romero and finally Barker. No forenames or ranks for the two investigators because Shepherd hadn't told me what they were, and no forename for Taylor because that was an on-going investigation.

The names took up a small corner of the board, leaving plenty of space for more suspects. I stepped back, looked at the five names, then swapped the black marker for a red one and put a line through Taylor.

A second line went through Fortier and a third through Shepherd. Both were too old, and both were preoccupied with other things. Fortier was looking for a way to vacate the sheriff's office, and Shepherd was looking for a way to jam his foot in the door.

I put question marks after Romero and Barker. They were in the right racial and age groups, but Barker was too small and Romero was too fat. I'd be surprised if either was our unsub, but wasn't ready to rule them out just yet.

I lit a cigarette and settled down on the bed with a glass of that thirty-year-old Glenmorangie. The whisky was everything I'd hoped for, and more. My laptop was showing the countdown, those white numbers moving inexorably towards zero, a steady stream of stick figures biting the dust.

04:03:32.

In a little over four hours another person was going to die. I still held on to the slender hope that we might be able to stop this guy, but that sliver was getting thinner with every passing second. Maybe the police would find the place Sam Galloway was murdered, and maybe I'd be able to take one look and work out who the killer was, and maybe we'd be able to hunt this unsub down before he killed again. But that was a whole lot of maybes, more than I was comfortable with.

It wasn't that far-fetched, though. Every once in a while you caught an eleventh-hour break, but those occasions were the exception rather than the rule.

The reality was that you couldn't save them all. I'd struggled with this when I was with the FBI, and it was a reality I was struggling with now. The countdown was going to hit zero on the stroke of midnight and someone else would die. I'd battle this one to the wire, but it wasn't looking good.

I phoned Hannah and asked her to bring up some coffee. A couple of minutes later I heard footsteps in the corridor, the rattle of dishes on a tray, a knock.

"Come on in," I called out.

The door opened and Hannah entered. She was dressed in jeans and still wearing the baggy Gutterpigs T-shirt she'd had on earlier. I nodded to the whisky bottle on the nightstand. "Like a drink?"

Hannah hesitated for all of a second, then dragged the chair over and poured herself a glass. She sat down and took a sip.

"Not bad."

"Better than not bad."

Her eyes narrowed. "Shouldn't you be working or something?"

I tapped the side of my head. "I am working. We're open for business twenty-four/seven, three sixty-five. Don't let my apparent lack of activity fool you."

Hannah laughed. "Well, from here it looks like you're getting paid to sit around on your ass, drinking whisky and smoking. Nice work if you can get it."

It was my turn to laugh. "I could say the same thing about you."

"Except I'm not smoking."

I crushed my cigarette into the ashtray and offered the pack to Hannah. She shook her head, said no thanks. I waited until she'd got settled, waited until she was nice and comfortable, then I clicked the laptop's keypad a couple of times to get the video running.

Hannah's coffee was good, but the film was the real reason she was here. I turned the computer around so she could see the screen better. Her eyes widened as she realised what she was looking at. A slight tremor appeared in the hand that held the whisky glass.

"Nanny cam." I nodded to the teddy bear on the dresser. "Six months ago a maid tried to steal some of my cigarettes. There were a dozen packs in my suitcase, she didn't think I'd miss one. She was wrong."

Even in low-res black and white there was no mistaking the woman who'd just come into the room. That short spiky DIY haircut was unmistakable. On screen, Hannah walked around, picking things up and putting them down again. She picked up the bear and her face became huge and distorted. A shake of the head, a puzzled frown, then she put it down. The picture jumped a little while she repositioned the bear to make sure it was exactly how I'd left it.

Next she unzipped my case and started going through it, carefully removing each item and putting it in a tidy pile. Then she put everything back exactly where she'd found it. She took one last look around then left the room.

"You didn't take anything. I'm not sure whether to be insulted or not."

"I'm not a thief."

"So what was that all about?"

Hannah ignored the question and said, "What happened to the maid who stole your cigarettes? Did she get fired?"

"The question's irrelevant. Nobody's going to fire you because you're the boss around here. So, what happened to your mother?"

"Who said anything's happened to my mother?"

"If nothing had happened to your mother, you would have said that nothing had happened to your mother. Instead you answered my question with a question."

"Nothing happened to my mother."

I shook my head. "Not buying. You're what? Twenty-two? Twenty-three? If your mother had you young she'd be in her forties. If she had you late then she'd maybe be in her sixties. Either way, statistically there's a high probability she's still alive. You're more than comfortable setting your own room prices. And I'm guessing Mom doesn't get a cut of that hundred bucks I gave you when I checked in. Or the hundred you conned from me. You're running the show around here."

Hannah grinned, but only for a second. She grabbed my cigarettes and Zippo from the bedside table and lit one. "My mother's got Parkinson's. She still deals with the admin, but that's about all she can manage these days. All of the physical stuff is down to me. And you're right. I'd sell this place in a heartbeat."

I studied her carefully, unconvinced. There was some sort of tragedy here, but it wasn't Parkinson's. I could call her on the lie, but even then I didn't think I'd get to the truth. Instead I decided to let it go. For now.

"Let's go back to my earlier question. Since you obviously weren't planning on stealing from me, what the hell were you doing in my room?"

Hannah flicked the dead ash from her cigarette, then walked over and picked up the teddy bear. She studied it closely, looking for the camera. Smiled when she found it. "I've got to admit that I did wonder about this. It didn't make sense. I thought it might have been a gift from an old girlfriend, but that explanation didn't sit well. Have you got a girlfriend?"

"Single and happy, and I'm the one asking the questions."

Hannah smiled. "It's a way of relieving the boredom and getting a bit of a buzz. That's one reason. The second reason is that I like to try and work out who the guests are, what makes them tick. Call it extreme people watching."

I laughed. "So what makes me tick?"

"If I didn't know better I'd say you were a serial killer."

Hannah laughed because she'd meant it as a joke, and I laughed right along with her because I didn't want her to know what I was really thinking.

We're the same.

"What makes you say that?"

"Six pairs of underpants, all neatly folded and all identical. Six pairs of socks, all neatly balled up and all identical. Six T-shirts that indicate a dubious taste in old-guy music, two identical pairs of Levis and two hoodies, one black, one grey. When you get dressed in the morning the only choice you need to make is which T-shirt and hoodie to wear, and since it's summer, you don't even have to worry about the hoodie, which reduces the choices you need to make to one."

"Maybe I'm just pragmatic."

"And one person's pragmatic is another person's weird. You've got to admit, it's a little bit OCD."

I reached for my cigarette pack and lit a fresh one. "I want you to come work for me. You're just the sort of person the new Dayton Parish Sheriff's Department is looking for."

Hannah gave me the look. "Two sentences filled with words I understand, but put them all together and they make no sense whatsoever."

I navigated through the laptop's files until I found the right one, then hit play. Dirt streaked concrete, and Sam Galloway hog-tied and panicked.

"Take a look, and tell me what you see."

CHAPTER TWENTY-FIVE

When Taylor turned up ten minutes later, Hannah was watching the film for the third time. "Gross" was her considered opinion the first time she watched it, which was accurate, and understandable, but not particularly helpful. The second time I asked her to watch more closely for anything that might help to identify the place Sam had been murdered. There wasn't, but that was to be expected since my question redefined the whole concept of the long shot.

Taylor came in without knocking and froze in the doorway when he saw us sitting shoulder to shoulder on the bed. Hannah had the computer resting on her lap, eyes glued to the screen, concentrating hard.

"What's going on, Winter?"

"Taylor, meet your new investigator. Hannah, meet your new boss. Taylor heads up our Criminal Investigation Division," I whispered to her *sotto voce*. "His first order of business was to requisition some investigators, so here you are."

Hannah snorted a little half-laugh. Her eyes remained glued to the screen. "My boss. Yeah, right."

I rolled my eyes and made a face. "Careful what you wish for, Taylor. So have you got that list of names?"

"No problem."

Taylor held up a sheet of paper. All I could see was a black blur of print on a white background, but I was happy to take his word on this one.

"What's the mood like back at the station house?"

"Tense, frustrated. Everyone's watching the clock and counting down the seconds. And should she be watching that, Winter? I mean, it is evidence."

"I figured that another perspective wouldn't hurt."

"But she's not a cop."

"Hannah, raise your right hand."

Eyes glued to the screen, Hannah raised her hand.

"Do you swear to blah, blah, blah. Et cetera, et cetera."

"I do," she replied.

"There, suitably deputised."

"She's not a cop, Winter."

"Guys," Hannah called out. "I might have something here."

I looked over at the laptop screen. Hannah had paused the film at a point where the picture was dominated by the fire-starter's bottom half, everything below the waist. Taylor came over and crouched down so he could see.

"Notice anything unusual?" she asked.

I looked for a second, saw what she was getting at, smiled to myself. "Got it."

"What?" said Taylor.

"Look at the shoes," Hannah told him.

Taylor didn't say anything for a second. He was staring at the screen, hating the fact that we knew something he didn't. His face suddenly brightened and he grinned. "They don't match."

"Exactly. They're both black, which was why you might have missed it, but when you look more closely you can clearly see that they're a different design."

"And who would go around wearing shoes that don't match?" I said. "Please don't all shout at once."

"A homeless person," answered Hannah.

"Which means our unsub is smaller than we thought. Originally, I said he'd be around the six-foot mark because it's difficult to control two people, but those shoes change all that. A soft lawyer and a homeless guy who's so far down that he doesn't even have matching shoes, a grandmother could control those two." I leant around Hannah so I could see Taylor. "Still think this is a bad idea? You know, if you're not careful your tenure as the head of the Criminal Investigation Division could be the shortest in the whole history of Dayton."

"Okay," Taylor said. "We know something new, but it's not necessarily a good thing, is it?"

"Why not?" asked Hannah.

"Because what Captain Taylor is getting at is that we're now looking for someone between five-seven and five-eleven. The average height for an American male is five feet nine point two inches. That's the median, the exact midpoint. Half of American males are taller and half are smaller. The further you get from the median, the fewer people you're going to find, until you find just one, and then none. It's a big deal being the world's tallest or smallest person. You get a certificate, and your picture and name ends up in the record books." I nodded to the sheet of paper Taylor was holding. "Our guy is going to measure in somewhere between five-seven and five-eleven, which, statistically speaking, covers most of the males on Taylor's list."

I walked over to the whiteboard and scrubbed out the red question marks next to Barker's and Romero's names. Looked like they were back in play. Taylor and Hannah followed me over. I plucked the list from Taylor's fingers and glanced at it. Names, dates of birth, addresses. I passed it back to Taylor.

"Okay, transfer the list to the whiteboard. Stick to white males aged between thirty and forty. Whoever's neatest can do the writing. By my reckoning we've got seventeen new suspects. Give me a shout when you're done."

The coffee was lukewarm, but lukewarm coffee has as much caffeine in it as the freshly brewed stuff, and right now it was caffeine I was after. I pulled the laptop across and replayed the silent movie of Sam Galloway's murder. Different shoes. I should have spotted that one. It made me wonder what else I might have missed. That was the problem when an investigation ran slow. The doubts began to creep in.

I finished my coffee and called Shepherd. He answered on the fifth ring, which meant his cellphone was closer to hand this time. Maybe even in the same room. He sounded excited to hear from me, until he realised I didn't have anything new. I heard a sigh and imagined him stroking his moustache even more furiously than usual.

They still hadn't located the crime scene.

There were two possible reasons, both of which could be contributing factors. One, they were looking for a needle in a haystack. Eagle Creek covered an area of twelve square miles, and Dayton was over six hundred square miles. That was a big old chunk of land. A lot of garages and barns and warehouses.

The second reason was that the unsub didn't want the crime scene to be found yet and was subtly steering the investigation away from it. The upside of this was that when we did find the crime scene, it could help to identify the unsub. I told Shepherd we'd be there soon and hung up.

"Seventeen new names exactly," Hannah called over.

I walked over to the whiteboard and stared at the names. Two neat columns, eleven names in each. Taylor, Fortier and Shepherd were out of play, but that still left nineteen suspects. Hannah was tapping the black marker pen against her leg, and studying the names on the board. Taylor was quietly staring, his face creased with fierce concentration.

"Any names jump out at you?" I asked him.

"Darrell Hodginson. But that's because he's an asshole, not because I think he's the unsub."

"What about you, Hannah?"

She shook her head. "Most of these people I don't know. I went to school with Dan Choat, but I can't see him being involved in something like this."

"Why not?"

"He was popular, bright, polite. That's the main thing I remember about him. How polite he was.

Whenever he spoke to the teachers he always called them ma'am or sir."

"And you've just described Ted Bundy."

Hannah's mouth made the shape of an O.

"Right now we have nineteen suspects. Our unsub is an expert at hiding in plain sight. He knows how cops think because he is one. He knows how investigations are run because he's been involved with so many. He knows about forensics and profiling. And he'll be doing everything possible to lead us in the wrong direction."

CHAPTER TWENTY-SIX

The sun had gone down, the temperature too. The evening was still warm, but it was a pleasant warm rather than Death Valley warm. My leather jacket was hooked on my finger and hanging over my shoulder for when it got cold later. Morrow Street was completely deserted. We were the only living souls. It was twenty to nine. In three hours and twenty minutes there was a very high likelihood that someone else was going to be burnt alive.

Hannah was back in the guesthouse because she had chores to do, which worked well since I'm pretty sure that Shepherd wouldn't be too impressed if we turned up with a sarcastic, spiky-haired ball of attitude wearing a Gutterpigs T-shirt. I made a mental note to Google Gutterpigs when this case was over. In my experience an interesting name didn't necessarily mean interesting music, but it was worth checking out.

"Keys," I held out a hand and made *gimme, gimme* gestures with my fingers. We were standing on the sidewalk beside the police cruiser. Taylor shook his head.

"Keys, *please*."

"No way, Winter. I'm driving."

I laughed. "Taylor, what you do can in no way be described as driving."

"I'm not giving you the keys."

"Look. You're only the head of the Criminal Investigation Division, so by default that makes me the sheriff around here, which means I outrank you. Also, my guess is that Shepherd ordered you to help me out in any way you can. And right now I would find it really, *really* helpful if you gave me the keys."

Taylor dropped the keys into my palm and we got in the car. He racked the passenger seat back as far as it would go, wriggled around a couple of times in a space that had been designed with an average-sized man in mind.

I dumped my jacket on the back seat and started the car, goosed the accelerator a couple of times, letting the engine scream until the rev counter was slamming into the red. Then I flicked on the lights, checked one last time to make sure the street was empty, rammed the car into gear, jammed my foot down on the gas pedal, and squealed away from the sidewalk. The amount of noise the car made, there had to be at least twenty feet of melted rubber left in our wake. A long black eleven and the stench of burning rubber.

"Jesus, Winter! Slow down!"

I slowed down when we reached the end of Morrow Street, checked the road ahead was clear then hit the gas again. Taylor was fumbling with his safety belt, trying to get it into the slot. We hit the train tracks at fifty, fast enough for all four wheels to lift off the ground. The car landed hard, the shocks grinding and complaining. Taylor was gripping the passenger seat, knuckles tight and shiny. We reached an intersection and turned left onto Main Street, heading south. I eased my foot off the gas and brought the speed down to a more sedate forty.

"You're going the wrong way," he told me.

"And that statement is based on the flawed premise that we're going to the station house."

"We're not? So where are we going?"

"Judging by Main Street, my guess is that Mayor Morgan has a zero-tolerance policy when it comes to the homeless. No bums, no hobos jumping from the midnight train, and any vagrants are shot on sight the second they step inside the town limits. Does that sound about right?"

Taylor nodded. "Yup."

"So, if you wanted to find a homeless person, you'd have to look elsewhere. Any suggestions?"

"Shreveport is probably your best bet. It's the closest big city. This time of day, it'll take about half an hour to get there."

"Half an hour, you reckon."

As soon as we reached the interstate, I switched on the blues and reds and stepped on the gas and watched the needle flick up past a hundred. We had both lanes pretty much to ourselves, a long, straight road heading west.

The old abandoned refinery appeared on our left. Dark, shadowy buildings that seemed darker than the night surrounding them. The facility was huge. It could have been a parish in its own right. It had been built back in a time when land was cheap and plentiful.

It looked totally different to when we'd flown over it earlier in the Gulfstream. Back then the harsh sunlight had made it look innocent, just another place that had outlived its usefulness. Now it looked sinister. There were plenty of places to hide a body, plenty of places to set someone alight without having to worry about the screams. Lots of hidden, secret spaces. Shepherd could send every man he had in there and it would take the best part of a month to search the place. Even then, they'd still miss something. Particularly if someone involved in the search wanted that to happen.

"How did you know Sam Galloway drove a Testarossa?" Taylor asked. "And I want a straight answer, Winter. None of your cryptic bullshit."

"I played the odds. There are more Testarossas on the road than any other Ferrari, so there was a higher probability that that's what he drove. Also, if you think of Ferrari, what's the first model that comes to mind? The Testarossa, right? Sam was more interested in the statement the car made rather than the car itself, so the chances were he'd go for a Testarossa."

Taylor looked over, an incredulous expression on his face. "You guessed."

"If you want to put it that way."

"You guessed," he said again.

"And I guessed right."

"But you could have guessed wrong. What if this had been something important? Like life-and-death important? This isn't a game."

"Look. What we do is an inexact science. The operative word there is *science*. Science isn't all logic and facts and empirical observations. Yes, those things are important, but some of the most important discoveries and breakthroughs have come about because some scientist in a lab somewhere looked beyond the facts and had the courage to take a leap of faith, a giant step into the unknown. Einstein once said that imagination is more important than knowledge, and I fully subscribe to that line of thinking. Sometimes you just need to believe that two and two can come together to make five, then you need to find a way to make that happen. Then you need to work out a way to make the rest of the world believe. Not so long ago people thought the earth was flat and that the sun revolved around it."

"But you guessed." Taylor shook his head in disbelief one last time, then went back to watching the road unfolding in the headlights.

Nineteen minutes later we passed the sign that marked the Shreveport city limits. Taylor had been born and raised in Eagle Creek and his family's roots ran deep. But Eagle Creek would have been too small a town for a teenager, particularly one who was the star football player. When Taylor and his buddies went out looking for weekend fun, I guessed they would have headed to the next big city. They'd know exactly where they wanted to hang out and they'd know which areas to avoid.

"I'm going to need you to direct me."

CHAPTER TWENTY-SEVEN

Ten minutes later we hung a right into a post-apocalyptic version of Morrow Street. All the buildings were boarded up, and this wasn't a new thing. They'd been boarded up and abandoned for decades.

The streetlights were all out, too, the bulbs smashed. Either the city hadn't got around to replacing them or, more likely, they'd given up because every time they replaced them they ended up smashed again. Grey, people-shaped outlines moved through the darker shadows. In places, the darkness was broken by flames licking up from oil drums that had been lit to provide illumination rather than heat.

We cruised slowly along the street, the eyes in the shadows tracking our progress. Halfway along I pulled up to the sidewalk, but kept the engine running. Not that I expected trouble. The car was covered in Dayton Sheriff's Department livery. The cops come calling in an area like this and everyone suddenly turns invisible and develops a bad case of amnesia.

"What now?" Taylor asked.

"I want you to go out there and talk to people. Find out if anyone's gone missing in the last forty-eight hours."

Taylor gave me the look. "You're kidding, right?" He stared at me, saw I was serious. "It's a complete waste of time, Winter. Nobody's going to talk to me. And who says this is where the unsub snatched his firestarter from anyway? Maybe he went east instead of west, headed over to Monroe."

"Just humour me, okay?"

Taylor shook his head and got out the car. There was a hefty dose of attitude in the way he slammed the door shut behind him. He walked around the front of the car and was momentarily lit up in the headlights, all six foot six and two-eighty pounds of him. Dressed in black and striding through the gloom, he looked more like a cop than ever. He moved like a cop. He walked like one. The people who hung out around here would smell him a mile off.

He walked up to a woman pushing a shopping cart that was overflowing with bottles and cans. He asked her a question and she shook her head. He asked another question and she started gesticulating wildly. Taylor crossed the street, heading towards one of the fires. A group of men were huddled beside it, passing a bottle in a brown paper bag. By the time he got there they'd all fled.

I shut my eyes and slid into the zone, imagined myself into the shoes of someone who got their kicks from watching flames burst and crackle, and skin melting.

Being a cop was this unsub's biggest asset, and also his biggest problem.

He could go to a thrift store and buy some clothes. He could rip them up and drag them through the dirt, and douse them in cheap whisky and urine. He could do all of that and he'd still never get mistaken for a homeless person.

There were a hundred details that would give him away. He'd be too well fed. He'd look too healthy. His teeth wouldn't be rotting away to stumps. Alcoholism and drug abuse showed up on the skin, and he wouldn't have any of the tell-tale signs. The jaundiced pallor and exploding capillaries of a drunk would be missing, the grey complexion and sunken eyes of a junkie. Being homeless was a way of life. It was not a part you could just step into.

So how did he do it?

He needed to separate his victim from the pack, and he needed them to go with him voluntarily. No fuss, no drama, nothing that would cause anyone to remember or take notice.

Maybe he pretended he was gay, a white-collar worker looking for a cheap, anonymous release. He'd be acting panicked and jumpy and sending out mixed signals, but that was nothing the people around here hadn't seen before. He could try to disguise the cop in him under a cloak of nervous ambiguity.

Except that wouldn't work either.

This guy was all about control. There was no way he'd relinquish that control, not for a second. He was confident enough to work with two victims at the one time, and he was confident enough to predict the time of his next murder right down to the last second. There was no way he could make a convincing submissive.

So, maybe he pretended to be a drug dealer.

Straightaway, that felt better. It was a more comfortable fit. Around here, dealers were practically cops anyway. They carried guns and laid down the law. It wouldn't be that big a stretch for him to step into that role.

He would choose his victim carefully. They needed to be desperate enough to go with him when he told them the good stuff was in the trunk of his car, but they couldn't be too desperate. Someone whose addiction had spiralled out of control wouldn't work. They'd be too jittery to play the part he had written for them, too unpredictable. He needed someone who still had enough of a grip on reality to come across as confident and in control when the camera rolled. He needed someone who cared whether they lived or died, since that's how he controlled them. Do what you're told and you'll get out of this alive.

The unsub would have gone straight to the trunk and popped the lid. He would have taken one last look around to make sure nobody was watching, then injected his victim with a powerful sedative. Firearms wouldn't work, nor would a stun gun. With both those methods, the unsub would need to restrain his victim with duct tape, and that would take time. The longer he was out in the open, the more likely it was that someone would see what was happening. It had to be a sedative.

So he drugged his victim, tipped him into the trunk, slammed down the lid and drove off, and nobody was any the wiser.

Taylor climbed back into the car and pulled the door closed. His expression was stern. Part pissed, part perplexed.

"A complete waste of time. Just like I told you. But you knew that before you sent me out there, so what are we doing here?"

I ignored the question and said, "Acquisition is the riskiest part of any abduction because the unsub is out in the open. There was a double challenge here because our guy is a cop. You saw the reaction they had to you. These people can smell a cop a mile away."

"So how did he do it?"

"He pretended to be a drug dealer."

"Wouldn't people be suspicious if a new dealer suddenly turned up?"

"But this unsub's a cop, remember. How difficult would it be for him to get the names of dealers who have been arrested around here? He drops a few names and people are going to be a lot less suspicious. Also, these are junkies we're talking about. At the end of the day they want their next fix, they don't really care where it comes from."

Taylor thought this through, then nodded to himself. "Yeah, I guess that could work. Okay, what now?"

"Do you know the way to the Shreveport Police Department's headquarters?"

CHAPTER TWENTY-EIGHT

Missing Persons was located in a small windowless basement office. The clock said twenty to ten, but without any sky to provide a reference point it could have been a.m. or p.m. This was one of those places that was permanently trapped in the Twilight Zone. The room smelled of scrubbed linoleum and unscrubbed people. It smelled stale. The striplights were dulled by dirty covers, dead insects dotting the plastic.

A wooden counter split the room in two. One third was on the public side, two-thirds on the business side. The woman behind the counter was Hispanic and in her late forties. Her shoulders were hunched, as though life had compressed her into submission, just squashed her right down and kept on squashing. Her name patch said Gomez, and she had sergeant's stripes, but considering her role and attitude it was unlikely that she was going to climb any higher.

We walked over to the desk and Taylor flashed his ID. Gomez glanced at it, then looked at us, eyes narrowed, giving us the once-over. She lingered on my white hair and the dead rock-star T-shirt.

"How can I help you gentlemen?" Her voice was harsh and grating, nicotine rough.

"I'm looking for someone."

She gave me a wry smile. Her top teeth were too straight and white to be natural, and her bottom teeth were too crooked to be anything else. "Take a ticket and join the back of the queue."

"White male," I went on. "Thirty to forty, around five feet nine. He went missing sometime during the last forty-eight hours."

"Anything else you can tell me? Name? Last known whereabouts? Star sign? Anything?"

"He's homeless."

Gomez laughed and shook her head. "Yeah, that really helps." She nodded to the ranks of tall grey filing cabinets behind her. "The number of homeless men back there that match your criteria, I can maybe count on two hands if you're lucky, and that's going back years. Homeless teenage girls I've got more of, but that's because they have family that comes looking." She shook her head. "A homeless white male in his thirties, you might as well be chasing the Invisible Man. Yeah, they might have family out there, but by the time they've got this far down the road, they're just a memory in a photograph. Occasionally someone will come looking, a brother or sister, sometimes a parent. But that's the exception rather than the rule."

"Can I see all the missing person reports filed in the last seventy-two hours?"

"Sure. But I'm telling you now, your guy's not in there."

Gomez pulled open the top drawer of the filing cabinet positioned nearest the counter. This cabinet would contain all the active cases, the ones they needed to get their hands on quickly. She reached into the drawer and pulled out a wad of brown Manila folders, brought them back over and dumped them down. They made a satisfying slapping sound when they hit the counter. The top folder had MISSING PERSONS and the Shreveport PD logo printed onto the cover.

"This got anything to do with that lawyer who got burnt alive in Eagle Creek?" She shook her head and made the sign of the cross. "That was a bad business. I've got a cousin over there, in the police department. He told me there was a film, some sort of snuff movie. He hadn't seen it, but he knows someone who had. It was pretty nasty by all accounts."

"We're working a different case."

"And you expect me to believe that? Nothing ever happens in Eagle Creek, so when something does happen everyone's going to jump to it. There's no way you're going to be out looking for some homeless guy unless that guy has something to do with the case."

Gomez had her right hand placed protectively on the folders. She wanted information, and I wanted a look at those folders. It was a negotiation, plain and simple. Everything in life was a negotiation.

"Can you keep a secret?"

Gomez nodded. "Sure."

"I don't work for the Dayton Sheriff's Department, I'm with the CIA."

She grinned. "I knew you weren't a cop."

"The lawyer who died, he was working for a Colombian drug cartel that we've been chasing down for years. He tried to rip them off and, like we both know, our Colombian friends do not take too kindly to that sort of thing."

"And the homeless guy?" Gomez's eyes were wide with childlike wonder. She was hanging on my every word.

"He was the lawyer's partner. He got wind that the Colombians were after them and did a runner. Last we heard, he was hiding out on the streets."

I nodded to the folders and Gomez followed my gaze. For a second she looked at her hand like she'd never seen it before, then her brain caught up and she jerked it away from the folders.

There were seven files in total. Four females and three males. Like Gomez had said, none of the males came close to being a match for our firestarter. There was one guy in his fifties who'd been married for almost thirty years. He'd told his wife he was taking the dog for a walk, and had never returned. He'd left the house with the dog one evening and just kept on walking, out of one life and into another. His disappearance had coincided with their youngest child going to college, and my guess was that it was motivated by a reluctance to pay alimony.

One guy was the right height and build. The problem was that he was Asian. The unsub had been careful to make sure the firestarter didn't show his face, but he hadn't been wearing gloves. The hand that had carried the jerry can had been as white as mine.

I pushed the folders back across the desk, waited until Gomez met my eyes, then mimed a zipper closing my lips shut tight.

"Not a word," she promised.

"Thanks for your time." I headed for the door. According to the clock on the wall it was just after ten to ten.

CHAPTER TWENTY-NINE

"The CIA?" Taylor gave an indulgent chuckle, like he was the parent and I was a kid who'd just done something unexpected and kind of cool. We were back in the car, bouncing out of the police department's parking lot.

"You know how fast gossip spreads through your offices. That's true for every station house. And I'm talking the whole world here. Wildfire can't touch it."

"That still doesn't explain the story you just told Gomez."

"Her career has stalled at sergeant, and she probably got that position based on years served rather than ability. So she's stuck there in Missing Persons and a couple of Eagle Creek cops come in asking about some homeless guy. It took her a millisecond to work out that this has something to do with Sam Galloway. So she's now got some gossip, you think she's going to keep her mouth shut?"

I stopped at a red light and took out my cigarettes. Taylor shot me a disapproving look from the racked-back passenger seat. The squashed pack got shoved back in my pocket, but the Zippo I kept in my hand. The brass was pitted, rough against my skin. The lighter was older than me. It dated back to the sixties, and it worked as well today as when it was first bought. I flicked up a flame, stared at it for a second, then snapped the lid shut and put the lighter away.

"You're no fun, do you know that, Taylor? You need to loosen up. Let your hair down. And before you say anything. Yes, I know you're bald."

"This has nothing to do with spoiling your fun, and everything to do with not wanting to die of lung cancer. I know how to have fun."

I raised an eyebrow.

"I know how to have fun, Winter."

"*Carpe diem*. Seize the day, Milhouse."

"My name is not Milhouse. Not now, not ever."

The light turned green and I put the car into gear.

"Gomez's credibility is hovering around zero. Let's face it, Missing Persons isn't exactly a prime assignment. She's stuck there until she retires. She knows that, and so does everyone else. Anything that can raise her status, she's going to use. A story about a couple of cops from Eagle Creek sniffing around, now that's believable, right? And it would be good for her credibility. That's going to raise her stock price by a few cents, right? Okay, so what happens if she starts going on about drug cartels, and conspiracies, and CIA agents, one with bright white hair and the other a bald black giant? What do you think the reaction to that's going to be?"

"Nobody's going to take her seriously."

"Exactly. There'll be a lot of eye rolling and whispers about how Gomez has really lost it this time, but nothing that'll get back to Eagle Creek."

I put my foot to the floor when we reached the interstate, turned on the roof lights. The road was empty and it felt good to have the highway disappearing so fast into the distance. I drove and thought about white numbers on a black background heading relentlessly towards zero. Most of all, I thought about how much organisation it would take to murder someone so publicly, and to such a precise timescale.

A couple of miles later I was thinking myself around in circles and getting nowhere. I found my cellphone and Shepherd answered on the first ring this time, which meant his cell was actually in his hand for once. He said a curt hello and there was tension in every syllable. Understandable. The clock was ticking and he was running out of options. Running out of time.

The downside of having your name in fancy gold letters on your office door was that they marked the place where the buck stopped. Sheriff Fortier and Mayor Morgan would be looking to him for answers, and making his life hell because he didn't have any.

"Have you found the crime scene?" I asked him.

"Still looking."

"You mentioned the old refinery earlier. That was a bust too?"

"We turned the place upside down, Winter. Nothing." There was a short pause, the sandpaper scratch of a moustache being stroked. "I thought you were coming back here."

"We are. We just needed to check something out."

"Anything worthwhile?" The pitch of his voice had risen by a semitone. A spark of hope? Desperation, maybe.

"No. It was a long shot. You've got to keep looking for that crime scene, Shepherd."

"Why are you so fixated on that?"

"Because that's what's going to help us catch this guy."

I killed the call and put my cell away. Taylor was squashed into the passenger seat, lost in thoughts of his own. An aura of dejection surrounded him, like the world had ended and it was all his fault.

"Penny for them," I asked.

"We're not going to be able to stop this guy killing again, are we?"

"I could lie, if that'll make you feel better."

He made a noise that could have been a laugh, or a sigh. He might have been a giant on the outside, but inside he was still enough of a kid to consider his teenage years to be the best years of his life.

"You can't save them all, Taylor. It would be crazy to think otherwise. Some days the good guy scores that home run at the bottom of the ninth to steal the game. Some days it's the bad guy."

"So why do we bother? Why do *you* bother?"

"Because someone's got to. What would have happened if our grandparents had taken that view and the Nazis had won the war? Do you think Hitler would have shut down all the death camps? Not a chance. New camps would have sprung up all over the place. Six million dead would have ended up looking like nothing."

"Yeah, I get that, but the problem is that you're hiding behind abstract concepts rather than dealing with specifics. The fact is that in less than two hours someone else is going to die."

"You can't let that darkness wear you down, Taylor. Let it into your soul and it will destroy you. You've got to keep fighting it all the way to your final breath."

"Easy to say, Winter, but how do you do that?"

"For me, it's music. When I listen to Mozart's Prague Symphony, I'm not in LA any more, or London, or Tokyo, or Eagle Creek, Louisiana. I'm right there in Prague and it's January 1787, and it's snowing outside, and the orchestra is tuning up and the world is about to hear this incredible piece of music for the very first time."

"And what if you don't have music?"

"Then you have to find your own happy thoughts. Okay, shut your eyes and think about the most amazing thing that ever happened to you. It could be the time your team won the title, or it could be your first kiss with the first girl you ever loved. I don't need to know what it is. I don't want to know."

Taylor gave me a sceptical look, then shut his eyes. To start with his face was tight, lips pursed, but gradually his features softened as a memory took hold. A small smile tugged at the corners of his mouth. He was no longer in a cop car speeding along I-20, he was holding up the trophy, or he was lost in that moment of eternal anticipation, wondering if he should kiss the girl or not. Or maybe he was lost in another memory altogether. It didn't really matter where he was, so long as he wasn't in a place filled with the stench of gasoline and burning flesh and the screams of the dying.

"Lose yourself in the memory," I said quietly. "Give yourself into it. What can you smell? What can you hear? What can you feel?"

Taylor's smile widened to show the tips of his teeth.

"Now imagine everything bathed in a bright white light. Paint everything golden."

I let a mile of blacktop roll off into the distance then told him to open his eyes.

"There you go. Your first Happy Thought. If things start getting on top of you, that's where you go."

Taylor stared through the windshield for a moment then turned to look at me. "Does this really work?"

"It works for me."

Taylor considered this, then said, "Thanks, Winter."

"Anytime."

CHAPTER THIRTY

I slowed up when we reached the abandoned refinery. There was something about the way it loomed out of the darkness that called to me. The west end was dominated by the old storage tanks, fourteen in total, all massive. They had to be at least a hundred feet high and sixty feet in diameter. The middle of the facility was dominated by the snaking pipes and towers of the distillation units. I switched off the flashing lights, hit the turn signal and left the interstate. The access road we turned onto led to the main gate.

"Small detour," I said in response to Taylor's questioning look.

"Shepherd's expecting us back at the station house."

"No, what Shepherd's expecting is a miracle, and he's looking for us to produce it, and that's not going to happen because miracles don't exist."

Taylor gave me the look.

"We've got under two hours until the countdown runs out. Now, we're agreed that when that happens there's a good chance this unsub will kill again?"

Taylor nodded.

"Which means that he must have already kidnapped his next victim?"

Another nod.

"In that case we're better off out here doing something, rather than being stuck in the station house doing nothing. You were there earlier. You saw what the atmosphere was like. Take that and multiply it by ten and that's what the atmosphere will be like now. Multiply it by a hundred and that's what it'll be like an hour from now. Multiply it by a thousand and you've got what it's going to be like as we close in on midnight. The tension is growing exponentially. Everybody's just waiting for the unsub to make his next move. They're sat there drinking coffee and getting strung out on caffeine and talking themselves around in circles. I know because I've seen it all before. Give me proactive over reactive any day."

Before Taylor had a chance to respond, his cell rang. He took it out and looked at the screen. "It's Shepherd. He's going to want to know where the hell we are, and what we're doing. What do you want me to tell him?"

"Tell him we're chasing down a lead and we'll be there soon."

"He's going to want details."

"So tell him I'll fill him in when we get there."

Taylor didn't look convinced. He glanced over one last time then connected the call. It didn't last long. He hung up and put the phone away.

"Don't look so worried, Herman. If Shepherd needs an ass to kick I'll make sure it's mine, not yours."

"It's not Herman, and why don't I feel even remotely reassured by that?"

I stopped in front of the main gates and got out. The cool breeze blowing up from the south was welcome after the fierce heat of the day, but I was glad I'd brought my leather jacket. I lit a cigarette, then walked over to the big double gates. Ten-foot-tall chain-link with razor wire on the top and wheels along the bottom.

The gates were clearly newer than the main fence and my guess was that they'd been installed when the facility was decommissioned. A lot of years had passed since then but it was easy to see where they'd been grafted onto the original fence.

Large signs made it clear what would happen to trespassers. None of what was promised sounded good. One of the signs had a large Alsatian on it. The dog looked feral. Sharp teeth and wildness in its eyes. That sign was worrying. Some places used dogs that had had their vocal cords removed. Stealth dogs. A patter of feet, then you're flat on your ass, razor-sharp teeth ripping into your throat.

I listened carefully. No barking or snuffling. The only sound was the soft whisper of the wind blowing around large buildings and structures, and pushing through narrow spaces, and whistling around the miles of pipework, a discordant chord that blended a dozen or so out-of-tune notes, some high, some low. The overall effect was eerie enough to send a shiver running up my spine.

The gates were secured with a thick chain and a large pad-lock. The lock looked heavy and daunting, but it was all for show. Inside there were a couple of small metal pins that needed to be persuaded to move aside. You're talking pins that were smaller than a quarter-inch. Learning to pick locks had been one of the more fun things I'd done during my time at Quantico. Locks are just puzzles that exist in the physical world rather than the cerebral. I love puzzles, love the challenge.

This lock had been oiled recently so all the parts moved smoothly. It took less than thirty seconds to pick.

I put the worn leather wrap containing my lock picks back into the inside pocket of my jacket, then tugged at the chain and rattled it off. Taylor grabbed the gate and dragged it open until it was wide enough for us to drive through. The gate moved easily and my guess was that this had nothing to do with Taylor's strength and size, and everything to do with the wheels having been oiled at the same time as the padlock.

We got back into the car and rolled slowly through the gap. Ten yards in we came to a barrier and a guardhouse. The barrier was up and we moved slowly past it. We hung a left and followed the perimeter road. Chain-link fencing stretched far into the distance on my side, shadowy grey structures rose up on Taylor's.

"Keep your eyes open for any signs of life," I told him. "Especially any vehicles. We're way off the beaten track here. Eagle Creek is a dozen or so miles to the north-east, and Shreveport's a dozen or so miles to the west, and in between those two points you've got a whole lot of nothing. I can't see our unsub walking or hitchhiking, can you?"

"You think he's here now?"

Taylor was almost whispering, as if the unsub might be hiding in the back of the car just waiting for an opportunity to stab us in the back.

"He's got to be somewhere. Unless he's mastered multi-dimensional travel."

"Why here?"

It was a good question. There was no evidence to suggest he was here. Except for the film clip of Sam Galloway going up in flames, and that computerised countdown, there was no evidence, period. This unsub had been careful to leave nothing behind. Except that wasn't entirely correct. Somewhere out there was a grey concrete place that would stink of charred flesh and gasoline. The reason we didn't have any real evidence was not because there wasn't any, it was because we hadn't found it yet.

"Why here?" Taylor asked again.

"Because it feels right."

"*Feels right?* What happened to facts and proof? You know, the sort of thing you can take to court."

"Sometimes you need to put two and two together to make five, remember. You need to take that leap of faith."

Taylor shook his head. "That's not the whole story, though, is it?"

"Okay, you've got me there." I smiled. "So what do we know about this unsub? We know he has a strong sense of drama. That film he produced for us was scripted right down to the last detail. He would have scouted out the location like he was making a

Hollywood blockbuster. He'd want a place that conveyed his vision."

"Somewhere like this?"

"Somewhere like this," I agreed. "Think about it. You're not going to find Dracula slumming it in a trailer park, are you? No way. He's going to have a big castle somewhere high on a cliff. And you can bet your ass that it's going to be in an area that gets more than its fair share of thunderstorms."

Taylor had his thinking face on.

"What?"

"I was just wondering if there was anywhere else around here that fit that description, but nothing springs to mind."

"No abandoned industrial parks? No old disused churches? No castles on cliffs?"

Taylor shook his head. "There are a few abandoned places, but nowhere dramatic enough for our unsub."

"If anything springs to mind, let me know and we can go check it out."

"Sure. So what now?"

"Now we search every square inch of this place looking for a car. When we find the car, we find the unsub, and so long as we find him in time, we save someone from being burnt alive."

We drove around the perimeter first, and ten minutes later we arrived back at the guardhouse. I gently pressed the brake pedal and the car drifted to a stop. No car. No guard dogs. No signs of life.

"Now what?" asked Taylor.

"Now we run a grid. We'll use the guardhouse as our start point. We'll go west to east to start with. If we find nothing there, we'll try going east to west."

We spent the best part of an hour and a half driving back and forth, burning gas while we searched every square inch. Anywhere big enough to hide a car, we checked out. The structures were all different sizes. Some were big enough to house a jumbo jet while others were so small you'd struggle to fit a desk inside. Some were positioned so close to their neighbours that there was barely enough space for a person to squeeze between, others were a football field apart.

Some of the roads we drove down were wide, some were narrow, some were dead ends. The one thing they had in common was that they were all as deserted as Morrow Street. No cars, no signs of life.

I pulled to a stop next to the guardhouse.

"We must have missed a turning in the dark," I said.

"Or, how about this? Maybe the unsub isn't here."

"Or maybe he's somewhere big enough to drive his car in."

"Or maybe you're clutching at straws because you can't bear to admit that you might be wrong. Face it, Winter. There's no one here."

I sighed, then drove through the gate and rolled to a stop. While Taylor pulled the gate closed, I dealt with the padlock. The wind had blown a thin layer of dirt and dust across the road surface and the faint outline of the gate's wheels was visible. I followed the tracks to the end of the gate then hunkered down and brushed a yard-long section of the dust flat. If anyone came through here after us, we'd know. What we wouldn't know was who that someone was. Still, right now I'd take all the information I could get.

"What?" I said in response to Taylor's questioning look. "Didn't you ever play spies when you were a kid?"

He gave me a *whatever* shrug, then got back into the car. I climbed into the driver seat and started the engine.

"Okay, let's go see if Shepherd's given himself a stroke yet."

CHAPTER THIRTY-ONE

It was eleven minutes to midnight when we arrived back at the station house. Eleven minutes until zero hour and that clock was ticking louder than ever. Every parking slot was taken. A line of police vehicles sat gleaming under the sodiums. Most belonged to the sheriff's department, but there were a few tan-coloured ones from the Eagle Creek PD.

In addition there were a couple of dozen civilian cars. Three stood out because there was no way a cop could afford them, not unless they were doing something illegal. If that was the case, they wouldn't be doing it much longer. The golden rule: don't flash the cash around, not unless you want to end up doing some serious prison time.

The three cars that stood out were a top-of-the-range Bentley, a bright red 1950s Cadillac Coup De Ville and a Porsche 911. The Caddy was well loved, the bodywork pristine. It was difficult to tell for sure in this light, but my guess was that it was in as good condition as the day it had rolled off the production line. I was also betting that both the Bentley and the Porsche were brand new. There was something about the way they sat there that made me think of car showrooms.

The media were here too. Three people can keep a secret, but only if two of them are dead, and there were a hell of a lot more than two people who knew about Sam Galloway. If you wanted proof of that you didn't have to look much further than Sergeant Gomez over in Shreveport.

For the moment there was just the one van. It was parked out on Main Street, as close to the station house as possible. A camera had been pointed at us as we drove past, but I doubt they got much, certainly nothing worthy of airtime. I hadn't recognised the acronym, but chances were it was a station broadcasting out of Shreveport. That's the way this game worked. The local media got hold of the story first, then, if it was big enough, it would go national. The next step was international, but there weren't many stories big enough to make that leap. What happened next would determine where this one stalled. If victim number two was another lawyer then the story wouldn't get much past Shreveport.

I abandoned our car as close as possible to the station house, then got out. Taylor got out the passenger side, slammed his door shut and started towards the building.

"Hold it a second," I called over.

He executed a neat about-turn and came back.

"Enemy territory." I nodded towards the station house. "We need a plan."

"What have you got in mind?"

I stared past Taylor's shoulder while I played out some moves in my head. Whenever I was short of cash at college I'd challenge my buddies to beat me at chess. On one memorable occasion I took on ten people at the same time. Ten games happening simultaneously, ten battlefields. The deal was that if any one of my buddies beat me, just one, I'd cough up twenty bucks to each competitor. If they all lost they'd pay me ten bucks each. That had been a good day. Any day where you end up richer than when you started was going to be a good day.

"There are nineteen suspects on the whiteboard back at my room." I nodded at the station house again. "This is the only show in town tonight. Anyone who's anyone will be here."

Taylor stood for a moment, thinking this over, waiting for me to say something else. I gave him all the time he needed. His eyes widened when the realisation finally hit.

"The unsub can't be in two places at the same time."

"Not unless he's working outside the four dimensions that keep the rest of us tied to this reality. Okay, time to play spy. I need you to use your cellphone to get pictures of any white males aged thirty to forty who've come to watch the show."

Taylor grinned. "And we compare those pictures with the list of suspects. Whoever's missing is our guy. That's brilliant, and so simple. This guy's really screwed up, and the beauty is that he doesn't even know it."

"They all screw up eventually. Don't let anyone work out what you're doing, though. Think you can manage that?"

"No problem. Everybody's going to be watching the countdown anyway. Six and a half feet tall and it'll be like I'm completely invisible. I guarantee it."

The station house doors suddenly banged open and Barbara Galloway strode out. She was accompanied by a man in his early sixties. It was almost midnight and he was dressed in a fitted suit, tie in place, the Windsor knot absolutely perfect. Shiny shoes, and a shiny gold watch, and a glimpse of shiny gold cufflinks with something sparkly set into them, something I strongly suspected were diamond rather than zirconium.

This guy had to be a lawyer, but he wasn't an Eagle Creek lawyer. The sort of wealth he was displaying made Sam Galloway look like a pauper, and Sam had been one of Eagle Creek's top earners. This lawyer was probably based in Shreveport or Monroe. Maybe even further afield. Dallas was only a couple of hundred miles west on I-20, which was no distance at all in that Bentley. Hit the road, set the cruise control, a little Bach on the stereo, and you'd eat up those miles in no time.

Barbara saw me and came to a halt. She looked older than earlier. It had only been six hours but it might as well have been six years. She looked exhausted, like she was running on fumes, and those fumes were dissipating fast. Even so, she looked good. There was something imperious about the way she was staring at me. Her husband had been murdered and her life had changed irrevocably, yet she was holding it together and I was more convinced than ever that she was going to survive this thing.

"Good evening, Mr Winter."

For once I didn't mind being called mister. It somehow sounded right coming from her.

"Mrs Galloway," I replied with a small nod.

"They think I had something to do with my husband's murder."

"Barbara," the lawyer said sharply. "You don't have to speak to these people."

"It's okay, Alan."

"As your lawyer, I strongly recommend you don't say anything else."

Barbara smiled at him. "I heard you the first time, Alan." She turned back to me. "My husband was having an affair. The police think I was consumed with jealousy and that I hired a hitman."

"It's just procedure. They need to check these things out."

"I wouldn't even know where to start looking for a hitman. Do they advertise in the Yellow Pages? On the internet?"

Alan the expensive lawyer was standing slightly behind Barbara, so she couldn't see the way his eyes had just widened. Her questions didn't blatantly indicate premeditation, but with some judicious manipulation they could be twisted to fit that concept.

"Like I said, it's just procedure. There's a possible motive there, so they have to check it out. That's all."

"It wasn't the first affair he'd had, you know."

"I know."

She looked at me, her expression blank and unreadable. "Do you think I had anything to do with my husband's murder?"

Alan took a sharp intake of breath. "I think it's best if we leave now."

"Shut up, Alan."

I shook my head. "You didn't have anything to do with your husband's murder."

"Captain Shepherd doesn't think that." She fixed me with her sad, tired eyes. "What makes you so sure?"

"Because it doesn't make sense. Judy Dufrene was no threat to you. The affair would probably have gone on for another two or three months before eventually burning out. For a couple of months afterwards Sam would have been attentive and guilt-ridden. The perfect husband, in other words. He'd buy you jewellery, take you away on an expensive vacation, treat you like a queen, and you'd be lapping up the attention. And then he'd get that itch again. He'd meet someone new and the cycle would start over. It's possible that somewhere along the line he might have met someone who'd give you a run for their money. If that happened then, yes, I'd seriously be looking at you as a suspect. However, so long as Sam was playing the game by your rules then everything was A-OK. It's only if he'd broken those rules that there would have been a problem. The bottom line: Judy Dufrene was a nice enough girl, but she wasn't a game changer."

"Thank you again for your honesty, Mr Winter."

Barbara walked off in the direction of the Bentley, Alan tagging along behind. The lawyer was doing a lot of talking, but Barbara wasn't listening. She was staring straight ahead, her face turning from orange to yellow as she walked through the sodium wash created by the lights.

Ten feet from the car, the driver got out and opened the back doors. Barbara got in one side, Alan got in the other, then the driver went around shutting the doors again. It was all done with the brisk efficiency of someone on double time, but who was still anxious for the day to be over. The Bentley eased out of the parking slot. It paused at the entrance to the lot, turn light flashing, then disappeared into the night. First stop, McArthur Heights. Second stop, wherever the hell Alan the expensive lawyer was staying tonight.

"Shepherd wasted no time there," Taylor said.

"Small-town cop, small-town motive. He couldn't help himself."

We went inside.

CHAPTER THIRTY-TWO

Everyone had congregated in the conference room because it was the largest room in the station house. There had to be at least fifty people squashed in there. It was standing room only, every seat taken. A laptop had been wired up to a projector, the image beamed onto a large screen. Blurred white numbers on a grey-black background, and blurred stick figures biting the dust. 00:04:33. Only twenty-eight stick men to go.

The three turned into a two and then a one, the countdown moving with agonising slowness. The numbers were huge, three feet tall and a foot wide. The stick figures were as tall as toddlers. Everything had been blown up to the point where the pixels were separating. Those numbers dominated the room.

The atmosphere was worse than I'd imagined. I'd never known a room containing this many people to be so quiet. It was like a funeral but without the music, prayers and eulogies. Just everyone staring at the coffin, waiting for something to happen.

Then there was the smell.

Most of the people here were involved in the investigation. They'd been out since dawn in temperatures that had hit a hundred plus. There might have been a few spare moments to grab a quick bite to eat and a coffee, fuel to keep you going, but not enough time to grab a shower. The stench that pervaded the room was a pungent mix of body odour and the deodorant that had been used to hide it. I was probably contributing to the smell. Taylor, too. We'd been out there in the hottest part of the day, sweating and toiling with the best of them.

"Romero and Barker are here," Taylor whispered in my ear. "Darrell Hodginson, too."

"Hodginson was the asshole, right?" I whispered back.

"That's right."

"Good. So that's three we can cross off the list straightaway. Only sixteen to go."

I glanced quickly around the room, taking in faces. Three people stood out because they didn't look like they'd been out in the noonday sun. They were sat together in a neat row and there was a couple of feet of space all around them, like they were protected by a force field. Everyone else's personal space had been compromised. Not theirs.

The old guy in the middle of that select group wasn't a cop, and he was obviously the most important person in the room because he had the best seat. He was wearing a black silk shirt that didn't have sweat stains under the arms, and he looked like the sort of person who'd drive a vintage Caddy.

I was betting that the middle-aged guy on the right was the Porsche owner. He was a younger version of the Caddy guy, heavier but obviously related. Same eyes, same nose. Father and son, without a doubt. The biggest difference was the attitude they projected. The old guy's authority was absolute. Nobody would think to question it, not for a second.

The younger guy wanted to believe he carried the same sway, but he didn't, and probably never would. This was someone who'd struggled his whole life to break out from the shadow of his father. Even when the old guy was dead and gone he'd still be fighting that one.

Sheriff Fortier made up the threesome. He looked stressed and exhausted and smaller than ever, crushed by the gravity of what was happening here. He was staring into space, locked inside his own bubble of silence. Right now, he was probably wondering why on earth he'd bothered running for sheriff in the last election.

"The guy up front with the Stetson on his lap," I whispered. "Jasper Morgan?"

"Got it in one. And that's Clayton beside him."

Jasper was staring at the screen, shoulders square, back ramrod straight. Nobody was speaking to him, and he wasn't speaking to anyone else either. Like Fortier, he just sat there in silence and stared at the screen. Jasper's tan was so deep his skin was like leather, lines carved into his face. He looked every one of his seventy-two years but there was something about him that gave the impression he could keep going for at least another thirty, which wasn't good news for Clayton.

"Okay, time to mingle, Taylor. Get some nice snapshots for me."

Taylor disappeared into the crowd, cellphone in hand, and I made my way over to the table where the laptop had been set up. The picture on the computer screen was better than the blurry representation being beamed from the projector, but the news was just as bad. 00:03:13. A limbless stick figure swung from the gallows beside the numbers.

"This is a nightmare," muttered a quiet voice behind me.

I turned and saw Shepherd standing there. If Barbara Galloway had aged six years, Shepherd had aged twenty. The stress was getting to him. It was in his muscles, it was in his eyes. Most of all, it was in every tight syllable he uttered. The neat uniform he'd been wearing when we first met was crumpled. There was a small greasy fingerprint smudge on the lens of his spectacles.

"I saw Barbara Galloway on my way in." My voice was as quiet as Shepherd's because the environment demanded it.

Shepherd snorted and shook his head. He straightened his glasses, his finger pressing down on the smudge. "That lawyer of hers is a piece of work. She didn't say a word to us. Not a single thing. She just sat there and exercised her right to be silent. Any questions we asked, the lawyer shut us down."

We were both staring at the laptop, counting off the seconds.

00:02:34.

"She's not involved in her husband's death. You know that, don't you?"

"Yeah, I know. But you know how these things work. Galloway was having an affair, so there's your potential motive straightaway. We needed to check it out."

"What was the reaction when news got out that you were bringing her in?"

"What do you mean?"

"Was anyone particularly vocal about it? You know, making a fuss, telling you that it wasn't a good idea."

"Only Mayor Morgan. He'd been best buddies with Galloway's father since way back when. His son had grown up with Sam. He didn't see that anything could be gained by bringing Barbara in, and I can understand his point. But like I said, there's that potential motive. We need to do this one by the book."

"Was there anyone who thought this was a good idea?"

Shepherd shook his head and I got that hitch in my stomach that always came when things didn't play out how I wanted. I'd been careful to make sure my last question sounded as casual as the previous one, and, judging by the fact that Shepherd didn't seem curious about why I'd asked, I'd pulled it off.

Not that it made any difference. It was another long shot, and it hadn't paid off. I'd given the unsub an opportunity to steer the investigation down a dead end, but he hadn't taken the bait. And when they don't bite it's back to the drawing board. I glanced up, searching for Taylor. He was on the other side of the room, one eye on the screen like he was watching the countdown with everyone else, one eye on his cell like he was checking for texts.

"How did your lead pan out?" asked Shepherd.

"It didn't."

"So are you going to tell me where you've been all evening, or is that a state secret?"

"I wanted to check out the old refinery."

"Find anything?"

I shook my head. "Nothing."

"Can't say I'm surprised. We ripped that place apart and didn't find a damn thing."

"I need to see that crime scene."

"I'm hearing you, Winter, and we're doing everything we can. We *will* find it, that you can guarantee. How's it working out with Taylor?"

"Good. He's a bright guy. He's got a great future ahead of him."

Shepherd stroked his moustache, then said, "So, what exactly have you two been up to?"

"We've been chasing our tails and getting nowhere."

"I know the feeling."

I rubbed my face, sighed. "It feels like I've spent most of today banging my head against a brick wall, and now we're about a minute away from someone else dying. I've had better days, that's for sure."

"You and me both."

We fell into silence, both of us fixated by the slow drag of those numbers on the laptop screen.

00:01:04.

The four turned into a three, then a two, then a one. Sixty seconds from now the countdown would hit zero and we'd be back in that concrete place again. There'd be a new victim hog-tied and struggling on the dirt-streaked floor. The homeless guy with the mismatched shoes was going to walk in with his jerry can and empty it out over the victim. Then he'd light a match. One small flame that would soon become an inferno.

And there was absolutely nothing we could do to stop that happening.

I'd never been so certain of anything in my life. It was the only scenario that made sense. The reason the big movie studios put out trailers for their films was so they could attract the biggest audience possible, and the reason they went to so much trouble came down to money. The financial layout for a major motion picture was enormous. Nine-figure budgets weren't unusual, and every single cent had to be earned back before the studios turned a profit, so you could be damn sure that they were going to use every trick in the book to get those theatre seats filled.

But this unsub wasn't motivated by money. His motivation was much darker. It wasn't enough for someone to die in the most hideous way imaginable, he needed the validation of an audience. And what better audience than one made up of the people who were hunting him? He wanted to rub our noses in it. He wanted us to acknowledge his genius. He was saying that he was cleverer than us.

He was wrong.

The first film clip had been the equivalent of a movie trailer, a way to grab our attention. And it had worked.

Every cop in Eagle Creek was here. Every cop except one.

They all screwed up eventually. All of them.

00:00:18.

The room had been quiet when I'd first got there. It was even quieter now. Everybody sat completely still, staring at the screen, waiting for something to happen. Willing something to happen. The only other time I'd ever known a roomful of cops to be this quiet was when news came through that the body of a kid had been found. That produced a different kind of silence, though. A stunned silence. This silence was anticipatory.

00:00:03.

I watched the three turn into a two. An eternity passed and the two turned into a one. Everyone was holding their breath and leaning forward.

The one turned into a zero.

CHAPTER THIRTY-THREE

Nothing happened.

I stared at the line of zeros on the laptop. Turned my head to look at the distorted numbers on the big screen at the front of the room. Back to the laptop again. Wherever I looked, I was seeing the exact same thing. Two zeros followed by a colon, then another two zeros followed by another colon, and then the last two zeros.

00:00:00.

Time passed and still nothing happened.

Three seconds, four seconds, five.

"Now *that* I wasn't expecting," I murmured.

"What the hell is this?" Shepherd muttered beside me.

And then all hell broke loose. Suddenly everyone was up and moving and talking at the same time. It was like a dam had burst. The tension just let go in one huge rush. After so much silence and stillness, all that sudden movement and noise was an assault on the senses.

"I don't get it," said Shepherd. "Why go to all this trouble? It makes no sense."

"The link to the website and the film clip, that was sent by email, right? Maybe the unsub's going to contact us the same way again."

"Good idea." Shepherd sat down in front of the laptop and went to work.

It wasn't a good idea, though. Not even close. Even as I'd made the suggestion, I knew it wasn't going to help. The unsub's first film had been all about getting an audience. He'd got his audience but, for whatever reason, he'd chickened out of his grand reveal.

If he had followed through, someone else would be going up in flames right now, and there'd be a crowd of cops staring slack-jawed at the screen. He would have posted the film on the countdown website. He would have talked to his guy in Mumbai or the Philippines or wherever and arranged it so that when the countdown hit zero the clock would have disappeared, and been replaced with the new film.

But for some reason that hadn't happened. Why? What had gone wrong? Because something must have gone very wrong, something significant enough for the unsub to pull the plug on a plan that he'd been putting together for a very long time.

"Nothing on email," Shepherd called out. "But maybe that's because he hasn't got around to sending it yet."

I shook my head. "Keep checking, but I'm telling you now that you're not going to get anything. That countdown was an absolute. The clock hits zero and something has to happen. That's how it works. It's like when an illusionist makes the girl disappear. The impact comes from the girl reappearing on the balcony at the exact moment the box is opened. Making her disappear is easy, getting the reveal right, now that's where the real skill comes in. There's no point in the girl reappearing ten minutes later, or an hour later when everybody's gone home."

"So what now?"

"I don't know about you, but I'm going to go and get some sleep. I'm exhausted. A few hours' shut-eye and I can come at this thing fresh tomorrow."

Shepherd looked disappointed, like this wasn't the answer he was expecting.

"There is a bright side," I added. "At least nobody else died."

"I guess that's something."

"It's definitely something. One less victim is always going to be a reason to celebrate."

I said goodnight and left the conference room then retraced my way back to the main entrance, the noise of fifty people speculating and theorising and getting nowhere fast dulling into the background. Outside, I lit a cigarette. The flicker of the Zippo flame made me think of Sam Galloway, and again I wondered what the hell was going on. What had happened to make the unsub abort?

I clicked the lighter closed and stared up at the night sky as though the answers might be hidden up there, somewhere in the infinity of space. That cool breeze was still blowing up from the south, a blessing after the fierce heat of the day. The moon was big and bright enough to dim the stars. Even so, there were plenty of stars up there. This was a country sky rather than a city sky. A big sky. The light pollution levels out here weren't high enough to steal the stars.

The station-house doors banged open. I turned expecting to see Taylor, but instead of a six-and-a-half-foot tall black giant, I was looking at a five-foot-ten white septuagenarian wearing a black silk shirt and a black Stetson. Jasper Morgan came over, arm outstretched. We shook.

"You're Jefferson Winter?"

"And I'm guessing you're the Glenmorangie guy."

He smiled at that. "It's a good whisky."

"It's a very good whisky."

"You're being looked after?"

"I'm getting the five-star treatment all the way."

"Good to hear. Anything you want, you just ask, okay?"

"Okay."

Jasper nodded to my cigarette. "Don't suppose you've got a spare?"

I handed him the packet and the Zippo and he lit one.

"I quit years ago, but you know." He shrugged and nodded towards the station house.

"Yeah, I know."

Jasper took a long pull and smiled to himself. He had the look of someone getting reacquainted with an old friend.

"What can I do for you, Mr Morgan?"

Jasper took another drag and glanced up at the endless sea of stars. At that moment he looked small and insignificant, just a sprinkling of cosmic dust that had coalesced into the shape of a man for the blink of an eye. The universe didn't care if he had a billion in the bank, and it sure as hell didn't care if he was the big man in Eagle Creek.

"I grew up with Joe Galloway, Sam's daddy. He was only forty-three when he passed, and that day was one of the saddest of my life. He'd been going for all those years with a dicky heart and didn't know. One day it just blew up on him. Forty-three is too young. Way too young. Anyhow, me and Joe had an arrangement. Anything happened to one of us then we'd look out for the other's family."

He took another long drag on the cigarette, blew out a cloud of smoke and looked heavenwards again, an old man lost in long-ago memories. I had no idea how it had gone down. Late-night drinks, perhaps, two good friends sharing a rare whisky. The talk turns philosophical, philosophical turns to hypothetical. A deal is struck, then sealed with the crystal kiss of glass against glass.

Or maybe they'd been out for the day, watching their boys play together, and got to wondering about all those apocalyptic what-ifs.

However it had gone down wasn't important. What was important was that the deal had been struck, and honoured. Arrangements like this were nothing new. I don't have kids, but if I did I'd want to know they'd be okay if anything happened to me. What parent wouldn't?

"Sam was like a son to me. I can't believe he's gone." Jasper dropped his half-smoked cigarette onto the ground and crushed it out. "Whatever you normally charge, double it. Hell, charge whatever you want, I don't give a shit. Just find the bastard who did this, okay?"

Jasper turned and strode off. His shoulders were as square as they'd been when I first saw him, his back just as straight, but he wasn't fooling anyone. I'd seen my share of hurt and grief, and Jasper Morgan was hurting bad.

He climbed into the Caddy and turned the key. The big engine growled to life and the dazzle of bright headlights flooded the lot. The car pulled gracefully out of its slot. It paused at the entrance, then hung a right, the red tail-lights glowing then disappearing. The doors of the station house opened again and this time it was Taylor. He was grinning like his lottery numbers had come up.

"Dan Choat," he said, breathless and still grinning.

"Our Ted Bundy clone?"

Taylor nodded.

"What about him?"

The grin widened. "He's not here."

CHAPTER THIRTY-FOUR

We'd phoned ahead and Hannah was waiting on the guesthouse steps when we got there five minutes later. Morrow Street was a graveyard. The bar owners had called it quits and shut up early for the night. The neon rocket on the front of Apollo's was switched off and the shadows behind the diner's windows got greyer and darker the deeper you stared.

Hannah climbed into the back of the car. She leant over into the front, her head bobbing between mine and Taylor's. She was holding a banana and motioning for me to take it, like I was a monkey in a zoo. "Got to watch your blood sugar, right?" she said in response to my questioning look.

I took the banana, peeled it, took a bite, and did my best to ignore the smug expression on her face.

"A thank you would be nice, Winter. Didn't anyone ever teach you manners? Someone gives you a gift, you smile sweetly and say thank you. That's the way it works."

"If it had been a candy bar you would have got a thank you. But it's not a candy bar."

"And there you go again with your awesome powers of observation." She laughed and got settled into her seat. "This is so cool. It's like being in the movies."

"Yeah," Taylor said from the passenger seat. "We've finally caught ourselves a lucky break. It's about time."

"There's no such thing as luck."

"So what would you call it?"

"Painstaking, methodical detective work."

"So, Dan Choat's our bad guy," said Hannah. "I always thought there was something suspicious about him."

"No you didn't. And I quote: 'I went to school with Dan Choat, but I can't see him being involved in something like this.' This was the guy who always called his teachers ma'am or sir, remember?"

Hannah ran a hand through her hair and stretched out on the back seat, getting herself comfortable. "Whatever. The point is that we know who did this, and we're going to go and bust his ass."

I finished the banana and dropped the skin into the door pocket. Then I put the car into gear and pulled away from the sidewalk, Taylor calling out directions. One a.m. and the streets we drove through were as quiet as Morrow Street. There was the occasional bedroom light, the occasional kaleidoscope flicker of a TV lighting up the drapes, but for the most part the houses were in darkness. We passed a park that had a baseball diamond marked out on it, a school that was as empty and lifeless as the old oil refinery.

Kennon Street was just inside the town limits, up on the north-east side of Eagle Creek. Dan Choat lived halfway along in a detached two-storey clapboard house. There was a small neatly kept yard out front, a single garage off to the side, flowers in the regimented beds, and a white picket fence. I slowed when we reached the house, but didn't stop. Cruised past. The lights were all off. Either Choat was asleep, or he wasn't here.

Fifty yards on I hung a right, then parked up and killed the engine. We got out and walked back to Choat's house, headed quickly up onto the porch. Kennon Street was dead. Not so much as a single light on in any of the neighbouring houses. I got Hannah and Taylor to bury themselves as deep into the shadows as they could get, then went to work with my lock picks.

Thirty seconds later we were inside, pulling the door closed behind us. Taylor had his Glock out. The gun looked tiny in his massive hand, like a toy. A big old Smith & Wesson would have looked like a toy. He went to say something and I pushed my index finger hard against his lips to shut him up.

For a second we just stood listening to the tales the house was telling us. A clock ticked loudly in one of the rooms. A refrigerator rattled to life in the kitchen. There was nobody on the lower floor. The place smelled clean to the point of overkill. Forest glades and ocean breezes and orange groves.

I put out my hand and gave Taylor a hard stare. It took a second for him to work out what I was asking. He shook his head. I made *gimme, gimme* gestures with my fingers and he shook his head again. I mouthed the magic word: Shepherd. He glared for a second, then handed me the gun butt first.

I pointed to the stairs and we went up together, the Glock leading the way, Taylor and Hannah at the rear. Three-quarters of the way up I hit a creaky floorboard. The sound of it giving way was as loud as an explosion.

We all froze. Nobody spoke. Nobody breathed. A wall of silence closed around us. At any second that wall was going to come crashing down and Dan Choat would come busting through the rubble, his service revolver in his hand, and demand to know what the hell we were doing in his house.

That wall of silence closed in tighter, and was suddenly shattered by a solitary tick from the clock. Time started up again and we all breathed a little easier. I nodded to the offending stair, made sure that Hannah and Taylor knew exactly which one to avoid. There were three rooms on the second floor: two bedrooms and a bathroom, their doors wide open. It took less than five seconds to confirm what I already suspected.

Dan Choat wasn't here.

CHAPTER THIRTY-FIVE

We went into the main bedroom and switched on the light. The bed was neatly made up and everything was properly squared away. There were no clothes lying around, no clutter.

And there was definitely no sign of Dan Choat.

I gave Taylor the Glock and he clipped it into his holster. "Okay, Hannah, time to do your thing. I want to know everything there is to know about this guy."

Taylor gave me a puzzled look.

"Extreme people watching," I said and his expression became even more puzzled. "You'll like this," I added. "She's got a gift."

I sat down on the bed to watch. Hannah started with the bureau. She opened the top drawer and carefully went through the contents. She lifted out a T-shirt, sniffed it, then put it back in the drawer exactly how she'd found it. Taylor was hovering in the doorway, uncertain what to do. His eyes kept flicking between Hannah and myself. He was looking like a kid trapped in a giant's body again. I patted the space on the empty side of the bed.

"Get your ass over here, Julian. Take a weight off."

"Julian? Really?"

"Still haven't worked it out then, Winter?" Hannah called over.

"Still haven't worked it out *yet*."

"Two hundred bucks says you don't."

"It'll be a pleasure to take your money."

I patted the bed again and Taylor came over reluctantly and sat down. "Tell me everything you know about Dan Choat."

"To be honest, I don't really know that much about him."

"Would you describe him as one of those people who keep themselves to themselves?"

Taylor nodded.

"Quiet and polite?"

Another nod.

"Always greets you with a cheery hello."

Another nod.

"The sort of fellow who's happy to help you out if you get stuck in a jam?"

Another nod.

"I'm liking the sound of this guy more and more."

"No you're not."

"He's the closest thing we've got to a suspect."

"Which is a totally different thing altogether," Taylor replied. "You don't think he's our guy, do you?"

"Let's see what Hannah has to say, shall we?"

I stretched out, hands behind my head, back against the headboard, toes pointing towards the door. Hannah had reached the closet and was riffling through Choat's uniforms. He had five in total, which, again, smacked of overkill. The most you'd ever need was three. One for wearing, one at the dry cleaners, and a spare. Each uniform was in its own black suit bag.

There was a rack with ten pairs of identical black shoes on it, four pairs on the top row, six on the bottom, all of them polished to a high sheen. Overkill again. There weren't enough shoes to put him in the same league as Imelda Marcos, but there were enough to make me wonder.

"Finished here," said Hannah.

"Go and check the bathroom."

Hannah left the bedroom and returned a minute later. I sat up on the bed and crossed my legs.

"Okay, tell me all about Dan Choat."

"Well, for starters, he's got serious mom issues. I mean, look at those drapes and that bedspread. Who the hell in their right mind would have something like that in their bedroom?"

She was right. The drapes were horrific. Fussy and floral, lots of pinks, purples and lilacs. The bedspread looked like a really bad impressionist painting.

"Also," she went on, "his underwear has been ironed. His *underwear*. T-shirts and jeans, too. Everything's so neat it's creepy."

"Maybe his mother is still alive," I suggested. "Maybe she does his laundry for him."

"No, his mother's dead. This used to be her room. That's the only explanation for those drapes. Even someone as terminally single as Choat wouldn't choose them."

"Terminally single?"

Hannah smiled coyly. "Don't act all innocent, Winter. That's why you had me check out the bathroom. If Choat had ever had a girlfriend then there would have been some evidence, either here or in the bathroom. And there was nothing. Not a single damn thing. Ergo, terminally single."

I turned to Taylor, "Admit it, she's good. So what have we got? We've got a white male who's terminally single with serious mom issues. He's a quiet, unassuming guy. Always polite, always cheerful. Someone like this goes postal and everyone just shakes their head in disbelief and tells the nice news reporters that they would never have expected him to do something like this, no sir, not in a million years. I've got to tell you, he sounds good to me. I'm sold. Let's go wake up a judge and get ourselves an arrest warrant." I smiled. "Okay, we're going to play a little game. Each of us is going to come up with a reason why this isn't our unsub. Taylor, you go first."

"Why me?"

"Because right now Hannah is kicking your ass into the middle of next week. If you're not careful she's going to end up in charge of the Criminal Investigation Division."

Taylor chewed his lip and stared at the horrific floral drapes. When they got too much, he stared down at his hands. Back to the curtains. Back to his hands. He stopped chewing and grinned to himself.

"Choat's the same age as Hannah, which means he's too young."

"Nice save. Your turn, Hannah."

She glanced around the room, ran a hand across her hair. She was thinking hard because she didn't want to get beaten by Taylor. And that was good. A little friendly rivalry never hurt.

"He's a neat freak," she said at last. "That bathroom was spotless. So clean it had to have been done recently, definitely within the last twenty-four hours. Then there's this bedroom. The bed's made up and everything's all tidied away. If you're in the middle of a killing spree, the last thing you're going to be worried about is whether or not you've done your chores."

I made a sour face and shook my head. "I'm afraid Taylor wins this round. Your reasoning is sound up to a point. The problem is that you're assuming the logic that dictates the actions of a serial killer can be measured against the logic a normal well-adjusted member of society would employ. In other words, you're comparing apples and oranges. I don't have a problem with the idea that a serial killer could go out and murder someone then come home and give their house a thorough clean. If that's part of his ritual, then that's what he's going to do. It might not make sense to you or me, but so long as it makes sense to the killer that's all that matters."

"You could have just said I was wrong."

"But that's the thing. You're this close to being right." I held up my hand, thumb and forefinger a quarter of an inch apart. "Burning someone alive is a messy way to kill someone. A neat freak like Choat is going to choose a nice tidy way to dispatch his victims. My money would be on asphyxiation. A pillow over the face or a plastic bag over the head. That way there's none of that yucky blood stuff to deal with."

"Your turn then, Winter," Taylor said. "Why are you so sure Choat isn't the unsub?"

"Because if something looks too good to be true, then it is too good to be true. Choat's been handed to us all neatly wrapped up with a pretty bow on top. There's no way he's our guy."

Taylor sighed and stood up and started pacing. He was biting his lip and shaking his head and thinking hard. He stopped and looked at me. "I really thought we were onto something with Choat. Now we're back at square one."

"You're kidding, right? This isn't a snakehead. Far from it. We've just gone shooting up a ladder. This is the best thing that's happened all day. The closest thing we've had to a lead."

Both Taylor and Hannah were staring like I was speaking in tongues.

"Big picture rather than little picture." Without another word, I headed for the stairs.

CHAPTER THIRTY-SIX

The guesthouse was quiet when we got back, so quiet I was beginning to wonder if I was the only guest. Except for Hannah, I hadn't seen any other signs of life. The overhead lights cast a dim glow on the red and white chessboard floor. Long-dead movie stars stared down at us from the walls.

Taylor and Hannah had started arguing and bickering back at Dan Choat's place. They'd kept this up all the way to Morrow Street and were still going at it now. They'd tried to drag me in a couple of times, but gave up when they realised I was ignoring them. There was something almost comical about the way they stood there toe-to-toe. Taylor towered over Hannah by at least a foot, but she was standing her ground, hands on hips and not giving an inch.

"The unsub's rattled."

That halted them in their tracks. They stopped looking at each other and turned to face me.

"The big question is why," I went on. "Why did the unsub feel it was necessary to present us with a viable suspect? And why did he chicken out with his grand reveal? He had everything and everyone in place, and then, at the last second, nothing. It was a total anti-climax."

Taylor and Hannah were still staring, neither saying a word in case they got the wrong answer.

"What's the matter? You both had plenty to say in the car, and now nothing?"

Silence.

"Okay, let's look at this from a different perspective. Imagine you're the unsub. You've spent years fantasising and planning. You've gone over everything again and again and again, rehearsing what you're going to do, checking for loose ends. Eventually you reach a point where you've done all the planning you can stand and it's time to take that fantasy and turn it into reality. But you don't make your move just yet. Once you step over the line, there's no going back. You're pretty sure how things are going to play out, but pretty sure isn't the same as absolutely certain. So you wait a little longer, driving yourself crazy with the anticipation. And then, when you really can't stand it any longer, that's when you make your move."

I went over to the counter and dinged the brass bell. B-flat, but ever so slightly sharp.

"Okay, folks, fingers on buzzers. Last night our unsub finally put his plan into action. This morning he would have woken up feeling like he was the king of the world. Yet tonight he's improvising like crazy and making mistakes left, right and centre."

"Making mistakes?" Hannah asked.

"Chickening out of his grand reveal was a mistake because it shows uncertainty, and uncertainty implies weakness. Dan Choat was a mistake, too, because if he thinks I'm dumb enough to buy that then it shows he's seriously underestimated me. So here's my question: considering that this guy has gone through all the variables a million times, what's changed? What's the rogue variable that's come into play here?"

Hannah and Taylor looked at each other, then at me.

"Very good," I said. "I'm the rogue variable. Bringing me into the investigation has changed the whole dynamic. It's made the unsub go back and reassess his entire game plan. And in the process of re-evaluating, he realised that his grand reveal wasn't going to work. Somehow he's got wind of the fact that we're looking for a cop. He realised that we'd be watching the crowd, and we'd notice he wasn't there, and that we'd have ourselves a prime suspect."

Taylor nodded. "So he sets up Choat to take the fall, joins the crowd and aborts his grand reveal. Yeah, that works for me."

"Considering the pressure he's under, it's not a bad move. Maybe he's certain we're looking for a cop. Then again, maybe he just suspects it. He's been keeping an eye on what we're up to and reached that conclusion. If that's the case, he's going to want confirmation that we're looking for a cop, and if we go after Choat that gives him his confirmation."

"So don't go after Choat," said Hannah. "That way we keep him guessing and he keeps on making mistakes. It's a no-brainer."

I dinged the bell again.

"Since Hannah's brought up the subject, let's move on to Round Two. What's happened to Choat?"

"He's being held captive," Hannah said.

"And as a little girl, I'm betting you dreamt of having your very own pet unicorn."

"What's that supposed to mean?"

Taylor fielded this one. "What Winter means is that Choat's dead."

He glanced over at me for confirmation and I answered with a nod.

"There's no reason to keep him alive, and a whole load of reasons to kill him. If he's dead, there's no chance of him escaping and identifying the unsub. Secondly, a dead body is lower maintenance than a live one. You don't need a deep, dark dungeon to hide your victim in, you don't need to feed them. You get the idea."

I dinged the bell a third time because I liked the sound, and the effect it had. Taylor and Hannah's attention snapped back to me. "So what do we do? Hannah's suggestion is one possibility. We do nothing. The problem with that strategy is that it's going to be a major stressor for the unsub. He's going to be sat there trying to double guess us, and treble guess us, and quadruple guess us, and that's going to drive him nuts. The more stress we pile on, the more unpredictable his actions become. Which is good because, like Hannah said, he'll make mistakes. But it's bad because it could push him to kill sooner than he would have done otherwise. Do either of you want that on your conscience?"

Hannah and Taylor shook their heads.

"The alternative is that we play along with the unsub. We go charging in, telling anyone who'll listen that Choat's the bad guy. Sheriff Fortier and Shepherd will rally the troops and before we know it every spare man will be out hunting Choat. While they're doing that we hang around on the sidelines and keep our eyes peeled for anyone who's looking particularly smug."

"So what do we do?" asked Hannah, echoing my earlier question.

"We sleep on it. We'll meet at Apollo's for breakfast at eight and make a decision then. Letting the unsub sweat it out for a few hours shouldn't cause a problem, and we're all exhausted. We need to sleep."

When I said we, I meant me, but Taylor and Hannah both looked as tired as I felt. Back in my room, I poured a glass of Glenmorangie, put on some Mozart and opened the window. A gentle breeze blew through, fluttering the drapes. I lit a cigarette then perched on the windowsill. With the room door closed, the outside world ceased to exist. The music and the whisky helped complete the illusion. And it was an illusion. At any moment my cell could ring, bursting my bubble. Midnight calls went with the territory. The people I hunted respected chronological constraints as much as they respected geographical borders.

The second movement of Mozart's one and only Clarinet Concerto was playing gently in the background. This was my all-time favourite piece of music. The way that clarinet sings, it's the loneliest sound in the world.

Show me someone who isn't moved and I'll show you someone who doesn't have a soul.

For a while I smoked and sipped my whisky and listened to the most beautiful piece of music ever written and did my best to shake off the day. My brain never switches off. The best I can hope for is that I can get it idling in a low gear. There was always something to think about, some puzzle to unravel.

This piece of music was a prime example. Western music uses a twelve-note octave, and somehow Mozart managed to blend those twelve notes into something so heart-rendingly beautiful that I don't understand how it can actually exist. I've picked this piece of music apart, examined every note, every phrase, and I still don't understand why or how it works. The only conclusion I can draw is that there are some things that exist beyond our ability to comprehend.

However, this doesn't sit comfortably since it leaves me trapped in a logic loop. Every question has an answer and every puzzle can be solved. Maybe one day I'll have a moment of enlightenment, that eureka moment where the pieces finally fall into place.

Then again, maybe you should be careful what you wish for. Once you know how the illusion is performed, the magic is lost for ever, and all you're left with are a bunch of gaudily painted plywood props and an assistant in a cheap costume who's wearing too much make-up.

The music drifted into silence and I switched off the laptop. I kicked off my boots and removed my jeans, chased a sleeping tablet down with some whisky then lay on the bed. For a while I stared at the shadows dancing on the ceiling, eyes heavy and my thoughts finally slowing to a more manageable level. Somewhere along the line, I drifted into an uneasy sleep.

CHAPTER THIRTY-SEVEN

I woke just after five, my brain turning at full speed. The thought that had got hold of me was that I was somehow responsible for Dan Choat's murder. Simply put, if I hadn't got involved in the investigation then Choat would still be alive now. Terminally single and trapped by his mom issues in his neat-freak life maybe, but still alive.

This idea was flawed from the foundation upwards. We cannot be held responsible for the actions of others. If a wife goes crazy and grabs a shotgun and shoots her abusive drunk husband dead, who do you blame? The husband for being a drunk? The shotgun manufacturer? Jack Daniel? You could try, but the truth of the matter was that she made the decision to pick up the shotgun, and she made the decision to pull the trigger. There were a dozen other ways she could have chosen to handle the situation, but that's the one she opted for.

I understood the logic and, when the sun came up, I'd buy into it. The problem was that at five in the morning what you believe and what you know are poles apart.

For a while I lay in bed, wishing for sleep. My watch ticked around to five-thirty and I gave up trying. As much as I wanted more sleep, it wasn't going to happen.

There was a small kettle on the dresser so I was able to make a coffee. I switched on my laptop and set the computer to play tracks at random, quietly, just in case there were any other guests. "Every Breath You Take" by The Police came on, a firm favourite of newlyweds and stalkers. All alone in a darkened room in the raw hours before dawn, the song seemed to take on a sinister edge that I'd always known was there but had never fully appreciated.

The kettle boiled and I fixed a coffee, adding three sugars to disguise the taste. I settled down on the bed and checked my emails. "Every Breath You Take" was replaced by "Riders on the Storm", an atmospheric old Doors song that was just as sinister. The mood I was in, it seemed prescient.

The email from Chief Olina Kalani in Honolulu included dozens of attachments. I'd asked for everything, and everything's what I'd got. Photographs, interview transcripts, autopsy reports, the works.

The media had christened this unsub the Clown Killer. I hated nicknames because their only purpose was to create mystique, and mystique was the foundation of legend. When that happened the atrocities committed by these assholes became glamorised. Before you knew it, you had magazine articles and books and TV specials, even movies. These people were monsters. Lock them in a dungeon and throw away the key. Don't give them bright lights and infamy. That's just wrong.

This unsub only targeted prostitutes. He attempted to rape them, then he stabbed them and painted their faces. An untidy, ragged red smile, a big red nose, thick black make-up around the eyes. The bodies were dumped in alleyways or behind dumpsters. No attempt was made to conceal them. This guy wanted his victims found.

The first thing that struck me was how needy this unsub was. Here was someone who craved the spotlight. His murders were performances. He wanted people to sit up and take notice. He wanted people to go, "Wow, look what the Clown Killer's gone and done this time!"

The second thing that struck me was how low his self-esteem was.

Prostitutes are low-risk victims. The nature of their profession means they'll go off with a complete stranger with little regard for their own safety, which makes them easy targets. That said, within this group there are sub-groups, each with a different level of risk attached. The riskiest prostitutes to target are your high-end escorts. If you're charging thousands of dollars an hour, then you can guarantee that your pimp or madam will make sure their investment is protected.

This unsub worked the other end of the scale. His victims charged nickels and dimes to blow you in your car or an alleyway. They were junkies. They were older. They'd gone past their shelf life. Consequently, they were easy targets.

His attempt at raping his victims was another indicator of low self-esteem. Reading through the autopsy reports, it was obvious that this part of the attack was over mercifully quickly. The downside was that this angered and frustrated him, and he then took his anger out on his victims. Each one had been stabbed at least twenty times. Deep, forceful, thrusts to compensate for what he wanted to do, but hadn't been able to.

In the background, Hendrix was singing "The Wind Cries Mary". I lit a cigarette and closed my eyes and thought things through. I could see a man in a hurry, fuelled by fury and self-loathing. And I could see a small boy whose life had been a hellish nightmare of beatings and abuse, whose only escape was into the perfect world promised on TV.

Hendrix faded out and Led Zeppelin came thundering in like the Four Horsemen. Even with the volume on low those four guys still managed to sound like the end of the world. I hit reply and started typing.

This unsub was a white male aged twenty to twenty-five, a failed actor or musician. He probably spent his life telling anyone who listened that he was on the verge of greatness. That the record companies were fighting to sign him up and turn him into the next big thing or the TV networks were lining up to get him to star in their next big series or his Hollywood agent had got him a part in next summer's big adrenaline-inducing blockbuster. The truth was a string of failed auditions and forgettable talent-show appearances.

And he was going to be easy to find because he would have been a face in the crowd at every crime scene. This unsub wouldn't have been able to stay away.

He'd want to witness the reaction to his work at first hand.

He wanted the applause. He craved the validation it brought.

Chief Kalani needed to get his people to check out news footage from the crime scenes. That's how they were going to catch this guy. Check the crowds for a bad actor who was doing his best to make out like this wasn't the best show ever.

CHAPTER THIRTY-EIGHT

I parted the drapes and looked out the window. It had just gone six-thirty and the sun would be up soon. The sky was beginning to lighten in anticipation of the main event, black turning to grey with a hint of purple. There wasn't a cloud in the sky, and the light breeze blowing in through the open window promised another hot one.

Apollo's was still closed and Morrow Street was as deserted as it had been last night. I shut the window, then hit the shower. I ran it as hot as I could stand to get rid of yesterday's grime before turning it to freezing to blast away the fatigue. Another couple of hours' sleep would have been good. Another six would have been divine.

By the time I'd got dried and dressed, Apollo's was open, the flickering neon rocket lit up blue and red and blasting off to wherever. I was the first customer of the day and I took the window seat I'd had yesterday. Lori looked exactly the same as she had the day before. Same make-up, same smile, same beehive hair-do. Same retro uniform as well, but this one was clean on and still smelled of fresh laundry.

"Early riser," she said.

"Borderline insomniac."

She smiled. "You and my Frank would get on just fine. That's him banging around in the kitchen. He's not a morning person, let me tell you. Like a bear with a sore head. Me, I sleep like the dead. My head touches the pillow and boom, that's me out until the alarm goes. Coffee?"

"That would be great, thanks."

There was a sudden loud crash from the kitchen followed by a whole lot of swearing. Lori shouted out, "It's right there at your feet, honey," and Frank swore some more, making her smile. She shook her head and started pouring my coffee.

"How long ago did your sister die?" I asked.

Lori paused mid-pour, then carried on. When she'd finished, she straightened up. The smile was gone. That was all the confirmation I needed. Up until this point I'd been ninety-nine per cent certain that Hannah had been lying when she told me her mother had Parkinson's. Now I was a hundred per cent certain.

"Cissy passed away almost a year ago." She shook her head. "I can't believe it's a year already. I still miss her every single day. She was my baby sister, and she'll always be my baby sister, and I loved her. Thing is, I'm going to get older and she's not, and that's just plain wrong. I was the older sister. It was my job to protect her. Have you lost anyone close to you?"

"I've lost people, yes."

"So you know what I'm talking about?"

I nodded because I did, but not from first-hand experience. Deal with death day in, day out and you get to see more than your share of grief. The truth was that I hadn't shed a single tear for either of my parents.

"What happened to Cissy?"

"Breast cancer. She'd done chemo, thought she had it licked, but cancer's a sneaky disease. It came back twice as bad and spread like wildfire. There was nothing Cissy could do. Nothing any of us could do except watch her wasting away."

Lori wiped her eyes, smearing her mascara.

"How did Hannah deal with it?"

"She was an angel. She nursed her mom all the way through to the end. And she managed to keep the guesthouse going."

"I take it Hannah's father isn't in the picture."

Lori shook her head. "He ran out when Hannah was still in diapers. Worthless no-good son of a bitch."

"The guesthouse doesn't seem that busy right now."

"Peaks and troughs. It's always been like that. A couple of weeks ago it was packed. No way you would have got a room. This week it's empty. It's not necessarily a bad thing, though. It means Hannah gets a break."

"She's on her own over there, isn't she?"

Lori nodded. "Me and Frank try to help out as best we can but we've got enough on our hands with the diner, so, yeah, she's pretty much running that place single-handedly. I've told her a hundred times to hire someone but she won't hear of it. It's almost like she's punishing herself, like she's blaming herself for her mother's death."

Lori sighed and pulled herself together in a way that made it obvious this conversation was over. She put down the coffee pot and took out her pad and pencil. "So what can I get you to eat?"

"Ham and eggs would be good." I smiled and clapped my hands together, making Lori jump. "So are you ready for the morning rush?"

"You're kidding, right? You saw what it was like yesterday. I don't know why we bothered opening. Not that I'm surprised. Something like this happens and folks are going to be scared. It's only natural. I mean, I'm scared. The idea that there's a killer out there somewhere frightens me half to death."

"People still need to eat, Lori. And anyway, Sam Galloway's already yesterday's news. A good night's sleep generally helps to restore common sense and get everything back into perspective."

"And I'm guessing you're a coffee-pot's-always-full kind of guy."

"Always."

Lori laughed and hustled back to the counter. She shouted my order through to Frank, and he shouted back that it would be his pleasure in that flat, world-weary voice. This was obviously a conversation they'd had a hundred thousand times over the years, a well-rehearsed double act. I stirred two sugars into my mug and took a sip. Then I took out my cellphone and made two calls. Taylor first because, theoretically, he had further to come, then Hannah since she only had to come from across the street. The conversation was the same both times: breakfast was being brought forward.

CHAPTER THIRTY-NINE

I'd just started eating when Hannah arrived. She smiled when she saw me, eyes sparkling, the stress, worry and years melting away. Today she was wearing a Death Parade T-shirt, another band I'd never heard of. I was wearing a Lennon T-shirt. She thumped down into the seat opposite.

The diner was already getting busier. There was a group of three guys in tan police department uniforms at a table opposite the till, and a single guy in a red plaid shirt had his head buried in the pages of the morning paper at a table in the far corner.

"Hi, Hannah," Lori called from the counter. "The usual?"

"Thanks, Aunt Lori."

Lori shouted the order through to Frank, and Frank shouted back that it would be his pleasure in that flat comic voice. Then she came over with the coffee pot, topped up my mug and poured a fresh mug for Hannah. They exchanged some small talk and Lori headed back to the counter.

"Tell me Taylor's first name and I won't take your money."

"And why would I do that?"

"Because I am going to work it out, and when I do you're going to be two hundred bucks out of pocket."

She grinned and shook her head. "No, Winter, you're not going to work it out, and I'm going to be two hundred bucks richer."

"I'll give you a hundred now if you tell me."

Hannah made the sign of the loser on her forehead, thumb and forefinger making an L.

"Okay," I said, "If you're so sure, let's make it four hundred."

"You're on."

There was no hesitation, which was a slight worry. Hannah could probably take a two-hundred-dollar hit, but four hundred would sting. Whatever Taylor's name was, she was convinced I wouldn't find out.

There was also a more intriguing implication to consider. Taylor wasn't advertising his name. If he had been I would have found out by now. He was acting like it was a state secret and he was the only person in the world who knew the truth, apart from his parents, of course. But Hannah was acting like she knew what it was. The way she'd jumped at my suggestion to double the wager, she couldn't not know.

The bell above the door *ting-a-linged* and Taylor came in. He said "Hi" and Hannah scooted along the seat to make space for him. Lori shouted over a "Hi" and made her way over with a Pepsi. According to my watch, it had been exactly five minutes since Hannah got here. I glanced out the window. A black sedan with sheriff's department markings had appeared outside the guesthouse. My money was on this being the same car we'd used yesterday.

"Anything you kids want to share?" I asked.

"We don't know what you're talking about," said Taylor.

"*We*," I said, with plenty of emphasis.

Hannah nudged Taylor in the ribs. "Idiot," she hissed.

Taylor made a what-did-I-do face. He looked so pathetic I almost felt sorry for him.

"Don't be too hard on him," I said to Hannah. "I already had it worked out before you guys got here."

"How?"

"The name thing was the big one. You know Taylor's first name, don't you?"

She nodded.

"Then there was the way you two were bickering last night. My first thought was that you were going at it like an old married couple. My second thought was that if a bird's making quacking noises, chances are it's a duck. Then there's Taylor's clothes. Yesterday I sent him away to change out of his uniform and he came back dressed like one of the Men In Black. He might as well not have bothered changing. Today he's wearing his off-duty clothes. Blue jeans, a grey T-shirt, sneakers. Those are the clothes he keeps at your place. You don't want him dressed like a cop when he's off duty, right?"

Hannah nodded again.

"The cop car was a nice touch. Last night when I headed up to my room, Taylor drove the car around the corner so I wouldn't see it from my window. Before he got here, he snuck out the back of the guesthouse and went and got the car and parked it across the street." I took a sip of coffee. "So when do I get my wedding invitation?"

"We don't advertise our relationship," Hannah said. "This isn't the fifties, but it is northern Louisiana. There are some people around these parts who wouldn't approve."

"You don't strike me as someone who'd care about something like that."

"And you don't strike me as someone who's ever tried to run a business in a small Southern town. Sometimes you need to play the game. I don't like it, but I'm not about to cut my nose off to spite my face."

"So how serious are you guys?"

"Serious enough for Taylor to get down on one knee."

"The old romantic. I take it you said yes."

"Of course I said yes. I'd be a fool not to. He's the best man I know."

"Guys, I'm sat right here," said Taylor. His cheeks were redder than I'd ever seen them. It was kind of endearing.

Lori arrived with two plates. Six blueberry pancakes for Hannah. Taylor had ten plain ones, and steak, and eggs. You couldn't see his plate for food. "Enjoy," she said, then headed off around the room, topping up coffee mugs. For a while we ate in silence. I finished first, drank some coffee.

"My guess is you guys are on a three-year plan."

"What are you talking about?"

"I know your mom's dead, Hannah."

For a second I thought she was going to deny this. She didn't. Instead, she stared at me with her big fawn eyes, then gave me an almost imperceptible nod to go on.

"The other thing I know is that you wouldn't be hanging around here working your ass off in the guesthouse unless you had a damn good reason. Reason number one is you need money. You're going to get a chunk of cash when you sell the guesthouse, but not enough to build a new life." I nodded to Taylor. "He's reason number two. For whatever reason he wants to be a cop, but he needs more experience, so you need to hang around here a while longer."

"You've got it all worked out, don't you?"

"It's what I do. So where are you going?"

"San Francisco," Taylor said.

"Nice city, if you like fog. And they get their fair share of murders too, so that'll keep you busy." I turned back to Hannah. "What about you? What are you going to do?"

"I'm going to start my own internet business. I'm going to buy stuff in cheap and sell it on for a profit. Anything and everything. Clothes, shoes, electrical gear, you name it. The one thing I'm not going to do is clean another toilet as long as I live."

"The American Dream made real for the twenty-first century."

"You'd better believe it."

"So what's the magic number? How much is enough to put your escape plan into action?"

"Half a million."

Hannah said this without any hesitation. She'd crunched the numbers so many times she could probably recite them by rote.

"How much would you get for the guesthouse?"

"The business is valued at a third of a million."

"And how much have you got saved?"

Hannah glanced at Taylor, then looked back at me. "Where are you going with this?"

"That's fine. You don't need to answer." I thought things through for a second then said, "Okay, you would have inherited some cash when your mom died, and you've been planning your escape for a while, so let's round it off at, say, seventy thousand. Does that sound about right?"

Hannah said nothing but her expression indicated I was in the right ballpark.

"If it's okay with you guys, I'd like to make a few alterations to our wager. *If* I don't work out Taylor's first name then I'll pay out a hundred grand. That should be enough to get you up to that magic half a million." Hannah went to say something and I put my hand up to stop her. "Also, I'll put in a good word for Taylor with the San Francisco PD. I've helped them out in the past, so they owe me."

"You can afford to lose a hundred grand?"

"First off, I'm not going to lose. Secondly, I wouldn't be out of pocket. Jasper Morgan would, but I wouldn't. As far as I'm concerned this would qualify as a justifiable business expense. And thirdly, if for some reason Jasper didn't pay up, and if by some miracle I lost the bet, I can afford to take the hit."

"That's a neat trick for someone working in law enforcement. Taylor can barely afford to make the repayments on his car."

"I like to dabble in the stock market."

"And, if you can afford to give away a hundred grand, you must be doing okay."

I shrugged and did my best not to look smug. "Yeah, I do okay. Anyway, that's beside the point. I have no intention of losing."

Taylor shook his head. "Maybe you can afford to lose a hundred grand, Winter, but we sure as hell can't."

"And the beauty of this deal is that you won't have to. If I do work out your name, you guys pay me a buck. You can afford that, can't you? A single dollar bill? One tiny little portrait of George Washington?"

Both Taylor and Hannah were staring at me like they were trying to work out what the catch was.

"Let me get this straight," Hannah finally said. "If we win, you pay us a hundred thousand. If we lose, we pay you a dollar."

I nodded. "And I'll help Taylor get a job with the San Francisco PD. Don't forget that."

Hannah and Taylor turned to each other and started discussing my proposal. They were communicating in their own secret language, lots of hand gestures and head gestures and whispering. I understood the odd word, but they might as well have been speaking Swahili. Taylor nodded. Hannah nodded. They turned to face me.

"There's no catch?" she asked.

"No catch," I assured her.

"Okay, you've got a deal."

I shook Hannah's hand first. It was small and her skin was rough from all those hours spent working in the guesthouse. Taylor's skin was smoother, his handshake much gentler.

"Right," I said. "Back to business. We're going to keep quiet about Dan Choat, make the unsub sweat."

"And what if that pushes him to kill again?" asked Taylor.

"Then that one's on my conscience since this is my call. You two are off the hook. Sometimes you've got to take risks. This is one of those times."

Reluctant nods from both Hannah and Taylor.

"Hannah, you get the day off from cleaning toilets and making beds today. You'll work with me and Taylor. Three heads are better than one."

"What about the guesthouse?"

"I'm the only guest, and I'll live if my bed doesn't get made and my suitcase doesn't get searched."

I smiled at Hannah and she fired a bright sunny smile right back at me.

"We need to find the place where Sam Galloway was murdered. That's our number-one priority. My money's still on the oil refinery."

"But we checked it out last night," said Taylor. "Remember we found nothing? Shepherd had some people checking it out yesterday as well, and they found nothing either."

"That place is huge. Judging by the maps, and what I saw when we flew in, you're looking at an area that's roughly twenty square miles. Five miles from east to west following the interstate, and four miles from north to south. We're talking haystacks and needles here. We could easily have missed something."

"Or maybe it's not the right place."

"It's the right place. The padlock was oiled recently. An old abandoned place like that, who the hell's going to oil the padlock? If you're the security firm employed to patrol it and the padlock gets all rusted up, you cut it off and go buy a new one. But that's not what happened here. Someone went to the trouble of getting a can of oil and spraying the lock. And that someone was our unsub. It had to be."

Taylor was shaking his head slowly from side to side. "Let me get this straight. You're basing this hunch on a padlock."

"It's not a hunch, it's a fact. And the padlock is only part of it. You saw how easy it was to pull the gate open. The wheels had been oiled, too. Believe me, nobody's going to do that, Taylor. Not in a million years. Our unsub wanted to get in quick, and he wanted to do that without making a sound. He didn't want the gates squeaking, so he oiled the padlock and he oiled the wheels."

"Why bother? That place is right out in the middle of nowhere. Nobody's going to hear him."

"And that's the third reason. This unsub redefines overkill. This is someone who kidnapped then coerced a street bum to burn up Sam Galloway so he wouldn't end up stinking of gasoline and barbecues. So, how long ago did the refinery shut down?"

"It's got to be twenty years. It was after I was born, but not by much."

"Good. That means there'll be someone still living around here who used to work there. Can either of you two think of anyone?"

Slow head shakes and frowns from the other side of the table.

"Aunt Lori," Hannah called out. "You got a minute?"

"Sure, honey."

Lori came over, a gentle cloud of perfume and coffee following in her wake. She topped up our mugs without asking.

"What can I do for you, sweetheart?"

"Do you know anyone who used to work at the old refinery?"

Lori put a hand up to her mouth and sighed through her fingers. She shook her head slowly and sucked in her cheeks. "Sorry, I can't help you on that one. That place closed down years ago. Anyone I can think of is dead now."

"How about Frank?" I suggested.

"He might know someone. I'll go get him."

"Don't bother. I need to stretch my legs."

I stood and headed to the counter, walked around it and peered through the hatch. The small kitchen on the other side was absolutely spotless. White porcelain and stainless steel shone under the bright lights. It reminded me of an autopsy room. The biggest difference was that it smelled better. A country song was playing quietly in the background on a small radio. Frank was over at the sink, scrubbing a pan clean. He was bald and red-faced, a large man who looked like he enjoyed his own cooking too much.

"Frank," I called over. "You got a second?"

"Sure."

He dried his hands and came across. I introduced myself and we shook through the hatch.

"What can I do for you?"

"Do you know anyone who used to work out at the old refinery?"

He shook his head slowly. "Sorry."

"You sure about that? Anyone at all?"

Another slow head shake. "No one comes to mind."

"Not to worry. And thanks for your time."

I'd almost reached the table when Frank shouted over from the hatch. "Hey, Lori, is Elroy Masters still alive?"

"Far as I know," she replied, nodding. "Yeah, he worked at the plant for a while. But he's got to be in his eighties by now."

CHAPTER FORTY

Elroy Masters lived out on Horton Street, down at the south end of Eagle Creek. He answered the door wearing a faded red-striped dressing gown and slippers. He looked suspiciously at the three of us standing on his stoop, eyes moving slowly from left to right, like he was behind one-way glass working his way along a line-up.

"The Jehovah's are really scraping the bottom of the barrel these days," he finally said.

"We're not Jehovah's Witnesses, Mr Masters," replied Hannah.

Elroy looked at her like he hadn't seen a woman for years, as though this was the first time he'd got up close to someone with multiple piercings and a nose stud and a Death Parade T-shirt. "Well, whatever damn religion you're selling, I ain't interested, you hear. I've lasted this long without having Jesus in my heart, I reckon I can make it through the few years I've got left without his interference."

I laughed. "Talking that way in this part of the world, it's a wonder you haven't been struck down by lightning."

Elroy narrowed his eyes at me. "If you're not selling religion, what the hell are you selling?"

Taylor held up his badge. "Sheriff's department."

Elroy put his hands up. "Okay, I admit it. I did it. I shot Kennedy. Surprised it took you so long to catch up with me."

I laughed again. I really liked this guy. He looked well into his eighties, but he was far from over the hill. He was sharp, and there was a youthful twinkle in those blue eyes. His skin was even more sun-blasted than Jasper Morgan's, and as thick as elephant hide. He gave the impression that the universe had thrown everything it could at him, yet he'd still managed to get the upper hand.

"We need your help with a case we're working on. Do you mind if we come in?"

"Sure. Knock yourselves out. It's not like my calendar's packed."

Elroy did an about-turn and we followed him down the hall. He had a spring in his step and moved like he was a couple of decades younger than he actually was. We filed into a small living room that hadn't been decorated since the eighties. The wallpaper was grimy and fading and peeling at the edges. The house smelled of microwave meals and was in need of a good airing.

Elroy lowered himself into the room's only armchair and waved towards a sofa that only had enough space for two. Hannah and Taylor sat down. I dragged the coffee table over to where Elroy was and set up my laptop. An old woman appeared in the doorway. She might have been older than Elroy, then again she might have been younger. It was impossible to tell. She moved stiffly, like someone with arthritis.

"Why didn't you tell me we had guests, Elroy?" She cinched her housecoat in a little tighter and smoothed out her grey morning hair. "You'll have to excuse my husband, he has no manners. My name's Rhonda, by the way. So what can I get you folks to drink?"

"Coffee with two sugars, thanks," I replied.

"Same for me, please," said Hannah.

Taylor shook his head and said he was good and Rhonda headed off to the kitchen.

"So how can I help?" Elroy asked.

"You used to work at the old refinery."

"For going on ten years until they shut the place down."

"What did you do there?"

"I was on the security detail."

"So you knew the layout of the place pretty well."

"Every square inch like the back of my hand."

I wanted to get excited, but couldn't. Twenty years was a long time, and memory was fluid rather than absolute, even more so the older you got. We fill the cracks in our remembrances with false memories all the time. That carpet in your childhood home you swore was blue was in fact brown. The steak you had at the meal to celebrate your twenty-first birthday was actually lamb.

I'm not immune to this phenomenon. The memories from my whole childhood had been warped by the actions of my father. I'm sure it wasn't as bad as I remember, but there were some things that were impossible to see past.

The laptop finished booting up and I loaded the film clip of Sam Galloway. I hit play, paused at a point where the background could be most clearly seen, then turned the computer around so Elroy could view the screen.

"Take a look. Could this be the old refinery?"

Elroy pulled a pair of reading glasses from the pocket of his dressing gown and studied the screen for a long time. When he'd finished looking he settled back into his armchair, the old springs creaking and squeaking to accommodate him. He pointed a bony finger at the screen.

"That's Sam Galloway."

I nodded.

"I heard he got murdered."

Another nod.

"So are you going to tell me what happened, or are you going to make me guess?"

"He got doused in gasoline and set alight."

Elroy sucked air through his teeth and let it out again. A shake of the head. "That's a hell of a way to go."

"You sound like you know what you're talking about."

"'Nam," he replied, like that explained everything. "You see napalm used, you're never going to forget that. And the smell. Sweet Jesus, you're not going to forget that, either."

"You're too old to have got caught up in the draft."

"Joined the Marines as soon as they let me, and stayed as long as they'd have me. Got a bronze star and a set of sergeant stripes for my trouble."

He rolled up a sleeve of his dressing gown to reveal a bony old-man arm. Up on the left biceps was an eagle with *Semper Fi* on the scroll underneath. The colours had faded and spread with time, but there was no mistaking the Far Eastern influence in the artwork. Rhonda came in with our coffees, handed one to me and one to Hannah. She'd dragged a brush through her hair and thrown on a faded grey dress that might once have been white.

"Did he have any family?" Elroy asked.

"A wife and three kids."

"That's too bad. So what did he do?"

"Nothing, so far as we can tell."

Elroy shook his head. "You're not going to do something like that to another person without a damn good reason."

"Nothing so far as we can tell *yet*. I'm with you on this one. You don't do something like this without a good reason."

He nodded to the screen. "It could be the refinery, but I can't say for sure. Sorry, I know that's not what you want to hear."

My heart sank. This was pretty much what I'd expected. Another long shot that hadn't played out.

"I take it you've got access to the refinery," Elroy added. "If we took a drive out there that might jog my memory."

The way he said this made me wonder what he'd actually seen on the laptop screen. The question sounded innocent but it wasn't. He had an agenda. What that was, I wasn't sure. Maybe something, maybe nothing, but it was worth exploring.

"Yeah, we've got access."

CHAPTER FORTY-ONE

Fifteen minutes later we were in the car, heading south. Elroy was riding up front, while Taylor was squeezed in behind me. I was pushed up hard against the wheel, my seat as far forward as I could manage, but there still wasn't enough room for him. Hannah was next to Taylor, her hand flat on the seat, their fingertips discreetly touching. She was smiling out the window, like a prisoner who'd just been paroled.

Elroy talked all the way to the old refinery, one story after the other. Some were funny, some were crude, some were sad. He was smiling, too, clearly having a ball, and I was starting to suspect that all Elroy wanted was to get out of the house. To get out from under Rhonda's feet. A ride in a cop car and a trip down Memory Lane would break the monotony of a life where every day probably played out exactly the same. TV dinners and arguments over which channel to watch, and regular checks of the obituaries to see if you'd lost any more friends.

The refinery slowly came into view, a tangle of tall forgotten metalwork that appeared out of the morning haze. The metal had dulled over the years but still had enough of a shine to make it glow in the sunlight. There was something other-worldly about it.

We got closer and the blurred shapes started to coalesce into something more solid and recognisable. The large storage tanks, the distillation units, maintenance sheds, admin blocks. The facility looked completely random, as if a giant had dropped all the parts from a great height and left them to lie where they fell. But looks could be deceptive. There was nothing random about this place. Once, this had been a complex living, breathing entity, each part reliant on all the others. Elroy fell silent and stared through the wind-shield, momentarily lost in his thoughts. A couple of seconds passed before he snapped back into the present.

"A hell of a thing, isn't it? I forgot how big it was."

"A hell of a thing," I agreed.

"I'm surprised they haven't bulldozed it into the ground by now."

"There's no point. The land isn't worth anything. It's useless as agricultural land, and it's on the wrong side of the I-20 for any developers to be interested. Then there are all the environmental issues to consider. A thousand years from now that refinery will still be here. Some of it will have probably crumbled into the dirt, but parts of it will still be standing, enough so you could work out what it once was. If mankind has managed to survive that long, you'll have historians and archaeologists crawling all over it and classifying it as a place of national interest. They'll be writing papers on the stupidity of a society that was so addicted to oil that it almost made itself extinct."

Elroy gave me the look, then laughed. "Whatever you say. The one thing I do know is that I ain't giving my car up for nobody. Anyways, I won't be around in a thousand years, so why should I give a damn?"

I pulled up outside the main gates and got out of the car. A little after ten and the heat was already getting up. A light breeze was blowing down from the north and the air smelled of burnt sand and exhaust fumes from the nearby I-20. I pushed my sunglasses as far back as they would go and just stood there for a moment looking towards the east. The sun was a dull yellow ball battling through the haze, but it was getting brighter.

The padlock opened as easily as it had the night before, the well-oiled parts clicking smoothly away from my pick. There were new wheel tracks cutting through the patch of dirt that I'd brushed flat, indicating that someone had been here since we left. The unsub? If it had been him, the big question was, where had he gone once he was on the other side of the gate? Alternatively, maybe he'd still been here when we left. If that was the case, then the question was, where had he been?

I rattled the chain off and ran the gates open on their well-oiled wheels, then climbed back into the car and drove through. We passed the gatehouse with its raised barrier, and pulled up at the T-junction.

"Left or right?" I asked Elroy.

"Left."

Even though it had been twenty years since Elroy was last here, he directed us as though it had only been a day or two. The first place he led us to was a maintenance shed that was built in the shadow of the storage tanks at the eastern end of the facility. I parked beside the rail tracks and the four of us got out.

Elroy stared up at the massive tanks and shook his head. "It just seems like yesterday. Time's a bitch, you know that? She sneaks up on you when you're not looking and takes a great big chunk out of your ass."

We walked over to the shed and I knelt down and checked the dirt by the door. The wind had blown it into a series of gentle ripples, but that was the only thing that had disturbed it recently. The lock was stiff and difficult to pick, and the door opened on creaky hinges. Clearly, it had been a while since it was last used.

Two decades, say.

The inside of the shed was grey and gloomy. A thick layer of dust covered every surface and the sunlight struggled to penetrate the grimy windows. The floor was peppered with mouse and rat droppings. I had one flashlight, Taylor had the other. Large, heavy-duty police-issue flashlights. Club someone over the head with one of these and you'd knock them out cold. Hit them hard enough and you'd be looking at murder one.

We played the beams across the interior. Large tins of paint were stacked up on the shelves against one wall, ladders, scaffolding and dust sheets arranged neatly alongside. One of the walls was fitted with shelves that contained boxes of tools. They'd been carefully arranged according to type and size. Hammers, monkey wrenches, screwdrivers, spanners.

I knelt down and brushed the dust away to reveal a patch of dirt-streaked concrete. It was impossible to say if this had been poured by the same contractors who'd laid the floor in the film clip, but I wasn't ruling it out.

"Where to next?" I asked Elroy.

The next place was another maintenance shed, this one at the west end of the refinery. It was the same story as before. Nobody had been there in years. We left the shed and I lit a cigarette, offered the pack around. Elroy was tempted. He looked longingly at the pack then shook his head. In the end, Hannah was the only taker. Taylor gave her a dirty look. Their body language indicated that this was an on-going battle, one that Taylor was going to lose.

I took a drag and looked to the east again. There was only a thin veil of haze left to burn away, and the sky was a glorious cloudless blue that stretched as far as the eye could see. For a while, I just stood and smoked and thought things through, and tried to get inside the mind of someone who got their kicks from watching a fellow human being going up in flames.

"He won't want to be out on the perimeter. It's too exposed. This place is like a maze, so he's going to want to be as near the middle as possible because it'll be harder to find him there."

Elroy was nodding like this made perfect sense. "Yeah, I can think of a couple of places."

The first two places he took us to were a complete bust.

The third place was a different matter altogether.

CHAPTER FORTY-TWO

The first thing I noticed was the car. It was a small white Nissan. Cheap to run and cheap to insure. The inside was spotless, and an air freshener dangled from the rear-view mirror.

The second thing I noticed were the tyre tracks. They were identical to the marks left by our car, which in itself proved nothing. The police had been all over this place yesterday. So had we. Lots of vehicles had this make of tyre.

But these tracks led all the way up to a rusting steel door, and there was more than one set, and as far as I could tell someone had been back and forth at least four times, parking in more or less the same place each time.

It was this last detail that got the hairs tingling on the back of my neck. We were down at the bottom of a dead end that had more than enough space for four separate cars to park in four separate places. I could accept that two cars might have parked in the same space, but not four.

The only reason for parking in the same place was because you'd been here before, and you'd worked out it was the best place for getting to the door as quickly as possible. This would be high on your list of wants if you were accompanied by a street bum who wasn't exactly thrilled at the prospect of being sedated, bundled into a trunk and brought here.

The three-storey building on our right had once housed offices. To our left was a tall brick wall that could have been anything. The wall continued around to form the bottom of the dead end. The only features were a line of windows at third-floor level and that rusting door.

The dust in front of the door had been kicked up to the point where it was impossible to see any footprints. Maybe it was just the one set of feet that had kicked it up. Then again, it might have been three sets. No one else had noticed the tyre tracks, or, if they had, they hadn't realised the significance. They were crowded around the Nissan like it was the Holy Grail.

The lock on the steel door had been oiled recently and was easy to pick. The door opened without a single creak. The smell that came out was a choking mix of spoiled meat that had been shot through with memories of barbecues past. It was a smell that stopped you dead in your tracks. A real attention grabber.

"You might want to get over here," I called out.

The others peeled away from the Nissan and hurried over. Hannah arrived first, closely followed by Taylor.

"Jesus," she whispered, her nose wrinkling. "That's not good."

"Wait here," Taylor said to Hannah and Elroy. "If this is a crime scene, I don't want you contaminating it."

Hannah looked like she was going to argue, but didn't. She took a step to the side where the smell wasn't so bad, and I went inside with Taylor. The rusty door opened onto a narrow corridor. The dust in the middle of the floor was all kicked up as well, but there were partial footprints at the edges. Frayed cobwebs danced in our flashlight beams up near the roof.

Ten feet on, there was a sudden ninety-degree turn to the right and everything dimmed to twilight. There was some reflected illumination from the walls, but not enough. We were pretty much on our own with the flashlights, and the smell was getting worse.

We reached an open doorway and stopped. Flies were buzzing in the dark room beyond. Lots of flies. I went in first and fired the flashlight into all four corners. The room was large and airless, and that smell was so bad you could taste it. This place had been used for vehicle maintenance. There was an inspection pit and a rusting hydraulic auto lift. The double doors were big enough for a decent-sized truck.

And there were two corpses in the middle of the floor.

The flies had congregated on the bodies, large, bloated, well-fed bluebottles and blowflies. They were buzzing frantically around the corpses, crawling all over them, searching for those soft, moist places.

"We need to leave," Taylor told me. "This is a job for forensics."

"You can go, but I'm staying. No way am I leaving until I've had a good look around. It's not going to happen."

"You'll contaminate the crime scene."

"I promise I'll be careful."

Taylor gave an exasperated sigh. "How certain are you that you can get me that job in San Francisco?"

"Getting the job is no problem, Wyatt, what you want to be worried about is winning that bet."

"Keep guessing, Winter."

Taylor turned and left. His footsteps faded down the corridor, the light from his flashlight bouncing up and down and gradually getting dimmer. The way the beam and the flies were interacting created the illusion that the bodies were still alive.

I waited until all I could hear was the flies, then walked over to the nearer body. My footsteps were deafening in the sudden lonely quiet. They ricocheted off the concrete walls, each one as loud as a gunshot. Every breath seemed to fill my head with noise.

But all those sounds were eclipsed by the hungry buzzing of the flies.

I moved the flashlight in a wide circle around the body, looking for blood. If you know how to read blood, it can tell all sorts of stories. This blood, and the way the corpse lay, shouted out that this had been an execution. I hunkered down and ran the beam from the top of the corpse's head down to the tips of its mismatched shoes.

White male, middle-aged, five-nine. His head was tilted to the left. Hollowed-out cheeks and hollow eye sockets and a week's worth of stubble. It was a lean, hungry face. A street face. His skin was lined like old marble, and the heat had increased the speed of decomposition, bloating his body.

There was an entry wound the size of a nickel in the middle of his forehead. The wound was cauterised from the muzzle flash, and the flecks of gunpowder residue that tattooed the surrounding skin indicated that the gun had been fired at point-blank range.

A large part of the back of the skull was missing, which meant the unsub had used a large-calibre bullet, something with enough of a punch to go into the skull and come out the other side. It was another example of overkill. This unsub wanted to be absolutely certain that this guy was going down and staying down.

CHAPTER FORTY-THREE

Up close, the buzzing of the flies was louder than ever. The smell was worse too. Barbecues, death, gasoline. Blood and brains had seeped from the exit wound and dried on the floor. The victim had been left where he'd fallen because the killer hadn't wanted to get the smell of gasoline on his clothes.

But how had the victim ended up here? What choices had led him to that point where he'd crossed paths with the unsub? And who was he? There was probably someone out there who knew the answer to that, a someone who'd once cared about him. A parent or sibling, maybe even an ex-wife. But for now he was just another dead John Doe. Since there was no one else to step up for him, that role had fallen to me. I wanted to know. I needed to know. Every victim deserves justice, and every victim deserves closure.

The second corpse was lying six feet away. I played the flashlight beam slowly from head to feet. Another white male, this one around five-ten and in his thirties. Fair hair, blue eyes, and a black sheriff's department uniform.

Dan Choat.

There were fewer flies because this corpse was fresher. Insects were pragmatic, the path of least resistance programmed into their DNA. The homeless guy was in a more advanced state of decomposition, which meant he offered an easier, tastier meal.

Choat was lying flat on his back, dead eyes staring up at the concrete roof. A Smith & Wesson was on the ground close to his right hand. I had no doubt that a ballistics examination would confirm this was the same weapon that had been used on John Doe.

There was a small entry wound in his right temple, and a pulpy mess where his left temple had been. That side of Choat's head had been obliterated a millisecond after the shot was fired. Large black flies buzzed around the wound.

A glimpse of white in Choat's shirt pocket caught my eye. I crouched down and pulled out a single sheet of notepaper with the tips of my fingers. It had been folded neatly in two. I unfolded it carefully, again using my fingertips, trying to touch the paper as little as possible. A single word was written across the fold. No capitals, no punctuation. The handwriting was neat, but the shake in the letters indicated a high level of stress.

sorry

I refolded the sheet of notepaper as carefully as I'd unfolded it, then put it back. The narrative being played out here was simple to follow. Choat had kidnapped John Doe then coerced him into setting Sam Galloway alight. He'd then gone back to his neat-freak serial-killer life in his neat-freak serial-killer house. The next day had taken place on autopilot, guilt eating him up. When the guilt got too much he'd come back to the scene of the crime and blown his head off.

It was an interesting narrative, and it would be interesting to see how it would play out.

It would be interesting to see how the unsub wanted it to play out.

The door in the back wall led to another room that was much smaller and had probably been used for storing vehicle parts. There was no ventilation and that smell of rancid barbecue seemed to be everywhere.

I shone the flashlight around and got glimpses of the room. Small flashes, like random snapshots. Even so, I recognised it straightaway from the film clip. That same dirty grey concrete floor. The same cinderblock walls. This was ground zero for that smell. There were no flies because there was nothing for them to feed on. All the good pickings were next door. It was another example of that DNA-inspired pragmatism. My flashlight found the incinerated remains of something that was once human.

"Hi, Sam."

CHAPTER FORTY-FOUR

Sam Galloway's corpse was black and charred and burnt to the bone. Muscles and tendons had shrunk in the flames, pulling him into a pugilistic pose. The phrase was a favourite of forensic anthropologists and arson investigators, and it was easy to see why. Sam's hands had clenched into fists and his arms were bent at the elbow, like he was squaring up for a boxing match.

I moved in closer and walked a tight circle around the body, my flashlight beam angled downwards. The black smears on the concrete had been caused by Sam's death throes. His face had melted into a mask of agony, an illusion caused by the flames. By the point this expression was created, Sam wouldn't have felt a thing. Whatever it was that had made him who he was had long gone.

I walked to the corner of the room and stood with my back to the wall, moving the flashlight beam from left to right then back again in an attempt to see the bigger picture. The problem with a crime scene like this one was that your attention was immediately drawn to the body. We're all fascinated by death. Drive past a car wreck and you're going to slow down to get a better look. If an ambulance screams past, you're going to try and see in the back.

The reason for this fascination is simple. All any of us can be sure of is that one day we will die. The big question is how. Will you end up broken and bleeding out in a car wreck, or will you end up crossing paths with a killer? Maybe you'll pass away peacefully in your sleep. Or perhaps you'll die of a brain aneurysm, a brief, nuclear flash of white light, and then oblivion.

However it happens, the one thing we want to know is whether we'll suffer. Given the choice, we'd all opt to slip quietly away. Nobody in their right mind would choose the hellish nightmare of being burnt alive.

I shone the flashlight around the room, studying every square inch. There were no windows and, aside from Sam's corpse, the room was completely empty. Fire was difficult to control. Once it was loose, it became a living creature. Self-perpetuation was its only reason for being, so it sought out oxygen to keep breathing, and it searched for food to sustain it. And it was utterly relentless in that quest. That was why so many fires got out of control so quickly. What started as a single spark could turn into an inferno in no time.

Concrete required temperatures in the thousands of degrees before it begins to melt, and there was no way it was going to get that hot in here. For the purposes of our unsub, this room was a large fireproof box. The only fuel was Sam, and the accelerant the unsub used. With that heavy door shut, the only oxygen was what was in the room to start with.

This unsub had wanted to contain his fire, and he'd done a good job. His aim was to torch Sam without setting fire to anything else. That's why he'd chosen this place. I wondered how long it had taken him to find it. Had he stumbled on it relatively quickly or had it taken a couple of visits?

Controlling the fire was the unsub's first consideration. Illumination was his second.

There were lights fixed to the concrete ceiling, but they were useless without power, and that would have been switched off when the refinery shut down. I shone the flashlight over the floor until I found what I was looking for.

Between the door and Sam was a patch of floor where the dirt and dust had been disturbed. I went over and took a closer look. There were two sets of markings, both describing the corner points of a triangle, one large, one small. This was where the unsub had positioned his tripods, a small one for the camera, a larger one for the light. The additional markings around the smaller triangle suggested that he had moved the camera around to find the best angle.

I made a frame with my fingers and crouched down until what I saw through my makeshift frame matched what I'd seen on the film clip. Then I stepped over to the bigger triangle and moved my flashlight up and down until the shadows were approximately the same. At a rough estimate, the camera had been on a three-foot-high tripod, and the lights were five feet up.

Next, I went over the likely chronology in my head.

The unsub would have chosen this place well in advance, maybe even months before he murdered Sam. A couple of days before the murder, he would have come back to check that everything was still okay. He would have brought the lights and the camera, and he would have set them up here. He would probably have brought the jerry can, too.

At some point during the next twenty-four hours he would have kidnapped John Doe. Maybe from Shreveport, or maybe from Monroe. Wherever John Doe had been abducted, it would have been somewhere that memories were short and people were happy to turn a blind eye.

The unsub would have brought John Doe here. He probably locked him in this room. I went over to the door and checked it out. The fixings for attaching a padlock looked brand new, which backed up that theory.

John Doe would have been locked up here in the pitch dark without food or water. The unsub was intending to kill him so there would have been no reason to feed him. Without any reference point to work from, John Doe would have had no way of knowing whether it was night or day.

He would also have been gagged and hog-tied like Sam Galloway to restrict movement and noise. This place was as remote as the dark side of the moon, but the unsub was into overkill. He didn't take risks. Even though there was nobody around to hear, he wouldn't have wanted John Doe banging on the door and screaming himself hoarse to be let out.

The other reason was psychology. By restricting John Doe's movement, the unsub was saying *I control you. I own you*. This would make it easier when it came to getting John Doe to light the match.

The next big event was Sam's kidnapping. The unsub had wasted no time there. He'd snatched him from his office after everyone else had gone home for the night and brought him straight here. Then there was a period of around four hours before he set him alight. During that time the unsub would have tortured Sam.

There hadn't been any signs of physical abuse on the film clip, but I could only see Sam's hands and face. There might have been injuries to his body, but it was unlikely. This unsub didn't like to get his hands dirty. John Doe and Dan Choat had been shot at close range. Quick and clean. All the mess would have been projected away from the unsub.

My money was on psychological abuse. Sticks and stones may break your bones but words can never harm you. Whoever coined that phrase hadn't understood the power of words. Words *could* hurt you. Used over a long enough time period, and aimed with enough precision, they could kill. Every other month you heard about some poor high-school kid who'd hanged themselves because the bullying had become unbearable. *That* was the sort of power that words held.

Sam's last few hours would have been a living hell. The unsub would have taunted and teased him, looking for Sam's vulnerable places. And when he found those places, he would have gone to town.

Barbara Galloway claimed that Sam had lived for his family, and the unsub would have been merciless there. He would have outlined in detail what he planned to do to Barbara and the kids. He would have promised pain, suffering and mutilation, even though he had no intention of carrying out those threats. In the days after Sam's murder, the police would be keeping tabs on the family, making it too risky. Also, killing women and children did not figure in this unsub's profile.

But Sam wouldn't have known that. He would have died believing that the unsub was going after his loved ones, and there was nothing he could do about it.

The unsub would also have spent time outlining exactly what he planned to do to Sam, revelling in every graphic detail. He would have explained how fire destroyed the human body a layer at time, eating away at it piece by piece.

He would have described how the heat would dry out the epidermis, the outer layer of skin, before incinerating it, causing first-degree burns. Then he would have told him that the next thing to go would be the dermis. The process was the same. The heat dried it out and the fire incinerated it, causing second-degree burns.

The dermis was where most of the nerve endings were and once this had been destroyed, Sam wouldn't have felt any pain. Third-degree burns extended through the dermis. Fourth-degree burns extended all the way down to muscle and bone.

A hell of a way to go.

No wonder Sam had been fighting and struggling to the end. I sat down on the floor with my back against the wall and stared for a moment at his charred remains. Sam Galloway, John Doe and Dan Choat. Three victims. This unsub had officially attained serial-killer status.

I switched off the flashlight and the darkness became all-consuming. The smell, too. My imagination projected flames onto the blackness, dancing oranges, yellows and reds. I could feel the fire burning me up from the outside in. I could hear the flies buzzing around the corpses in the workshop.

Most of all, I could hear Sam Galloway's haunted screams.

CHAPTER FORTY-FIVE

The police arrived fifteen minutes later. Heavy feet hammered on the dirty concrete floor and echoed off the walls, making it sound like an invading army. Flashlight beams fired in all directions, like searchlights looking for enemy aircraft. Someone whispered a breathy "Jesus Christ" when they caught sight of the bodies.

Shepherd came into the storeroom first, closely followed by Barker, Romero and Taylor. Almost twenty-four hours had passed since I arrived in Eagle Creek and the pecking order remained exactly the same. All four men froze when they caught sight of Sam Galloway's remains. They were wearing all-in-one white crime-scene suits. Latex gloves on their hands, and rubber bands around their bootees to make it easy for forensics to tell the difference between their footprints and anyone else who might have been in here.

For the longest time nobody moved. They just stood and stared, mesmerised. Barker whispered another breathy "Jesus Christ". He had a hand over his mouth and was shaking his head from side to side in disbelief.

I stood up and switched on my flashlight, making everyone jump. Shepherd looked like he was about to have a heart attack, and Barker looked like he was about to lose his breakfast.

"Jesus, Winter." Shepherd stared at me from behind his spectacles, then took a deep breath and pulled himself together. "You shouldn't be here."

"And where should I be?"

"You know what I mean. This is a crime scene, goddamn it. There are protocols that need to be followed. Protocols that have been put in place for a good reason. You can't just go wandering around a crime scene. That's how evidence gets destroyed."

"I'll make sure your guys have my fingerprints and an impression of my boot tread so you can eliminate me from the investigation. See, no damage done."

"Not the point. You should have waited."

"Follow me. There's something you need to see."

We headed next door to the workshop. Shepherd looked pissed and I didn't blame him. Everything he said was true. I should have waited. The thing was that I'd always had a problem with that concept. I hunkered down beside Dan Choat's corpse and pointed to the note in his pocket.

"Take a look at that."

Shepherd hunkered down beside me and used a pair of tweezers to remove the note. He unfolded it as carefully as I had, then read what was written on it. Barker, Romero and Taylor were all crowding around him to get a better look. Taylor glanced over, a dozen questions in his eyes, but he kept his mouth shut. Judging by the widened eyes and the sharp intakes of breath, the other three had all leapt to the same conclusion. No great surprise there. It was a compelling narrative.

"Did you touch this?"

"I was careful to hold it by the edges."

Shepherd glared at me through his heavy-framed glasses. His mouth was a tight thin line and all the muscles in his face were tense. He looked like he wanted to punch me out. "Christ, Winter, what other damage have you done?"

"That's it. Just the letter."

Barker said, "I don't believe this. There's no way Choat killed Galloway. No way in hell."

"Why? Because he was quiet, polite, friendly? What you seem to be forgetting here is that some serial killers are experts at hiding out in plain view. Also, Choat fits the profile. A white male, college-educated."

"You knew all along that the unsub was a cop, didn't you?" There were accusations in Barker's voice, a ton of questions.

"Yes, I did."

"Shit," hissed Shepherd. "Why the hell didn't you say something?" He shook his head, stroked his moustache. "This is so screwed up. A complete and utter mess."

"I'm going to hang around until tomorrow in case you have any questions. Then I'll be moving on to my next case."

I held out my hand and waited for Shepherd to shake it. He just stared at it.

"Look on the bright side. Not only have you got a crime scene, you've got yourself a dead bad guy as well.

If nothing else this is going to save the taxpayer a fortune. No lengthy trial, no jail time. The only losers are the lawyers."

Shepherd was still staring at my hand and making no move to shake it. "Don't leave town," he said finally.

I lowered my hand and walked out the workshop, and had almost made it outside before Taylor caught up.

"You're going to hang out here," I whispered. "Watch everyone. Anyone you see acting suspiciously, I want to know straightaway. Anyone taking an unhealthy interest in what's going on here, I want to know. The unsub's got an idea of how he wants this to play out, and he's going to be pushing to turn that idea into a self-fulfilling prophecy. He's going to screw up. It might be a big mistake, it might be a small one, but he is going to screw up, and we're going to be all over him when he does."

"What are you going to do?"

"I'm going back to Choat's place with Hannah to see if we missed anything."

CHAPTER FORTY-SIX

We detoured via Horton Street to drop off Elroy Masters and arrived in Kennon Street a little after noon. This was a typical suburban street in a moderately prosperous area, an area where most residents were on an upward trajectory rather than a downward one. Detached one- and two-storey clapboard houses sat in their own compact parcels of land. All had porches where you could sit and watch the world go by.

The front yards gave a good indication of who owned the houses. Green grass and tidy colourful flower beds indicated a retiree, someone with both the time and the inclination to fight off the effects of a long hot summer in northern Louisiana. A parched, recently mown lawn indicated someone who worked during the week and struggled to find time at the weekend to keep up with their chores. Toys strewn across the yard obviously indicated kids.

We parked outside Choat's house. The sun was beating down through the windshield and the temperature was pushing ninety degrees. I let the air-conditioner run, enjoying the cool air for as long as possible.

The pretty little picket fence surrounding Choat's house had been newly whitewashed, the grass had recently been mown and was a healthy green, the flowers were blooming. The garage was in good condition and the driveway was free of weeds. This was an old person's yard. It was not the yard of a twenty-something single guy who had a full-time job.

A banana landed in my lap, startling me from my thoughts. I looked up and saw Hannah grinning.

"You haven't eaten since breakfast."

"What is it with you and all these bananas? Have you got shares in a fruit importers or something?"

"They're good for you, and they're packed with potassium."

"Whatever." I went to put the banana down.

"Eat," Hannah ordered. "We're not going inside until you do."

I peeled the banana and started to eat it.

Hannah waited until I'd finished then said, "Let's go."

I killed the engine and we got out. The sun was burning through my T-shirt. It was hot and sticky, and it was only going to get hotter and more humid. We started across the sidewalk to Choat's front gate.

"So, how long have you and Taylor been together?"

"Why do you want to know?"

"Why so defensive?" She shot me a hard stare and I added, "I'm just curious, that's all. I like you, and I like Taylor, and I think you're good together. Also, I'm a sucker for a good love story."

Her expression softened and she looked at me for a second longer. "We've been together since his last year in high school."

"Cradle snatcher."

"Hey, I wasn't the one doing the snatching. Taylor came after me."

"Slowly and carefully and no doubt taking his own sweet time."

Hannah laughed. "Okay, once I realised he was interested I had to steer him in the right direction, but that was kind of fun. The guys I'd been with before were all typically Southern, and they didn't last long. Taylor was different. Despite his size, he's the gentlest gentleman I've ever met. And he is a gentleman, Winter. The last of a dying breed."

We reached the top of the narrow path that led through Dan Choat's neat garden and climbed the stairs to the porch. Hannah shielded me from any curious eyes while I went to work with my lock picks. Twenty seconds later the last pin gave way and I pushed the door open just enough for us to squeeze inside. Hannah pulled the door shut behind us. Slashes of sunlight cut through the window, making sharp angles on the wooden floor.

"How did you meet?"

"We bumped into each other in town one day. He said he liked my hair. I had a go at him for being a sarcastic, chauvinistic brain-dead jock. He almost died on the spot. That's when I realised he was being serious, and that's the point that *I* wanted to die on the spot. I offered to buy him a coffee by way of an apology."

"And he had a Pepsi."

Hannah laughed "Yes, he had a Pepsi. We got talking and before we knew it four hours had disappeared. Turned out he wasn't a brain-dead jock, after all."

"No he's not."

"We spent the whole of that summer together. Saw each other every day. I was working at the guesthouse but my mom was still alive, so I had plenty of free time. I'd just got back from spending a year travelling and I was killing time before going to college."

"The same college as Taylor?"

Hannah nodded. "I managed to swap colleges so we could be together."

"And then your mom got sick."

Another nod, this one accompanied by a sigh. For a moment she looked much older. This was an aging process that resulted from hard experience. Sometimes when I looked in the mirror I'd catch the same look in my own eyes.

"Taylor went to college and I stayed behind to care for Mom. He said he'd be faithful, and I thought *yeah, right*. He promised, but that just wasn't going to happen, was it? I mean, he was at college. There would be plenty of partying and plenty of temptation, particularly for one of their star football players. He even got down on one knee and did the whole proposal thing, and I just told him he was being ridiculous."

"But he was faithful, wasn't he?"

Hannah nodded, then smiled, then laughed. It was a warm sound, the sound of a woman who loved her man and would do anything for him, someone who'd lay down their life if it ever came to that. This wasn't the romanticised love you saw in the movies, or the pragmatic love that had existed between Sam and Barbara Galloway, this was the real thing. For better or worse, for richer or poorer, in sickness and in health.

"Yes he was. He's a good man, Winter. Too good for me."

"And you're selling yourself short. He needs someone like you as much as you need someone like him."

"What about you? Who do you need?"

I laughed. "That is so the wrong question."

"And what's the right question?"

"Who would put up with me?"

I laughed again, but Hannah wasn't laughing. She was staring at me with an expression that was part pity and part sadness. It felt like she was looking right through me and finding me wanting. Before she could say anything else, I said, "I want to know what Dan Choat was hiding."

"How do you know he was hiding anything?"

"Because everybody's hiding something. You, me, everyone."

"And what are you hiding, Winter?"

Hannah was still staring, the silence between us growing more uncomfortable by the second. She wasn't just expecting an answer, she was demanding one. I thought about the swirl of guilt that had run through my gut yesterday when she joked that I was a serial killer. And then I thought about my father lying strapped to a padded prison gurney, aiming his last words at me. *We're the same*.

More staring. More silence.

"Dan Choat was hiding something." I said finally. "We're going to find out what."

CHAPTER FORTY-SEVEN

We started downstairs. Hannah took the kitchen while I searched the living room. I could hear her going through the cupboards in the next room. She was doing her best to keep quiet but that's hard in a kitchen because there's so much metal.

The living room hadn't been changed since Choat's mother died. Floral patterns dominated, a swirling kaleidoscope of pinks, violets, yellows and greens that would give you a headache if you stared too long. The bookcase was filled with hundreds of brightly painted porcelain animals and figurines. There wasn't a single book because there wasn't space for any. I ran a finger along one of the shelves. Not a speck of dust.

There was one book in the room, though. A large well-thumbed bible sat on the coffee table in easy reach of the living room's only armchair. It had a cracked black leather cover that the years had faded to a dark green. The gold leaf had rubbed off long ago, leaving a dark shadow of the letters. The bible could easily be a hundred years old, maybe even two hundred, a family heirloom passed down through the generations.

On one wall was a reproduction of Da Vinci's *Last Supper*. On another was a large crucifix. There was no

TV, but there was a radio. A heavy Bakelite model that dated back to the early sixties. I switched it on and a hollering good-time Baptist preacher demanded to know if I'd let Jesus into my heart yet. I quickly switched it off.

Choat had made one addition to the room since his mother passed away. He'd commissioned an artist to paint his mother's portrait. The end result was almost as horrific as the floral drapes. The picture hung above the sofa and had been positioned directly opposite the armchair.

The portrait was huge, four feet by three feet, way too big for this room. It wasn't even remotely flattering. Choat's mother looked as severe as the most extreme of the Old Testament prophets, ancient and desiccated. You could almost smell the fire and brimstone.

This had to have been commissioned by Choat. It was the only explanation that made sense. Usually when you commissioned a portrait you'd ask for something that made the subject look good. You'd maybe get a decade or two shaved off the age, and you'd lose the wrinkles, lines and imperfections. You would not waste money on something that looked like this.

My guess was that this was the way Choat remembered his mother, the way he thought about her, which would explain plenty. It was not the way she would have wanted to be remembered. This wasn't the way anybody would want to be remembered.

It was easy to imagine Choat in here on his days off, listening to sermons on that old Bakelite radio and reading bible passages. I could see him dusting the ornaments while his mother gazed disapprovingly from the painting.

Was Choat gay? The more I thought about it, the more likely it seemed. If he was, then he'd been buried so deep in the closet he would have suffocated under all the guilt. I'd only been in the house for a short time and already I could feel the walls closing in. What must it have been like to spend your whole life living here?

I sat down in the armchair. There was a notepad beside the bible, the edges absolutely parallel. Next to the pad was a pen. This had been positioned parallel, too. Bible, pad, pen, all laid out in a neat row. The top sheet of the pad had the imprint of a single word in the middle, right where the fold would go. Lower case, no punctuation: *sorry*.

That narrative just kept unfurling, new details being added all the time. This room encouraged guilt. There was guilt written large in the pages of that big old family bible. One look at that portrait would have an innocent man confessing to sins he'd never committed.

It was easy to see how the unsub wanted the narrative to play out.

Choat had spent his last hours in here. He'd done a lot of pacing and a lot of thinking, the guilt eating him up. He might even have done some dusting. And then, when the guilt got too much, he'd sat down and written his suicide note, folded it neatly, tucked it into his shirt pocket and then driven out to the old oil refinery.

There was a grey area, though. A potential plot hole. Why would Choat murder Sam? What was the motive?

Chances were that the unsub had a whole narrative strand unfurling there too. One that we hadn't uncovered yet.

Jealousy was a possibility. I could imagine Choat being stuck here in his locked-down neat-freak life, the pressure building. He would have seen Sam swanning around town in his Ferrari, without a care, playing the big man. Sam would have been the perfect focal point for Choat's rage. The pressure would have carried on building until he finally snapped and killed him.

I could think of a dozen other possible motives off the top of my head, but until we had more information it was just so much speculation. One thing I did know was that this unsub was too careful to leave a plot strand dangling. If anyone bothered to dig deep enough they would find something.

Hannah came in from the kitchen. She saw the portrait and stopped dead.

"That's really, really bad," she said in an awed whisper. "And a little bit scary. I told you he had serious mom issues."

"You told me. So, how did you get on?"

She shook her head. "Nothing, I'm afraid. Not unless it's a crime to eat Cheerios when you reach your twenties. How about you? Did you find anything?"

"Yes and no. I'm building up a clearer picture of Choat, but I still haven't found what I'm looking for." The unsub had something on Choat, something embarrassing enough to use against him. Something that he could use to control him."

Hannah nodded at the painting. "And that's not embarrassing?"

"Not embarrassing enough. I'm talking something so embarrassing that Choat would rather die than have it revealed. Something that would make him drive out to an abandoned oil refinery to meet up with the unsub."

I led the way up to the second floor, Hannah a few steps behind. Halfway up, my cellphone trilled, making us both jump. Even though the house was empty, we'd slid into a burglar's silence. Sneaking around like this, it was inevitable. Hannah swore under her breath when she realised what the sound was, her relief evident in every clipped syllable.

I checked my cell and saw that a text had come in from Taylor. The only reason he would text us was because he'd found something and didn't want to call in case he was overheard.

I held the phone up. "It's a text from Taylor."

She crowded in closer to get a better look and a second later the message flashed up on the screen. It was only two words long, and it was my turn to swear. *nothing yet*. I texted back, telling him not to contact us unless he had something worth sharing, then put my phone away.

I took the main bedroom while Hannah checked out the spare room. It didn't take me long. Hannah had searched it last night. If there had been anything worth finding, she would have found it. When it came to breaking and entering, she was a natural.

Hannah was on her hands and knees looking under the bed when I caught up with her. This room looked like it belonged to a teenager. Except that wasn't quite right. What it actually looked like was an idealised version of a teenage boy's room. And not a modern teenager. This was a kid from the fifties or sixties.

Models of fighter planes hung from the ceiling, handmade and hand-painted, a real labour of love. Choat had spent ages working on them. The bookcase was filled with detective and war stories, the spines cracked from use. The small desk pushed into the corner under the eaves was empty. There was a faded blue quilt on the single bed and matching faded blue drapes on the windows. What I found most interesting was what was missing from the room. There was no TV, no CD player, no music collection, no posters.

Unlike the rest of the house, this room hadn't been cleaned recently and there was dust everywhere. My guess was that Choat had moved into his mother's room when she died, and hadn't been in here since. When he'd shut the door for the final time, he'd been effectively trying to close off this part of his life.

"Come and take a look at this," Hannah said.

She'd got up off the floor and was standing next to the bed. She picked up a framed photograph and a box from the nightstand and handed them to me. The man in the photograph was wearing a full-dress army uniform and standing proudly to attention. There was enough of a resemblance to conclude that this was Choat's father. The box contained a Purple Heart.

"Anything else?" I asked.

"Sorry that's it."

I let out a long sigh.

"Maybe he didn't have any dark secrets, Winter. Maybe it's exactly what it looks like. Maybe he was just a sad, lonely guy with mom issues."

I shook my head. "No, there's got to be something. Okay, here's a scenario for you. The unsub comes here, gets Choat to write the suicide note, knocks him out, dumps him in the trunk of his car, drives him to the refinery, shoots him, arranges everything to make it look like suicide, then drives home. What's wrong with this version of events?"

"The Nissan. Someone had to drive it to the refinery, and it couldn't have been the bad guy because how did he get home? You're not going to commit a murder then hitchhike, are you?"

"Exactly. Choat had to drive the Nissan out there, and the only reason he would have done that is if the unsub had coerced him. And before you say anything, there wasn't a second shooter up there on the grassy knoll. This is a one-man show."

"Well there's nothing here. I would have found it."

"I know you would have. That's what's so weird. I was so sure we were onto something".

"So what now?"

"I don't know," I admitted.

We headed outside and walked back to the car in silence, both of us thinking hard. I was still trying to figure out what would make Choat drive to the refinery. With the right leverage you could encourage anyone to do anything, you just had to work out which buttons to push. And that didn't necessarily mean using violence. In fact, it was often better if you could avoid that.

One prop that Ted Bundy had used was an arm cast. He'd park his van at the sidewalk and pretend that he was having trouble loading something into the back. His victims would take one look at the cast and the pathetic, puppy-dog expression and actually climb into the back of the van to help him.

This unsub hadn't used the threat of violence to get Choat to drive to the refinery. It didn't play out. He might have been able to coerce him to go to his car, but once he got there Choat would have just driven off. The only way that would work was if the unsub had travelled in the car with him, which he couldn't do because how did he get back from the refinery? Choat didn't have any relatives the unsub could threaten. No lovers, either.

But there was something, some sort of leverage. There had to be. The question was what? We reached the car and I opened the door and took one last look at the house. Hannah was beside me, looking at the house, too. A sudden smile lit up her face.

"There's one place we didn't look," she told me.

It took a second before I worked out what she was getting at. We hurried back to the house. At the top of the path we turned right instead of left. It took all of ten seconds to crack the lock on the garage.

CHAPTER FORTY-EIGHT

The garage door opened easily. Not that I'd expected anything less. The world outside the picket fence might be a whirlwind of chaos and heading all to hell, but Dan Choat had made sure that everything on this side was running with the smooth, ordered efficiency of a Swiss watch.

For a moment we stood on the threshold. The sun was directly behind us, burning into our backs and lighting up the interior. The garage looked like it was bathed in an otherworldly glow, making the mundane and the everyday appear somehow special. There was a clear open space directly in front of us, which meant Choat had been a part of that minority group who actually kept their car in a garage. The concrete floor was whitewashed and there were no oil stains, or dirt streaks, or dust. It glowed in the sunlight, throwing off blinding reflections. Choat hadn't just swept the floor, he'd scrubbed it until it shone.

Hannah's expression was part bemusement, part disbelief. "This place is cleaner than my kitchen."

"Which tells us that he's dealing with major guilt issues."

"And you got that from the fact that his garage is tidy? You're good."

"It's not just the garage. His mother was a religious nut who just kept piling the guilt on. It was a dynamic that existed in their relationship right from the start, but she would have gone into overdrive when her husband passed, and it would have kept going until she died. Even then Choat wasn't free. Everywhere he looked in this house there were memories of his mother, and lurking behind the memories was all that guilt."

I snorted a laugh and shook my head, and Hannah said, "What?"

"I was just thinking how crazy this world can be at times. There's a good chance that the unsub did the residents of Eagle Creek a massive favour when he murdered Choat. And the irony is that he doesn't realise."

"How so?"

"Choat would have maybe kept going for another year or so before the guilt and pressure got too much. Best-case scenario, he would have ended up committing suicide. Worst-case, he would have gone postal and marched into the high school and shot up a load of kids." I stopped, thought about this, shook my head. "No, not a school, a church. He'd wait for Sunday to come around and then go into the busiest church in town and shoot as many people as he could before he ran out of ammunition. He would have saved the last bullet for himself, though."

We went inside. It was stiflingly hot and there wasn't any oxygen. Garden tools hung on the left-hand wall. A spade, hoe, fork, all positioned level and parallel. The large workbench that stretched the length of the back wall had been there for years and the wood had darkened with age. Cupboards on the bottom level, a single line of drawers above that, and then the workbench. Tools hung neatly on the wall above, ordered by type and size, screwdrivers at one end, hammers at the other.

Hannah started at the left end of the bench, while I started at the right. The plan was to search the cupboards and drawers and meet in the middle. The first drawer I tried opened smoothly and had a tray that looked like it contained every type of screw known to man, all separated into their own little partitions. The cupboard underneath contained coils of rope of varying thickness and length.

"I think I've found something," Hannah called out from the other end of the bench.

I went over to where she was crouched down beside one of the cupboards.

"Now, why do you think this cupboard would have a lock when none of the others do?" she asked.

I looked along the line of cupboards and saw she was right. A small keyhole had been cut out of the door underneath the knob. I took out my leather wrap and selected the smallest pick. The lock was small and fiddly and it took a couple of attempts to crack it. I opened the door with a flourish.

The cupboard was empty.

"I don't get it," said Hannah. "What's the point in having a locked cupboard that's empty?"

I shrugged. "Maybe he lost the key."

"In that case either there'd be something in here that wasn't worth breaking the door down for, or we'd be looking at a busted lock. It's not just the fact the cupboard's locked, Winter, it's the fact it's empty. You don't lock an empty cupboard. That's the bit that doesn't make sense."

I leant into the cupboard to get a better look. There was something different about this cupboard and it took a second to work out what. It was slightly smaller than the one I'd looked in at the other end of the bench. I rapped a knuckle against the bottom shelf and heard a hollow echo. I pressed the shelf at the back and the front rocked upwards. Underneath was a stash of magazines.

Hannah pulled out the top one and held it up. There were two men dressed in leather on the front cover. One of the men was on all fours, a ball gag wedged tightly into his mouth, a studded dog collar around his neck. She flicked through the magazine, shaking her head. Her expression was difficult to read. There was no disapproval on her face, but there was a kind of sadness and some anger, too. She closed the magazine and shook it at me.

"Nobody should die because of something like this. So what if he was gay and into S&M? It was his life."

"Except that's not going to be the majority view around here. That's why the unsub was able to use it as leverage."

Hannah turned to face me and there was only one emotion left on her face. The anger had eclipsed everything else. "I hate this town. The sooner I get out, the better."

CHAPTER FORTY-NINE

We put the magazine back, repositioned the false floor and locked the cupboard. I took one last look around to make sure everything was exactly as we'd found it, then we went outside, closed the garage and headed back down the path that led through Choat's yard. I stopped at the sidewalk and put my sunglasses on, scanned the yards on the other side of the street.

"So what have we got?" The question was aimed as much at myself as Hannah. "We've got a spooked unsub who's making mistakes. We've got a crime scene. And last night we saved someone else from getting torched. This guy's on the ropes and he doesn't even know it."

"But we still don't know who he is."

"We don't know who he is *yet*," I corrected. "Okay, the next thing we need to do is work out exactly how and where Choat was abducted."

I took out my cell and called Taylor. His phone rang out and went to voicemail. I left a short message asking him to find out if Choat was on duty yesterday and, if he was, to see what shift he was working. I hung up and tapped the phone against my chin.

"What are you thinking?"

"With crimes like these, the abduction phase is always the riskiest because the unsub needs to come out into the open. It doesn't matter how careful you are, as soon as you do that you run the risk of being seen, which in turn increases the chance of being caught. That's the catch 22. You can sit at home and fantasise all you want and stay safe, but if you want to be a real player then you need to get out there and find yourself a nice warm body to have some fun with. But you're not stupid, so you do everything possible to reduce the risks."

"You think Choat was abducted here."

I was still staring at the yards on the opposite side of the street. From left to right they read: young couple with kids, working couple, retirees, working couple. "It makes sense. He lives alone, and you saw how easily we managed to break in."

"But the bad guy would still need to be out in the open, even if only briefly."

A drape opened an inch at the retirees' house, then quickly fell back into place.

"Exactly." I started walking. Hannah had caught up by the time I reached the opposite sidewalk. "How are you at impersonating a police officer?"

"Can't say it's something I've ever done."

"It's easy. You just need to stand there looking as intimidating as possible. And let me do the talking."

This yard was as neat as Choat's, and the picket fence looked like it had been whitewashed in recent memory. We walked up the path and knocked on the door. I used the midnight cop knock. Loud and insistent and impossible to ignore. Someone knocks like this and you come running, your heart thundering in your chest because you know instinctively that there's bad news on the way. This was a knock that interfaced directly into some primal part of our programming.

The hurried footsteps in the hall were followed by the dead-bolt being unlocked, then the Yale. Any protection they offered was illusory since anyone who was halfway competent with a set of picks could be inside within a couple of minutes. And if you didn't have two minutes, you could always go in via a window. Security on windows was generally pretty substandard. The harsh reality was that if someone wanted to break into your house badly enough, they'd find a way.

The door rattled open as far as the intruder chain allowed and a woman's ancient face peered through the gap.

"What do you want?"

"Just a few minutes of your time, ma'am. We're from the sheriff's department."

The woman looked at us like we'd just claimed to be aliens. I didn't blame her. We looked nothing like cops. Neither of us had cop hair, then there were the T-shirts.

"I'll need to see some ID."

I patted my pockets and made a face. "I must have left it back in the car."

Her eyes narrowed to slits. "So I'm supposed to take you at your word?"

I stood aside and nodded to the cop car, gave her a second to take in the markings. I was wishing Taylor was here. At least, I was wishing his badge was. A badge would make this situation a whole lot easier.

"Ma'am," said Hannah.

The old lady's sharp eyes zoned in on her. They were eyes that didn't miss a thing.

"All due respect, missy, you look even less like a cop than he does."

"You heard what happened to Sam Galloway? The lawyer?"

"Yeah, I heard."

"Well we've been brought in from Shreveport to help with the investigation. The reason we're dressed like this is because we were working undercover. As soon as we closed that case, me and my partner came rushing over here to help out. We didn't even have time to get changed."

"Yeah, but you'd still have ID."

"Ma'am, we were working undercover, chasing down some really bad people. If they'd found ID on us they would have killed us."

The old woman glanced past us at the car, then the door slammed shut in our faces. A couple of seconds later there was the rattle of an intruder chain being unlatched.

"I was supposed to be doing the talking." I whispered.

"You're welcome," she whispered back. I raised an eyebrow and she added, "If I'd left it to you, Winter, we'd still be standing here at Christmas."

The door opened and we turned to face the old woman wearing our best smiles. In the bright sunlight, the woman didn't look as old as I'd first thought. Late sixties, early seventies. Her cheeks were sunken because she'd lost most of her teeth, making her look older, an effect that had been compounded by the gloomy hallway. She nodded to Choat's house.

"You think Daniel did it, don't you? You think it was him who burnt up that lawyer?"

"What's your name, ma'am?"

"Annie Dufoe. What's yours?"

"I'm Detective Winter." I nodded to Hannah. "And this is my colleague, Detective Hayden."

"Well now we've got all the niceties out the way, howabouts you answer my question?"

"Yes ma'am, he's a suspect."

Annie nodded like everything was clicking into place, like this all made perfect sense. "There was always something strange about that boy. He was so quiet and polite. It wasn't natural. Then again, it wasn't his fault."

"What makes you say that?"

"A boy needs his father. I don't know if you know this, but his daddy died when he was young."

I nodded. "He was a war hero."

"He was, but he didn't die in no war, if that's what you're thinking." She nodded to the garage. "He blew his brains out in there. It happens. Some people go to war but only a part of them makes it back, and not the good part. Lord knows, I've got nothing against a person enjoying a drink, but some people can take it too far. They don't know when to quit."

I knew exactly what she meant. I was thinking about my mother and her slow dive into the darkness at the bottom of a bottle. "Daniel found his father's body, didn't he?"

Another nod. "Any other kid would have run out of there screaming. They'd have run a mile in the other direction, got away as quick as they could. Not Daniel. He went and got a bucket of soapy water and scrubbed that floor clean while his daddy was turning stiff less than a foot away. His poor mother found them both in there when she got back from work. She told me later that he was just sat there with the bucket between his knees, staring into space."

"When did you last see Daniel?"

Annie sucked in her cheeks and squashed her lips together with her thumb and forefinger. "Last night. It was a little before seven. I remember because I'd just finished washing up after dinner and my stories hadn't started on the TV. My kitchen window looks out over the street."

"Was it unusual for him to go out at that time of night?"

A shake of the head. "He worked shifts so he was always coming and going at all sorts of hours."

"Did you notice anything suspicious happening over there last night?"

Another shake of the head. "I'm generally in bed by ten. Once I'm asleep nothing can wake me."

"Thank you for your time, Mrs Dufoe," I said.

"I hope you catch him soon."

"Well, until we do, you make sure that door's locked up nice and tight."

"You don't have to worry about that."

The door slammed shut and the locks engaged one after the other. The intruder chain went on last, rattling back into place.

CHAPTER FIFTY

"Smoke and mirrors."

We were back in the car with the engine running and the air-conditioner going full blast, the temperature slowly dropping. The sun was burning through the windshield and my T-shirt was sticking to me.

"What are you talking about?" Hannah asked.

"The unsub has created an illusion. However, illusions only work if the audience buys into them. The magician can't tell an audience what to believe. All he can do is make suggestions. He can take them by the hand and invite them to go where he wants, but they have to make the decision to go with him. In this case, we have a body, a gun and a note. Put it all together and it adds up to suicide."

"I'm hearing a 'but'."

"But there's always going to be that sliver of doubt. If you make a woman disappear and then reappear in exactly the same spot you can work out a dozen ways the trick might have been executed. Maybe there's a false panel in the box, maybe there's a trapdoor in the stage. However, if the woman reappears on the upper balcony in defiance of the laws of time and space, then we start to believe in the magic. So, what's the detail that turns this illusion from a run-of-the-mill parlour trick into a top level piece of magic?"

Hannah scrubbed a hand through her spiky hair, thinking hard. She shook her head. "Sorry. No idea."

"The notepad."

She shot me a disbelieving look.

"The notepad is a stroke of genius. That's what connects the illusion to the real world. Without that connection we'd always be wondering, because without it everything happens on stage, or, in this case, a garage in an old abandoned refinery. It all goes back to our disappearing woman. By having her reappear on the balcony the illusionist is bridging the gap between the stage and the real world. So, how did the notepad get into Choat's house?"

"Maybe it belonged to Choat and the unsub found it in his house."

I shook my head. "No way. The unsub took it there. If forensics bother to count the sheets of paper they'll find that only one is missing, the one that was all neatly folded up in Choat's pocket. So how did this play out?"

Hannah chewed at her lip and stared through the windshield at the haze rising from the road surface. I was staring too, thinking this one through. *How did it play out?* In my mind, I'd travelled back in time to yesterday.

My first thought was that the unsub had gone to Choat's house, got him to write the note, then told him to drive over to the refinery. Once he'd got him there, he shot him in the head, put the note in his pocket and arranged everything to make it look like a suicide.

Except that doesn't work. If Choat had written the note at home, there was no way he would have driven himself to the refinery. He would have driven away in the opposite direction as fast as he could. But Annie Dufoe had said that Choat left just before seven. If the unsub had arrived before then, she would have seen him.

Scenario number two: the unsub told Choat to meet him at the refinery. He told him if he didn't, then he was going to share his secret with the whole world. So Choat drove over there and parked the Nissan outside the garage, and that was part one of the illusion complete. And the beauty of this was that the unsub hadn't gone anywhere near the car. No fingerprints, no DNA, no fibres.

Things started moving quickly after that. The unsub didn't want to give Choat the opportunity to think. He wanted him flustered and scared. He wanted him to jump when he said jump. He ordered him to go inside at gunpoint, and one of the first things Choat would have seen was the dead homeless guy. He would have been terrified, and from that point on he would have done everything the unsub said without argument, anything to buy some time.

So the unsub got him to write the note and then he shot him in the head.

I was still staring straight ahead, watching the wisps of heat rising from the road, there but not really there. For all intents and purposes I was in that concrete garage again, surrounded by the smell of burnt flesh, my ears filled with the buzzing of the flies.

The use of a large-calibre bullet was another example of overkill, but this time it was justified. If you're serious about shooting yourself, you put the barrel in your mouth and fire upwards. If the unsub had tried to force Choat to do that, there would have been bruising around his mouth, probably a couple of broken teeth, too. If that had happened the illusion crumbles there and then.

Shooting yourself in the side of the head is risky, because there's an outside chance that you might survive and end up in a vegetative state, and there's an even slimmer chance that you're going to survive with all your faculties intact. The smaller the bullet, the more chance there is of that happening. And that's why he'd used a large-calibre bullet.

After killing Choat and planting the note, the unsub had headed back to the station house, where everyone was waiting for the grand reveal. And much later, at some point during the early hours, he had headed over to Choat's house and planted the notepad, completing the illusion.

I clicked back into the present, took a moment to go through everything in my head one more time, then ran this theory past Hannah.

"The unsub caught a lucky break there," she said when I'd finished. "Admit it. If Annie Dufoe had been an insomniac, she would have seen the unsub when he came back to plant the letter. She would have been able to ID him."

"Luck doesn't come into it. This illusion was well thought out. It wasn't something thrown together at the last minute. This unsub is a cop, remember. He knows about surveillance. He would have taken the time to learn Choat's habits, to learn the rhythms of Kennon Street. He would have known that Annie Dufoe was someone he needed to avoid. It took us all of two seconds to work that one out."

Hannah thought this over. "Why Choat?"

"Because our guy's into overkill. There was always a possibility that the cops might get too close for comfort, so he looked around for a scapegoat. He might not have needed one, but he wanted his bases covered. Choosing a cop was an inspired move. The police wouldn't be expecting the killer to be one of their own, so it would send them into a state of shock and disbelief. So the unsub looked around and decided that Choat seemed a good bet. Then, when he started investigating him, he found he'd struck gold. Choat's private life made him the perfect decoy. If things had turned out differently this case would now be closed and everyone would be happy. The unsub would have given it a couple of months for things to quieten down, then quit and moved to another part of the country where he could start killing again."

Hannah nodded to herself. "Yeah, that makes sense. Okay, where to now?"

I smiled. "That one's easy. My body clock's telling me it's past lunchtime. I vote we head on over to Apollo's."

CHAPTER FIFTY-ONE

I lit a cigarette and passed the pack to Hannah. Then I put the car into gear and eased away from the kerb. The car quickly started to get smoked up, so I cracked open a window. Any benefit from the air-conditioner was immediately lost as a wave of hot air came rolling in.

For a while we drove and smoked. Random snippets of Mozart played inside my head. Concertos, arias, overtures. I focussed on the music and tried to block out any thoughts of the case. I was getting too close and needed some distance. Some breathing space. We finished our cigarettes and put the windows back up.

Outside, the buildings were getting closer together. Every house had the drapes drawn or the blinds down, anything to keep the relentless heat out. I hit the blinker and stopped to let a battered Ford pick-up past, then took the next left.

"Is there any way that Choat could be the killer?" Hannah asked. "Any way at all? Annie Dufoe didn't have a problem jumping to that conclusion. And I've got to say, I could easily imagine Choat doing something like this. If I turned on the news right now and heard he'd been arrested for Sam Galloway's murder it wouldn't be a shock or a surprise."

"That's not what you said yesterday."

"That was yesterday and this is now."

I raised an eyebrow.

"Okay, I guess I'd be a bit surprised, but only for a second, and once I'd gotten over my initial shock, I'd be a believer. It's the quiet ones you've got to watch out for, right?"

"Sometimes," I agreed. "And sometimes it's the noisy ones. But loud or quiet, the ones you really have to watch out for are the intelligent ones. Now, they're especially dangerous because they're your chameleons. They blend into their environment and you don't even know they're there."

Hannah thought this over for a second.

"Surely they can't be totally invisible. Somebody must suspect something."

"Eventually. That's how they get caught. But some killers can go for years before that happens."

"I still don't get it."

I hesitated a second. "Okay, take my father, for example. He killed for years and nobody suspected anything. He could be outgoing when he wanted to be. He'd go to bars with his buddies. He could laugh and joke with the best of them. He definitely wasn't your quiet neighbour. Although, that said, he was always polite and cheerful, and he'd help you out if you needed him to."

"Taylor told me about your father. I'm sorry."

"Why?"

"Because it must have been hard."

I shook my head. "That's the thing, it wasn't. My early childhood was pretty average. It certainly wasn't anything worth paying a therapist to sort out."

"And how does that work? Your father was a murderer, he killed all those young women, yet you're sat there telling me you had a normal childhood. Sorry, not buying."

"A *relatively* normal childhood. I don't know what a normal childhood is. I don't think anyone does."

"You must have suspected something, though."

I shook my head. "Nothing. Not a single thing. My mother didn't suspect anything either. Nobody did. The first we knew about it was when the FBI arrested him."

"How could you not know?"

"It's all about compartmentalisation. Sometimes he was a father and husband, sometimes he was a math teacher, and sometimes he was a killer. What he did very well, and what helped him avoid capture for so long, was to make sure that those personas never overlapped. There was no grey whatsoever. It was all very black and white. Family man, teacher, killer."

"You said your early childhood was average. What about afterwards?"

I thought this over for a second, remembering the nightmare that had followed my father's arrest. At the time it seemed like it would go on for ever, but it hadn't. Eventually I found a way out. At any rate, I found a way to live with myself, which was as much as you could hope for. Unfortunately you were never going to be completely free from something like this. Those ripples were going to be felt all the way to the grave, diminishing in intensity as time passed, but always there.

"My mother never really came to terms with what my father did and we ended up moving around a lot. Going to a new school is hard at the best of times. When you're intelligent and your father's a serial killer, well, let's just say that I had some interesting moments."

"It couldn't have been easy for you."

I shrugged. "Does anyone have an easy time of it? I mean, look at you. Your father ran out on you when you were a kid and your mother died of cancer, and you're working dawn to dusk while you chase your dream."

"Is this the point where you tell me that life's a bitch?"

I shook my head. "No, that would be a cop-out. Life can be hard, I'm not going to deny that. But it can also be beautiful and joyous and fun. You need both the highs and the lows, otherwise you're flat-lining. That happens, you might as well be dead."

My cellphone trilled in my pocket. A new text had arrived. I pulled the phone out and thumbed it to life, one hand on the wheel, one eye on the road. The number wasn't Taylor's, or one that I recognised. I opened the text. There was no message, just a picture. It took a second to process what I was seeing. My brain caught up with itself and I jammed on the brakes. The seatbelt cut into my chest and bounced me back into my seat.

I was vaguely aware of Hannah saying something, but couldn't work out what. The air-conditioning was pumping hard, but that wasn't the reason I felt so cold. This was more than being cold, this was a freezing numbness. I looked at the picture on my cellphone again, hoping I'd imagined it.

I hadn't.

CHAPTER FIFTY-TWO

"What's going on? Why have we stopped in the middle of the road?"

There was no disguising the panic in Hannah's voice. She was looking to me for answers that I didn't have. At least, I didn't have any she'd want to hear. I glanced at my cellphone and wished this was some mistake. It wasn't. This wasn't an hallucination, and it wasn't my imagination. This was as real as it got.

"Talk to me, Winter."

I tried to find something to say, words to reassure, words to comfort, but nothing came out. I just stared at the picture on my cell, wondering how things could have gone so wrong.

"Let me see that cellphone."

"You don't want to see this."

My voice sounded calm, but that wasn't how I felt. Far from it. My emotions were pinballing all over the place, swinging from one extreme to the other. Anger to impotence. Fury to uselessness. My heart was thundering in my chest and the excess of adrenaline flooding my system made me feel sick.

Hannah snatched the cellphone and looked at the screen. Her eyes widened and the cell tumbled into her lap. She took a sharp intake of breath and her hands flew up to cover her mouth. It was almost like she was trying to push all her questions back in because then she could pretend this wasn't happening. As soon as she started talking everything would become real. The words would turn fantasy to fact and there would be no going back.

"Is he dead?"

The question came out in a stuttering whisper.

"I don't think so."

There's a time for white lies, and there's a time for black lies. If Hannah lost it now she'd be no use to me. I reached for the phone and studied the picture and did my best to pretend this was just any old crime-scene picture, but the image of Taylor's broken body kept pulling at me. I took a deep breath and made myself focus, studying the background for clues.

Dust on the concrete floor.

A blank concrete wall.

And right at the edge of the frame was the partial image of a section of scaffolding.

"I know this place. It's the first storeroom that Elroy took us to." I passed Hannah my cellphone. "Call 911. Get them to send the paramedics and the police."

"He's going to be all right, isn't he?"

The combination of desperation and hope in her voice broke my heart. I nodded. Another black lie. I put the car in gear and hit the accelerator. It took ten minutes to reach the refinery, a journey that would normally take between fifteen and twenty. I drove as fast as the roads would allow, ran red lights, anything to shave a few seconds off the journey.

Not that it made any difference. However fast I drove, however quickly we got there, Taylor would still be dead.

The refinery gates were wide open and I drove through them at forty, the security hut and the barrier passing in a blur. I braked for the T-junction, skidded left, the car's back end fishtailing. The perimeter road was long and straight and I hit the gas and roared through the gears. Forty, fifty, sixty. The old storage tanks were getting bigger in the windshield.

We turned into a side road that led to a wide open area and came skidding to a halt in front of the storeroom. I wrenched open the driver's door, jumped out and broke into a run.

There were marks on the ground from where someone had dragged something heavy into the building, disturbing the dirt and partially obliterating our footprints from earlier. There was a new set of tyre tracks, too. The patterns they made were consistent with someone performing a K-turn and then backing up as close to the entrance as possible. The door was unlocked, and it crossed my mind that this was a trap. The unsub might be in there right now, just waiting to shoot us.

Except that didn't fit with what we knew about this guy. He was careful. He wasn't going to make a mistake like that. He would have known that we'd call 911. It's what anyone would have done in this situation. It was something that had been conditioned into us from the cradle. Bad stuff happens, dial 911. He would also have known that 911 would track us through my cellphone. Ambushing us here was too risky. The paramedics and cops would be all over this place in no time. Even so, there was enough doubt to make me wish I had a gun.

I crashed through the door, moving from the nuclear glare of the day into the twilight gloom of the storeroom. The scuff marks in the dirt ended where Taylor was lying on the floor.

The sight of him knocked all the fight out of me. My bones turned soft and I reached for the wall to support myself. My head was pulsing in time with my racing heart. I took a couple of deep breaths and told myself that this crime scene was no different from the hundreds I'd seen over the years.

Another lie.

This couldn't have been more different. The sense of detachment I got when I stepped into a crime scene was absent, the emotional distance that enabled me to do my job. I'd only known Taylor for a day, but that was long enough to make a world of difference.

A high-pitched noise brought me back into the present. It was part screech, part scream, part sob. It sounded more animal than human. This was the sound of someone being ripped apart by grief, the raw noise of open wounds being smeared with salt. All the colour had drained from Hannah's face and she was using the doorframe to hold herself up. She stared at me, hate blazing in her big brown eyes.

"You said he was alive."

Her hands curled into fists and she punched me in the chest. She punched again and again, and I just stood there taking it. Tears streamed down her face, accusations poured from her mouth. Her blows gradually got weaker, then stopped altogether. I pulled her into a hug and held her tight, hot tears soaking into my T-shirt.

Taylor's face had been beaten to pulp. Multiple blows had caused both eyes to swell up and clamp shut. His lips were swollen and cut and there was blood everywhere. His clothing hid the damage the unsub had done to his body, but I was betting it was there. Taylor's face looked bad, but those injuries alone weren't enough to kill him.

His grey T-shirt had turned black where the blood had seeped through. That's where the real damage was. Internal injuries. A ruptured spleen, liver damage, broken ribs, maybe even a punctured lung. No bullet wounds, though. There wasn't enough blood for that.

He was lying on his left side with his right foot tucked under left calf and his right hand draped over his left arm. The pose was very deliberate and obviously staged. This wasn't how Taylor had died. The unsub had left him like this and he'd done that for a reason. I'd seen this pose before. It took a second to realise where.

The last time I'd seen someone laid out like this wasn't at a murder scene, it was in a medical textbook. Taylor had been left in the recovery position.

CHAPTER FIFTY-THREE

I broke away from Hannah and ran over to Taylor, knelt beside him and pressed two fingers against his carotid artery. My fingertips tingled with a flutter that was as gentle as the flapping of a butterfly wing. His chest was barely moving, but it was moving.

"He's alive?" Hannah whispered behind me. The question was made entirely from breath. There was no weight to the words.

"Barely. Call 911 again. Tell them to hurry up with that ambulance."

"Is he going to be okay?"

I glanced down at Taylor, then looked at Hannah. I didn't like the way Taylor was breathing. Every time he exhaled, I expected it to be the last time. Every breath was an effort. It crossed my mind to tell another black lie, but I couldn't do it. "I don't know. Just call 911."

I pulled Taylor onto his back, quickly wiped the worst of the blood from his mouth, then started giving him CPR. The taste of metal touched my tongue and it was hard not to gag. I told myself that if the positions were reversed Taylor would have done the same for me. Then I started pumping his chest, counting off the compressions. When I got to thirty, I gave him two more breaths, then thirty more chest compressions.

"Where the hell's that ambulance?"

"It's on its way. It'll be here soon."

I fell into a rhythm. Two breaths followed by thirty quick chest compressions. Taylor's blood was smeared over my lips and my arms were aching. I lost track of time. Hannah was on her knees beside me. She was holding Taylor's hand and whispering over and over that everything was going to be all right. The promises came out as a stream of words. The way she was talking, it sounded like she was trying to convince herself rather than reassure Taylor.

A siren in the distance, getting closer.

My arms were so tired I couldn't feel them. My knees were numb from pushing into the concrete floor. I didn't know how long I could keep this up for. And then I glanced down at Taylor and knew I'd keep this up as long as he needed me to.

More mouth-to-mouth. More chest compressions. More whispered words of encouragement from Hannah.

The siren stopped. Footsteps outside.

"In here," I shouted.

Two paramedics rushed into the storeroom and I shuffled out of the way so they could do their thing. I felt completely redundant. After all that frantic activity, I didn't know what to do with myself. Hannah was still on her knees, still whispering, her fingertips touching Taylor's. The room suddenly felt tiny. There was too much drama going on, too many people crushed into too small a space. It was more than these four walls could hold.

I slipped outside and the heat hit me. It was like a physical blow, as though I'd been punched in the gut. The contrast of gloom to brightness made my head throb. The harsh sunlight made me squint. The taste of Taylor's blood filled my mouth. My skin was contracting where it had been coated.

I walked over to the police cruiser and sank into the driver's seat, reached up to the sun visor and flipped open the vanity mirror. The face staring back was like something from a disaster movie. There were smears of Taylor's blood all over my mouth and chin. It was on my hands as well. Red streaks stained the white cotton of my John Lennon T-shirt.

There were no hand wipes in the car, no tissues or napkins, nothing I could use to clean myself up. Not that I'd expected anything different. This was a cop car. Right now, all I wanted was to get Taylor's blood off of me. I wanted to get in a shower and run it as hot as I could stand for as long as I could stand, and to stay in there until all trace of it had been scalded away.

I got out of the car and went over to the ambulance. The back door was unlocked. Twenty seconds of rummaging and I'd found what I was looking for. A tub of wipes, and a blue medical top that was still in its cellophane wrapper. The paramedic business could get messy at times, so it made sense to carry these things.

I used the wipes to scrub away the worst of the blood. Even when I managed to get a patch clean I could still feel it pulling my skin tight where it had dried. That was the thing with blood. It didn't matter how hard you scrubbed, you could never get rid of it all. I got as clean as I could and swapped my blood-stained T-shirt for the blue medical top.

Then I went and found a shady spot and waited to see who'd show up.

CHAPTER FIFTY-FOUR

I was sitting in the shadow of a wall when the first cop car arrived thirty seconds later, lights strobing, siren wailing. It screeched to a halt behind the ambulance. The car was a black sheriff's department sedan with Barker driving and Romero in the passenger seat. Barker was leaner and fitter and got out first. Romero was a good ten seconds slower because of his bulk. Barker spotted me.

"Is he alive?" he called over.

"Just about. They're inside."

Barker and Romero disappeared into the storeroom and I kept my vigil.

Over the next five minutes almost every cop in Eagle Creek turned up. I recognised most of the faces from the station house the night before. The area in front of the storeroom soon resembled the parking lot at a cops' convention. The black sedans and 4×4s of the sheriff's department were abandoned next to the tan-coloured police department vehicles. It was completely understandable. One of their own had been taken down and they all wanted a piece of the son of a bitch who'd done this.

All except one.

Shepherd and Sheriff Fortier arrived together and went inside. I gave it another minute for any latecomers to turn up, then positioned myself where I could see as many cops as possible, both inside the storeroom and out. I thumbed through the call log on my phone, stopped when I reached the number the photograph had been sent from. Then I connected the call and watched for someone to reach for their cell.

Five seconds passed, ten seconds, then a disembodied voice told me that the phone I was trying to call was switched off. That would have been too easy, but it would have been crazy not to try. It had been a long shot, and like most long shots it hadn't paid off. This guy was too clever to make a mistake like that. I sighed and rubbed at my face. I could still feel Taylor's dried blood pinching my skin.

This was a taunt, the unsub's way of telling me he was smarter. But he wasn't as smart as he thought. Even if you were using a burner phone, the smart thing to do would be to withhold the number. This was a sign of overconfidence, and overconfidence was the breeding ground for mistakes.

Sheriff Fortier came out on his own and stood for a second, squinting in the sunlight, one hand up to shield his eyes. He saw me and walked over. He looked more stressed than ever. Somehow smaller, too. This was someone who wished he could be anywhere but here. There wasn't even a glimpse of the young guy who'd signed up to serve and protect all those years ago.

"What can you tell me?"

"Not much."

I outlined what little I knew. It didn't take long. The picture had arrived, we'd called 911, we'd rushed over here as fast as we could and I'd performed CPR until the paramedics got here. That was about it. When I showed him the photograph, he asked to keep my phone as evidence. I told him no. He looked like he was going to argue, then thought better of it. Fortier wanted to know what Hannah was doing here, and I couldn't see any reason not to tell him. If he was surprised that Hannah and Taylor were a couple, it didn't show.

"Choat's not our guy, then?"

"Choat was never your guy."

"You didn't think to mention this?"

"I figured you'd work it out sooner or later."

Fortier wasn't happy with this answer, but he didn't push it. "Why send the picture to you?"

I shrugged. It was a good shrug, one that conveyed the impression that I didn't have a clue. I underlined my puzzlement with a head shake. "I don't know."

"Have you got any idea who this guy is?"

I shook my head. "The profile still stands, though. You're looking for a white male, five foot nine. He's in his thirties, slim-built and college-educated. What you can add is that this unsub's a game player. He's got a Machiavellian streak a mile wide and right now he's getting off on the fact that we're running around like a bunch of headless chickens."

Fortier stared up at the massive storage tanks, then turned back to me. "Why's he doing this? What's his motivation?"

They were good questions, questions I didn't have answers to. What happened to Taylor had changed the whole landscape of this case.

"He's a serial killer." I opted for a stock answer, one that I knew I could deliver convincingly. "He's driven by his fantasies. He wants to watch his victims suffer. He wants to control and dominate."

"But why?"

"There's no *why*, not really. It's just the way he's wired. Yes, you can blame his childhood, and how he was brought up, and, yes, those things undoubtedly have an influence, but not everyone who has a lousy childhood goes on to become a serial killer. The difference is in the wiring."

"So this guy's been a killer from day one."

"Pretty much. When we catch him, ask him if he killed and tortured animals as a kid. You'll find out he did."

There was a sudden bustle of activity over at the door and we both turned to look. A second later the medics came out pushing a gurney, Hannah a few steps behind. Taylor was strapped to the gurney. If anything, the sunlight made his injuries look even worse. By the time I reached them the medics already had the back door of the ambulance open and were pushing Taylor inside.

"Hannah."

She turned to look at me. Her face was paler and more drawn than ever.

"You want to stay with Taylor, and I get that, but there's nothing you can do for him. Whether he lives or dies is down to how good these guys are. I'm going to find the bastard who did this with or without your help. If you help me, I'm going to hunt him down more quickly. The quicker we catch him the less chance there is that someone else will end up hurt or dead."

She looked at me in disbelief. "You want me to leave him."

"I need your help."

"Taylor needs me."

"No, he doesn't. He's unconscious. He might even be in a coma. Hannah, he doesn't even know you're here."

"We've got to go," one of the medics called out.

"I'm sorry, Winter."

The medic went to shut the door and I pushed it open. I stared straight at Hannah.

"When you were nursing your mother you felt completely powerless. She was dying and there was nothing you could do to help her. You would have done anything to take the pain away. You considered killing her, but you couldn't even do that because there was too big a risk of getting caught, and you knew that no matter how much pain she was in, she'd never forgive you for throwing your life away."

The medic told me to move. He tried to push the door closed again, but I pushed back harder.

"Day after day you watched her fading away until there was nothing left. If you hadn't been there, would that have changed the outcome? The answer's no. Your mother would still be dead, and you'd still be feeling guilty because you're convinced there must have been something you could have done differently. Something you could have done to make things better. You have that chance now. Help me."

Hannah was staring like she wanted to kill me. I didn't blame her, not one bit. "You bastard," she hissed.

The medic gave me a hard shove and I staggered backwards, landing on my ass. The door slammed shut and the ambulance pulled away, the siren howling, lights flashing.

I stood up, brushed myself down, then went back to the car. I got inside, fired up the engine and turned the air-conditioning to full. Then I sat there with my cellphone in my hand and counted off the seconds. I reached fifty-seven before it rang. I connected the call, pressed the phone to my ear.

"Where are you?"

CHAPTER FIFTY-FIVE

Hannah was waiting in the shade of the guardhouse at the refinery entrance. She stomped over, wrenched the passenger door open, got in, slammed the door shut. I pulled away from the guardhouse and drove out the gates. For a while we just sat in silence and stared at the world on the other side of the windshield. Hannah was lost in her thoughts. I was lost in mine.

"Why did the unsub attack Taylor?" I asked as we drove up the ramp on to the interstate.

"Don't you want to know how Taylor's doing?"

"How's he doing?"

Hannah just glared. "Don't you care what happens to him? Even a little bit?"

"Of course I care. Taylor's a great guy and I hope he pulls through. But there's nothing I can do to affect that outcome, not a single goddamn thing. That one's down to how much Taylor wants to live, and how good the surgeons are in this part of the world."

Hannah hit me with another icy look. "You really are a bastard, Winter. How did you get to be so cold?"

I could still taste Taylor's blood, and the ache in my arms would be there for the rest of the day. This had nothing to do with being cold, and everything to do with wanting to catch the guy who did this. I'd never wanted anything so badly. Call it revenge, call it whatever the hell you wanted, but someone was going to pay for this.

Unfortunately, there weren't enough words in the world to make Hannah understand that. She was angry and she wanted someone to blame, and I was as good a target as anyone because I was there. I understood that anger because I'd felt it myself.

Hannah was still glaring. "I thought you were supposed to be good at this sort of thing." She shook her head. "I've got to say, I'm not impressed. This guy's been one step ahead of you all the way."

"He has," I agreed.

For the next few minutes I let her talk herself out. I didn't listen to a word she said. There was no point. If she was going to be any use to me, she needed to vent. And if I was going to be any use to Taylor, I needed to let her vent without taking it personally. So I just nodded at the appropriate points and offered a "yes" or a "no" when she paused for breath and was expecting a response.

Because Taylor *would* want me to catch this bastard. That's the way he was wired. He didn't do this for the glory or the backslaps or because he wanted his picture in the papers, he did this to put the bad guys away. We were the same in that respect. Kindred spirits recognised one another.

While Hannah vented, I thought things through, and the one question I kept circling back to was why had the unsub chosen to attack Taylor now? What was the trigger?

As we approached the outskirts of Eagle Creek I noticed a change in Hannah. Her anger was gradually shifting from the external to the internal. This was my cue to intervene. She'd be just as useless to me if she was beating herself up.

I hit the blinker and turned into a residential street that was filled with tidy, well-cared-for detached clapboard houses that were painted in shades of white, blue and grey. I parked at the sidewalk and killed the engine.

"Let's take a walk. I need to stretch my legs."

Hannah stopped talking and looked at me. It was the first thing I'd said in a while, and it obviously wasn't what she was expecting. I got out of the car, lit a cigarette and started walking away. The street was narrow, the houses squashed up together. It was approaching two and the shadows were short. There was very little shade and absolutely no breeze. The blue medical top was sticking to me before I'd gone even a dozen feet.

A car door slammed. Hurried footsteps behind, coming closer. Hannah fell into step beside me and I offered her the cigarette pack and lighter. She took them without a word, removed a cigarette, straightened it out and lit it.

"It's a beautiful day," I said. "Don't you just love the feel of the sun on your skin?"

"No, Winter, it's way too hot and way too humid." She sighed. "I shouldn't be here. I should be with Taylor."

"So, why did the unsub attack him?"

"No idea. Maybe he just did it for the sheer hell of it. Maybe he did it because he could. And anyway, since when does he need a reason?"

"Believe me, there's a reason behind everything he does. Which leads us neatly onto question number two. Why didn't he kill Taylor? Now, that's the real puzzler. He's responsible for three deaths, why not make it a fourth?"

"Maybe he thought he had killed him. I mean, I thought he was dead when I first saw him."

For a second Hannah looked as though she was going to lose it. She struggled to get that last sentence out. She took a deep breath and squashed her emotions down.

I shook my head. "There's no way this guy would make a mistake like that. He's into overkill, remember. His first three victims were most definitely dead. There was no grey whatsoever. It was totally black and white. Two shot in the head, one burnt alive. Believe me, if he'd wanted Taylor dead, he'd be dead. Secondly, and this is the clincher, if he wanted Taylor dead, why leave him in the recovery position? You don't do that if your endgame is to kill someone, you do that if you want to keep someone's airway open and make sure they don't choke on their own blood or vomit."

Hannah said nothing. She had a faraway look on her face, like she'd slipped back into the storeroom.

"Hannah," I said, sharply. "I need you here." I softened my voice, then added, "Taylor needs you here."

"What if he dies, Winter? I don't think I could live without him. And don't tell me that won't happen. I saw the way the paramedics were looking at him."

I stopped walking and turned to face her, placed a gentle hand on her arm. "If he dies, then at some point you'll want closure. The only way that's going to happen is if we catch this asshole. You've chosen to be here, which means a part of you understands that. However, if you're going to be any use to me I need you to actually be *here*. If you can't do that, then say the word and I'll drive you over to the hospital right now."

For a while we just stood there in the searing heat and stared at each other. Sweat was trickling down my sides and back. I wiped my forehead with the back of my hand and it came away soaked. The muscles in Hannah's face were tight and her lips were two thin strips. There was a battle going on behind those eyes. She wanted to be with Taylor and she wanted to help me catch this bastard, but she couldn't do both and that was tearing her apart.

"Okay, why didn't he kill Taylor?" Hannah's voice was so low I could barely hear her.

"Because he thought we'd go to the hospital with him. If we're at the hospital, sitting there waiting to hear if he's going to pull through or not, then we're not hunting him. Even if I didn't go, he reckoned I'd be knocked off my game. Anyway that's not the important question."

"So what's the important question?"

I guided Hannah over to a patch of sidewalk where there was a modicum of shade. The temperature dropped by a couple of degrees, which was nothing when it was a hundred plus.

"Why now? He staged Choat's death to make it look like a suicide, and everyone seemed happy with that explanation. So everyone relaxes, lets out a great big sigh of relief. The cops have a dead bad guy and a story that makes sense. The unsub buys himself some time and space to work out what to do next. But then he goes and attacks Taylor. What's the point in staging Choat's suicide then going and doing that? As far as the cops are concerned I'd solved the case and I was about to head off into the sunset. The unsub should have just lain low, but he didn't. Why?"

"Because he knew we'd worked out it was a hoax."

"Exactly. But how did the unsub know we'd worked it out? We were careful. It wasn't like we advertised the fact. The way I see it there's only one possibility that makes sense. The car's bugged."

Hannah glanced over at the cop car, then looked at me like I was crazy. "You're kidding, right?"

"Never been more serious. Either it's hidden under the driver's seat or under the passenger seat. The unsub will have gone in from the rear seats, though. To make it harder to find. Usually it's only the bad guys who ride in the back of cop cars, and they don't tend to be rummaging around under the seats looking for bugs. Everyone else travels up front. If he'd hidden the bug under the dash or in the glove box then that would increase the likelihood of it being found."

Hannah just stared at me.

"There is another alternative. Either you or Taylor told him, because I know I didn't."

"And I can tell you for nothing that neither Taylor nor I have breathed a word."

"So the car's bugged. It all comes back to Occam's razor: the simplest explanation is usually the solution. You said yourself that the unsub is one step ahead of us. If he's listening in to our conversations then that would explain how he's managing to do that."

"Okay, assuming you're correct, why the car?"

"It's not just the car. He's probably got my room at the Imperial bugged, too. But that one doesn't count because I've been staying at your place."

Hannah thought this over, then nodded to herself like she'd come to some sort of decision. "We can use my car."

"Not a good idea. If we do that then the unsub will know we're on to him. For now, we just need to be careful what we say when we're in the car."

I smoked my cigarette and tried to ignore the heat while I considered my next move. Then I thought about the moves I'd already made, and the assumptions I'd made that had led us to this point. I homed in on one particular assumption, and the more I thought about it, the bigger it grew, until it was all I could think about.

Despite the fact that my skin felt like it was on fire, a cold wind was blowing through me. A house built on shifting sand was a disaster waiting to happen. Except, in this case, the disaster had already happened. The fact that Taylor was fighting for his life bore testament to that.

"I got it all wrong," I whispered to myself. "This guy is not a serial killer."

CHAPTER FIFTY-SIX

"If he's not a serial killer, then what is he?"

Hannah was staring at me, waiting for an answer. We were still outside, about fifty yards from the car. Far enough away so that any listening device wouldn't pick up what we were saying. The sun was burning down furiously and my skin was melting.

"He's just a murderer."

"Just a murderer," Hannah echoed in a dead whisper. There was no emotion, no inflections. "You make it sound like he's a grocery bagger."

"This is good news, Hannah. It changes everything. And it gets better, too. This isn't a hot-blooded murderer we're dealing with, remember, this guy premeditates, which means we're dealing with one of the big three motives: revenge, money or belief."

I was thinking out loud, talking at the speed of my thoughts.

"We need to take another look at the victims. We can forget about Choat and our homeless John Doe because they were victims of circumstance. Those two can be filed away under wrong place, wrong time. Sam Galloway is a different matter, though. He was very much in the right place at the right time. All we've got to do is work out why Sam was murdered and we'll have this guy nailed."

I turned and walked quickly back to the car. For the first time since arriving in Eagle Creek I felt we had a handle on this thing. In more innocent times my father had taught me to hunt. What I remembered most was that feeling when you finally picked up the scent of your prey, the way your blood turned hot. That's how I felt now. My blood was hot and I had the scent of prey in my nostrils.

Hannah was matching my speed step for step. Physically she was right beside me, but mentally and spiritually she was locked in her own private hell. I had a good idea what she was going through, but I wasn't kidding myself that I knew how she felt. Grief was such a personal thing. It was different for everyone.

We reached the car. I pushed a finger against my lips and shook my head, waited until Hannah nodded that she'd got the message. Then I opened the back door and pretended to rummage around on the seat. I glanced under the driver's seat and saw nothing, glanced under the passenger seat and saw a small black box attached to the underside. It was half the size of a cigarette pack, maybe smaller. There were no blinking lights, and it didn't have any distinctive markings. It didn't have *any* markings. It was just a plain black box. If I hadn't been looking for it, I would never have found it.

I got in and started the car. Hannah was already buckled into the passenger seat. She asked a question with her eyes and I nodded to her seat. Her eyes widened with surprise and she shook her head in disbelief. I pictured a map of Eagle Creek and plotted the quickest route to McArthur Heights, then put the car into gear and pulled away from the kerb.

We shared some small talk for the first mile or so. Hannah was good. She sounded natural without sounding contrived, and she didn't give anything away. I imagined the unsub listening in. Would he know what we were up to? I didn't think so.

He might not know what we were up to, but he'd work out where we were going soon enough. All cop cars were fitted with tracking devices, even this far out into the middle of nowhere.

We drifted into a silence that was as natural and uncontrived as the small talk. After what had happened to Taylor, it would be understandable for Hannah to be quiet. This was something that worked in our favour, possibly the only positive in a situation that was overloaded with negatives. The less talk, the less chance there was of us giving anything away.

While I drove, I thought about Taylor lying on that dirt-streaked concrete floor and the memory of blood filled my mouth. The what-ifs pushed in on me, and I pushed them back. It would be easy to make this my fault. Way too easy, and pointless. What would it achieve? Nothing. Sinking into a pit of self-incrimination and guilt was not going to change what had happened. If anything, it would make things worse since I wouldn't be able to do my job.

A cellphone went, the ringtone muted. It wasn't mine. My first thought was that the unsub had hidden a phone in the car and was calling to taunt us. Except that didn't fit with his profile. This unsub wasn't like Chief Kalani's talent-show reject He wasn't looking for recognition or headlines. He flew way below the radar.

Hannah was fumbling around in the passenger seat. She pulled a cellphone from her jeans and the ringtone brightened. She connected the call and said "Hi". I only got half the conversation, but it was enough to work out that she was talking to Taylor's mother. Taylor had arrived at the hospital in Shreveport and been rushed into surgery. He was expected to be there for a while. Hannah asked for an update as soon as there was anything, then hung up.

She sat for a moment, staring out the windshield, gazing into the middle distance. The phone was clutched tightly in her hand, and she was tapping it against her leg in a way that made me doubt she was aware she was doing it. Her left leg was vibrating from all the adrenaline. It was like she was dreaming of running away. Maybe she was dreaming of San Francisco. If she was, I hoped Taylor was with her.

"How is he?"

"He's still alive."

"Which is a good thing, right?"

"Yeah, that's a good thing." Hannah's voice was flat and she didn't sound convinced. Not because she didn't think it was a good thing, but because she was wishing and praying that none of this had ever happened. "The next few hours are going to be critical," she added. "If he gets through that then he might be okay."

We fell into an awkward silence. Hannah had made no attempt to disguise how big that "if" was. By the sounds of things, Taylor needed a miracle. The problem was that miracles didn't exist. I wanted to tell myself that he was getting the best treatment possible but that would be a lie. This was northern Louisiana. Shreveport was a city, home to 200,000 people, but however good the medical facilities were, you had hospitals out there that were a damn sight better. Johns Hopkins in Maryland and Massachusetts General up in Boston sprung immediately to mind.

We passed through the town limits and left the houses behind. Trees and fields stretched as far as the eye could see, the leaves glowing in the sunlight.

While I drove, I thought about what might be motivating this guy. Revenge? Money? Belief completed the trinity, and I considered that for a split second before ruling it out. If the unsub had been part of a terrorist group or some ultra right-wing organisation he would have chosen a target that tied into his agenda, whatever that was. Al-Qaeda attacked the American Dream. It wanted to make grand statements and grab headlines. That's why they hijacked passenger jets and flew them into buildings. That's why they sent suicide bombers into places where they knew innocent people would be killed.

Sam Galloway just didn't fit. He dealt in divorces and wills. There was no real statement to be made from his murder, no headlines to be grabbed. His death might be big news in Eagle Creek, but it would only merit a couple of minutes on the regional news, and would probably be passed over altogether by the national news. As for the international news channels, forget it. The only people who were going to get all teary about Sam being burnt alive were his wife, kids and friends.

CHAPTER FIFTY-SEVEN

We reached the wide tree-lined streets of McArthur Heights and cruised slowly through the heat. Everything up here was about personal space and personal wealth, and letting the world know how important you were. I turned into the Galloways' driveway and stopped in front of the tall, imposing wrought-iron gates. The window buzzed down and the hot air rushed in. I reached through and hit the buzzer.

Silence was replaced by static, and a voice asked, "Can I help you?"

It was the same voice as before, the sound through the small speaker just as distorted. This time I knew it was the maid straightaway. The rhythm of the voice was all wrong for Barbara Galloway.

"Jefferson Winter to see Mrs Galloway."

"One minute, please."

I closed the window. It had been open for less than forty seconds, but that was long enough for all the cold air to get sucked out. One minute stretched into two and it had reached the point where I was beginning to wonder if we'd ever be let in when the gates slowly swung open.

We headed along the driveway, undulating plains of pristine green grass stretching out on either side of us. The house looked even more perfect than yesterday. The paintwork seemed whiter, the windows gleamed more brightly, and everything was just somehow more real, but real in a way that made it feel artificial. It reminded me of a film set. If I looked around the back I wouldn't have been surprised to see a wooden frame.

I drove around to the side of the house and parked in the same spot as yesterday. The Mercedes hadn't moved. We got out and walked around to the front. The maid was waiting for us in the open doorway. She welcomed us with a "good afternoon" and asked us to follow her. We went inside, into the cool gloom, our footsteps echoing through the house's large reflective spaces.

Barbara Galloway was waiting in the same room as yesterday. She appeared momentarily perplexed by my appearance, then her conditioning kicked in and she offered a polite hello. She was acting like having someone who looked as if they'd been dragged from a car wreck turn up on her doorstep was an everyday occurrence.

Her gaze followed me across the room, all the way to the Steinway. I laid a hand on the lacquered wood. It felt cool to the touch. "Do you mind?" I asked.

It took a second for her to work out what I was asking. There was confusion in her eyes. Hannah was looking puzzled too. For a moment I was convinced that Barbara was going to say no, but her conditioning kicked in and she nodded her assent.

I sat down on the stool and rattled off a couple of quick scales. The piano was more or less in tune, but the acoustics in the room were atrocious. The walls were smooth, the floors uncarpeted, the ceiling too high. It was a musician's nightmare. All those large, shiny unbroken surfaces created too many aural reflections. The notes hung too long in the air, clashing with one another and creating an unpleasant wave of dissonance.

Like everything else in this room, the Steinway was for show. Maybe one of the kids had piano lessons once, and maybe the Galloways had bought this piano to encourage them. If that was the case, then I didn't doubt for a second that their intentions had been good, but the truth was that anyone who was halfway serious about their playing would not have put the piano in this room, and they would have made damn sure that an instrument this fine was kept in tune.

I stretched my fingers and went straight into Mozart's Turkish Rondo. To make up for the dreadful acoustics, I played the piece pianissimo throughout. Less volume meant fewer reflections. The tune was bright and cheerful and completely wrong for the mood of the room. Hannah and Barbara were both locked into their own little pockets of despair, and I was filling the gaps in the darkness with playful bursts of sound.

I was six when my mother taught this to me. I remember sitting on the stool beside her, concentrating furiously on the dots on the page, working my way through the piece a bar at a time, my mother encouraging me when I needed encouragement and making suggestions when I struggled with the trickier phrases. Once I'd gone through it a couple of times, I didn't require the music any more. If I needed to see the dots all I had to do was shut my eyes and they'd be lit up inside my head.

After half an hour of practising, I still couldn't get it right. All the notes were in the correct place, all the phrases were note perfect, but there was something wrong and I couldn't work out what. My mother must have sensed my frustration because she told me to stop and look at her. She smiled, then touched the side of her head. "Music doesn't come from here, Jefferson." She tapped the left side of her chest. "It comes from here. Always remember that."

She told me to scoot over. Then she placed her hands gently on the keys, shut her eyes and started playing. The notes were exactly the same as the ones I'd been playing, the phrases identical, but that's where the similarities ended. Her fingers flew effortlessly across the keys and her smile grew wider and the sound that filled our tiny music room was the sound of pure joy.

Every time I hear this piece I think of my mother, and I think about what she taught me that day, and I silently thank her for that lesson. This piece of music is everywhere. You hear it in elevators and on commercials and in stores. A thousand kids' toys have this melody programmed into them. Most versions you hear have all the heart taken out, but that doesn't matter. Whenever I hear this piece, wherever I am, I'm transported back to that long-ago day, and all I can hear is the sound of my mother playing.

Eyes closed, I did my best to switch off my brain and play from the heart. For a short while I was back in that tiny music room with my mother sitting beside me. It would be another five years before our world was irrevocably torn apart. I was back in the days when we still had good times, and this was one of the best times of all.

So I played for my mother, and I played for that six-year-old kid who didn't have a clue what was just around the corner. Most of all I played for Taylor. Sometimes the only way to fight the guilt and the grief is to pretend it doesn't exist. Sometimes the only way to save yourself from the darkness is by sprinting headlong towards that thin glimmer of light without worrying about the repercussions, or the future, or the what-ifs and what-might-have-beens.

Sometimes you need to make yourself play from the heart, even if that's the last thing you feel like doing.

I reached the end of the piece and for a moment I just sat there, my hands resting lightly on the keys. Then I turned and looked Barbara Galloway straight in the eye.

"Sam had a secret. Something worth murdering him for. What was it?"

CHAPTER FIFTY-EIGHT

"I don't know what you're talking about."

There was no hesitation. I'd asked my question and Barbara Galloway had answered immediately. It was like she'd been expecting the question and had her answer ready and waiting, just in case. Her response was respectful and polite. It was a conditioned response that was informed by her upbringing and generations of breeding. Her grandmother would have been a Southern belle back in the days when the term still meant something, her mother would have been influenced by that, and that influence would have been passed all the way down to Barbara.

"You're lying," I said.

"And I'd like you to leave now." That politeness was still there, but the words were cut from ice.

"Do you remember Officer Taylor?"

"Of course I remember him."

"Right now he's in the OR over in Shreveport and it's touch and go whether he's going to pull through."

"What's that got to do with me?"

"The person who attacked him was the same person who murdered your husband." I gestured for Hannah to step forward. "This is Hannah Hayden. She's Officer

Taylor's fiancée. They've got a whole future planned together. Except that might not happen now."

"You can't blame that on me."

"It's not me you need to worry about. No, what you need to worry about is that little voice inside your head that you call your conscience. That voice has plenty to say when you sneak into the fridge to snack on something you shouldn't, so what do you think it's going to make of this? It's going to have a field day. It's going to haunt you with this until your final breath. It's going to wake you up in the middle of the night to torture and accuse you, and when that happens do you think your denials are going to count for anything?"

"Mrs Galloway," Hannah broke in. "If there's something you know that could help, I'm begging you, please tell us."

Barbara broke eye contact and looked at Hannah. "How long have the two of you been together?"

"Four years."

"And you're going to get married?"

"One day."

"What about children? Are you going to have children?"

Hannah nodded. "Not right now, but, yeah, in a couple of years, we'd like to start a family."

"How badly injured is your fiancée?"

"It's bad." Hannah sniffed back a sob. She wiped her mouth, scratched a hand through her spiky hair. "He might die."

Barbara took a moment to process this, then said, "I'm sorry. Really I am. But there's no dark secret."

"That's a lie," I said again. "If that was true you'd be acting very differently. For one thing, you'd be on the phone to the police right now demanding they arrest us for trespassing. Hell, you'd probably have grabbed a gun and be exercising your Second Amendment rights. But you're not doing either of those things. Instead you're just standing there making empty threats, while I'm standing here calling you a liar."

Barbara was staring at me again, her eyes ever so slightly narrowed. This was as close to a glare as her conditioning would allow.

"By the way," I added. "The way you hinted that Sam was having an affair when we first met was a nice touch. Very clever. It gave us something to look into while the big secret remained hidden."

"There's no secret, Mr Winter. How many times do I need to tell you that?"

"Sam was killed for revenge or money. Which one was it?" I took out a quarter, flipped it in the air, slapped it down on the back of my hand. "Heads we take a look at revenge. Tails we look at money."

Barbara stared for a second then glanced down at my hand. Her eyes met mine again. I lifted my hand, peeked underneath, then took my hand away with a flourish and let her see the coin.

"Tails it is. So, did Sam owe anybody money? Did he have a gambling problem?"

I watched Barbara carefully. Neither question elicited a response. This had nothing to do with that conditioned cool detachment and everything to do with being way off the mark.

But there had been a reaction when the coin came up tails. It had been so slight anyone else would have missed it. A tiny flash of something in her eyes, a microscopic tightening of her lips. Money was involved, but it wasn't the main reason Sam had been murdered.

"Okay. Let's move on to revenge, then."

Barbara displayed both the tells she'd displayed earlier. They were there and gone in the space of a heartbeat. That flash in her eyes, the fractional tightening and relaxing of her lips.

"Maybe Sam cheated someone out of some money. It would have to be a ton of cash to merit burning him alive, though. How does that sound? Am I in the right ballpark?"

I was watching carefully again. Barbara didn't react to this suggestion. Nothing, not so much as a twitch.

"How about this, then? Maybe he was involved with the Russian mafia. Drug smuggling, people trafficking, arms dealing."

"That's ridiculous."

"Not as ridiculous as you might think. When it comes to dreaming up ways to get even, the Russians can be pretty imaginative. Dousing someone in gasoline and setting them alight would fit with their MO."

"Sam was not involved with the Russian mafia, or the Italian mafia, or any form of organised crime."

"Maybe so. But you live in this big house and you have a garage full of luxury cars. The money had to come from somewhere. Now, I'm sure Sam was a great lawyer, but I just don't see him earning that sort of money in a town this small."

"Family money, Mr Winter. His father played the stock market and made some good investments."

"And how much of that money is left?"

"Enough."

"Okay, if he wasn't involved with the mafia, then that leaves his love life. I'm happy to accept that you're not responsible for Sam's death, but what about all those women he slept with over the years? Maybe one of Sam's mistresses didn't handle being dumped as well as he thought."

"And what? She hired a contract killer to kidnap and murder him? I went through all this with Captain Shepherd, and I'll tell you the same thing I told him. I just don't see that happening."

"I'm not convinced. The wronged wife sticking up for her husband's lovers. Not buying."

She sighed. "Sam had a type. His mistresses were all young and naive, and shallow enough to be impressed by his money."

"And you know this because you got someone to check into their backgrounds."

"Yes I did. I needed to be sure that Sam wasn't going to leave me. Can you understand that?"

I nodded. "You needed to protect your investment."

"That's not how I would have put it."

"So what did you find out?"

"Nothing that gave me any sleepless nights. Some of the girls had money problems, but nothing particularly serious, and certainly nothing that was going to lead them to blackmail Sam. Or arrange to have him killed. A couple of them had been through therapy."

"That could be significant."

Barbara shook her head. "They thought they were sad and unhappy, so they paid someone to tell them that they weren't. These girls were a long way from being sectioned."

"How can you be so sure of that?"

"Because the private investigator I hired was the best money could buy. He came highly recommended."

"Hacking into someone's medical and financial records is a crime. You do realise that, don't you?"

Barbara almost laughed. "Mr Winter, you've met my lawyer. If that was some sort of threat, it was pretty lame."

I turned back to the Steinway and let my fingers run over the keys. They danced from one random melody to the next, little snippets of sound, like someone was dialling through the stations on a radio. I stopped as suddenly as I'd started, thanked Barbara for her time, then made for the door, leaving a stark, sudden silence in my wake. A couple of seconds passed before I heard Hannah's hurried footsteps coming up behind me.

CHAPTER FIFTY-NINE

We talked about Barbara Galloway on the journey back to town, but there was no substance to our conversation. If the unsub was tracking us he'd know we'd been at the Galloway place, and that we were there long enough to have talked to her. It would have been suspicious if we hadn't talked about her. So we put on a show, both of us playing our parts.

But I could tell Hannah's heart wasn't really in it. The guilt was eating away at her. Even though none of this was her fault, she'd managed to rationalise it so that it was. She was going back and forth over the last few hours looking for something she could have done differently, anything. It was a common reaction in these situations, one that bordered on the superstitious. We all believe that we're at the centre of our own little universe, that we can somehow predict and control everything that happens in our lives. We can't. Sometimes things happen that are beyond our control and there's not a damn thing we can do.

The conversation reached a natural conclusion and the silence that filled the car was thick and awkward. Hannah took out her cell and called Taylor's mother.

Taylor was still in surgery and there was nothing to report.

"No news is good news," I offered.

"No, Winter, being told that he's survived the surgery and is going to pull through is good news."

We drove the rest of the way in silence. From time to time I'd glance over at Hannah. Her brow was creased and the shine had gone from those big brown eyes. The stress was taking its toll. Hannah was tough, but it was a learned toughness rather than a part of her nature. You didn't need to dig deep to discover that she had a heart as big as the sun.

What happened to her mother could only have shaped and changed her, and not necessarily for the better. For her sake, I hoped Taylor pulled through, I hoped they made it to San Francisco, and I hoped they ended up with a cosy little house that they could fill with kids and laughter and good times.

I drove into Morrow Street and parked in front of the guesthouse. We got out and crossed the street to Apollo's. The blue and red neon rocket flickered dimly in the bright sunlight. The bell jangled above out heads when we walked in. Lori saw us and broke away from the customer she was serving. She came over, wiping her hands on her apron. Concern filled her face and her eyes were heavy with worry.

"I heard what happened to Taylor. How are you holding up, honey?"

"I'm doing fine, Aunt Lori."

She studied Hannah carefully, unconvinced.

"I'm fine," Hannah repeated. "Don't worry about me."

"And if I don't worry, who's going to?" Lori tried for a reassuring smile and missed by a mile. "How's Taylor?"

"He's still in surgery. His mom and dad are over there with him. I'm just waiting to hear something."

"He's going to be fine, honey. He'll pull through, I just know it. Do you think he's going to leave you all alone?" Lori shook her head. "No way. That boy would go to hell and back for you. He loves you so much."

Hannah excused herself to use the restroom, leaving Lori and me standing there. Lori waited until Hannah was out of earshot then said, "How's she really doing?"

I rocked my hand from side to side. *So-so*. "I'm trying to keep her busy. I figure that's better than her sitting around at the hospital worrying."

"You're probably right." Lori was staring in the direction of the restrooms. "That girl's already been through so much. She doesn't deserve this. Why does God punish the good ones? What's that about? If this is part of His grand scheme, then it makes you wonder if He knows what He's doing. Some days it's difficult to keep believing."

Lori looked like she was going to say more, so I gave her a second. She was staring towards the back of the diner, lost in thought, looking without seeing. Suddenly she snapped out of her trance and asked if she could get me anything. It wasn't what I was expecting. At the same time it was exactly what I would have expected. When things get tough we often slip into the roles we're most comfortable with. Sometimes it's easier to lose yourself in the familiar rather than face up to reality. You can call it denial, or avoidance. I prefer to call it self-preservation.

"I'll have a burger and fries, thanks. Hannah's going to tell you she's not hungry, so just bring her whatever you think she'd like. Maybe she'll eat, maybe she won't."

"Will do, honey."

Lori went back to the counter and shouted the order through to Frank. He responded that it would be his pleasure. His voice sounded flatter than normal, even more world-weary. There was no acting involved this time. He was trying to put on a pretence of normality for Lori, but he wasn't fooling anyone.

I took my usual table by the window and got settled in. There were a couple of dozen people in the diner and the place was filled with noise. People talking, chairs moving, cutlery scraping against the china. Pans banged in the kitchen, something sizzled, and the gentle refrain of a country ballad drifted through the hatch, quiet as a whisper. It was the busiest I'd seen the place. Proof that life did go on.

Lori came over with the coffee pot and two mugs. She poured, then left me alone. Any talking we needed to do had already been done. Hannah reappeared and sat down in the seat opposite.

"We're good to talk," I told her. "Unless our guy's out there with a listening device pointed at the window."

Hannah almost smiled. Her expression turned serious, harder, older. "Barbara Galloway knows something, Winter."

"Yeah, I know."

"O-kay." Hannah stressed both syllables and managed to inject the word with a hefty dose of sarcasm. "If that's the case, then what the hell are we doing here? Why aren't we back there getting her to tell us what she knows?"

"Because she'd die before she gave up Sam's secret. She's got her future to consider. Her kids' futures, too."

Hannah breathed out another of those sarcastic o-kays. This one was part sigh, part word. "Correct me if I'm wrong but isn't this something else you're supposed to be good at? Getting information from people."

"And what do you suggest? Do you want me to get out the thumbscrews? Pull out her teeth? Her fingernails? Threaten her kids?"

"Of course not."

"It's not all doom and gloom, Hannah. Barbara told us plenty without realising."

"Like what? From where I was standing it looked like she was calling the shots."

"And looks can be deceptive. The only way we were going to get anything from her was if she thought she was in charge."

"So what you were doing back there was all an act." A shake of the head. "Sorry, not buying."

I grinned.

"Okay, so what did you get?"

"Well, we now know that Sam was definitely hiding something, and that that something was big enough and bad enough for Barbara Galloway to choose to have her fingernails pulled out rather than tell us, and we also know that that something was big enough and bad enough for someone to burn Sam alive."

Hannah shrugged and shook her head and made a little disdainful snorting noise, the three gestures all happening simultaneously. "You're the ace detective and that's the best you can come up with? If we don't know *what* she's hiding, how the hell does any of that help us?"

"You've been watching too many cop shows. Most crimes are solved with baby steps rather than huge leaps. Light-bulb moments rarely happen in real life. That's the reality of the situation. Baby steps. Before we went to see Barbara Galloway we suspected Sam was hiding something, now we know that for certain. We're finally on the right track, and that's progress."

"Okay, let's go back there and beat it out of her."

I smiled. For a second there I caught a glimpse of the old Hannah. "It wouldn't help. She's not going to give up what she knows."

"Arrest her and question her until she confesses."

"That could work. Except this unsub is a cop, so I don't want her anywhere near a station house. It's catch 22. We know Barbara's got the information we need, but we can't get it without alerting the unsub, and, since we don't know who he is, that's the last thing we want. He's already acting unpredictably."

I didn't expand on that last statement. I didn't need to.

"Look, Hannah," I added. "If there was any way of getting the information from Barbara, we'd have it."

"There has to be a way."

I shook my head. "There isn't."

Lori arrived with our food just in time. My blood sugar had taken another dip and I was starving. Aside from the banana that Hannah had force-fed me back at Dan Choat's place, I hadn't eaten anything since breakfast. There was a toasted sandwich on Hannah's plate, a burger and a double helping of fries on mine. Lori tucked the tray under her arm and took a step back.

"What's this Aunt Lori? I didn't order anything."

"I ordered for you," I replied.

"I'm not hungry."

"You need to eat, honey," Lori put in. "You've got to keep your strength up."

"Whatever."

Lori bit back whatever she was going to say, flashed me a worried look, then walked away, leaving us to it. I picked up a handful of fries and shoved them into my mouth.

"How can you eat at a time like this?"

I shrugged. "I missed lunch and I need to eat."

"You know what I mean."

"Starving yourself won't help Taylor, and it won't make you feel any less guilty."

Hannah went to say something and I put up my hand to stop her.

"Eating."

I picked up my burger.

CHAPTER SIXTY

I ate and did my best not to think about the case. The idea that this unsub wasn't a serial killer changed everything. I needed some distance, needed to clear my mind and come at this thing afresh. I stared out the window at nothing in particular and roamed through my memories.

One memory kept coming up, and I kept pushing it back down, but it was restless and didn't want to be ignored. Hannah hadn't touched her food. She was staring out of the window as well. Maybe she was lost in a memory, too, and, if she was, I hoped it was a good one. I wasn't kidding myself, though. More likely she was trapped in a prison built from guilt, whipping herself raw. Or she was back at the refinery, looking down at Taylor's broken body and wishing it was her lying there instead of him.

The memory tugged again, and this time I surrendered. I was a kid, eight going on nine and I was out in the woods with my father. We'd followed a deer to a clearing and were going in for the kill. Ancient trees stretched up on three sides, making the animal look tiny. We were on our bellies, down with the stink of dirt and dead leaves, hardly daring to breathe.

My father nudged me, then pushed the rifle in my direction. I shook my head. This was one of those rite-of-passage moments and I'd known it was coming. I'd known it was coming from the moment my father suggested this trip. On the surface, the way he'd asked was no different from any other time he suggested we go camping. Except it *was* different. There was a brightness in his voice I'd never heard before, something in his eyes I'd never seen.

I took the rifle and looked through the sight, slowed my breathing. The forest came alive all around me. Sounds, smells, colours. The leaves were dappled with sunlight. Our bodies had compressed the dirt, squeezing out a damp, loamy smell that rose up all around us. I trained the scope on the deer's head. Its eyes were wide and brown. And kind. The animal had no idea we were there, that in a few seconds it would be dead. It was grazing peacefully without a care in the world.

Beside me, my father was breathing slowly, all his attention focussed on the deer. Neither of us made a sound because even the slightest noise would spook it. I moved the rifle until I was staring at the large brown mass of her body, aimed for the spot my father had told me to aim for. My hands were still, my breathing steady. My finger tightened on the trigger.

For a fraction of a second time froze, and in that frozen moment I saw the deer fall, and I saw the light in her eyes die. My father was concentrating so hard on the deer I might as well not have been there. It was like he was the one holding the rifle. I shifted my aim ever so slightly and squeezed the trigger. The gun bucked hard against my shoulder and a puff of dirt exploded beneath the deer. She froze, startled, then darted into the trees.

My father looked at me. He didn't say anything, but he knew. And the fact he knew and wasn't saying anything got to me more than if he had said something. His silent disappointment hurt me more than any words, and he knew that, too. He held out his hand and I gave him the rifle. It was the same rifle he used when he went hunting on those long moonlit nights.

The next time we went hunting, I killed a deer. After that first time it got easier. Almost too easy. I was a natural. In no time I was matching my father kill for kill.

"We need to go back to the very beginning and start again."

That got Hannah's attention. She looked across the table at me, her eyes filled with more sadness than any one person could bear. I don't know how long I'd zoned out for, but the burger was gone and I'd eaten most of the fries. Hannah's toasted sandwich lay untouched on her plate.

"Assumption number one: this guy's a serial killer. That's why I came to Louisiana in the first place. It was the combination of the film clip and the countdown that led me to that conclusion. Take the countdown out of the equation and you've got some guy who's been burned alive. It's just a murder. Yes, it's an extreme way to kill someone, and, yes, there are easier, less messy ways, but, when all's said and done, it's still just a murder. It was the countdown that turned it into theatre. That's what convinced me. Some serial killers get off on all that stuff. They want to parade their work. They want people to sit up and take notice."

I picked up a cold fry and ate it even though I wasn't hungry any more. I needed something to do with my hands, something to distract me.

"Assumption number two: this guy's a cop. That one still stands."

I didn't expand any further. The fact that Dan Choat was dead and Taylor was in surgery was all the proof we needed to support that theory. I drank some more coffee and looked out the window. I needed to come at this case cold. If I was presented with these facts for the first time, how would I react? What assumptions would I make?

The first time I did this exercise was in my hotel suite in Charleston. Back then all I had to go on was the film clip and the countdown. Now there was a whole chronology of events that started with Sam Galloway's abduction and led all the way through to this moment. A lot more information. And somewhere amongst all that information was the key to solving this puzzle.

"What other assumptions have you made?" Hannah asked.

"I assumed that the unsub's kill room was at the old refinery, and that one played out fine."

"Anything else?"

I shook my head, about to say "no", but stopped myself at the last second with the word lodged in my throat.

"What is it, Winter?"
"Maybe something, maybe nothing."
I stood up and headed straight for the door.

CHAPTER SIXTY-ONE

Five minutes later we were driving along Main Street. Storefronts gleamed and windows shone in the afternoon sunlight, and everything was as perfect as Disneyland on a hot summer's day. Hannah's questions had gone unanswered, and had dried up completely by the time we turned out of Morrow Street. That's how far down she was. The old Hannah would have kept going at me until she got her answers. Nothing would have stopped her.

The person sitting in the passenger seat looked like Hannah, and sounded like her, but something fundamental had been stripped away. She was gazing blankly through the windshield, seeing without really seeing, Taylor never far from her thoughts.

We reached the town square and I could feel Randall Morgan glaring down at me from his plinth. Glaring and laughing his ass off. A century further down the line and another black man had just been lynched in his town. Things move on, but some things just stay the same. The big difference was that the white guy who did this would be held accountable. He was going to pay for what he did.

I parked in front of the police department's HQ and got out. Hannah was buckled into her seat, not moving, just staring out the windshield. I leant back into the cool of the car and she turned to meet my eye.

"Are you coming?" I asked her.

"Not until you tell me what we're doing here."

"Suit yourself."

The car door closed with a bang and I hopped up onto the sidewalk. Five seconds later a car door opened and closed, and five seconds after that Hannah was at my side. The building next to the police department building was the mayor's office. The walls were whiter than white. Even with my sunglasses on they were dazzlingly bright. The big double doors were made from a heavy dark wood.

Inside it was gloomy, the temperature comfortable. The smell of beeswax seemed to be everywhere. Our footsteps ricocheted around us, bouncing from floor to wall to ceiling and creating a confusion of echoes.

The woman behind the reception desk was in her mid-thirties. Brunette, hazel eyes, hair scraped back from her forehead into a tight, efficient ponytail. She was conservatively dressed and had mastered the receptionist's smile. Warm, pleasant, bland. She looked at us, taking in Hannah's piercings and T-shirt, taking in my white hair and blue medical top and the smudges of Taylor's blood, and her smile didn't falter, not even for a second.

"I'm here to see Mayor Morgan."

"Do you have an appointment?"

"No, we don't have an appointment." I nodded to a corridor that led deeper into the building. "I take it his office is down this way?"

The receptionist followed my gaze and the smile faltered. That was as good as a yes. I started walking, the smell of beeswax getting stronger with every step. It was a smell that reminded me of museums and art galleries. Hannah was following a couple of steps behind.

"Sir," the receptionist called after me. "You can't go down there."

"I can and I am," I called back.

"Mr Morgan isn't in today."

"Sure he isn't."

"He phoned in sick this morning."

Something about the way she said this stopped me in my tracks. I turned and walked back to the reception desk.

"Is he often ill?"

"Sorry, who are you?" She was doing nothing to hide the fact that she was staring now. She was looking at me like I might be a murderer or a madman. I didn't blame her. Given my appearance I could have passed for either.

"My name is Jefferson Winter and I'm investigating Sam Galloway's murder, and I really don't have time for this. So I'd appreciate it if you could please just answer the question."

The receptionist shook her head, flustered. Her perfume smelled expensive, and it crossed my mind that it might have been a present from Jasper. Maybe it was, maybe it wasn't. Maybe I was being too suspicious for my own good. That was the problem with this job. Spend long enough looking for the worst in people and there was a danger that that was all you'd end up seeing.

"He's never ill," she said eventually.

"What? Not even a cold?"

"He's had colds, but he comes in anyway. That's the sort of person he is. He just soldiers on."

"So, when you spoke to him he sounded like he was at death's door, right?"

The receptionist shook her head.

"How did he sound?"

"A bit quiet and subdued."

Subdued was not a word I would use to describe Jasper Morgan. He was the town's alpha male, and had been for years. What's more, he knew it. Quiet and subdued, not a chance.

"He's not normally quiet, is he? Usually he's barking out orders and marching around like he owns the place, which, if you think about it, he probably does." I smiled. "That must have got you worried. The fact he was so quiet."

The receptionist almost returned my smile. She nodded. "I guess so."

"So, he didn't have a cold or a sore throat? Nothing like that?"

Another shake of the head.

"Tell me what he said as best you can remember. Try and use his exact words."

The receptionist thought this over for a second. "He said he was feeling a little under the weather and wouldn't be in today. He asked me to cancel all his appointments."

"That's what he said? That he was a little under the weather?"

The receptionist nodded. She was smiling like she'd just been told to go to the top of the class.

"Did he say when he was going to be back in the office?"

Another shake of the head.

"Did he say anything else?"

Another shake of the head. "No, that was all. It was a short conversation."

"Thanks," I said, and headed for the front doors.

Outside, I lit a cigarette and put my sunglasses back on. The sun was brighter and hotter than ever, searing through the thin material of the blue medical top, cooking me alive. Hannah held out her hand and I passed her my cigarettes and Zippo.

"Don't you have your own?"

"I'm trying to quit."

"Since when?"

"Since Taylor."

"You're not doing a very good job."

"If he pulls through, then I'm going to quit. This time I promise."

Hannah lit a cigarette. There was a slight tremble in her hand when she passed back the pack and the bashed-up Zippo.

"Are you going to tell me what Jasper Morgan's got to do with all this?"

"Maybe something, maybe nothing."

"That's what you said back at the diner."

"Except now I'm veering more towards something rather than nothing. The conversation Jasper had with his secretary was all wrong. If you're ill you'll say you've got flu or a cold or you're sick. Something along those lines. You don't say you're feeling a little under the weather, not unless you're in an old black and white film from the forties. Also, you always give some indication of when you're going to be back. You say you'll be in tomorrow, or in a couple of days, or a couple of months. You don't leave it open-ended like that. Nobody does. People need to factor the inconvenience of a colleague's illness into their own lives, and they can only do that if they have a time frame to work within, even if that time frame is fictional. And if you're the most important person in Eagle Creek, and you've never had a day off, you're definitely going to let people know when you'll be back."

Hannah smoked her cigarette, thinking. "So we need to go and speak to Jasper Morgan."

"That's exactly what we need to do."

CHAPTER SIXTY-TWO

Jasper Morgan's house was shielded from the rest of the world by its own private forest, a massive swathe of woodland that could be measured in square miles rather than acres. The land had probably been bought up during Dayton's oil rush at the start of the last century. Randall Morgan had no doubt paid a fraction of what it was worth, and hadn't lost a wink of sleep in the process.

The driveway wound between the trees, following the undulations and geography of the land, a long thin road that was as well maintained as Main Street. We came over a rise and dropped down into a wide open valley.

The house was at the bottom end of a large teardrop-shaped lake, butted right up against the water. It was large enough to make the Galloways' McMansion look like a shack, a massive structure made from wood and stone. The wood had been painted a cool grey and the blockwork was as white as the municipal buildings in the town square.

Overall, the house had the look and feel of a New England hotel, but change the angle slightly and you'd see a turret or roofline straight from a French chateau. From another angle you'd see something more severe that wouldn't have looked out of place in medieval Germany. The huge fountain at the front of the house was the sort of thing you saw in the piazzas of Rome. Two large stallions were erupting from the water, naked women riding them bareback. The difference was that this fountain would have looked right in Rome. Here it just looked tacky. This house was a good argument in favour of the maxim that money didn't necessarily buy good taste.

I pulled up as close to the front door as possible. Before the engine had a chance to rumble to a stop, two security guards came out and started walking down the wide staircase. They'd probably been watching us since we turned into the driveway.

This place was like a fortress. There would be cameras hidden in the trees and motion sensors embedded in the road. The driveway was a mile long, the only way in and out. It was so long that you wouldn't need security gates. By the time anyone reached the house the whole world would know they were coming. Approaching through the trees wasn't impossible, but it would be hard work, and there were probably cameras and sensors hidden there, too.

Both guards had Glocks strapped to their waists, and they looked like they knew how to use them. They were wearing black shirts, black trousers, polished black boots. Uniforms that were almost identical to the casual clothes Taylor had been wearing yesterday.

We got out of the car and the guards met us at the bottom of the stairs. They were both larger than me, but smaller than Taylor. Six-two, six-three, somewhere in that region. The younger one was in his late thirties, his buddy maybe ten years older.

Ex-military, without a doubt. They moved like they were marching. Backs straight, shoulders straighter. Their eyes were constantly on the move, looking for danger, hands hovering near enough to their guns to draw them in a heartbeat. Special Forces was my guess. When you could afford a Gulfstream, a house like this, and you had a billion in the bank, you didn't skimp on personal security.

In my experience, money has the capacity to buy as much grief as happiness. I'd worked a number of high-ransom child kidnappings during my FBI days. I'd witnessed the moment when the news broke that the kid wasn't coming home. On a couple of occasions I'd delivered that news myself.

There aren't enough words to describe that moment when a mother realises her baby is dead. It's heart-breaking. It rips you apart. And the thing is, this isn't even your kid. You didn't know them, you'd never played with them, never laughed with them. You knew them as a face in a photograph, and a few second-hand guilt-soaked remembrances, and that was all. And it still got to you.

The older guard stepped into my personal space. An alpha male defining his territory. This was the point where I was supposed to step back. I didn't. Instead, I stood my ground and fought the temptation to look up. The guard's chin was at eye level. It was a strong chin. A GI Joe chin. If this guy wanted, he could pick me up and snap me in two, and he wouldn't even break a sweat.

"Can I help you?"

Now I looked up. "Sheriff's department. We're here to see Jasper Morgan."

The guy scoped me up and down. The white hair, the blue medical top, the jeans and the worn work boots and the smears of dried blood. He glanced over at Hannah and gave her the once-over as well, starting at her spiky hair, moving down past the Death Parade T-shirt and finishing at her scuffed sneakers. His face said that he didn't believe us for a second.

"I'm going to need to see some ID."

I nodded towards the police car. The guard looked over the top of my head, following my gaze.

"I'm going to need to see something more official."

I patted my pockets, shook my head. "I must have left my badge in my other jeans."

"I'd like you to leave now."

"Not going to happen. Not until I've spoken to your boss."

"He's not here."

"Yes he is. His receptionist said he was feeling a 'little under the weather'. Where else is he going to be other than tucked up in bed convalescing?"

The security guy was staring down at me. The angle must have been making his neck ache by now, but he couldn't step back because that would show weakness, and this guy had been programmed never to show weakness in the face of the enemy. I was fine. I could quite happily talk to his chin all day.

"Tell him Jefferson Winter is here to see him."

"Mr Morgan doesn't want to see anyone today."

"I'm sure Jasper would make an exception for me. Tell him I've come to give him an update on the Sam Galloway case."

The guard didn't move. He just stared down at me, his neck getting stiffer by the second.

"You can let him through, Smithson."

The voice came from the top of the stairs. It wasn't a shout and it wasn't loud, but it was authoritative, a voice that ended arguments. We all turned towards it. Jasper Morgan waved for me to come on up, and I dodged past Smithson and headed for the stairs, Hannah hot on my heels.

"We'll be in the lake room, Smithson."

"Very good, sir."

The three of us went inside, Jasper leading the way. We walked in silence through wide, bright corridors. There were reminders of Jasper's wealth everywhere. Expensive paintings on the walls, expensive statues on plinths, expensive marble beneath our feet.

The view from the lake room was breathtaking. The main wall was made almost entirely from glass, creating the illusion that you could dive right into the lake. The water stretched all the way to the tip of the teardrop. Beyond, the land rose up into a steep bank that disappeared into the trees. The room was sparsely furnished, just a couple of large sofas in front of the window, some side tables, and that was it. The rug was a shade darker than the light grey marble floor tiles. This room was all about that view.

Jasper waved us towards the sofas and we sat down. I studied him closely, looking for signs of stress, and saw nothing. He wasn't fidgeting or fiddling with his hands. He was calm and relaxed. It crossed my mind that I might be wrong, but if that was the case why would he be here instead of at the office? Why would he have called in pretending to be sick?

"You're looking well."

Jasper smiled a politician's smile, his tanned, leathery face folding and creasing. "And you've been talking to Susan back at the office." The smile disappeared. "You didn't come all the way out here to enquire about my health, did you?"

I shook my head.

"Okay, here's what's puzzling me. Last night at the station house, the countdown hit zero and nothing happened. At the time I assumed that the unsub had got spooked and aborted whatever it was he had planned."

Jasper was looking straight at me, not saying a word, just letting me talk.

"But what if that assumption was wrong? What if everything happened exactly how he had meant it to happen and I just hadn't noticed? What if he'd made his grand revelation and I missed it?"

"Then it obviously wasn't that grand."

"Not to me, but it's all a matter of perspective. I was expecting a rerun of Sam Galloway's death. Like everyone else in that room, I was expecting to see someone being burned alive."

Jasper had flinched ever so slightly when I mentioned Sam Galloway. The gesture was small and, on the surface, so insignificant that it could easily be written off as the result of sunlight reflecting in his eyes. It wasn't. This was the first indication that I was on the right track. He shrugged, his eyes still locked on mine.

"I was there," he said, "and I've got to say that, to me, it looked like nothing happened."

"I don't think so. There were fifty people in that room, but the unsub was playing to an audience of one. You. It was a perfect performance. Even down to the way the seats were set out. You had the best seat in the house."

"But nothing happened."

"Exactly. Nothing happened. It was a huge anti-climax. Everyone had been drawn there by the promise of blood, but nobody really wanted that to happen. Sam Galloway's death had taken the number of murders in Dayton over the past century up to twenty-one, and everyone was happy for there not to be another one. Go back a hundred years and murder wasn't that big a deal. Find a likely suspect, go through the motions of a trial, then hang them as quickly as possible. These days it's hard work. There are procedures to be followed, paperwork that needs to be filled out. It takes months to get to trial, years even. And then, when the bad guy is found guilty, he spends the next twenty years in jail waiting for the state to finally get around to executing him."

"What's your point?"

"Nobody likes murder, especially cops."

Jasper shook his head, a confused expression on his face. "I'm not following."

"After the countdown hit zero and everyone realised nothing was going to happen, the overriding emotion in the room was relief. People were laughing and joking and acting like it was a party. And you were in a party mood, too. When I spoke to you outside the station house, you were dancing up there on cloud nine."

"Nobody else had been killed, of course I was happy about that."

"Of course you were, but you're the mayor. You need to be seen to be above these sort of things, yet there you were acting like one of the boys."

"You're reading too much into this."

"Am I? This was personal for you, that's why you acted the way you did. If it hadn't been personal, you would have acted differently. You would have been aloof, distant. You would have acted cool. You wouldn't have joined the party. You're the big man around here. The richest man in town. You're not one of the boys. So, what did you think was going to happen when the countdown hit zero?"

We were staring at each other. All that mattered was the distance between us. The room had shrunk until it was big enough to hold just the two of us. That fantastic storybook view of the lake and the forest had blurred into insignificance. Even Hannah had ceased to exist.

"You actually had a pretty good idea of what was going to happen, didn't you? And things played out exactly how you imagined they would. That's why you were on such a high. You thought you'd outsmarted the killer. So, how did that work out for you, Jasper?"

CHAPTER SIXTY-THREE

Jasper sat staring out over the lake for the longest time. We'd reached a junction and this conversation could go one of three ways. Either we'd get as much of the truth as Jasper knew, or we'd get a sanitised version of the truth, or Jasper would start shouting for his lawyers and his security people. I was aware again of Hannah beside me. She was breathing gently, keeping her thoughts to herself.

"You're guessing," Jasper said finally.

"I am. But judging by your reaction, I'm in the right ballpark. There are some things I know, some things I think I know, and in-between there's all sorts of speculation and assumptions."

Jasper turned to face me. He looked much older than he did last night. "Okay. Let's start with what you know."

"Sam Galloway is the key to all this. He always has been, right from the start."

Jasper flinched again at the mention of Sam's name. The expression was almost non-existent, the tiniest twitch of his facial muscles as a spark of electricity burst through his nervous system. He tried to hide it, but couldn't quite contain the emotion. If this had been a poker game, if the stakes had been lower, he would have managed it. He had a great poker face.

"You told me that Sam was like a son to you."

I watched carefully, and caught another of those facial twitches. I was thinking on my feet, using those tiny twitches to lead me closer to the truth. A big piece of the puzzle suddenly dropped into place. It fitted so perfectly it had to be right.

"Sam wasn't just *like* a son, was he? Sam *was* your son."

It was almost as if Jasper grew bigger in front of me. For a moment I thought he was going to fight me on this one, and then he suddenly deflated, crumpling in on himself. He put his head in his hands and sighed a long sigh. When he took his hands away he no longer looked like the big man, he just looked like any other parent whose child had been brutally murdered. This was someone who had been cut adrift in an empty, infinite universe with no chance of finding their way back home again, because the place they'd once called home no longer existed.

"Yes, Sam was my son," he confirmed quietly.

I nodded like this explained everything. It didn't. It explained a lot of things but not everything. It explained how a small-town lawyer like Sam could afford such a lavish lifestyle. Basically, he couldn't afford it. He was being bankrolled by Jasper. That in turn explained why Barbara was so desperate to protect Sam's secret. She had a standard of living that she was keen to maintain.

"Sam wasn't the real target here," I continued. "He was murdered to get at you. If he hadn't been your son he'd be alive right now, living the illusion of domestic bliss. He'd probably have a smaller house but it would still be in McArthur Heights, and he'd be driving something a little less snazzy than a Ferrari, but at least he'd be alive."

I stared out at the lake, puzzle pieces tumbling randomly around my head. They fell into place, fell out of place, ideas in a state of constant motion. Some parts of the picture made sense, other parts didn't. In some places I was too close to the picture and all I could see were the blurred curves and lines of the joins between the pieces.

"That's why you kept Clayton close by last night. You'd lost one son, you didn't want to lose another."

Jasper nodded. "When I saw that clock counting down, I figured that whoever did this would probably go after Clayton next. Clayton doesn't have kids. At the moment he's the last of the Morgans. He dies, the family name dies with him. Anyone who knows me knows that would hit me hard. I've been on at the boy to start a family for years, but he's always telling me it's not the right time. It's never the right goddamn time."

"You also figured that the safest place for him to be when the clock hit zero was in a roomful of cops. That's why you were so confident that nothing would happen."

"I'm not going to deny that. I want to protect my family. Since when has that been a crime?"

"Where's Clayton now?"

"He's here at the house. He's been here since last night. Him and his wife. I've doubled my security detail, too. We're safe here."

"Okay, let's talk motive. Revenge or money? Which one is it?"

Jasper's face twitched as he tried to suppress another spark of electricity flashing through his nervous system.

"What are you hiding, Jasper? If I'm going to help you then you need to be straight with me. I can catch the person who did this, but I need your co-operation."

"Can I have a cigarette?"

"Sure." I handed over the pack and the lighter. He shook out a cigarette and lit it.

"It's money. When I got home last night there was an email in my personal account telling me that Clayton would be next unless I paid twenty million dollars. There were details for a Swiss bank account that I'm supposed to wire the money to."

"You haven't paid the money yet?"

"Not yet. It takes time to get that sort of money together. I've been given until midnight, but I'm almost there."

"Don't pay."

Jasper just stared at me. "Why the hell not? If anything happens to Clayton, then how am I going to live with myself? Of course I'm going to pay. It would be crazy not to."

He stopped short of saying it was only money. It wasn't. Twenty million was a significant amount of cash to lose. Even for a billionaire.

"No, what would be crazy is making that payment. If you do that, what's to stop the blackmailer coming back for more? Because that's the way blackmailers operate. The first payment is the hardest one. That's the hook. Once you've paid the first time it gets easier. Before you know it, you're dangling from that hook and the blackmailer just keeps coming back for more. Also, nobody's going to kill Clayton."

"You can't know that for sure."

"He knows about Sam Galloway, right?"

Jasper nodded. "I told him everything."

"When?"

"Yesterday afternoon."

"And you're certain that he didn't know anything before that?"

"I'm certain."

The words projected confidence, but his tone betrayed the tiniest amount of uncertainty. Doubt was sneaky and cancerous. Given the opportunity, it could eat into even the strongest of beliefs.

"And how did he take the news that he had a brother?"

"He was angry that I hadn't told him sooner, but he accepts my decision not to say anything."

"From what I've heard, Clayton has spent years accepting your decisions. Ever since he was born you've told him what to do and what to think. It might say CEO on his door but everyone around here knows who really calls the shots. Deal with that crap day in, day out for long enough and you're going to end up really pissed."

"What are you saying?"

"I'm saying that I want to talk to Clayton, and I want to talk to him now."

CHAPTER SIXTY-FOUR

Jasper left the room to go find his son, and I got up and walked over to the window. Even right up close, the illusion that you could lean forward and tumble into the lake still held. The glass was hot under my hand, the sun blazing down. The water was a bright Mediterranean blue around the edges, dark and forbidding in the middle where it was deepest.

Hannah was on the sofa, reflected in the glass. She had her cellphone pressed against her ear and, judging by the lack of facial expression, there was no news on Taylor. No relief, no grief. No emotion at all. Head down, she stared stony-faced at the pale grey rug.

I didn't care what she said. Right now, no news was good news. The longer this went on, the longer Hannah would remain tethered to her old life. Once the call came through to tell her Taylor was dead, she'd be the one who was cut adrift with no way home. Sometimes the final cut came via the telephone, or that midnight knock on the door, and sometimes the FBI came swooping in and you discovered that someone you thought you'd known your entire life was a complete stranger.

I took out my cell and called Shepherd. He answered almost immediately.

"I've found your unsub."

"Who?"

"Clayton Morgan."

There was a momentary hesitation while he processed this. A sharp intake of breath. "Is this some sort of joke, Winter?"

"No joke. Clayton's your guy. How long will it take you to get to Jasper Morgan's place?"

"I can be there in ten minutes."

"If you've got someone close by send them up here to block off the driveway. You're also going to need to get someone out to the airfield. The Morgans own a helicopter and a Gulfstream. I don't think Clayton's a flight risk but let's not give him the opportunity."

"No problem." There was a heavy sigh on the other end of the line. "Clayton Morgan. You're certain about this?"

"No doubt whatsoever."

"Jasper Morgan's not going to be happy."

"Not my problem. My job is to catch them. Once that's done, I'm out of here, and you guys get to clean up the mess."

"Ten minutes." Shepherd hung up.

Hannah had come up alongside me while I was talking. She was staring out the window, lost in the landscape.

"How's Taylor?" I asked.

"Still in surgery. He's had his spleen removed." Her voice was as dead as her eyes.

"If he's in surgery, he's still alive, Hannah."

"And if this is leading up to a glass-is-half-full lecture, save your breath."

If Taylor didn't pull through, there was a good chance that she wasn't going to make it either. She wasn't like Barbara Galloway. She didn't possess her hardness, or her ruthlessness. Hannah projected strength, but a lot of that strength came from Taylor. He was her talisman. He was the magic feather that made it possible for her to fly.

Hannah stared through the glass. No doubt she was wishing that today had never dawned, praying that this was all a nightmare and she was going to wake up at any second.

"You said he was a cop." Hannah was speaking to her reflection.

"I was ninety-nine per cent certain he was a cop."

"Is that your way of saying you're wrong?"

"No, it's my way of saying that it's time to make things right again."

"If Clayton Morgan was here all morning, how was he able to attack Taylor?"

"Jasper *said* he was here. That's not the same thing. People lie all the time. Would, Jasper would lie to protect his son? Of course, he would."

"But what if he's telling the truth? What if Clayton was here?"

"Then he paid someone else to do it. Throw enough money at a problem and you're eventually going to find a solution. Clayton's the CEO of a billion-dollar corporation, he's got access to more than enough cash to find a solution to that particular problem."

Hannah turned to face me. "Okay, but if Clayton's got all that money, why blackmail his father?"

"I'd rather not get into all that now since I'm going to have to go through it all again when Jasper and Clayton get here."

Hannah's eyes were blazing, like the lights had suddenly come back on. Her anger was righteous and justified, and a vast improvement on self-pity.

"You'd 'rather not get into it'? Jesus, Winter. This isn't some game, you know."

"But that's exactly what it is. A game. The unsub makes a move, we make a countermove, and at the end of it all someone wins and someone loses."

"But people get hurt. People die."

"Do you think the bad guys worry about any of that?" I shook my head. "Of course they don't. And if I'm going to catch them, I can't either. There's a time for emotion, and that time is after they've been brought down."

Hannah sighed and turned away. She stared at her reflection for a moment, stared at the view, then turned back to me.

"What if you're wrong about this one, too? What if Clayton's innocent? What then?"

"You need to have a little more faith, Hannah. Trust me, I know what I'm doing."

Hannah snorted and shook her head in a way that made it obvious she wasn't a believer. I looked out at the view, losing myself for a moment in the vastness of the landscape. The water, the sky, the trees. There was something grounding about having all that nature so close.

I adjusted my vision so I was staring at my reflection. Faint traces of Taylor's blood still remained on my face. Dressed in dirty jeans and old work boots and that cheap blue medical top, I looked a mess. This outfit was as far removed from the uniform I'd worn when I was with the FBI as it was possible to get. The dark G-men suits, the shiny black shoes, the impenetrable sunglasses. The only thing I'd kept from those days were the shades. I shut my eyes and felt Taylor's chest compressing under my hands, felt the faint rhythm of his pulse in my fingertips.

"You'd better know what you're doing," Hannah muttered behind me.

"Watch and learn," I whispered to her reflection. "Watch and learn."

CHAPTER SIXTY-FIVE

I was standing with my back to the room, using the window as a mirror, when Jasper arrived with Clayton. I didn't turn around, didn't say a word, just watched them file into the lake room through the wide double doors. Hannah was beside me again, looking out over the lake.

The two men chose to stand, which was an obvious and understandable power play. I was standing, therefore they needed to stand as well. Sitting would have put them at a distinct psychological disadvantage.

I hadn't paid much attention to Clayton last night. Despite his job title he'd seemed so insignificant next to his father, a lost little boy rather than a CEO. The shadow cast by his father was large and looming, and had completely eclipsed him.

The idea that Clayton was Jasper's puppet was easy to buy into. It was hard to imagine Clayton ever having an original thought. Jasper would have done his best to squash that out of him years ago. And the sad thing was that Jasper probably thought he was doing him a favour. Spare the rod, spoil the child. What a crock.

I was paying plenty of attention to Clayton now. He looked nervous, and he looked more lost than ever.

He looked like he'd just been given a good scolding by his father. His head was down and he was glaring at the rug. His face was bleached white and he didn't know what to do with his hands. There was plenty of repressed rage there, and he didn't know what to do with that, either. He was in his early forties, but the stress of the situation made him appear much older.

All that was missing were the cops. According to my watch it had been nine and a half minutes since I'd spoken to Shepherd. Their cars would have been picked up by the cameras when they turned into the driveway. The fact that Jasper and Clayton had chosen to turn up now meant they must almost be here.

The silence that filled the room was stretched to breaking point. Every now and again there would be a slight disruption. A movement, a clearing of the throat, the scratch of a shirtsleeve against skin when someone checked their watch. It's impossible for four people to stay completely silent, particularly when they're trying to stay quiet.

John Cage understood that. 4′33″ was his most controversial composition, and his most misunderstood. People assume it's four minutes of silence. It's not. The noise created by the audience is the music. It's a genius concept. Minimalism taken to its ultimate conclusion.

The cops arrived a couple of minutes later, long enough for almost half of Cage's masterwork to be performed. They came into the room in single file. Sheriff Fortier was first, then Shepherd, Barker and, finally, Romero.

Fortier marched straight up to Jasper. There was a good half a foot difference in their heights. The sheriff's eyeline was level with Jasper's mouth. "I'm sorry about all this, really and truly. We'll be out of here as soon as possible and you folks can get on with the rest of your day."

"Wait a minute." I turned from the window. "We've got ourselves a viable suspect here. We've got motive, opportunity and means. What you're going to do is escort Clayton back to the station house so we can question him."

Fortier marched up to me. His face was red, his blood pressure through the roof. We were standing toe-to-toe, and he had to angle his head up to meet my eye. I looked a mess, but his uniform was as immaculate as ever, creases in all the right places, shoes shining and not a single hair out of place.

"Let me tell you exactly what's going to happen here. We're going to leave these good folks in peace, and then I'm going to personally drive you over to Shreveport and make sure you get on the first flight out of here." He turned to Jasper. "Once again, I can't apologise enough for this misunderstanding."

Jasper waved the apology away like it was something inconsequential, like this sort of thing happened all the time. Like it was no big deal that his son had been accused of murder.

"Big mistake," I said, and Fortier glared at me. "You were brought up in Eagle Creek, right?"

Fortier nodded. "What the hell's that got to do with anything?"

"So you've known Clayton since he was a boy. And Jasper's known you since you were a boy. That's the way things work around here, right? Everybody knows everyone else's business. The Clayton you know couldn't be involved in something like this. No way. Now, the problem with that line of thinking is that it's based on the idea that we can truly know another human being. We can't. Most of us don't even know what's going on in our own hearts and heads, never mind what's going on in someone else's."

"Clayton Morgan had nothing to do with Sam Galloway's murder. I'd stake my life on it."

I let my gaze drift around the room, studying each face in turn. Taking it all in. Jasper and Sheriff Fortier looked ready to blow. Shepherd looked like a man who knew he had the law on his side. Barker and Romero looked like they were waiting to be told what to do. And Hannah looked destroyed. The room was big, but there were still too many mixed emotions competing for space.

"Is nobody interested in what I've got to say?" I asked. "No one?"

"I am," said Hannah, earning a glare from Sheriff Fortier.

I looked at Jasper. He called the shots around these parts.

"So what do you say, Jasper? If you're so sure your son's innocent, what have you got to lose? I say my piece and it turns out I'm wrong, then you guys end up vindicated and I end up looking like a fool." I smiled. "But what if I'm right? What then? How's that going to reflect on you? I'll tell you exactly how that one's going to look. It's going to look like you were covering up for your son, and that's bad for business. Whatever you choose to do, Clayton will need to be investigated. One way or another, the truth will come out."

Jasper sighed and shook his head. For now, he was keeping a lid on his temper, but it was a real effort. His fists were clenched tight, the whites of his knuckles contrasting against his sun-blasted skin.

"You're wrong. There's no way my boy's involved in this. But, what the hell. Knock yourself out. Say what you've got to say, and then I want you the hell out of my house."

"Okay, let's talk motive. We've got a blackmail demand for twenty million dollars, so this must be about money, right?" I shook my head. "Wrong. This one's all about revenge. It's beautiful really. What's the one thing that means the most to you, Jasper? And I'll give you a clue. It's not your family, and it's not Eagle Creek."

Everyone was staring at me, nobody saying a word. The room had gone very quiet. Not completely silent, though. This was a silence that John Cage would have understood, and appreciated. It was a dark silence, one filled with foreboding.

"The answer is Morgan Holdings. The company is your legacy. It was here long before you were born, and you want to believe it'll be here long after you're gone. And you want it run by a Morgan. That's important to you. The fact that Clayton hasn't produced an heir really pisses you off. Your son is implicated in a murder and you still find time to be angry that there aren't any grandchildren running around the place. That's pretty screwed up if you ask me."

I looked away from Jasper and turned to face the rest of the room. Six pairs of eyes stared back. I could smell my own sweat and, beneath that, the faint aroma of Taylor's blood. It would take a week of showers to get rid of the smell of his blood, maybe longer. Maybe I'd never get rid of it.

"For those of you not up to speed, Jasper received a blackmail demand for twenty million dollars last night. Now *that's* the really cool part of Clayton's plan. That first payment is just the start. Its main purpose is to get the ball rolling. Clayton would have chosen that figure carefully. It needed to be big enough to hurt the company, but not so big that it would kill it. If that had been the case, Jasper would have had no choice but to escalate this and bring in the FBI. Right now, he wants to keep things as quiet as possible. He wants to keep this in-house. If it gets out that he's being blackmailed, that's going to be bad for business."

"You need to make your mind up," Fortier put in. "One second you're saying this isn't about money, the next you're saying it is."

"And you're not paying attention. The blackmail demand is a means to an end. Clayton hates his father. He despises him. He wants to destroy him, and that means destroying the thing he loves most. The company. Work it through and you'll see I'm right. Jasper pays up, then a few months later another demand comes through. A smaller amount this time.

Five million, say. So Jasper liquidates some more assets and pays up. And so the cycle continues, the company slowly eroding away until there's nothing left. It doesn't matter if you're dealing with millions or thousands, that's how blackmailers operate. You get that ball rolling, then bleed your mark dry."

I paused, gave it another second for everything to sink in. All eyes were still on me, and the room was as quiet as the station house just before the countdown hit zero. Clayton met my eye, then quickly looked away. His hair was a mess from running his hands through it, and his frown lines ran deep. Given another decade or two they'd be as deep as the trenches that lined his father's weatherworn face.

"But Jasper's not stupid," I went on. "He's an astute businessman. He's going to hire an army of private investigators to hunt down the blackmailer. And these will be good, competent men. Former cops, ex-FBI, the best money can buy. Except nobody's going to look too hard at Clayton, and why should they? Why the hell would Clayton be trying to destroy his own company?"

I nodded to myself. "It's a good plan, and what I love most is the way Clayton has manoeuvred himself into a position where Jasper is actually protecting him. That's genius. Absolutely brilliant." I grinned at Clayton. "Your father seriously underestimated you, didn't he?"

"That's crazy. I had nothing to do with Sam's murder, and I'm not blackmailing my father."

I studied Clayton carefully. Again, he met my eye for the briefest of seconds before looking away. "You're a good liar. I'll give you that much."

"I'm not lying."

"You hate your father, though, don't you?"

Head down, Clayton bit his lip and said nothing.

"And there's your motive right there."

"But where's the proof?" said Fortier. "Where's the evidence? So far all I've heard is speculation."

"You guys are the cops, you go and find the evidence. My job was to hunt down Sam Galloway's killer, and that's what I've done." I put my hands together like I was about say a prayer, pressed my fingertips against my lips then took them away again. "If I was in your shoes, I'd want to get Clayton into an interview room double-quick and see what he has to say for himself."

"Winter's got a point, sir," Shepherd broke in. He was stroking his moustache, his face thoughtful. "We don't have enough to charge Clayton, but he does have motive. We need to at least talk to him."

Fortier stood paralysed for a second, then he shook his head and let out a long weary sigh. It was a sigh burdened by the weight of an unfair and unforgiving world. "I'm really sorry about this, Jasper, but we're going to have to take Clayton in. Don't worry, though, we'll get this sorted out. We'll have him back by suppertime, I promise you that."

Shepherd waved Barker and Romero forward, and nodded in the general direction of Clayton Morgan. The two cops walked over to him.

"I'm real sorry about this, Mr Morgan," Barker told him.

Clayton just stood there, shaking his head from side to side. "I'm not going anywhere."

"Look, I don't want to handcuff you, not in front of these folks, but if needs be, I will."

Clayton was staring at his shoes like they were the most interesting things in the room, even more interesting than that spectacular view. I'd seen plenty of broken people over the years. Clayton looked totally beaten down, like life had finally knocked him into submission.

And he looked as guilty as hell.

I waited until the three of them reached the door, then said, "Hold it a second. I've changed my mind. Clayton didn't do it. He's innocent."

Six pairs of eyes stopped looking at Clayton and turned to look at me.

CHAPTER SIXTY-SIX

"That's the thing with lies. Inject them with just the right amount of truth and you can make anything sound plausible. You can make believers out of anyone."

Everyone just stared. Jasper Morgan and Sheriff Fortier looked as furious as ever, but there was a touch of uncertainty that hadn't been there before. I could see a faint reflection of my face in Shepherd's glasses. The corners of my mouth were turned up into an expression that could easily become a grin if left unchecked. It mirrored how I felt, but it was inappropriate for the situation. I swapped it for my best game face. Serious, unflinching, challenging.

"You guys remember Dan Choat, right? The guilt-ridden cop who committed suicide after murdering Sam Galloway? That was a good attempt at creating a plausible lie. Most people believed it, and the reason they believed was because the unsub made a good choice with Choat. All the ingredients were there. The messed-up childhood, the overbearing mother, classic stuff."

I stopped talking and shook my head.

"Unfortunately that little illusion was built on shifting sand. That's the other thing with lies, you need to get the fine details right. Where our unsub screwed up was the suicide note. The reason you leave a suicide note is because this is the biggest thing you've done in your whole miserable life and you need people to understand why you're doing it. If you don't want people to understand, you don't write a note. It's that simple. Now, when you sit down to write that note, do you think you're going to find the right words straight off? No way. You're going to write and rewrite and rewrite. You're going to end up with a wastepaper bin full of false starts. But not Choat. His note was written on the first sheet of the pad. He got it right first time."

I stopped talking and smiled. The room was so quiet that if a pin had dropped it would have sounded as loud as a church bell.

"That was mistake number one. Mistake number two was the content of the note. Nobody's going to leave a one-word suicide note. *No one*. It's as pointless as decaffeinated coffee. After all his deliberations, the best Choat could come up with was 'sorry'. Sorry for what? Sorry to whom? Like I said, the whole point of a suicide note is to explain why you're killing yourself. To justify the act. To try and inject some meaning into your existence."

"What the hell is this?" Jasper bellowed. "And why am I listening to this bullshit? Someone get this idiot out of my sight now."

Jasper had finally found his voice. It had taken a while but he'd got there in the end. He looked like he'd be happy to shoot me dead where I stood.

I put my hands up in mock surrender. "Hey, you should be the happiest man on the planet right now. Your son's innocent. He's not going to prison. You've got someone to make sure the family firm keeps running long after you're dead and gone. Yes, he hates you, but at least he didn't try to destroy you. Not that that was ever really on the cards. We both know he doesn't have the balls for that. Any fight he had in him, you'd knocked out by the time he was in kindergarten."

Jasper turned to Sheriff Fortier. His hands were clenched into fists again, the knuckles shining white. He looked like he wanted to hit someone or something. It didn't really matter what, although I had the distinct impression that I would be his first choice for a punching bag.

"I want him out of my house now. Do I make myself clear?"

Barker and Romero had moved away from Clayton and were coming towards me. Barker was reaching for his gun. Romero was reaching for his handcuffs. I put my hand up to stop them, but they kept coming.

"Before you kick me out, I need to say one last thing. Most of you bought that story about Clayton blackmailing Jasper, but that was flawed from the ground up, just like Dan Choat's suicide. Doesn't anyone want to know why?"

"Get him out of here," Fortier shouted. The sheriff looked almost as furious as Jasper.

"It's because the guy you're looking for is a cop."

I was watching Jasper carefully, studying him. Right now he was the only person in this room who mattered.

Barker and Romero had stopped dead and were just staring around, waiting for instructions.

"Okay that's enough," Shepherd said. "You're clutching at straws. There's no way this guy's a cop."

I walked up to Shepherd and stopped in front of him. We were so close our noses were almost touching, close enough that I could smell his aftershave. I was invading his personal space, but he was standing his ground.

"You had no problem believing that Choat was the unsub. Okay, it turned out that he wasn't, but that doesn't mean another cop can't be behind this. You, for example."

Shepherd laughed and shook his head. "Like I said, you're clutching at straws."

"This explains why Taylor's in hospital. That one really bugged me, you know. The actual why is straightforward enough. You wanted a distraction. However, because of Taylor's size, the how was trickier to answer. If Barker or Romero or anyone else had tried to take him out, he would have knocked them into the middle of next week. It'd be them in the hospital, not him. And he would have been watching out for a move like that." I smiled at Shepherd. "You're a different matter, though. You could have caught him off guard. You were one of the first names that went up on our list of suspects, and one of the first names that had a line put through it. So how did you do it?"

"If this is another one of your stunts, it's not funny."

We were more or less the same height. One second I was looking into his eyes, the next I was staring at my reflection in his spectacles, my perspective shifting and changing. I gave him a second to respond but he just stood there staring, his mouth shut tight.

"Okay, I'll tell you exactly how you did it. You waited until everyone else was busy, then asked Taylor to go fetch something from the trunk of your car. Then you wandered over, pretending like there was something else you needed. You were smiling and chatting and doing your best to keep him off guard. As soon as you were close enough, you injected him with a tranquilliser, something powerful enough to take down an elephant, and tipped him into the trunk. Then you drove around to the storage shed and parked as close to the door as possible and dragged him inside. Then you beat him half to death and headed back to the crime scene before you were missed."

"You've got an overactive imagination, Winter."

I laughed at that, and saw a flash of anger spark behind those spectacles. It was there and gone so fast I could have imagined it. But I hadn't. That reaction was as good as a confession in my book.

"And that's the wrong response. Someone in your position gets accused of something like this, they come out fighting. They're going to tell you they didn't do it in no uncertain terms. They're going to be shouting from the highest rooftop."

"What's my motive?"

I took a step back and turned to Jasper. "That's a good question. So what's his motive, Jasper?"

"How the hell should I know?"

"Because your first reaction was to look at Shepherd. By my reckoning he should have been third on the list. Clayton comes first, then Sheriff Fortier because he's the most senior police officer in the room. And then Shepherd because he's the second most senior officer. But you didn't do any of that. You looked straight at Shepherd. Why?"

I glanced at Shepherd, glanced back at Jasper. Another glance at Shepherd. Another glance at Jasper. Comparing and contrasting. I looked over at Clayton, then turned my attention back to Shepherd.

"It's the eyes. There's obviously a dominant gene there. The glasses and the moustache are a nice touch, by the way. They take the focus away from your eyes."

"What's he taking about?" said Clayton.

"Meet your other half-brother."

Clayton just stared at me as though I'd proclaimed Shepherd to be the reincarnation of Elvis. He had a dumb expression on his face and his mouth kept opening and closing like there were words trapped in his throat but he didn't know how to get them out.

"Bullshit," said Shepherd. He nodded to Barker. "Get him the hell out of here."

"It's okay, I'll go. But first I want Jasper to tell me I've got this one wrong." It was Shepherd's turn to glare at me like he wanted me dead. I looked at Jasper. "The floor's all yours."

Jasper walked slowly over to Shepherd and stopped in front of him. Standing together like that, more similarities became apparent. The shape of their noses, the cut of their cheekbones. They were the same height.

Jasper's hair was as white as mine. Shepherd's was heading in that direction.

"Why?" Jasper asked.

There was a long silence. Shepherd was looking at Jasper, Jasper was looking at Shepherd, and everyone else was watching the two of them, just waiting for something to happen. Shepherd broke the spell by laughing. His laughter was dry and brittle and completely devoid of humour.

"You really don't get it, do you?"

"I don't, but I want to understand. I *need* to understand."

Shepherd sighed and shook his head like he couldn't believe he had to spell out something that was so obvious.

"Sam had that big house up in McArthur Heights and that Ferrari, all paid for by you. You could even argue that you bought his wife. A loser like Sam, if he hadn't had your money to spend there's no way he would have been able to afford a woman like that. Then there's Clayton. When you die he gets everything. Where does that leave me?"

"I've always made sure you were all right. You wanted to be the next sheriff. I was going to make that happen."

"And you still don't get it." Shepherd shook his head and snorted. "I want the Ferrari and the Gulfstream and the big house, but even though I'm your son I can't have any of that. A cop buys a Ferrari and people ask questions."

Jasper's eyes widened in disbelief. "This is about money?"

Another shake of the head. Another snort of laughter. "Of course it's about money. When you get right down to it, everything's always about money."

"You should have said something, I would have given you money."

"And you're still not hearing me. What was I going to say when people started asking questions? That I'd won the lottery? I guess you could have told the truth about me being your son. Except that wasn't going to happen because then you'd have to acknowledge your relationship with my mother. The fact you fathered a child with a waitress really wouldn't do your public image any good, would it? How's that one going to look up at the golf club?"

"I always made sure your mother was well taken care of."

"No, you bought her silence. Big difference."

"A quick question." The two men turned to me, surprised. They were so wrapped up in their own drama that they had forgotten there were other people in the room. "Your mother's dead, right? And I'm betting this happened fairly recently."

"She died last month," said Shepherd. "But what the hell's that got to do with anything?"

I nodded to myself as another piece of the puzzle fell into place. "That figures. If you're going to go crazy and start burning up your half-brother just because he's got a better car than you, then there's got to be some sort of trigger. As far as triggers go, a bereavement is right up there near the top of the list."

Shepherd stared at me, eyes blazing, cheeks red. He looked like he wanted to kill me, and I realised that I'd inadvertently crossed that line again. Then his expression softened, but what it changed to was worse. One second his face was twisted with fury, the next there was a kind of blank serenity there. I'd seen that look before on some old CCTV footage during my FBI days. This was the face of a suicide bomber a second before the explosion.

In the time it took my brain to catch up with what was happening Shepherd already had his Glock out. I started moving towards him with no idea what I was going to do when I got there. The instructors at Quantico had tried to teach me about self-defence and hand-to-hand combat. Tried and failed.

Before I'd covered half the distance it was already too late. The first bullet hit Jasper in the chest, and the second took the back of his head off.

CHAPTER SIXTY-SEVEN

Shepherd swung the gun towards me and I skidded to a halt in front of him. He reached out and grabbed a fistful of the blue medical top, then spun me around and dragged me into a tight embrace. The Glock drilled into my right temple, hot metal burning into my skin. Shepherd ducked behind me so he could use my body as a shield. We were right up against that wide panoramic window, so close that Shepherd must have been touching the glass.

There was a patter of footsteps, and Smithson and his buddy ran into the room. The two security men already had their guns out and were aiming in our direction. They looked pissed at having read this one so wrong, but they also looked serious, like they were anxious to make amends. Barker and Romero were fumbling with their holsters, panicked looks on their faces, guns popping out one after the other.

I could see Hannah in my peripheral vision. Her eyes were wide open and her mouth was frozen into an O. Jasper was lying off to my left, his blood draining out onto the expensive rug, red appearing black against the pale grey background. An average male has around eight pints of blood. All nice and tidy when it's contained, but it makes a hell of a mess when it gets out.

The smell of Jasper's death filled the room. Death, the great leveller. It didn't matter if you were a homeless guy wearing odd shoes or one of the richest men on the planet, there was little dignity in death.

Shepherd pushed the gun harder into my temple. His left arm was snaked around my throat, restricting the blood flowing through my carotid artery. There wasn't enough air getting into my lungs. I felt strangely weightless, like I was about to float away. My legs were tingling, my vision was turning to grey static, and I was getting close to unconsciousness.

I fought the urge to struggle, fought the urge to fight. Do that and I'd just be using up precious oxygen. It wasn't easy. I wanted to run, wanted to fight, but I still had enough of a grip on the situation to know that wouldn't get me anywhere. I locked eyes with Smithson. The security guy was moving his gun around, searching for a clear line of sight. His face was expressionless. If he was frustrated, it wasn't showing.

"Shoot him." My words were aimed at Smithson. They were desperate and barely audible, the volume crushed to nothing by Shepherd's arm.

Shepherd drilled the gun even harder into my temple. It felt like he was pushing the gun right into my brain. "He does that you're going to die. Is that what you want?"

"Shoot him," I hissed again.

It was all I could manage, and even that was too much effort. I had more to say, words that could buy my freedom, but they were lodged in my throat, lodged in my brain. Given time, I could unravel this puzzle. There was always a solution. I could find a way out of this. But my brain was slowing down and I couldn't think straight. Nor could I see straight. Everything was a blur. I was vaguely aware of Smithson, vaguely aware of Hannah.

The world was getting darker. Any second now it was going to turn black and that would be that. I was attached to this world by the thinnest of threads, and when that thread finally snapped I was going to float right through the glass and get picked up by the water, and then I was going to float right on out of here.

A sudden blur sparked in the left side of my field of vision. This was it. This was the moment when the lights went out for ever.

A single gunshot.

The sharp high-pitched insistence of glass shattering.

The thread snapped and I was floating through the air. Far in the distance, I heard the haunting sound of Mozart's clarinet and I had time to wonder if I was finally going to get the answer to that particular puzzle.

One by one the lights winked out until there was only darkness left.

CHAPTER SIXTY-EIGHT

I stood in front of the hospital with my face turned up to the sun, enjoying the moment. When you come face to face with your own mortality, for a short while afterwards you become hyper-aware. Your senses explode with the sheer majesty of the world around you. Sights, sounds, smells, taste, touch, everything is brighter and more vivid.

It doesn't last long, a couple of days, a week at most. Slowly the dials are wound back down until your feet touch the ground again and you discover that you're just one more person amongst seven billion other souls, and like everyone else out there you're just doing your best to get through another day.

Nothing lasts for ever, everything is in a constant state of flux. That's one of the basic truths that the universe turns on, and I accept that. For now, though, I was happy to enjoy the feel of the sun on my skin, and the symphony created by the world going on around me. I was happy to lose myself in the simple smells of a hot summer day.

I really thought I'd died.

Twenty-four hours had passed since then. I'd had a whole day to work out what had happened, to get some sort of perspective, and I'd filled in most of the blanks.

It was Hannah who'd saved my life. She was the blur of movement I'd caught out of the corner of my eye just before I lost consciousness. She'd charged Shepherd, knocking him off balance, and giving Smithson the clear line of sight he needed to take his shot. The bullet had gone clean through Shepherd's skull and shattered one of those big panes of glass, then the three of us had tumbled out and ended up in the lake.

I'd already regained consciousness by the time I was pulled coughing and spluttering from the water. Somehow I'd escaped without a scratch. My throat was sore from where Shepherd had crushed it and there was a small burn mark on my temple from the Glock, but they were my only injuries. Hannah hadn't got off so lightly. She'd caught herself on the broken window and had needed stitches. If I could have taken those injuries for her, I would have done so in a heartbeat. That girl was my hero.

Taylor would have been proud.

I walked into the hospital, a cheque for a hundred thousand dollars made out to Hannah Hayden folded into the back pocket of my jeans. Unfortunately, the money was coming out of my account. Jasper wasn't around to sign off on my expenses, and Clayton was being an asshole. He blamed me for his father's death and was withholding my fee.

I could afford to take the hit. I had my stocks and shares, I earned good money, and my outgoings were negligible. Day-to-day expenses were covered by whoever I was working for. Hotel bills, meals, whisky.

My mortgage was paid off, and since I hadn't been back to Virginia in a while, my utility bills were next to zero. A nominal amount went out on electricity since the lights were on a timer to deter burglars, and I paid a security firm to look in on the place from time to time, and once a month a groundskeeping firm tidied the yard. And that was about it.

The only thing I had to buy were my cigarettes.

The elevator stopped at the third floor and I walked into a wide, brightly lit corridor that was filled with hospital noises and smells. A black couple were coming towards me. They were in their late forties. Tall, fit, lean. The woman smiled when she saw me. She was dressed in bright reds and yellows and had a large silver crucifix on a chain around her neck. She held her hand out and we shook. She kept hold of my hand in both of hers. It was warm and soft. She smelled faintly of lavender.

"It's so good to meet you. Taylor has told us so much about you. I'm Rosa, by the way." She smiled at her husband. "And this is Malcolm."

"Good to meet you both. How's he doing?"

"Better." Rosa was still clutching my hand like she might never let go. "Thank you for saving my son."

Rosa smiled at me a while longer before finally letting go. Then it was Malcolm's turn to take hold of my hand and shake it. He was almost as big as his son, only an inch or two shorter. In his face I caught a glimpse of the man Taylor would become. It was a good face. There was strength there, pride, integrity.

Malcolm's hand engulfed mine, his skin rough from a lifetime of hard, manual labour.

"Thank you," he said.

I didn't know what to say, or where to look. I'm not good with praise, and this praise was unjustified. If I'd read the situation better then Taylor wouldn't be here. These people were thanking me when they should have been chasing me out of town.

"Is he awake?"

"He drifts in and out," Rosa said. "But he was awake when we left and I'm sure he'd love to see you."

We said goodbye and they walked over to the bank of elevators. I walked on for a couple of steps then came to a dead stop. Something Rosa said had just registered. If I hadn't been so preoccupied I would have picked up on it sooner. I hurried back to the elevators and got there just as the door was opening.

"Rosa," I called out.

She turned around. "Is everything all right?"

"Yeah, everything's fine. When we were talking just now, you called your son Taylor."

She gave me a puzzled look. "That's his name. What else am I going to call him?"

"No, you don't understand. You're his mother. Mothers always call their kids by their first name. And no contractions, either, they always use the whole thing. Robert instead of Rob. Michael instead of Mike. I think there might even be something about it in the Constitution."

She nodded and smiled, understanding lighting up in her eyes. "Taylor is his first name."

It was my turn to look puzzled.

"It's probably best if Malcolm explains this one."

Malcolm shook his head in a way that made it obvious he'd been here before, many a time. "Twenty-two years and she still won't let me forget. Are you married?"

"No, I'm not."

"Well, if you ever do get married be careful what you say. Everything gets filed away. *Everything*."

"I'm not following."

"The day I went to register Taylor's birth I stopped at a bar and had a drink."

Rosa snorted. "One drink would have been fine, but it wasn't one drink, was it?"

"What? A man gets a son, he's not allowed to celebrate?"

"Celebrating is one thing. Getting falling down drunk is another matter altogether."

"Anyway, when I filled in the form, I filled it in wrong, wrote Taylor for both his first name and surname. We meant to change it, but a newborn's hard work. We kept calling him Taylor and it became a joke between us. By the time we'd gotten over that initial spell of sleep deprivation and worked out which way was up, the name had stuck, so we never got around to changing it."

"I wanted to call him David," Rosa cut in. "But that name just didn't fit. He was Taylor, and that was that."

"Yeah he's definitely a Taylor," I agreed.

CHAPTER SIXTY-NINE

I left Rosa and Malcolm by the elevators and walked along the corridor to the Intensive Care Unit, smiling all the way. There is no better feeling than the buzz you get when you finally solve a baffling puzzle. Taylor was asleep in the second bed along. He looked better than the last time I saw him, but not by much. His upper body was wrapped in bandages and his face was a mess. His eyes were puffy and bruised, his lips swollen. Shepherd had really gone to town on him.

He was breathing without a tube, though, and, according to the monitor, his heart rate was good. Hannah sat beside him holding his hand and I was reminded of the way she'd stuck to his side while the paramedics were saving his life.

"How's he doing?" I whispered.

Hannah turned and smiled a tired smile. She was wearing a Tangleweed T-shirt, yet another band I'd never heard of. Both her arms were bandaged up, and there were scrapes and scratches on her face and hands.

"Good," she whispered back. "The doctors say that if he keeps on improving then he should be able to get out of here in a couple of days and move downstairs."

"That's great news. What about you? How are you doing?"

"I'm fine."

"Yeah, right. When did you last sleep?"

"How am I supposed to sleep?"

"Being a martyr won't help Taylor. You need to look after yourself."

Hannah laughed. "Really? And you're the best person to give *that* advice."

"Actually, I probably am."

We drifted into a silence that was punctuated by the subtle sounds of machinery going about the business of keeping people alive. The huff and puff of a respirator a couple of beds down, the gentle buzz of cooling fans. There were no beeps. That one was a myth. The only time the machines in an ICU made a noise was when there was trouble.

"Thanks for saving my life."

Hannah laughed again. "Don't flatter yourself. What I did had nothing to do with saving your life. I just wanted to take down the asshole who put Taylor in hospital. If there was a phrase that meant the opposite of collateral damage then that's what you'd be."

"Whatever. Thanks anyway."

"Hey, Winter. Is that you?"

Taylor's eyes opened a quarter-inch, just enough to show his dilated pupils and a glimpse of the irises.

"You're looking good, Taylor."

"No I'm not, I look like crap. They won't even bring me a mirror, that's how bad I look."

"Better a hospital bed than a coffin."

The corners of Taylor's mouth turned up. This was as close to a smile as he was going to manage for now. "Shepherd, huh? I never saw that one coming."

"No kidding."

The corners of his mouth turned upwards again. His sense of humour seemed to be working fine.

"He asked me to go and get some lights from the trunk of his car. Next thing I remember was waking up here."

"Don't beat yourself up. Shepherd had us all fooled."

"Not you."

"I didn't work it out quickly enough, though."

"Hey, don't you go beating yourself up either. The thing is, you did work it out."

My smile was as small as Taylor's, but that was because my heart wasn't in it. Taylor was trying to make me feel better. Given the circumstances, that just wasn't right.

"Hannah told me what you did," he continued. "Thanks. Things could have turned out very different."

He didn't define "different". He didn't need to. His eyelids were flickering and he was struggling to keep them open. His voice had turned thick and lethargic. He was like a little boy who was trying to stay awake in case he missed something exciting. The first time I met him he'd reminded me of a kid trapped in a grown-up's body. Nothing had really changed since then, yet, at the same time, everything had changed.

"We got him," Taylor mumbled, the words trailing off as he drifted back into a morphine-induced sleep.

"Yeah, we got him," I whispered, but he was already gone.

"This is what he keeps doing," said Hannah. "Waking up, then sleeping."

"His body needs time to heal."

"This is going to change him, isn't it?"

I sighed. It wasn't a case of whether or not there'd be any lasting damage, it was a question of how much damage had been done. A thing like this, you never fully got over it. You could kid yourself you had, but that was just delusion and denial.

I'd seen this before, too many times. Basically, you got your victims, the ones who didn't make it. Then you got the secondary victims, the ones who did make it. The ones left behind. Parents, lovers, friends. People like Taylor who'd come face to face with a killer and survived. My mother had never recovered from what my father did and I'd be lying if I claimed that I hadn't been affected.

"These next few months he's going to need you more than he's ever going to need you," I told her.

"I'll be there for him."

"I know you will. You two are good together."

"You're leaving, aren't you? This is you coming to say goodbye."

I nodded. "Maybe we can catch up next time I'm in San Francisco."

"I'd like that."

I pulled the cheque out of my back pocket and handed it over. Hannah unfolded it, looked at what was written on it, then held it out to me.

"I can't accept this."

"You can and you will. You won it fair and square. If I'd won, I'd have had no problems collecting my winnings. All one hundred cents of it."

She studied me for a second, those big brown eyes getting right under my skin.

"How did you work it out?"

"I don't know what you're talking about."

She ripped the cheque in half, then into quarters, then into eighths. The action was very deliberate. The sound of ripping paper was louder than any other sound in the ICU. She tipped her hand over and the pieces fell to the floor.

"Taylor's parents," I said. "I met them in the corridor."

"Me and Taylor, we're going to be okay. We're going to get to San Francisco, and we're going to get married, and we're going to have a dozen kids."

"I don't doubt that for a second."

"See you around, Winter."

"Yeah, see you around."

I turned and headed for the door. The whispering low chord created by the machines followed me into the corridor, a sound that slowly faded into the background. I took the elevator down to the lobby and went outside.

I'd hired a black Corvette convertible from Hertz, and fifteen minutes later I was on the interstate heading east, the top down, my sunglasses on. I had no destination in mind, no plan other than to keep on driving until I was tired then book into a motel.

When one case finished I usually moved straight on to the next. That had been my MO since quitting the FBI. My default setting was to keep moving forward but, for now, I was happy to tread water. There were places I could be heading for, monsters I could be hunting down, but there was nowhere I *needed* to be.

Chief Kalani had caught his rapist, so I didn't even need to be in Hawaii any more. In the end, the bad guy had turned out to be a failed actor rather than a failed musician. Not that it mattered. The only thing that mattered was that he was in custody. Kalani's people had gone back and checked news footage from the earlier crimes and there he was, acting as though it was Christmas.

The depressing truth was that if I stepped off the merry-go-round for a few days, it wouldn't make much of a difference. The number of active serial killers in the US could be as high as a hundred, maybe even higher. Some of those monsters would be out there right now, dreaming up new ways to kill, maim and torture. Some would actually be turning those fantasies into reality. Then there was the rest of the world to consider. It didn't matter what colour your skin was, it didn't matter where you lived or what language you spoke, that evil was out there just looking for a way in.

And it was never-ending. No matter what I did, or how many of these monsters I stopped, it would never be enough. But that wasn't a reason to quit. A wiser man than me once said that you begin saving the world by saving one life at a time, and that's all I was trying to do here. That was all I could do.

I found a rock station on the radio and turned the volume right up. Then I hit the gas. The needle crept past eighty, ninety. It hit a hundred and I just stared at the road stretching long and black into the distance, lost in the music and enjoying the way the breeze was blowing across my face. The whole world seemed more alive than I'd ever known, and, for once, it was enough just to kick back and enjoy.

Acknowledgements

First and foremost, I couldn't do this without the love and support of my family. Karen, you are the best thing that ever happened to me. And Niamh and Finn, you're the coolest kids on the planet . . . you make me proud every single day. Love you guys now and always.

Camilla Wray constantly amazes me. As well as being an incredible agent, she's a fantastic first editor. Jefferson Winter couldn't ask for a better champion . . . nor could I.

Once again Katherine Armstrong at Faber has done a brilliant editing job. She has an eye for detail that really is second to none.

Nick Tubby is a great first reader and one of the world's last true gentlemen.

Darley's Angels get an extra-special mention. In particular, Clare Wallace and Mary Darby for doing such a fabulous job of finding homes for Winter out in the big wide world, and Sheila David for that TV deal. You guys rock!

And finally I'd like to thank Kate O'Hearn and K.C. O'Hearn for their suggestions and comments.